D0035503

Also by Sally MacKenzie

What Ales the Earl
When to Engage an Earl
How to Manage a Marquess
What to Do With a Duke
Loving Lord Ash
Surprising Lord Jack
Bedding Lord Ned
The Naked King
The Naked Viscount
The Naked Baron
The Naked Gentleman
The Naked Earl
The Naked Marquis
The Naked Duke

Novellas
In the Spinster's Bed
The Duchess of Love
The Naked Prince
The Naked Laird

The Merry VISCOUNT

SALLY MACKENZIE

ZEBRA BOOKS
KENSINGTON PUBLISHING CORP.
www.kensingtonbooks.com

ZEBRA BOOKS are published by

Kensington Publishing Corp.
119 West 40th Street
New York, NY 10018

First Printing: October 2019
ISBN-13: 978-1-4201-4672-1
ISBN-10: 1-4201-4672-6

ISBN-13: 978-1-4201-4675-2 (eBook)
ISBN-10: 1-4201-4675-0 (eBook)

10 9 8 7 6 5 4 3 2 1

Printed in the United States of America

With thanks to my brilliant, long-suffering editor,
Esi Sogah. Someday, maybe, if we wish upon a star,
I'll hand a book in early . . . or at least on time.

For Kelly—welcome to the MacKenzies.

And, once again, for Kevin.

Chapter One

Caroline Anderson gave up her attempt to protect her space and shifted closer to the stagecoach wall, away from the beefy thigh pressing up against her.

The owner of the thigh spread his legs wider.

Blast! She glared at the cloth-covered appendage, her fingers itching to pull her knife out of her cloak pocket and prod the encroaching body part back into its own—

No. There was no point in making things more uncomfortable than they already were. She'd been lucky this coach was wider than normal and could squeeze six people inside, because she certainly didn't want to spend another night in London. And the man wasn't dangerous—his wife was seated on his other side, after all. He was just male and oblivious.

She'd be in far worse straits if the weaselly-looking fellow sitting diagonally across from her were in Beefy Thigh's place. The Weasel had been staring at her as if she were a tasty sweetmeat ever since they'd left London. Fortunately, two other men were wedged onto the bench next to him, preventing him from sliding any closer.

She turned her head to stare glumly out the window.

Oh, hell!

Could things get any worse? The snow, which had been lazily dusting the buildings when they'd left Town, was now falling in thick curtains. It covered the grass and decorated the trees. If it kept up at this rate . . .

No, the road *had* to remain passable. She needed to get back to the Benevolent Home for the Maintenance and Support of Spinsters, Widows, and Abandoned Women and their Unfortunate Children today. It was almost Christmas Eve.

She let out a long breath, fogging the window. She could do with a little luck, but luck—or at least the good variety—had not been her companion on this journey.

She'd had *such* high hopes when she'd set off from Little Puddledon yesterday. Mr. Harris, the owner of the Drunken Sheep in Westling, had again increased his order of Widow's Brew, the ale she produced with her fellow residents of the Home. Even better, he'd told her he'd visited his brother in London and had persuaded *him* to give their ale a try. She'd been so thrilled, she'd almost hugged the man. Getting Widow's Brew into the London market had been her dream ever since she'd perfected the recipe. Here, finally, was her chance.

Some chance. She pulled a face at the passing scenery, her stomach knotting in anger and frustration. *Oh, what a* colossal *fool I've been.*

The pasty-faced man seated directly across from her sneezed, a great, wet eruption—and only then pulled out his handkerchief to give his nose a honking blow.

Splendid. That was all she needed—to come down with a horrible head cold. It would quite put the final flourish on this fruitless jaunt.

She frowned. It wasn't as if she'd gone running up to London only to fulfill her personal ambition. The Home needed the money. The more ale she sold, the less they had to depend on the whims of their noble patron, the Duke of Grainger.

Well, *patrons* now. When Pen Barnes, the Home's former hop grower, had married the Earl of Darrow in August, the earl had promised to lend his support to that of his friend, the duke.

Ha! Caro had learned from sad experience to trust a peer only as far as she could haul a full hogshead of ale—which meant not at all.

Her frown deepened to a scowl. Apparently, she could trust a London tavern keeper even less. The Westling Mr. Harris had very much mistaken the matter. Yes, his London brother had been eager to discuss terms, but the commodity he'd wished to purchase had not been her ale.

Her lips twisted into a humorless smile. She'd made good use of her pocketknife then. The dastard would think twice before putting his hands on the next businesswoman he encountered.

For all the good that does me.

Her shoulders slumped. To be brutally honest, the bounder's bad behavior wasn't the real cause of her dismals. No, her spirits were so low because she'd finally realized that her dream of breaking into the London market was pure self-delusion. Pen and Jo—Lady Havenridge, Baron Havenridge's widow and the founder of the Home—had tried to tell her that, but she'd refused to listen. She'd had to slam her head into the truth before she'd believe it.

She'd last been to London when she was seventeen, thirteen years ago. She'd forgotten how large and busy and overwhelming it was. Even if she could somehow brew ten times—a *hundred* times—the quantity of ale she did now, her output would be only a tiny drop in the enormous vats of the London breweries. And if she *did* get any orders, she'd never be able to deliver reliably. Little Puddledon was too far from Town.

Oh, Lord. How I wish—

The coach lurched, skidding a foot or two.

"Lawk-a-daisy!" That was Beefy Thigh's wife. "We're gonna end in a ditch, Humphrey. See if we don't."

Beefy Thigh—or, rather, Humphrey—put his large hand over his wife's. "Don't fret, Muriel. The coachman knows what he's about."

Caro heard the quaver in his voice if Muriel didn't.

He turned to the somberly garbed man sitting directly across from him. "Ain't that right, Reverend?"

The clergyman looked up from his book—a Bible—opened his mouth and—

Was interrupted by an expressive snort from Pasty Face, who then had to make quick use of his handkerchief.

"I'm getting off at the Crow," Pasty Face said. "*I* don't want to break me neck."

Muriel sucked in her breath and then moaned.

The clergyman gave Pasty Face a reproachful look before smiling at Muriel. "Now, now, madam. Remember what the Good Book says." He patted his Bible. "'Be not afraid, neither be thou dismayed, for the Lord thy God is with thee whithersoever thou goest.' Joshua chapter one, verse nine."

Pasty Face snorted again, this time with handkerchief at the ready. "The Lord can go with me into the Crow."

The reverend scowled. "Sir, you border on blasphemy."

Pasty Face shrugged. "As long as I border on a nice, warm fire with a pint in me hand, I'm good."

Caro's thoughts veered off on a new path. The Crow wasn't London, but it *was* on the main coaching route and closer to Little Puddledon. If she could persuade its tavern keeper to serve Widow's Brew, word would spread. She might find a larger market that wasn't *too* large.

Should I get off and talk to—

No. Mr. London Harris's wandering hands—it was truly shocking how different two brothers could be—and the Weasel's wandering eyes had reminded her of the dangers a woman traveling alone faced. If she stopped, chances were good she'd be stranded at the Crow for several days. Even if the tavern keeper himself wasn't a lecher, she was certain to encounter more than one drunken, lascivious lout on the premises. Her poor pocketknife would be worn to a nub.

Not to mention coaching inns were terribly expensive, and she was short of coin. *And* she was needed back at the Home.

Muriel was still whinging. "Humphrey, maybe we should get off, too."

"But yer sister is expecting us, dumpling. She'll worry. Ye know that."

"Y-yes. But what if we *do* end in a ditch? What if we freeze to death? What then?"

"Zounds, woman! It's just a little snow." The Weasel finally stopped staring at Caro long enough to scowl at Muriel.

Caro looked out the window again to confirm that the "little" snow had now given the stone walls running along the road white caps.

Pasty Face snorted again and dabbed his nose. "Mebbie it's not much if yer a polar bear. I don't have a big white fur coat. I'm gettin' off at the Crow and sittin' in front of the fire, warmin' me coattails."

That *did* sound appealing.

"What is your opinion, madam?" The clergyman suddenly turned to Caro. "Do you think the weather too, er, *uncertain* for further travel, especially for delicate females such as yourself and this lady?" He nodded toward Muriel.

Caro blinked at him. *Delicate* female? She'd wager she could work longer, harder hours than this sermon-writing, Bible-toting parson. And there was nothing uncertain about the weather. But she couldn't afford—on any level—to take shelter at the inn, and if Muriel and Humphrey got off, the Weasel was certain to move over and sit next to her. Ugh!

"I'm not getting off the coach," she said as they rattled into the innyard.

"Well, *I* am," Pasty Face said. And, true to his word, as soon as the coachman unlatched the door and pulled down the steps, Pasty Face was out and heading toward the Crow's light and warmth and liquid refreshment.

Caro looked longingly after him, tugging her cloak's collar closer in a vain attempt to keep out the cold. She'd like to be sitting by the fire—

Remember the lubricious louts.

"If ye need to use the privy, do it straightaway," the coachman said. "We're not stopping long. I want to make it to Marbridge afore the weather worsens."

"Do ye think it's safe to go on?" Humphrey asked, Muriel gripping his arm and peering anxiously around him.

Caro held her breath.

The coachman nodded. "Aye. The road's good—straight and flat—and the horses are steady. The snow's not too bad . . . yet. But the sooner we leave, the better." He scowled at them. "So be quick about yer business. I won't wait fer ye if ye dillydally."

The coachman stepped back, and Humphrey, the clergyman, and the Weasel clambered out, the Weasel managing to "accidently" brush his hand over Caro's knees as he passed.

"Pardon me," he said, sending a noxious cloud of stale breath her way.

She forced a smile, fingering the knife in her pocket, and decided she could forego the jakes. Braving the cold and, more to the point, the filth of the public outhouse wasn't appealing, but she especially didn't want to risk being caught alone by the Weasel or to open herself to the possibility that he could rearrange the seating while she was gone.

Muriel must have come to the same conclusion, at least about the outhouse.

"So, yer traveling alone, are ye?" she asked after the men

left, eyeing Caro with a nervous mixture of curiosity and suspicion.

Mostly suspicion.

Caro was tempted to say, no, she had an imaginary companion by her side, but bit her tongue and forced a smile instead. She was a good saleswoman and selling herself—that is, her skill and dependability as a businesswoman—was often part of convincing skeptical tavern keepers to take a chance on her ale. She'd use those skills now. "Yes. I'm going home for the holidays."

No need to clarify that home meant the Benevolent Home for the Maintenance and Support of Spinsters, Widows, and Abandoned Women and their Unfortunate Children.

"Did I hear you're visiting your sister?" She'd also found that throwing the conversational ball back to her inquisitor usually worked very well—as it did this time.

Muriel's face lit up, and she rattled on about her sisters Mildred, Mirabel, and Miranda, who all lived just outside Marbridge, and how she went back every Christmas to celebrate the holiday with them.

Caro nodded and made encouraging noises to keep the woman talking, counting the seconds until the men returned and they could resume their journey. One of the things she most hated about Christmas was the way people dug up their old, moldering memories and dressed them up with garlands and candles and nostalgia. The past was best left in the past. Fortunately, most of the women at the Home agreed with her.

Humphrey and the Weasel returned then. Humphrey climbed right in, but the Weasel loitered in the cold.

Oh, Lord. He's going to try to take Pasty Face's place.

Caro gripped her knife, ready to pull it out the moment any part of the Weasel touched her. If he thought she'd bear his insults politely, he was going to be very *painfully* surprised.

Humphrey turned into an unwitting ally. "What are ye doing out there, sir?" he said. "Get in afore ye freeze yer arse off."

The Weasel shrugged—or perhaps shivered. "I'll g-get in when the reverend comes back. No need to s-sit longer than I have to."

"But ye'll catch yer death out there," Muriel said.

"Naw. I'm used to the c-c-cold."

That was definitely a shiver. In any event, the coachman appeared just then to put an end to the Weasel's plot.

"Get in, man." His voice had an edge to it. "We need to be off at once. The coachy coming from Marbridge said the roads are getting worse."

"But what about the reverend? He's not back from the privy."

The coachman put his hands on his hips. "Are ye wanting to keep him company? Because ye shall if ye don't get in the coach *right now*."

There was a momentary standoff, and then the Weasel grumbled and climbed in. He leered at Caro the moment his rump hit the other bench.

"Why don't ye join me?" He patted the spot next to him.

"Good idea," Humphrey said.

"Do move over, dear." That was Muriel. "We'll all be more comfortable."

Ha! Caro would be vastly more *un*comfortable—as everyone else would, too, after she stabbed the Weasel in the leg.

She was saved from violence by the clergyman, who came stumbling up at that moment, still buttoning his fly.

"Just in time, Reverend," the coachman said. "We were going to have to leave ye here."

"Sorry." The clergyman hoisted himself in, forcing the Weasel to slide over. "Balky bowels."

That was more information than Caro wished to have, but she welcomed anything that forced the Weasel away from her.

The coachman started to put up the steps—

"Wait! Oh, please, sir. Wait."

He stopped and looked—they all looked—toward the inn. A young woman, carrying a small satchel, and a young boy, about six or seven years old, half ran/half slid over the snow-slick cobblestones.

"Sir," the woman said, her voice tight and breathless, "I've a ticket for an inside seat. They said I might have a place here, since the gentleman got off."

The coachman frowned, hesitating.

"There's only one seat and two of you," the clergyman said. "You won't fit. Go back to the inn."

Now *there* was Christian charity.

The coachman scowled. "Now see here, Reverend. This is my coach. I'll be the one making the decision about who rides and who doesn't."

"I'm the one who has to sit next to them."

The coachman's scowl deepened. "Unless ye wish to get out and stay at the Crow—or take a seat on the roof."

"Have her sit on the outside if she needs to travel."

The Weasel and Humphrey began to grumble as well. The matter was clearly getting out of hand.

Caro spoke up when Muriel didn't. "A child can't sit on the roof."

The man of the cloth—and the balky bowels—shrugged.

The young woman didn't waste her time with the clergyman. She addressed the coachman again. "Please, sir. We need to get to Marbridge afore Christmas, and yers might be the last coach to get through."

The coachman looked at her a moment longer and then

let out a long breath. "Very well. But the boy will have to sit on yer lap. No crowding the reverend."

The woman nodded and handed the coachman her satchel as the boy scrambled in. Then she followed awkwardly. Her right arm must be injured. It was hidden under her cloak as if in a sling, a lump that she made no attempt to use.

Caro expected the reverend to inch over toward the Weasel; there wasn't much room, but the boy was as thin as a reed. Instead, the fellow gave the woman a sidelong glare and opened his Bible, not budging a hair's breadth.

The atmosphere in the coach dropped to rival the temperature outside—well, that wasn't so surprising as the coachman was still holding the door open, waiting for things to sort themselves out. But it wasn't just the frigid air causing the chill. It was also the icy stares Humphrey and the Weasel gave the newcomers. Muriel sniffed and made a show of pulling her skirts back, not that she was close enough to risk being touched by either of them.

Caro looked back at the woman. The other people in the coach weren't members of the *ton*—far from it. Their clothing wasn't any grander, though the woman's and the boy's were visibly threadbare. But what emboldened her companions to treat the poor mother with disdain must be the air of defeat and desperation that clung to her.

It was the same air that clung to so many women when they first arrived at the Benevolent Home.

The boy pressed against his mother and, once she'd managed to sit, climbed onto her left leg, careful not to jostle her injured arm. She gave him a small smile that did nothing to dispel the dark shadows under her eyes or the tightness of her expression and hugged him close.

Much to Caro's surprise, she felt a flood of compassion.

She frowned. Jo was the tenderhearted one, not her. Caro

was the Home's clear-eyed, practical businesswoman. A tender heart could be a liability when striving to make a tidy profit.

The coachman heaved a relieved sigh. "All right, then. We'll be on our way." He started to close the door.

"Wait!"

This time it was two loud, boisterous young men, swathed in multi-caped greatcoats, who pounded across the innyard, skidding to a stop just before they knocked the coachman over. One had to use the coach to break his forward progress, setting the vehicle to rocking.

"Are you going to Marbridge?" the one not leaning on the coach asked, his words slurring slightly.

"Aye." The edge was back in the coachman's voice.

"Splendid," the other man said. "That's where we're going." He reached for the door.

Surely the coachman wasn't going to evict one of them—well, *two* of them? The mother threw Caro a panicked look. The woman guessed, likely correctly, that she would be the first one thrown out. Caro was afraid she'd be the second.

Just let them try.

Fortunately, Caro didn't have to defend her seat. The coachman stood his ground—and held onto the door, keeping it from opening any farther.

"As ye can see, I'm full inside. If ye want to leave today, ye'll have to ride atop."

The men shrugged.

"All right. We've got coats"—the first man lifted a bottle—"and brandy to keep us warm."

Muriel gasped. "Humphrey, say something," she hissed as the coachman finally closed the door. "It can't be safe to have those drunken bucks riding with us."

"Likely they're the ones at risk," the Weasel offered. The coach swayed as the men hauled themselves up to their seats. "Though if they're drunk enough, they won't feel it when they fall off and hit the ground."

Muriel stared at the Weasel, and then elbowed her husband. "*Say* something," she hissed again.

It was too late. The coach had lurched into motion.

And the young mother's cloak started wailing.

The reverend jerked his eyes off his Bible, a mixture of alarm and disbelief in his expression, and scowled down at her. "Good Lord, woman, what have you got there?"

"That's my sister, Grace," the boy said, as his mother uncovered a very small, very young infant. "She's a baby."

The clergyman snorted all too expressively—he obviously thought "Grace" a vastly inappropriate name—and transferred his scowl to the boy, who bravely raised his chin and held his ground unflinching.

Meanwhile, the mother was trying to soothe the baby in the limited space she had. "Shh." She jiggled the infant. "Shh."

"Grace is only four weeks old." The boy's young, clear voice dropped each word like a pebble into a still pond, sending ripples of consternation through the coach's other occupants.

The mother, clearly all too aware of the disapproval building in the confined space, leaned closer to whisper to her son. "Hush, Edward. Don't bother the people." Then she shifted her arm with the infant closer to the stagecoach wall, trying to make more room for her son on her lap.

The poor woman. It was bad enough she was traveling in a snowstorm, on the public stagecoach, with a young boy and a baby only a month after giving birth. She didn't need to feel alone and judged by everyone around her.

"Here, let me hold the baby for you," Caro said.

The woman hesitated, clearly nervous about entrusting her precious child to a stranger.

"Don't worry. I've lots of experience."

Caro was the fifth of eleven children and the only daughter. Her poor, beleaguered mother had put her to work tending her siblings as soon as she was old enough to rock a cradle. And then when she was seventeen, she'd gone to London to work as a nursemaid—

No. She shoved those memories back into the box she'd made for them and slammed down the lid.

Baby Grace let out a thin wail, and her mother gave in.

"Thank you," she said softly. She leaned forward, and Caro scooped the small bundle out of the crook of her arm. "Careful with her head."

Caro nodded, wondering again what would force a new mother out into the snow just before Christmas.

Ah. The moment she felt the baby's warm weight—the mite couldn't be even as heavy as a tankard of ale—Caro's hands remembered how to hold such a young child. She settled the baby against her shoulder, patting her and humming, feeling a surprising calm flow through her as she soothed little Grace back to sleep.

Women needed to band together to support one another. That's what they did—most of the time—at the Home. Caro looked at Grace's mother. Did she need the Home's refuge? Caro could—

No, unfortunately she wouldn't. Space at the Home was very limited. There wasn't room for two separate dormitories for boys and girls. Jo had made the decision early on that they couldn't take in mothers with sons past babyhood.

If there were only Grace, the Home's doors would be wide open. But there was also Edward.

An uneasy silence had settled over the coach—no one wanted to be trapped in a small space with a howling infant—but once it became clear Grace was going back to sleep, everyone seemed to relax. The clergyman went back to his Bible; the Weasel and Muriel looked out the window on their side of the coach. Humphrey—perhaps afraid he'd jostle the baby awake—slid his bulk away from Caro as best he could. The young mother and her son fell into what must have been an exhausted sleep.

Caro shifted the baby slightly, patting her bottom when she whimpered. The snow was still coming down, but so far, the coach was moving along, thank God. Perhaps she *would* reach Marbridge in time to catch the one coach that would take her on to Little Puddledon.

And then Grace started making little snuffling, hungry noises.

Oh, blast. How could Grace's mother nurse a baby in this cramped carriage of disapproving men? But there was no arguing with a hungry infant. Grace was going to start screaming soon unless . . .

Perhaps a trick Caro had learned tending her siblings could buy them some time.

She gave Grace the knuckle of her pinkie to suck on.

Ah. She'd forgotten how surprisingly strong and rhythmic an infant's sucking was. The sensation made her feel . . . odd. Almost as if she wished she had a baby herself.

Nonsense! What she really wished for was a miracle, that she could keep Grace content until they got to Marb—

"Tallyho!"

The coach suddenly picked up speed amid a storm of shouting and cursing from the roof.

Oh, hell. The drunken bucks must have taken the coachman's reins.

Caro tightened her hold on the baby.

"Humphrey!" Muriel screamed. "Make them stop."

"Good God, woman, how am I supposed to do that? I'm stuck in here with you."

The Weasel was swearing quite creatively, and even the

reverend addressed the Lord in less than polite terms as they careened down the road.

"Wh-what's happening, Mama?"

The young mother hugged her son. "I think the men riding on top have taken over driving the c-coach, Edward." She tried to speak calmly, but Caro heard the slight quaver in her voice.

Muriel didn't even try to mask her alarm. She grabbed her husband's arm and screeched, "Lord help us, we *are* going to end in a ditch!"

"H-hold on to me, Edward." The mother's eyes, tight with desperation and entreaty, went to Caro.

"I've got Grace." Caro gripped the baby as securely as she could and braced herself against the coach wall. She was not much for praying—she'd found relying on herself rather than a distant and inscrutable Deity usually served her best—but nevertheless she sent a quick, sincere entreaty to the Almighty in case He was listening.

She'd no sooner formed a mental "amen" than the coach started to slide. Everyone except Caro and, blessedly, the baby screamed. Caro was too busy trying to curl her body around Grace's. If the coach landed on its side, it was going to be very hard to keep the baby safe.

The slide seemed to go on forever, and then finally there was a jolt, a shudder, and the coach stopped, still upright.

And then the floor dropped a foot, eliciting more screams and curses.

"What was that, Humphrey?" Muriel squeaked.

The Weasel answered instead. "Feels like the axel broke. Looks like we ain't getting to Marbridge today." He glanced at the clergyman and nodded at his Bible. "But at least we needn't be afeard since the Lord is traveling with us, eh, Reverend?"

The clergyman scowled. "You are offensive, sirrah!"

"I'm cold and hungry, and now I'm stranded in the snow

who knows where." The Weasel shrugged. "I'll probably freeze to death, so I suppose I can lodge a complaint with yer God all too soon."

Muriel shrieked.

"Hold yer tongue," Humphrey told the Weasel sharply.

Yes, indeed. Didn't any of these idiots give a thought to the boy? He was looking up at his mother, eyes wide, face pale. "We'll be all right, won't we, Mama?"

His mother forced a tense smile and smoothed back his hair. "Aye, Edward. As long as we're together, we'll be all r-right."

That was all very well, but the truth was they had to get out of this cold, particularly poor little Grace. Sitting around moaning and arguing wasn't going to accomplish that goal. Someone needed to have a word with the coachman.

Obviously, that someone was Caro.

Caro pushed the carriage door open and looked out. The axel had indeed broken; the ground was well within reach. "I'll be right back," she told Grace's mother. "Don't worry. I'll keep Grace warm."

The mother, holding her son tightly and looking wan and defeated, nodded weakly.

Caro climbed out, pulled her cloak snugly around the baby, and approached the coachman, who was trying, along with the two bucks, to unhitch the horses. They were not having a great deal of success.

"Sir, I need a word with you, if you please."

The coachman glanced at her and then went back to his work. "Get back inside the coach, madam. One of these men"—he glared at the miscreants who had put them in this position—"is going to ride on to the next stop and bring back help as soon as we can get a horse free."

She eyed the blackguards. At least the accident seemed to have sobered them up. "And how long will that take?"

The coachman scowled at her. "Likely an hour or more."

She shook her head. "Too long. It's far too cold for the children to wait here. The baby, especially, needs to get inside by a fire immediately."

The coachman's brows shot up. "*Baby?!* Where the bloody—that is, pardon me language, madam, but . . . a baby?"

"She was under her mother's cloak when they got on at the Crow. She's only a few weeks old and needs to be warm by a fire immediately."

The coachman looked annoyed—and desperate and helpless, too. "How are ye going to manage that, may I ask? These idiots can't sprout wings and fly, ye know."

"I know that." What *was* she going to do?

She looked around at the snow-covered landscape, the fat flakes falling thickly around her. There was a break in the stone wall nearby and what appeared to be a snow-covered drive leading to a faint glow. . . .

"What's that light over there?"

The coachman looked in the direction she was pointing. "Oh, Lord Devil must be at home. Ye don't want to go anywhere near him."

Lord Devil?

An odd jolt of nervous excitement shot through her, a mix of dread and eagerness akin to what she felt when she was getting ready to meet a tavern keeper for the first time in the hopes of selling him some Widow's Brew. *That must be Nick. . . .*

No! What was the matter with her? She'd thought herself cured of any sort of romantic foolishness. She'd not seen Nick—if this was indeed Nick—for . . . She did a rapid calculation.

For seventeen years. She'd been thirteen, a naïve child, the last time he'd come home from school with her brother Henry. Her feelings for Nick then had been puppy love.

He'd been the only one of her brothers' friends who hadn't ignored or teased her.

That was all this odd feeling was—a faint echo of her old hero worship.

"You mean the new Lord Oakland?"

"Aye."

She wasn't afraid of Nick. "Well, if he has a warm fire, I most certainly do wish to go near him. Even a devil wouldn't turn away a tiny baby." And certainly not the Nick she'd known.

It's been seventeen years. People change.

Yes, they did. But Nick couldn't have changed *that* much.

"I wouldn't be so certain," the coachman said, but she'd already turned away. There was no time to waste.

She stuck her head back into the coach briefly to address Grace's mother. "There's a house nearby. I'm taking Grace there and will send back help."

The woman frowned but must have concluded that the sooner Grace got inside, the better, because she nodded. "All right. Do hurry."

"And close the blasted door," the clergyman snapped. "Do you want us all to freeze?"

Muriel moaned, Humphrey glared at her, and even the Weasel's look was annoyed rather than amorous.

"Right." Caro pushed the door closed and started through the snow toward the house.

Chapter Two

Nicholas St. John, Viscount Oakland, or, as some called him, Lord Devil, averted his gaze from the Honorable Felix Simpson, sprawled in the red upholstered chair by the fire with Polly kneeling between his legs. Fortunately, Polly's body blocked Nick's view of precisely what she was doing, but from the way her head moved and the quality of Felix's moans, Nick could venture an educated guess.

Sadly, there wasn't a safer spot in his sitting room to rest his eyes. Bertram Collins, occupying the settee with Fanny, looked to have his tongue so far down the girl's throat he could sample the luncheon she'd consumed several hours earlier.

"Oh," Felix gasped. "That's it, luv. Faster now. Fast—ah. Ah. Yess."

Blast. Sticking his fingers in his ears and humming would be too obvious. Nick would have to endure the noises of sexual passion as best he could without cringing.

Cringing?! What the bloody hell is wrong with me?

He should turn to clever Livy, patiently stroking his arm—his still jacket-covered arm—and get busy with some carnal fun of his own.

His most carnal organ shrunk—literally and figuratively—at the thought.

It's Oakland. The damn place casts a pall over everything.

He took another sip of brandy, hoping the alcohol would blunt his discomfort and make him numb enough to engage in the amorous activity Livy clearly expected.

Why the hell did I think hosting a Christmas orgy at Oakland was a good idea?

He hated Christmas *and* Oakland. Usually he stayed in Town for the holiday, where the noise and dirt and the wide offering of activities—polite and extremely impolite—helped take the edge off the revoltingly merry season. But two nights ago, he'd made the mistake of hosting a party at his townhouse.

Well, the party hadn't been a mistake. The mistake had arrived with his neighbor, Myles Gray. Myles had been walking Rufus, his large dog of questionable pedigree, when he'd heard the revelry and decided to have a look-in. Myles *should* have tied Rufus to the gate first, but he hadn't thought of that.

Once the butler opened the door, it was too late. As bad luck would have it, a footman had been passing through the foyer at that precise moment, carrying a tray piled high with plates of ham, sausage, bread, and cheese.

Rufus had given a great, deep woof of joy and charged, jerking his leash from Myles's hand. The footman had emitted a loud—piercing, really—yelp of surprise and alarm and had thrown up his hands, sending the tray airborne. Food and cutlery had rained down upon them, plates shattering on the black-and-white tile floor.

Rufus was surprisingly nimble and quick for such a large animal. And smart. He clearly knew he'd lose out if he gobbled the treats at the scene, so he grabbed as many as he could and bolted.

In retrospect, Nick should have sent someone in pursuit of the dog at once. Myles had started after Rufus, but slipped on a slice of ham and went crashing to the ground. Nick's other guests were too drunkenly entertained by the drama unfolding before them to catch the dog, and the servants were focused on helping Myles and the hapless footman and cleaning up the mess before someone else hit the floor.

By the time they'd got everything sorted out and gone looking for Rufus, the dog had consumed—and disgorged—all his plunder, mostly in Nick's bedroom. The stench was quite remarkable. Nick had had no choice but to decamp while his carpets and bedding were washed and aired.

So, he'd hatched this plan to bring two of his least responsible friends and their favorite light-skirts to his detested country estate for his most loathed holiday. How better to thumb his nose at everyone than by celebrating the Roman Saturnalia in place of Christmas here?

Old Pearson, the estate manager, Brooks, the butler, and Mrs. Brooks, the housekeeper, had been suitably appalled when the carriages had pulled up yesterday and he and his disreputable guests had tumbled out.

And I was unsuitably dismayed at their reaction. Why the hell had that been? I wanted *to be outrageous.*

The dismay had lasted only a moment, however. All it had taken to dispel the feeling had been hearing his uncle's thin, nasally voice echo in his head—just as Nick heard it again now.

This is not the way a viscount behaves.

He gritted his teeth. *Shut* up, *Uncle Leon.*

Was he ever going to be free of the man? His father's older brother had been dead for almost a year now—and Nick had been grown and as independent of him as he could manage for much longer than that—and yet he *still* heard his uncle's censorious voice, especially when he came to

Oakland. In a blink, Nick was no longer thirty-two, but a boy of eleven, just orphaned, snatched away from the sun and warmth of Italy and dumped into cold, dark England—into Oakland's cold, dark halls—to face an equally cold, dark man.

Papa had been so different, always laughing and smiling. He'd been on his Grand Tour when he'd fallen in love with Venice—and with a young Italian woman—and had decided to end his journey there, where he could enjoy the warm sun and blue water and spend his days painting. Nick had grown up speaking English and Italian—though mostly Italian—surrounded by his Italian aunts and uncles and cousins.

And then the fever had taken his parents.

It had been horrible; he did not like thinking about it even now. Then, a few months later, Josiah Pennyworth, a tutor passing through Venice, had called at his grandfather's house to inform them that he'd been engaged by Viscount Oakland to convey Master Nicholas back to England and away from everyone and everything he'd ever known.

So, Nick had gone from a happy, effusive extended family to a dark, empty house with a stiff, unsmiling old man—though, doing the math later, he realized his uncle must have been only in his forties.

Which had seemed ancient then.

Livy was nuzzling his ear now. Her fingers had moved from his sleeve to his fall. "Don't you want to play, too, Nick?"

"Mmm." He *should* want to play.

He forced himself to look at Livy and smile. He liked her. She was by far his favorite whore, inventive in bed and agreeable out of it. Maybe if he went through the preliminary motions, his cock would bestir itself.

It didn't last night.

Oh, God.

He pushed that mortifying memory away and leaned toward her—

Bang! Bang! Bang!

"Someone's at the door." Livy stated the obvious.

"Brooks will get it."

No, he wouldn't.

His butler did *not* approve of orgies. He'd been playing least in sight ever since they'd arrived.

Perhaps the person would go away.

Nick smiled at Livy—

Bang! Bang! Bang!

Whoever it was had a strong arm and sounded extremely determined.

"Who the hell is out on a day like this?" Felix asked. Polly was sitting on the floor now, exposing Felix's spent cock for all in the room to observe.

Nick averted his gaze—noting in the process that Bertram had reclaimed his tongue—and looked out the window. The light was failing, and the snow was still coming down heavily. Ah. This obviously wasn't a social call.

"I'll go see." He stood and headed for the entry, calling over his shoulder as he left, "You might want to put yourself to rights, Felix, in case it's someone I can't send directly to the stables."

Bang! Bang! Bang!

The noise was even louder in the entry.

Good God, the man's going to pound a hole in the door if he keeps hammering away like this.

"All right, all right. I hear you." Nick hurried across the floor, slid the bolt free, and pulled the door open.

Oh.

The person standing before him was swathed in a cloak,

hood pulled low, but the hand raised to pound on his door again did not belong to a man.

"It took you long enough," the woman said as she pushed past him. "One would think a house this size would be better run."

It was proof of his surprise that he didn't try to stop her. Not that he would ever leave a poor, defenseless woman shivering in the snow, of course.

The woman shook off her hood and met his gaze squarely.

Perhaps not so defenseless—or at least not at all discomfited at being alone in a strange house with a strange man.

A small frown of puzzlement or confusion appeared between her brows, but vanished almost at once as if she'd dismissed whatever thought had occurred to her. "The stagecoach has had an accident. You must organize the other servants and set off at once to the rescue."

She thinks I'm the butler.

I did *answer the door.*

"There are two women, a young boy, and five or perhaps six men, including the coachman, stranded in the cold."

Where have I seen those eyes before?

They were a remarkable deep blue and large with long, dark thick lashes. Her hair was dark, too. She was quite beautiful.

I wouldn't forget such a female. I couldn't have met her before.

And yet, those eyes . . .

"Sir!"

His attention was recalled to the present by her sharp tone. She was glaring at him.

"What is the *matter* with you? Did you not hear me? You need to organize a rescue party *at once*. I assure you your master would wish you to do so."

"My master?" She spoke as if she knew him—or, rather,

as if she knew Lord Oakland. Since she didn't recognize him, she must think his uncle was still alive.

But that didn't make any sense either. Word of Leon's death must have reached even the smallest village by now—he'd been in his grave almost a year. And Nick would be shocked if the old grumbletonian had ever met this woman. She was far too young to have been part of Uncle Leon's circle—not that he'd had a circle of any sort that Nick knew of.

But most of all, he'd be shocked if *anyone* had thought Uncle Leon would bestir himself to help some common travelers.

No, that wasn't fair. Leon might have been a sour old man, but he'd not been so heartless as to let anyone freeze to death outside his gates.

I think.

"Yes. Lord. Oakland. The. Viscount." She was now speaking slowly and distinctly as if addressing a halfwit.

Who is *she?*

And then her cloak began to wail.

Zeus, he *must* be drunk, but he hadn't thought he'd had that much brandy.

He watched in stupefaction as she reached inside the cloak's warm folds and pulled out a baby.

A very small baby.

He took a step back.

She took a step forward. If she hadn't had her hands full of infant, he was certain she'd have poked him sharply in the chest with an emphatic finger.

"Are you deaf, sirrah? Didn't you hear me say there was a young boy involved? People's lives are in danger!"

"Er, yes." Babies made him nervous. Not that he'd had any actual contact with them, but just seeing one made him feel very large and clumsy. This one looked to be hardly longer than his forearm. "How old is your child?"

She scowled at him. Clearly, she was not a person to suffer fools. "What has that to say to the matter?"

Her eyes are beautiful even when they are shooting daggers.

Beautiful and familiar.

He'd puzzle out who she was eventually.

Or you could just ask her . . .

The baby, who had stopped its yowling when it emerged from the cloak, started crying again—a thin, piercing, blood-curdling sound that caused his brain to freeze with panic.

"Shh." The woman cupped its head, pressed it against her chest, and started to perform an odd little swaying, dipping dance. The infant must have found it comforting or at least distracting because, blessedly, it stopped howling.

He sighed in relief—and the woman's right brow winged up.

Is that a glint of calculation in her eyes?

"She's hungry. Any moment now she'll start *really* screaming."

Definitely calculation. She knew exactly what would most strike terror into his heart.

He tried to wipe his sweaty palms discreetly on his breeches. "Can't you feed her?"

The woman smiled—rather evilly, he'd say.

"No, I can't. She's not mine. I brought her with me when I came to get help because she's too young to be out in the cold for any length of time." She scowled again. "And we are wasting precious seconds. Her mother and brother—as well as the others—are still in the coach. If you cannot help, sir, tell me where I may find someone who can."

Right. He could sort out who she was later. "I'll get some men and go at once. Where precisely is the stagecoach?"

She smiled briefly, her expression easing. "Just past the

gates. We were on our way to Marbridge when some drunken idiots took the reins and sent us into a ditch, breaking an axle."

No using the stagecoach to tow the travelers up to the house, then.

"Are there any injuries?" That would make things more difficult.

"No, thank God. The coach stayed upright. Everyone is all right, but cold"—she scowled again—"and getting colder."

It was his turn to frown in puzzlement. "But if they aren't injured, why didn't they come along with you?"

That provoked a snort, startling the infant.

"Shh." The woman bounced and soothed the baby before replying. "The coachman thinks your master is too cold-hearted to care about people"—she glared at him—"in *desperate* need. He told me not to bother coming up here for help."

Now it was Nick's turn to snort. Coldhearted described his uncle to a T. The man had been a stiff-necked, supercilious, sanctimonious zealot who sucked the faintest glimmer of fun out of any room he entered. His face would likely have shattered had he smiled.

But the coachman must know I'm the viscount now. . . .

Good God, I've not become Uncle Leon, have I?

The woman frowned. "I cannot believe any Englishman—even a peer . . ."

Even *a peer?*

". . . would turn away children in need, but if you fear your master might, I will be happy to have a word with him"—she speared Nick with her lovely eyes—"*after* everyone is safe."

Should I tell her who I am?

Too late. His guests, likely wondering what was keeping him, spilled out into the entry.

"What's going on, Nick?" Bertram asked.

The woman sucked her breath in sharply at his name. Her eyes widened with . . . horror? Disappointment?

Definitely recognition—and beyond the simple acknowledgement that he was the viscount. She knew his Christian name. They *must* know each other, but then why couldn't he remember who she was? He didn't usually forget beautiful women.

Felix let out a long, low whistle. "Well, look what the snow blew in."

The woman scowled at Felix and then addressed the others. "There's been an accident," she said. "I was trying to get *Lord* Oakland—"

That was definitely said with loathing. What did she have against the peerage?

"—to mount a rescue. There are several people stranded in the cold, including this baby's mother and young brother."

The infant started squawking again—Nick wouldn't put it past the woman to have given the child a little poke—to underline the need for haste.

"The poor mite's hungry," Polly said.

"Yes." The woman glared at him again. "And will just scream louder and louder until *someone* rescues her mother."

"Right." Whoever she was, she was correct—it was past time to take action. He looked at the other men. "Bert, Felix, will you come with me? I need to alert the servants to harness the sleigh and prepare for our new guests, and then we can set out."

He did his best to repress a shudder at the thought of going out into the cold snow.

He looked back at the woman. "I'm on my way to the coat room. Do let me take your cloak, Miss . . ."

She was looking at the baby. "Anderson," she said.

Anderson . . .

Good God!

Don't jump to conclusions. It's a common name.

But those eyes—

Now he knew where he'd seen them before. It had been years ago, in a young girl's face.

From the time he was eleven until he turned fifteen, he'd avoided the echoing halls of Oakland by going home at school holidays—except Christmas—with his friend, Henry Anderson. The Anderson house had still been in England, of course, so still cold and damp and dark to a boy raised in Venice. But it had also been crowded and noisy and full of activity. Henry had three older brothers and many younger siblings—the next younger one being this woman.

Caroline . . . Caro! That was her name. She'd been strong and fearless then, too, and had insisted on being included in all their activities. He'd liked her—had come to think of her as just another boy, which back then had been rather a compliment.

She didn't look anything like a boy now.

He slipped her cloak off her shoulders as she juggled the baby. The fabric was heavy enough to be warm, but it wasn't luxurious by any means, and the cloak's style and cut—and that of her dress—were serviceable rather than fashionable.

"*Will* you hurry along?" she asked as soon as she was free. The sharpness of her tone must have bothered the baby, because it—no, *she*—started to cry again. "Shh, Grace." Caro shot him a look before addressing the baby again. "The *nice* man will get your mother very soon."

Well, he'd been given his marching orders, hadn't he?

"On my way. Go into the sitting room and get warm by the fire. I'll send the baby's mother in as soon as we get back."

She gave him a pointed look that promised a rain of hellfire if he didn't make haste, and then she and the other women disappeared into the sitting room.

"Come on." Nick gestured for Felix and Bertram to follow him.

"Now *there's* a very fine piece," Felix said as they strode down the corridor. "Those eyes. That skin. Those—" He held his hands open at chest level, fingers curved. "The dress is a fright, but I'll wager a good sum that what's underneath is well worth the unwrapping."

A surprisingly strong bolt of annoyance shot through Nick. "Watch your tongue."

Tongue . . .

Oh, hell, what was the matter with him? It was a bloody figure of speech. He shouldn't suddenly be thinking of tangling tongues with Caro—if the woman was indeed the Caro Anderson he'd known. She'd likely bite him hard enough to draw blood and then, for good measure, knee him so his voice rose an octave.

Felix's—and Bertram's—brows shot up.

"Have your eye on her yourself, do you?" Felix shrugged. "Well, then, of course I won't try to seduce her."

"I do *not* have my eye on her." At least he wouldn't admit it. "And neither should you." He wouldn't tell them who he thought she was. "She seems to be a respectable female, not available for any sort of dalliance."

Felix snorted. "Traveling alone on the stagecoach? I think not."

"It does seem unlikely, Nick," Bertram said.

Nick frowned, opened his mouth to argue—

And stopped. He hadn't seen Caro in over a decade. He knew nothing about *this* woman.

"We don't know she's alone. She could be the baby's nanny." Ah, yes. That must be it. He had a vague memory of Henry telling him, when their paths had crossed several—well, many—years ago, that Caro had gone to London to be a nursemaid.

The woman certainly seemed to know what she was doing with the baby and was fiercely protective of it.

What else is she fierce about?

An extremely salacious image of her blue eyes and smart mouth smiling up at him, hair spread across his pillow, as he—

Stop it!

He was years beyond trying to get under the skirts of every woman he met. He'd played the rake for a while, in large part to shock and embarrass his uncle. Not a comfortable or admirable thing to admit, but true. When his uncle had died, the mad urge to fornicate at every opportunity had left him. Mindless swiving didn't give him any real pleasure, but instead left him feeling oddly empty and dissatisfied.

"Nannies need a bit of tupping, too," Felix said. "She's not a young girl, Nick, and likely not a virgin. Too much fire to her." He grinned. "I wager she'd scorch my sheets. Don't be a dog in the manger. If you aren't interested, let me give her a go."

Nick swallowed the sudden, inexplicable fury that threatened to choke him. "She's a guest under my roof. I'll not have her insulted." And if she were indeed Henry's sister, that was even more reason to protect her.

Not that he could imagine her needing his protection. She struck him as being quite capable of protecting herself.

"I'm not going to rape the woman, Nick. I think she's old enough to know her own mind"—Felix's lips slid into a grin—"and needs. Frankly, she seemed overly agitated. She likely wants a good plowing to calm her and balance her humors."

Felix is an annoying idiot. Why did I invite him here?

"Polly might not like it if you focus your attentions on this new woman, Felix," Bertram said.

Felix laughed. "This is an orgy, Bert. Polly knows she doesn't have sole claim to me"—he grinned with a bit of swagger—"not that I can't keep more than one female happy at a time."

Once I get back to London, I am cutting this connection.

Their voices echoing off the hard, tile floor and bare walls must have been loud enough to alert one of the servants that something was afoot—something other than an orgy—because Brooks appeared from the depths of the house just as they started pulling on hobnail boots, coats, hats, and mufflers.

The butler's eyes widened. "Milord, you aren't going out, are you?"

There would be no other reason for him to be putting on all his blasted outerwear, would there? And yet he understood Brooks's surprise. It was no secret Nick hated the winter weather.

"Unfortunately, yes." One would think after more than twenty years in England, he'd have grown used to the cold and damp, but it still cut him to the bone. "The stagecoach has had an accident, and there are people in need of rescuing. Can you ask Walters to harness the sleigh and take it down to the road to collect the passengers? And tell Mrs. Brooks we'll have extra people to house and feed—"

They heard a high, thin, furious wail that could only be coming from the sitting room.

Poor Brooks so far forgot himself as to widen his eyes. "Milord?"

"Yes, that's a baby. Its mother is still with the coach. The, er, nursemaid brought the infant up with her when she came looking for help." Nick slammed his beaver hat on his head. "We're going to hike down there now to see what's what and let them know help is coming. If we can, we'll guide some of the men back on foot, but we'll likely need the sleigh to fetch the women and the boy and all the luggage."

Brooks nodded. "Yes, milord. I'll see to it at once."

The baby wailed again, spurring them all to action. Brooks hurried off to send some hapless footman to the stables and to alert Mrs. Brooks to prepare for the new arrivals. Nick led the way to the door and threw it open.

A blast of frigid air and snow hit him in the face.

God, I hate English winters.

He gritted his teeth and plunged out into the bloody cold.

Chapter Three

That was Nick.

Caro stood in front of the fire, held Grace firmly to her shoulder, and swayed and dipped. Her little dance quieted the baby again, but if the idiot men didn't hurry, soon not even a spirited Scotch reel would keep Grace from howling.

How did I not recognize him at once?

The answer was obvious. She'd been focused on the emergency not the man. And it had been almost twenty years since she'd last seen him. He'd gone from being an awkward boy to a full-grown man.

A full-grown, handsome man.

She frowned. And an irresponsible one, apparently.

She'd known the moment she'd seen his guests what sort of a party she'd interrupted. The men—including Nick—were disheveled and . . . *relaxed*. That was the best word she could come up with to describe the casual familiarity of what was clearly not a family group.

Well, Nick didn't have any family now, at least not in England.

But beyond that, years of living in the Home among former prostitutes had made it obvious to Caro what sort of work these women did.

It's none of my concern if Nick wishes to fornicate in his country house. Why wouldn't he? Oakland has never felt like a home to him.

Except now he was Lord Oakland. It was his duty to care for the estate and its people.

She felt a heavy sense of . . . what? Disappointment?

Ridiculous. How Nick chose to live his life was none of her concern. Except . . .

Her stomach dropped. She *did* care what sort of man Nick had become.

She'd read about his escapades over the years, but she'd thought she was doing it simply to keep abreast of an old friend's life. When she'd seen the report of his uncle's death, she'd thought—*hoped*—that assuming the title would give Nick a purpose and a focus he'd lacked.

Apparently not.

A cold, hard knot formed in her stomach. She bounced Grace a little faster.

"She's so tiny."

One of the women hovered near Caro as if she wanted to touch Grace but was afraid to do so. She was young, likely younger than Grace's mother, and quite plump, her ample breasts on the verge of spilling out of her dress. Her head was a riot of blond ringlets and her eyes—

Her eyes were gray with yearning.

"Would you like to hold her?" Though holding a hungry infant wasn't a very pleasant experience unless you could also feed her.

The girl shook her head, and her eyes suddenly welled with tears. She pressed her lips tightly together as if that would keep her face from crumpling.

"It's all right, Fanny." One of the other women—the one with red hair, a broad face, and a smattering of freckles—put a comforting hand on Fanny's arm.

"Fanny lost a baby in the spring," the third woman said. She was the shortest and oldest, likely about Caro's age.

Fanny swallowed, gulped, and nodded, still unable to speak.

"I'm so sorry." Caro had thought, when she was young, especially after—

She shied away from the memory.

When she was young, she'd thought miscarriage would be a blessing for an unmarried woman who found herself increasing, but since then she'd learned the matter was far more complicated. Some women *were* relieved to escape a difficult situation, but others were distraught, and almost all were sad to some degree.

And now she knew that being an unmarried mother didn't have to be a curse, especially for women who managed to make their way to the Benevolent Home. Look at Pen. She'd raised her daughter for nine years by herself until August when, in an absurd fairy-tale ending, she'd married Harriet's father.

At least Caro *hoped* the fairy tale was a happy one, and the earl didn't prove to be a beast at heart.

She patted Grace and jiggled her some more.

Well, all right. Caro wasn't especially proud to admit it, but she'd be just a little happy and a lot relieved if Pen's marriage did *not* work out. They'd yet to find a new hop grower, and without a good crop of hops, there'd be no Widow's Brew.

"Are you the baby's nursemaid?" the older woman asked pleasantly. Her expression was friendly, but her eyes were sharp. Shrewd.

The businesswoman in Caro recognized that look—and she could guess what the woman was hoping to sell her. Surely, she didn't think she could charm Caro into joining her stable of light-skirts?

Perhaps she was assuming a motive that wasn't there. The question was a reasonable one, after all.

"No. I just offered to hold Grace. It was crowded in the coach, and her mother needed help."

"Ah." The woman's gaze grew sharper. She smiled. "I'm surprised your husband let you travel alone—or is he still with the stagecoach?"

Oh, Lord. Please *let me be wrong about this.* "I'm not married."

"I see." Her smile widened, her voice growing thick with flattery. "You must know your figure, your face—especially those lovely blue eyes—are very striking. Have you ever wished to live and work in Town? I could find you a splendid position."

Blast, blast, blast. I was *right.*

"I already have a position."

After spending years living and working with retired Cyprians—the "abandoned women" in the Home's name referred not just to females who had been abandoned by their families, but also to those who'd abandoned Society's rules—she felt no moral outrage. A woman alone had to resort to whatever means were at her disposal to make her way in the world. But she also felt no desire to join the ranks of the fashionable impures. She would have to be on death's doorstep to let a man touch her that way again.

"But this position would be much, much better. You'd be surrounded by only the best of Society." The woman's smile turned sly. "The best *gentlemen* of Society. With very little effort, you could have wealth and independence beyond your wildest dreams."

Caro's stomach twisted at the memory of what that "effort" entailed.

"It's true," the redheaded girl said. "Livy knows all the swells."

Fanny nodded. "I worked as a barmaid afore I fell in with Livy. This is much better." She grinned. "It's not really work."

The older woman—Livy—smiled. "I know any number of gentlemen—some lords, even—who would be very happy to make your acquaintance."

Caro's stomach twisted again. Fortunately, it was empty or she might have punctuated her refusal quite dramatically.

"Thank you, but I'm quite content with my current situation. I'm the brewster at the Benevolent Home for the Maintenance and Support of Spinsters, Widows, and Abandoned Women and their Unfortunate Children in Little Puddledon."

All three women blinked. Hearing the Home's name for the first time often had that effect on people.

"My name is Caroline Anderson." The baby squeaked, and Caro bounced her a bit more vigorously. The men had better get back with Grace's mother very, very soon. She couldn't distract the poor infant much longer. "And you are . . . ?"

"Olivia—Livy—Williams," the older woman said, and then introduced the others. "Fanny Taylor and Polly White." She smiled slowly, her eyes watchful, still hopeful of a sale. "We're here for a Christmas orgy."

Oh, hell.

Caro had known this was a scandalous gathering, but she hadn't realized it was quite *that* scandalous. Apparently, Nick had fully embraced the life of a degenerate peer.

"There's no reason you couldn't join in. If the snow keeps up, you'll be stranded here for a while. You might as well get a taste of the life I could offer you. If you like it . . ." Livy raised her brows and shrugged.

"We get paid very well," Polly said.

Livy nodded. "You'd have a very hard time finding work that pays half as well—and with such reasonable hours and delightful, er, *companionship*."

How could Caro get through to the woman? Perhaps if she spoke slowly and distinctly. "I. Really. Am. Not. Interested."

And she really, *really* hoped Nick would get back soon. Surely, enough time had elapsed for him to tramp down to the stagecoach and back. It wasn't as if he were hiking to Marbridge.

Livy's too-shrewd eyes were still studying her. "I think you might be just what Nick needs. He's seemed a little bored recently—a little, er, *limp* in the bedroom, if you know what I mean?"

No! She didn't want to know anything about Nick and bedrooms. If she weren't holding a baby, she'd stick her fingers in her ears and hum.

No need for that. Baby Grace finally lost patience. Her wails of hunger, sharp and insistent, ended all conversation.

Nick pushed open the front door in time to hear Livy's voice, coming from the sitting room. He caught only a few words—*bored, limp, bedroom*—but that was enough to cause a hot flush to flood his face and ears and—

Hell, likely his entire body, including his poor, maligned cock.

Zeus! Who's Livy talking to?

Cold horror quickly replaced mortification.

Dear God, don't let it be Caro.

And then the baby started to wail.

"Grace!" Grace's mother, still wearing her coat, pushed past him, hurried across the entry—tracking snow over the tile floor—and disappeared into the sitting room.

"Grace is hungry," Grace's brother said.

Nick nodded and closed the door, shutting out the arctic air. He and Bert and Felix had found the woman and her son halfway up the drive, fighting their way through the deep snow, following the path Caro had made earlier. Grace's mother had told them the others were still with the stage-coach, that the coachman had told her to stay, too, but she couldn't—she knew her baby needed her.

Why none of the men had felt the smallest spark of chivalry and come with the poor woman and child once it was clear they were setting off was beyond Nick's understanding. They would all have to come here eventually. The snow, which had got even worse in the short, miserable time he'd been out in it, must have made the roads completely impassible, even for a horseman. Oakland was their only hope of shelter—of survival, to be blunt about it.

So, he'd sent Felix and Bert on to the coach while he turned back, carrying the boy piggyback and going ahead of the woman, tamping down the snow for her as best he could. He'd seen the sleigh go by just as they reached the front door, so the others would be arriving soon.

Oh, blast. Now the boy was shivering, his teeth chattering so loudly, Nick could hear them. He'd have to—

"Lord Oakland!" Caro came striding toward him, the mother's still-dripping cloak draped over her arm, the mother with the still-screaming baby following behind her. "We need a room with a—ayiee!"

Caro slipped on a wet tile, got tangled in the cloak, and started to go down.

Nick lunged and caught her, pulling her tightly up against his chest.

Mmm. This is nice.

Caro fit into his arms perfectly. Her mouth was just the right distance from his that he could kiss . . .

Right. And get himself soundly slapped or, more likely, kneed in the groin.

He set Caro away just as she pushed against him. Her cheeks were flushed, and she wouldn't meet his gaze.

Interesting . . .

Suddenly he didn't feel at all bored—or limp, for that matter. Though it was a mystery how he could be feeling anything but a pounding headache with the infant shrieking.

"Mrs. . . ." Caro looked back at the woman. "What is your name, madam?" She had to raise her voice to be heard.

Ah. So, she's not the baby's nursemaid.

"Emma Dixon," the woman shouted back.

Caro nodded and turned to him. "We need a room at once with a roaring fire so Mrs. Dixon can get warm and dry and have some privacy in which to nurse Grace." She looked at the boy. "And Edward needs to get warm and dry, too."

Nick nodded. So, what was he to do? It was so hard to think with the baby wailing.

The only bedrooms with banked fires and sturdy doors were already assigned. The others were in Holland covers, though he supposed poor Mrs. Brooks and the chambermaids were feverishly working to get them ready. Still, none would have fires going.

There was only one answer: he'd have to let them use his room.

"Come along." He led the way up the stairs, the boy trotting at his side, the mother and Caro following behind with the screaming infant.

Harboring stranded travelers—especially a woman and her baby—is more in the spirit of the season than an orgy.

Eh, where had that thought come from? It was true, he supposed, if the holiday being celebrated was Christmas rather than Saturnalia, but housing a hodgepodge of strangers was also far more annoying and less entertaining.

It's not annoyance *you feel for Caro.*

Yes, but the odd excitement and anticipation—if those were what the feelings roiling his gut were—could easily end up turning to disappointment and painful, ah, frustration. As far as he knew, Caro was a virtuous woman, uninterested in any sort of dalliance.

Though there had *been those flushed cheeks . . .*

No. Remember, this is Henry Anderson's sister.

Not that he'd seen Henry in years. Nick had stopped

going home with Henry shortly after he'd turned fifteen and Uncle Leon had forced him to spend every school holiday at Oakland. And Henry had never been part of the rather wild set he ran with in London.

And then Henry had married young and retired to the country to raise horses and children.

Nick felt a twinge of regret. He'd liked Henry. *I shouldn't have let our friendship go.*

But people changed. Had different priorities . . .

And what are my priorities? Raking and carousing and wasting time?

Guilt slithered through him, as it had more and more often since his uncle's death.

That's just because Pearson has been yammering at me to sit down with him and go over the boring estate books.

In any event, he had more pressing problems at the moment. He could feel the eyes of the strong-willed woman behind him burning a hole in his back, willing him to move faster.

It wasn't just the fact that Caro was Henry's sister that demanded he treat her with respect. He might be Lord Devil and not the best landowner, but he hadn't lost all sense of propriety or, well, kindness. She was a woman forced to take shelter in his home. That was enough to guarantee her safety from him or any of his guests.

Unless she doesn't wish to be safe.

Ha! He knew a self-serving rationalization when he thought one.

Where had she been all these years? He vaguely remembered she'd gone to London. . . .

Ah, yes. She'd found a position at Dervington's London house as a nursemaid, hadn't she? Nick remembered being concerned about her when he'd heard that, as Dervington hadn't the best reputation, but by the time he'd got around to inquiring about her, she was gone. Under a bit of a cloud, he thought.

Guilt brushed his soul again.

"Why are there s-so many empty sp-spots?"

"What?"

Edward pointed to the walls, to the large rectangles of darker wallpaper where clearly paintings had once hung. "P-pictures are m-missing."

The poor boy's teeth were chattering so he could barely get the words out. He needed to get in front of a fire at once.

"I had them taken down. I didn't like them."

The first thing he'd done upon becoming Viscount Oakland was to relegate all the dark, cheerless paintings to the attics. It was bad enough having to walk the cold and gloomy halls without also having generations of dyspeptic—and poorly painted—ancestors frowning down at him. They'd given him nightmares as a boy. He'd used to pass them with his eyes trained on the floor.

He'd often wondered how his charming father, always cheerful and carcfree with a ready laugh, had descended from such dour people. And while it was possible some of the artists had misrepresented their subjects—he was enough of a connoisseur to recognize clumsy, pedestrian brushwork when he saw it—he'd had his uncle as a living example of the breed's stern, sullen temperament.

And it wasn't just the stiff, unsmiling faces he'd packed away. All the pictures of dead birds, hunting dogs tearing into fallen stags, avenging angels casting sinners into hellfire—all had been carried off to the attics.

He *had* kept one painting, though—a bright, happy landscape of the Grand Canal that he'd found tucked in the back of his uncle's dressing room. The moment Nick had seen it, he'd been transported back to Venice and his early boyhood, to the sun's warmth, the shouts of the gondoliers, the splash of the water.

And then he'd looked at it more closely and seen his father's mark in the lower left corner.

Why had his uncle hidden it away where only he could see it? More to the point, why had he kept it at all?

Perhaps there'd been a spark of joy somewhere in the man's dark heart.

The painting now hung prominently in Nick's bedchamber, on the wall across from the foot of his bed where it was the last thing he saw each night and the first thing he saw each morning. He'd thought of bringing it to London, but he hadn't wanted to risk damaging it in transport. It was all he had left of his father.

And Nick needed it more here. It made Oakland almost bearable.

"Oh. And you don't like Ch-Christmas either?"

He didn't, actually. He'd liked it as a boy in Venice, with the masks and music and street fairs. But here in England?

No.

Well, perhaps that wasn't completely fair. He likely didn't know what a proper English Christmas was. Here at Oakland, growing up with his stern uncle, Christmas had been a religious holiday only, meant to be spent in prayer and repentance.

But the boy wouldn't know that. "Why do you think I don't like Christmas?"

"There's no gr-greenery." Edward wrinkled his nose. "It doesn't smell like Christmas."

Hmm. Greenery. Mistletoe . . .

Neither Livy nor Polly nor Fanny needed a vegetative excuse to pucker up—or to do anything else of an amorous nature—but Caro . . .

It might be fun to see if he could find some mistletoe.

"It's not Christmas Eve yet. We'll hang some greenery then." He'd had no intention of decorating, but since it looked as if the boy would be stranded here for the holiday,

Nick should try to make things festive. He didn't want to turn into a killjoy like his uncle.

They finally arrived at his rooms.

"Here we are." He pushed open the door.

The boy gasped and looked around, his mouth hanging open for a moment before his teeth started chattering again. "It looks like a palace."

The room *was* large—and drafty, a huge waste of space. He'd much preferred his little room in his father's house in Venice, with its bright, white walls and view of the sea.

"It's hardly a palace." He went over to the hearth to wake the fire. The baby, still howling, wasn't far behind. The faster he got the fire going, the sooner the infant could be fed—and their hearing saved.

The boy followed him. "D-do you have it all to y-yourself?"

"Yes." Usually. He *had* entertained Livy here last night.

Or he'd *tried* to entertain her.

His stomach twisted, and he bent down to examine the fire. If anyone observed him now, he hoped they'd ascribe what he suspected was his heightened color to his proximity to the glowing embers.

He'd planned to put Livy in what was nominally the viscountess's bedroom that adjoined this one, but Mrs. Brooks hadn't thought to have it made up.

Well, perhaps she *had* thought of it and decided against it on the grounds that it offended her sense of decorum or moral rectitude. He'd considered taking the matter up with the woman when he'd discovered the problem, but he'd been too drunk on Christmas spirits—*alcoholic* spirits—to discuss the issue. By morning, reason—and sobriety—had reasserted themselves.

Asking Mrs. Brooks to countenance a Christmas orgy was bad enough, but forcing her to put a light-skirts, even a superlative one like Livy, in what had once been Lady Oakland's room would likely be more than she could tolerate.

He certainly didn't wish to push the woman to quit. Finding a new housekeeper here in the country, especially if he'd managed to alienate the local people, would be extremely difficult.

And she'd likely prevail upon her husband to leave, and then he'd be out a butler as well.

He honestly didn't want to upend Mrs. Brooks's life. She was a good sort. She'd grown up on the estate and had been a chambermaid when he'd been a boy here. She used to bring him sweets when she came back from visiting her family. She had a brother around his age.

Not that his uncle would let him play with the boy or with any of the other local children. Oh, no. It wouldn't do for his heir to rub elbows with the lower classes, especially given Nick's deplorable—in Uncle Leon's view—pedigree. Not only had Nick's mother been Italian, she'd been a lowly baker's daughter.

And it hadn't mattered about the room. Livy was just steps down the corridor, and in any event . . .

Eh, it might not reflect well on him, but he'd taken a great, twisted pleasure in inviting Livy into his puritanical uncle's bed.

He grimaced. Thumbing his nose at his uncle's ghost had been the *only* pleasure he'd taken last night.

Livy had kindly blamed his, er, lack of *spirit* on the vast quantity he'd imbibed, but drink had never affected him that way before. And earlier today in the sitting room, before Caro had arrived, his cock had again been completely unmoved by Livy's invitations.

His stomach twisted again. *I'm only thirty-two. I'm too young to give up sexual congress.*

It *must* be the curse of Oakland. He hadn't had this problem in London. Once he got back to Town all would be well.

And yet . . .

If he were being brutally honest, there'd been too many times of late when sitting home reading a good book appealed more than going out raking.

Of course it did. He wasn't a randy boy any longer. He was just selective in his bed partners.

You selected Livy and still couldn't rise to the occasion.

Bleh! Well then, his current, er, *droopy* mood *must* be due to Oakland and the bloody English cold.

"Lord Oakland."

He started. That was Caro's voice, sharp with impatience and coming from directly behind him. The infant's screaming must have drowned out the sound of her footsteps. Was she going to urge him to hurry along with the fire just as she'd pushed him to set off on the rescue mission?

He'd grant she'd been right about the rescue, but some things couldn't be rushed. Coaxing this fire back to life was one of them.

Making love was another. . . .

Ha! Last night he couldn't coax his poor cock to do anything, fast or slow.

He glanced over his shoulder at her. "Just let me be certain the fire is going well, Miss Anderson, and then I'll leave."

Caro dismissed his words with a wave of her hand. "I can tend to the fire. What we need now are some blankets and towels. Mrs. Dixon and Edward should get out of their wet clothing as soon as possible."

"Right." The fire was burning nicely now, so he stood and—

Where the hell am I going to find extra blankets and towels?

He'd no idea where to look. He'd just arrived yesterday—

No, he could have been here for years, and he still wouldn't know where the extra linens were kept. Linens and blankets and counterpanes had always just appeared on his bed.

"Milord?"

Thank God! Mrs. Brooks was at the door. He felt like falling on her neck, he was so relieved to see her, but he restrained himself and simply smiled.

At least the boy and his mother were now standing by the fire and not shivering, so he didn't look completely incompetent. Even the baby had been lulled to silence by the heat.

Or perhaps she was just gathering her strength to start wailing again. In any event, it was easier to think without the piercing noise.

"Mrs. Brooks, you are just the person we need. Mrs. Dixon and her son, Edward, require towels and blankets and perhaps a rack to hang their clothes to dry before the fire."

"Of course, milord." She smiled at the woman and her son. "Just come with me. I'll get you both settled in your own room and make you comfortable. The men are back with your bag, Mrs. Dixon, so you and your son can change into something warm and dry at once."

Mrs. Brooks looked at him as Mrs. Dixon and Edward walked past her. "Milord, after I attend to Mrs. Dixon and her son, where would you like me to put our other new"—she swallowed—"guests?"

Lord, who *were* they taking in? Not that he had any choice in the matter; he couldn't bar the door and have the poor souls freeze to death. He just hoped one of them didn't make off with his valuables.

Though perhaps he should fear more that they'd steal his peace and sanity. His Christmas orgy was definitely ruined—not that it had shown much promise before their surprise guests' arrival.

"Put them wherever seems best to you, Mrs. Brooks. You know the rooms better than I."

She nodded—and looked at Caro.

Oh, no, Mrs. Brooks wasn't taking her away. He needed Caro to tell him about their surprise company.

"And then please come back and let me know where things stand. Miss Anderson and I will await your return here."

He heard Caro give a small squawk of surprise or disagreement, but it was quickly drowned out by Grace's far louder and more insistent squawk from the corridor.

Mrs. Brooks was already in motion. "Very well, milord," she said, and then closed the door behind her.

"Lord Oakland—"

He held up his hand. "Miss Anderson, please. I need you to help me sort out whom I'm taking under my roof." He gestured for her to take one of the wingchairs facing the fire.

She stayed standing and frowned. "I-I don't know anything about them."

"You know more than I do. You, at least, were in the coach with them."

"Yes, but—" She pressed her lips together, swallowed, and then said, a distinct quaver in her voice, "It's not p-proper for me to be h-here."

He felt his brows shoot up and his jaw drop. Not proper? This was the first sign he'd had that the woman who'd burst into his house, berated him in his own entry hall—even after she knew he was the viscount—and spent several minutes with three light-skirts without resorting to a fit of the vapors, gave a fig about propriety. She was no wilting wallflower.

The Caro he'd known hadn't given a fig for propriety.

He remembered the first time he'd met her—the first time he'd come home with Henry. Uncle Leon had dumped him at school at the beginning of second term. He'd been the only new boy there and, with his dark hair and eyes, clearly not one hundred percent English. Henry had been one of the few to befriend him.

Henry really had been a capital fellow. I shouldn't have let our connection break.

So, when he'd gone home with Henry that first time, he'd been surprised by Caro. She'd been around the same age as his cousin Maria, but she'd been nothing like Maria. Maria had liked lacy dresses and dolls, hated mud, and run screaming from frogs and spiders. Caro, on the other hand, hadn't thought twice about pulling on one of Henry's old shirts and a pair of breeches he'd outgrown, tying back her hair, and going exploring through fields and woods whenever she could sneak past her mother. She'd been strong and fearless and determined.

She *couldn't* be afraid he was going to attack her, could she?

Shock—and yes, affront—surged in his breast, quickly followed, he was embarrassed to admit, by a tinge of relief. If that *was* her fear, it could not have been his lamentable lack of bedroom vigor Livy had been describing when he'd come back with Mrs. Dixon.

"I'm afraid *proper* wasn't invited to this party, Miss Anderson. Surely, you've discerned Livy's and the other women's profession?"

"Yes. Of course."

That was better. Now she sounded annoyed rather than alarmed.

"You have my word I will not harm you. I wouldn't harm any woman, but unless I miss my guess, you are Henry Anderson's sister. We knew each other as children, did we not?"

She didn't look surprised, so she must already have made the connection.

"Yes, but we are not children any longer."

True. And women, as the weaker sex, were at a physical

disadvantage. Perhaps she would feel more at ease if she had some sort of weapon at hand with which to defend herself. He glanced around. . . .

His eyes fell on the marble statues on either side of the mantel clock. One of those would do splendidly. He grabbed the nearest one, hefted it—it was heavy, but not too heavy for her to manage, he hoped—and handed it to her.

She was strong. She took it from him without any difficulty.

"What's this for?"

"To brain me with if I suddenly forget myself." He smiled in what he hoped was a reassuring manner. "Now, please do take a seat. May I pour you a glass of brandy?"

Chapter Four

"Oh, very well."

Caro dropped into the chair rather gracelessly. She was annoyed with herself. She didn't care if Nick's guests were proper or not, and she certainly didn't care what anyone thought of her own actions. She'd never been one to dance to Society's restrictive tune. But now that she was a mature woman, living among other women who had been forced by circumstances or their own choices to step far, far outside Society's ballrooms, she saw *propriety* for what it really was: Society's whip to keep women where it wanted them—subservient and powerless.

No, she'd foolishly let fear ambush her simply because she was alone with a strange man in a secluded situation without her knife. In all the hubbub, she'd forgotten to get it out of her cloak pocket.

Nick is not *a strange man. He won't hurt me.*

She hoped. She hadn't seen him in years—so many years that she hadn't recognized him at first. He'd been a boy then; he was a man now.

A very handsome man.

Yes, and an irresponsible one, remember?

She'd admit to having had a schoolgirl crush on him years ago, but she wasn't a schoolgirl any longer.

So why have you scoured the papers for any mention of Lord Devil all these years? And why were you so disappointed that he was hosting an orgy?

Oh, all right. Perhaps it *was* more than a schoolgirl crush, but that made it even more foolish. She wasn't usually one to build air castles. She couldn't afford to. She dealt in concrete matters—hops and malt, pounds and pence.

Except for your dream to sell Widow's Brew in London. That *air castle was bigger than a London brewery.*

Defeat settled heavily on her heart, but she quickly pushed it aside. She didn't have the luxury of curling up for a good cry. She needed to move forward, to look for the silver lining in this dark cloud. At least this unfortunate journey would cure her of her ridiculous London plans *and* this silly infatuation. That was good. Painful, but good.

In any event, the point was she *had* read every mention of Lord Devil she'd happened upon in the papers—and she'd never seen any accusations that he'd forced himself on a woman. And now Livy had said the poor man was a bit of a gelding. A . . . What was the word? Eunuch. Not literally, but functionally, which was all that mattered.

So why have a Christmas orgy?

Excellent question. Perhaps he wished to throw people off the scent. She hadn't seen any hints in the papers, but there might well be rumors circulating through the *ton* about his . . . problem. In her very brief time in London, she'd seen how the *ton* loved to gossip.

She felt a stab of sympathy. Men took such ridiculous pride in their amorous prowess. To be unable to perform at all must be extremely lowering.

Lowering—ha!

And to be an impotent peer must be the biggest curse of

all. That sort's main purpose was to procreate so they could pass their titles and wealth on to the next generation.

Perhaps the affliction runs in the family. Nick's uncle was childless.

She felt the last bit of tension drain out of her shoulders. She put the statue Nick had given her on the table next to her chair. How nice not to have to worry she was going to be assaulted at any moment.

She frowned. At *this* moment. There was still the Weasel and the other men to consider. They'd likely be snowbound for days. Nick's home was large, with far too many isolated spots. She'd remember to keep her pocketknife with her from now on, but she'd rather not have to stab any of the other guests—or have to be constantly on her guard.

What can I do?

An obvious, if outrageous, solution presented itself.

If Nick's willing, I can pretend we have a liaison.

It would ruin her reputation, but then her reputation—her *social* reputation—had been ruined years ago. Even people who hadn't heard the sorry tale of her time in London assumed the worst of her, given her advanced age, her unmarried state, and the fact that she lived at the Benevolent Home for the Maintenance and Support of Spinsters, Widows, and Abandoned Women and their Unfortunate Children.

But if Nick wished to hide his, er, problem, her scheme would suit far better than the one he'd devised. He certainly couldn't pretend he was an enthusiastic orgy participant if Livy was going to tell everyone about his affliction. And if she'd told Caro within moments of meeting her, she would tell anyone.

Caro studied his profile as he poured their brandy. Now that she knew who he was, she could see the soft curves of the boy's face under the hardened planes and angles of the man's. His jaw hadn't been outlined by stubble when he'd been young—even at fifteen, he'd still had a boy's smooth skin—but his dark brown hair had tumbled onto his forehead just as it did now. And while his eyes hadn't changed, the skin around them was more weathered, with faint lines and creases.

It was his distinctive dark brown eyes that had given her the feeling of familiarity when she'd stood in the entry, thinking he was the butler and ranting at him to mount a rescue.

He turned toward her then, offering the brandy glass and smiling.

Ah! She'd forgotten the dimples. They'd been attractive enough in the boy's face, but in the man's . . .

They were devastating. Her insides did an odd little fluttering dance.

It was really too bad Nick was impotent. He could seduce any woman he wanted with those dimples.

Though not me, of course.

Er, right.

She released the unsettling feeling in a long breath and smiled back at him. It was time to negotiate.

"So, am I safe then? You aren't going to use that marble statue to bash my head in?" Nick's voice was teasing.

"Not this time," she teased back. It was so . . . freeing not to have to worry he'd take her tone as encouragement and attempt unwanted liberties. Even the light of male admiration she saw in his eyes didn't alarm her, since she knew he was incapable of acting on any amorous feelings.

Though it's a little disappointing, too . . .

No, it wasn't. Other women might find male attentions enjoyable, but she didn't. They were uncomfortable—painful, really—and embarrassing.

"But I put it here on the table just in—oh!" She'd finally *looked* at the thing. Had Nick known what he'd handed her?

No, apparently not. His eyes held confusion rather than

suppressed glee. She'd grown up with too many brothers not to be very familiar with *that* expression.

"What is it?" he asked.

Some things had to be shown rather than told.

She handed him the statue. He gave her a puzzled look and then glanced down—

"Whoa!" His eyes widened, brows shooting up.

Whoa, indeed. The statue was of a shepherdess—or at least, that's what Caro guessed she was, given the crook she was inexplicably straddling and the devoted sheep gazing up at her. A very buxom, oddly blissful shepherdess who had misplaced most of her clothing.

"To think old Uncle Leon had *this* in his room."

"You've not seen it before?"

Nick shook his head. "Well, I must have *seen* it. I can't imagine Mrs. Brooks or one of the other servants would have put it out especially for this visit. But I've never actually *looked* at it before." He glanced at the mantel, frowned again, and walked over to inspect the other statue. "Gah."

"What is it?"

"You don't want to know." He grabbed the statue, shoved it and the shepherdess into a cabinet, and firmly closed the door.

"Perhaps I do." She did not appreciate being treated like a child.

On the other hand, she didn't really wish to examine lewd sculptures either.

"Trust me, you don't. I wish *I* hadn't seen it." He dropped into the other chair and stared at the fire, stretching his legs out toward it as if he wanted to be as close to the warmth as he could.

Ah, yes. She remembered how he'd always tried to stay near the hearth when he'd come home with Henry. Her mother had said Nick's blood was thin because he'd been born in Italy.

He let out a long breath. "I just cannot believe it."

Wasn't he overreacting? Obscene statues and drawings weren't that uncommon among the men of the *ton*. Even her father had had a book of salacious prints that he'd hid on the top shelf in his library—and which her brothers had quickly discovered.

She opened her mouth to tell Nick that—and then bit her tongue. Something about the bleakness of his expression suggested this wasn't really about the statues.

"My uncle was a harsh, puritanical zealot," he finally said, his voice rough. Tight. "He hated the fact that his heir was the product of his younger, easygoing, artistic brother and a wanton"—he glanced at her—"in *his* view"—he looked back at the fire—"hot-blooded, emotional Italian woman. Not that my uncle ever met my mother. His opinion was built solely on narrow-minded prejudice."

Nick's jaw flexed as if he were clenching his teeth.

"Um." Caro didn't know what to say, so she just nodded and made what she hoped were encouraging sounds. "Mm."

"He tried his best to cure me of any influence she'd had, any scrap of fun or joy I'd managed to hold onto, and turn me into a cold, hard-hearted replica of himself. He'd have drained my mother's blood out of me if he could have. I *hated* him."

He said "hated" with such an intense, controlled violence, it made her both shiver with unease and ache with compassion.

"I'm sorry." She remembered now that she'd sensed sadness in him even when he was a boy, but she'd never asked him about it.

Asked him? Boys didn't talk about feelings, at least not the boys in her family. . . .

You don't talk about feelings either, do you?

Oh. She blinked. Perhaps not. Well, what was the point? Talking never got things done.

Nick shrugged off her sympathy and smiled again, though this time the dimples were absent and the expression didn't reach his eyes. "Perhaps you can see now why I so enjoyed spending school holidays with Henry. Your house was full of life."

She snorted. "I'd have called it full of chaos."

That made him laugh, bringing back the dimples. "What boy doesn't like chaos?" He glanced at the mantel and frowned again. "I thought my uncle an unpleasant, self-righteous, mean-spirited man, but I've always given him credit for living by his wrongheaded convictions." He shook his head. "Now I discover he was also a colossal hypocrite."

She heard the bitter anger in his voice and again felt a pang of compassion. She wanted to make things better. . . .

Are you mad?

Nick was a man, a peer with the money and power that went along with that position. He didn't need her sympathy. *Need* it? Ha! He'd laugh at her should she be bold enough—or totty-headed enough—to offer it.

And yet sympathy still tugged at her heart.

Nick shook his head as if that would free him from his unpleasant memories and then looked back at her. "How *is* Henry? I'm afraid I lost touch with him once he married."

"I assume he's well." Henry and the rest of her family had cut ties with her—and she with them—after her disastrous time in London, but there was no need to share those details now, or ever. "He's not the best correspondent, at least not when it comes to writing his sister."

Especially since he has no idea where I am.

"And, frankly, I'm not much of a letter writer myself." She should be fair and not lay all the blame on Henry.

Nick's brows rose in a look of shock and surprise. "I can't imagine your losing touch with your family like that. If I—" He paused. Frowned. "Well, yes, I *have* lost track of my Italian relatives, but that's largely because my uncle wouldn't let me write them when I was a boy. And I suspect if they wrote me, he threw their letters on the fire."

"You're not a boy any longer. You could write them now." Perhaps it was rude of her to point that out, but. . . .

But you aren't a girl any longer, either. You could write to Henry. It's possible he and even Papa and the rest of them would forgive and forget.

Possible, but unlikely.

Nick was nodding. "I'm sure you are right, but after a while, my life in Italy seemed no more real than a pleasant, hazy dream." He took a swallow of brandy and smiled at her. "I did envy Henry his, as you say, chaos. There was always someone at hand to play with."

"Or fight with."

He laughed. "That, too."

Caro had loved her brothers, but there had been so *many* of them. Almost every year had brought a new baby boy. For the longest time, she'd desperately wanted a sister, and then she'd just wanted time alone—an impossible feat with so many people, so many *boys,* crammed into one house. So, she'd taken to escaping outside, to the fields and woods, to find peace—and, yes, to avoid some of the childcare that fell to her as the family's only female besides her mother.

Her father had soon put an end to her solitary ramblings, though. It wasn't appropriate or safe for her to wander the countryside by herself, he'd said. Her mother had agreed.

To be honest, Caro had agreed, too, if grudgingly. Even though her father was the local squire, and she had an army of brothers to defend her, she'd no longer felt safe by herself. Grown men had started to stare at her—especially at her bosom—and to whistle and catcall. It had been maddening, but there'd seemed to be nothing she could do to change matters.

"And how have you been?" Nick asked.

Did she hear a note of false heartiness in his voice? She looked at him.

He looked at the fire. "I—" He cleared his throat. "I think Henry told me years ago that you were coming to London to be a nursemaid." He glanced back at her. "I'm sorry I never looked you up to see how you went on."

Was that . . . Did she see *pity* in his eyes?

Dear God! He doesn't know what happened, does he? He can't. If he does. . . .

No. She couldn't think about that now.

She took a deep breath and forced herself to smile. To speak calmly. Briefly.

The less said about her stay in London, the better.

"I *was* a nursemaid for a very short while, but I found the position didn't suit me. Now I live in the village of Little Puddledon at the Benevolent Home for the Maintenance and Support of Spinsters, Widows, and Abandoned Women and their Unfortunate Children."

"The . . . what?" Nick's brows furrowed.

She did hope he wasn't trying to puzzle out if she were a spinster or an abandoned woman, though if he *did* know the sorry tale of her time at Dervington's. . . .

Shame and guilt, feelings she'd thought she'd long cured herself of, twisted in her stomach.

She ignored them.

"Jo—the former Baron Havenridge's widow—started the Home after her husband died. We have over two dozen women and children living there now. We depend on the Duke of Grainger's support—and now the Earl of Darrow's also." Might as well be bold. "You are welcome to contribute, too, if you have the interest."

She smiled and swept on. No need to pick his pocket

at this precise moment—it was enough to have planted the seed.

"We do try to support ourselves as much as we can. A few years ago, we hit upon the idea of selling ale. We got the manor's old brewhouse working, and we now supply the village tavern and a few other local establishments with Widow's Brew, the ale I developed. I'm the brewer, you see." She smiled—persuasively, she hoped. "I discovered I'd much rather tend ale than babies." *Or dodge randy fathers.*

Though, to be painfully honest, she hadn't done enough dodging. That had been the worst of a bad story.

"That's why I was in London. I went up to see if I could interest a tavern keeper there—a man whose brother carries Widow's Brew in his establishment in Westling, near Little Puddledon—in adding our ale to his offerings."

"Oh." Nick was clearly struggling to keep up. "And how did that go?"

Horribly. "I'm afraid he decided against taking any at this time." And since she was never going to darken his door again, *this time* meant *ever*.

She shrugged. "It's just as well. I hadn't focused on how far London is from Little Puddledon. It would be very difficult—likely impossible—for us to keep any London tavern adequately supplied."

Nick nodded. "Even without the distance, I can't imagine your operation would be large enough to compete with the London breweries. A vat in one of them gave out a few years ago, and the force of the escaping beer broke through the back wall, flooding the surrounding neighborhood and killing several people. It was the talk of London for quite a while."

Caro nodded. She'd read the newspaper accounts of that disaster when it had happened—or at least when the London papers had finally found their way to Little Puddledon.

"And there might be laws or regulations or other sorts of official red tape that would give you problems," Nick said, "even if everything else was in your favor."

Caro let out a long, discouraged breath. Oh, blast. Getting Widow's Brew into the London market *had* been a mad dream. She'd known it all along, she supposed—she wasn't a complete cabbagehead—but she'd refused to admit it.

And, yes, Pen had pointed out the plan's impracticability again earlier this year. That had only made Caro more determined. Growing up with so many brothers had—possibly—encouraged her to obstinacy.

She would just have to come up with some other scheme to increase the Home's income. Perhaps she could learn something from how things were managed at Oakland.

"Do you mind if I talk to your brewer and look around your brewhouse?"

Nick stared at her for a moment and then shook his head. "As far as I know, the brewhouse has been turned over to storage. My uncle was very much against the consumption of alcohol, even beer"—he glanced at the mantel—"or at least I thought he was. He certainly ranted at me enough times on the subject."

"Oh." Perhaps she shouldn't be surprised. Most of her Widow's Brew went to pubs. The Home's residents drank tea, coffee, and chocolate.

Of course, the Home's residents were women and children.

"Any beer or ale we have, I suspect we get from those large London breweries, but you may quiz Mr. Pearson, the estate manager, if you like. He would know the details."

"Thank you, I will. When would be the best time to—"

Hold on. She'd let herself get distracted. She hadn't intended to discuss Widow's Brew or her past. No, it was the immediate future she needed to address.

Best get to the point before his housekeeper got back. Even if Mrs. Brooks was aware of Nick's affliction—and from Caro's short stay in a peer's home, she'd discovered the servants usually knew everything that went on within its walls—Caro couldn't see Nick wishing to have the matter discussed in front of the woman.

Well, he likely didn't wish to discuss it with Caro, either, but there was no help for that.

A sudden case of nerves caused her to use his title. "Lord Oakland—"

Nick raised his hand to stop her. "Please, call me Nick. My friends do." His lips twisted. "I rather loathe being called by my uncle's title. I feel his soul-sucking ghost hovering over me whenever I hear it."

She felt another tug of sympathy.

"Oh, yes. I see." She'd never considered what it would be like to set aside the name you'd grown up with and answer to something totally different.

Of course she hadn't. She spent very little time pondering the peerage—with the exception of the time she'd spent this summer plotting how to persuade the Duke of Grainger to continue his support for the Home.

Nick was smiling now. "I don't know how long we'll be stranded here together, Caro, but at a minimum it will be several days. We may as well dispense with the formalities."

Right. They were stranded here. *She* was stranded here with the Weasel and other assorted men who she feared would be eager to dispense with *all* formality.

Dispensing with formality with Nick was precisely what she'd thought might solve her problems and his.

"And we were childhood friends of a sort, weren't we?" he said.

"Yes. We were." Of a sort.

Perhaps she could play upon that sentiment. She leaned toward him as if being physically closer would help persuade him.

Caro would admit that, once or twice, she'd resorted to a

little flirting to sway a wavering male into trying Widow's Brew. But she was always careful to do so only when she had a clear path of escape in case the fellow misunderstood and thought she was offering something more than ale.

Fortunately, she didn't have to worry about that here.

"I need your help, Nick."

Chapter Five

"Of course you may count on me," Nick said. "What do you need me to do?"

Concern—an admittedly foreign emotion—swirled through him, mixing with regret. It sounded as if Caro had broken off all contact with her family and had banished herself to the country. Perhaps if he'd done something all those years ago when he'd first heard the Dervington rumors. . . .

And yet, what could he have done? He wasn't Caro's relative. She had a father and brothers.

But none of them are members of the ton *or even frequent visitors to London. They know very little about Society.*

And, well, much as he appreciated Caro's father welcoming him into his home all those years ago, he'd always suspected part of the reason for his hospitality had been that Nick would one day be Viscount Oakland. There'd been an undeniable whiff of toadyism about Mr. Anderson. Would he have taken his daughter's part against a marquess?

I should have written Henry.

Except . . .

He frowned. They'd all been more than a little judgmental, hadn't they? Not as bad as Uncle Leon—that would be well-nigh impossible—but bad enough that they might blame Caro for whatever had happened.

He suddenly wondered if it was not he but Henry who'd broken the connection between them.

He'd admit some of—a lot of—his own behavior *was* offensive, but he was in an entirely different league than Caro.

He studied her as she cleared her throat, shifting in her chair as if she were suddenly uncomfortable.

I hope she hasn't blamed herself all these years for what happened.

If anything *did* happen. All he knew for certain was she had left London under a cloud.

In any event, she'd clearly made the best of her situation. She was still assertive—her big, blue eyes still threatened to swallow you whole and spit you out in little pieces if you were acting like a fool. But it couldn't have been easy to go off on her own.

He smiled to himself. He was quite sure Caro would scoff at easy.

"It concerns my fellow travelers—well, one traveler in particular. Or I hope only one."

Ah. And now they were finally back to the place where this conversation had been supposed to begin. "As I have no idea who was in the stagecoach—and who is now in my house—you will have to be a bit more explicit."

Caro frowned briefly and then nodded. "Yes. Well, as I said before, I actually know next to nothing about them. There's the coachman, of course, and the two men who got on at the Crow"—she scowled—"and sent us into the ditch. They rode outside, so I got only a very brief glimpse of them when they ran up just as the coachman was closing the door and then again after we crashed. And then there's Mrs. Dixon, of course, and her children. They boarded at the Crow also."

Ah, Mrs. Dixon. Now there was a puzzle.

"Why is she traveling with such a young baby at

Christmastime—and in a snowstorm?" He didn't know anything about children, especially infants, but common sense would counsel—and events as they had unfolded had proven—that it would have been far wiser for her to have stayed safe at home or, if she'd already been on the road, then safe inside the warm, dry Crow.

Caro's brows wrinkled. She looked as puzzled as he was. "I don't know. She told the coachman she had to get to Marbridge before Christmas, but she didn't give a reason."

Another problem. He let out a long breath and took a sip of brandy. "Very well. I assume she'll tell us once she's settled—or her son will. He seems an articulate child. If it's truly something that can't be delayed, I might be able to send her and her family on in my sleigh, but it's still snowing, and Marbridge is farther than I would think anyone—especially a woman with a baby and a young son—would wish to travel in an open conveyance."

And he was relatively certain it was farther than Walters would wish to drive—or, more to the point, wish the horses to travel. Nick didn't know Walters well—he hadn't been on the estate when Nick was growing up—but every head groom Nick had ever known valued horses far more than people.

Caro nodded. "If she doesn't, I'll ask. Perhaps it is a matter we can address here."

He knew Caro meant "we" in a general sense, but he was surprised at the pleasure he felt at hearing her say the word.

Ridiculous. They weren't and would never be a "we."

Why not? You could marry—

Alarm sprang awake in his chest. It tried to get his heart pounding and his thoughts rushing to the battlements with a supply of evasions and arguments.

Alarm was unsuccessful. Perhaps it was the fire or the solitude or the brandy, but his heart and thoughts, like cows chewing their cud as walkers passed through their field, placidly watched alarm rush by.

Ha! Alarm said huffily. *Just see. If you aren't careful, you'll get caught in parson's mousetrap.*

Absurd. Being alone with a mature woman who wasn't a whore, enjoying her company in a completely non-amorous way—

Well, not *completely* nonamorous. He wasn't dead. Of *course* his heretofore somnolent cock was awake and interested, but in a pleasant, lazy sort of way, since it—and he—knew Caro was not available for dalliance. He would just enjoy the thrum of desire, and perhaps tonight he would be able to entertain Livy properly.

Thinking idly—*very* idly—of marriage did not mean he'd be waiting at the altar soon—or ever.

Though talking to Caro did *soothe the pain of seeing that bloody statue and discovering Leon's black-hearted hypocrisy.*

He'd never before talked about his uncle like that with anyone.

True, but he'd vowed years ago never to wed. If he married, he might have a son, and he didn't want to give Leon the satisfaction of continuing his direct line.

Uncle Leon is dead.

Nick frowned. Yes, but the principle still held.

In any event, he thought Caro was just as uninterested in marriage as he. And should he be foolish enough to attempt anything of a lascivious nature, he was quite confident she'd firmly and unequivocally make her displeasure known, even without access to a heavy, lewd statue with which to whack him.

"We don't want her fretting," Caro was saying. "It might affect her milk, and that would be very bad for little Grace."

Nick grunted. He had no opinion—nor any knowledge—about nursing mothers.

But if you married Caro, you might.

Zeus! What *was* the matter with him?

It must be his cock talking.

Blessedly, Caro moved on from Mrs. Dixon.

"There's an older, married couple," Caro said. "Humphrey and Muriel. I don't know their family name. They're on their way to Marbridge for the annual Christmas gathering of Muriel's sisters." Her lip curled. "And then there's the clergyman."

Aha! They must have finally reached the problem. People did not usually look quite so disgusted by the clergy, though he'd certainly encountered one or two or three whom he'd not be surprised to see hobnobbing with Uncle Leon in hell.

She scowled and leaned closer. She really was rather splendid when she was incensed.

All right, she was rather splendid all the time—she just seemed to be incensed rather regularly.

"When Mrs. Dixon tried to get on the stagecoach, the scoundrel said there was no room and that she and Edward should sit on the roof or go back into the inn!"

Shock caused Nick to sit up straighter.

"It's true there was only one seat," Caro was saying, "but Mrs. Dixon isn't large, and Edward takes up only a sliver of space."

"Indeed." Even Nick, who knew nothing about children, was appalled by the man's—and a man of the cloth at that—callousness. "Sit on the roof with a boy and a baby? And in a snowstorm?!"

Caro nodded as if she approved of his reaction. "To be fair, he didn't know about the baby at that point. Mrs. Dixon had covered Grace with her cloak." Her brows slanted down. "But I doubt it would have made a difference to him if he *had* known."

The more Nick thought about it, the angrier he got. Edward seemed such a quiet, well-behaved boy. Not that it would be right to put even an unruly youngster on a stagecoach roof, of course, but Nick might be better able to understand the wish to do so. But any man or woman with a heart would swallow that urge.

And it was Christmastime, for God's sake. One would think a member of the clergy, especially, would be charitable to children and young mothers in hardship, forced to travel at such a time. Had the man skipped over the Nativity story in his Bible?

He'd grant he might feel a special degree of sympathy here. It had been Christmastime when Nick—a few years older than Edward was now and freshly orphaned—had had to leave the warmth of Italy and his Italian aunts and uncles and cousins for the icy cold of England and his English uncle.

"Fortunately," Caro was saying, "the coachman set the man straight." She shook her head, frown deepening. "But the clergyman didn't move over even a whisker to make room for the boy. Edward had to sit on his mother's lap. That's why I had Grace. I couldn't bear to see Mrs. Dixon trying to juggle two children."

"Quite right." What other woman of his acquaintance would have seen the problem, let alone offered to hold a stranger's infant? Livy or Polly or Fanny might, he supposed, but he couldn't think of a single Society miss who would.

Not that he spent much time with Society misses. They gave him hives.

"So, what do you want me to do about the clergyman? Banish him to the stables? There's a certain poetic justice in that."

Well, perhaps not. In the Bible story, it was the Savior, not the Devil, who'd slept in such humble surroundings.

Still, a bit of hay in the clergyman's drawers might serve as a barnyard version of penitential sackcloth, provoking the man to piety.

Caro smiled briefly. "I doubt that's necessary now. He doesn't have to inconvenience himself to accommodate anyone, though he might drive you mad with his annoying habit of tossing Bible verses into the conversation."

That Nick could handle. "I'll turn him over to my friend Bertram Collins. He considered a life in the church before he came into an inheritance." Nick grinned. "I'll wager Bertram knows a verse to undercut any the reverend might offer. The Holy Book can be remarkably contradictory if one has a mind to make it so."

Caro grinned back at him, her eyes gleaming with mischief—and he felt a . . . connection. Something he'd not felt for a woman before.

No, not *for*. With. Something he'd not felt *with* a woman. There was a mutuality about this. He wasn't hunting. She wasn't luring. They were sharing as equals.

It was an odd, confusing sensation.

Or perhaps he'd merely had too much brandy. He looked at his glass.

No. It was still half full.

"So," he said to break the odd rapport, "is there anything else you need me to do?"

She stared at him blankly—and then shook her head. "Oh, it's not the clergyman I need your help with—or at least he's not my main concern."

"No?"

"No. It's the Weasel I'm most worried about."

It was Nick's turn to stare blankly. "You have a vermin problem?"

Her eyes widened—and then she laughed. "I don't mean a *real* weasel. I mean a *human* weasel—the last man in the coach. *He's* the one I need your help with. He, ah."

Her face suddenly flushed. She looked away and took a sip of brandy—her first, he thought.

"I think . . ." She looked back at him. "That is, I feel certain . . ."

Bloody hell. This did not sound good. And yet what could be the issue? If Caro didn't know the fellow's name, he couldn't be a previous acquaintance. And it was hard to see what mischief a man could cause in a crowded coach. The only possibility Nick could imagine was that the fellow had let his hands wander, but Caro must have corrected his mistake at once. As a girl, she'd never been shy about putting an idiot male in his place.

"Stop hemming and hawing and just spit it out," he said, likely a bit too roughly, but it did the trick.

"I'm afraid he'll attack me."

Nick's jaw dropped. He felt as if he'd been kicked in the gut.

"Uh. That's . . ." He cleared his throat. "I mean, don't you think you, er, might be"—he cleared his throat again—"overreacting?"

"No." The forceful, uncompromising word was accompanied by a piercing glare. There wasn't the faintest hint of uncertainty in her eyes.

"Women have to develop a sixth sense about such things, Nick. From a very early age, we learn to keep our eyes open, to be aware of everyone near us." She gave him a slight, pained smile. "Like mice, we're always ready to dart for safety the moment we sense the hawk's shadow above us."

That sounded unpleasant—and a bit hyperbolic, frankly.

"I usually carry a small knife in my pocket when I'm meeting with tavern keepers. I had to use it in London. The man thought I wished to sell him something other than Widow's Brew."

Well, she *had* been alone with the fellow. No, that

shouldn't be taken as an invitation, but Nick could see how a man might make such a mistake.

She must have read his thoughts from his expression, because her color rose. He wouldn't have been shocked to see steam come from her ears.

"You don't believe me, do you? Of course you don't. Why would you? You're a *man*." She managed to inject the word with an impressive amount of venom.

He tried to lighten her mood. "I'm glad you noticed."

She didn't take his weak joke well. Her lip curled. "*And* a peer."

She clearly did not care for the nobility, but this time her prejudice was quite unfair. "Was your tavern keeper a member of the nobility?" he asked. "Or is this Weasel?"

Though he might agree with her low opinion of the peerage.

Oh, it was true some titled fellows were serious men, dedicated to the good stewardship of their land and people. Some spoke eloquently in the House of Lords and worked to solve the many social and political issues the country was grappling with now that Napoleon had been defeated: famine, high food prices, unemployment, parliamentary reform. But many others were ne'er-do-wells, interested only in their own pleasure, drinking, and whoring, and gambling, and—

And which one am I?

Zeus! Where the hell had *that* thought come from?

His situation was different. He wasn't supposed to be the viscount. He wasn't even supposed to be in England. If the damnable fever hadn't taken his parents, he'd be happily elsewhere. Perhaps Italy or Greece. Definitely somewhere warm and sunny with—

No. It wasn't his *parents'* deaths that had exiled him. It was Papa's. Even if Mama had survived, he was all too certain Uncle Leon would have demanded she ship Nick to

England. His bloody uncle would never have let his heir be raised by "foreigners."

Familiar anger simmered in his chest. Well, Nick would get his revenge. Uncle Leon might have had the power to drag him away from his home and family, but he'd had no power to force Nick to marry and continue the succession—not while he'd been alive and certainly not from the grave.

Some fellow hidden among the leaves of the family tree would become the next Viscount Oakland once Nick was put to bed with a shovel. The poor chap was welcome to the bloody title.

And who's going to manage the estate in the meantime?

Good Lord! He'd known coming to Oakland for Christmas had been a mistake. Well, in his defense, he wouldn't be here if Myles's dog hadn't erupted all over his London townhouse.

The estate was in perfectly good hands now. Pearson did a fine job, far better than Nick could do.

But he's not the viscount. He can't take a seat in the Lords.

Nick poured himself more brandy. He'd drown these silly, annoying, guilt-inducing notions in short order.

"No, they weren't, but it makes no difference," Caro said. "You are all the same."

He frowned. He'd lost the train of her thought. "I beg your pardon?"

She was scowling at him. "You have *no* idea what it's like to be a woman." She underlined the "no" by jabbing her finger at him. "I could tell I was in danger by the way the Weasel stared at me. The way he brushed against me. The way he tried to get me to sit next to him."

Uneasiness threaded through Nick and twisted in his gut. He'd seen behavior much like this. Oh, not in Society's halls. There were too many fathers and brothers and uncles watching over those girls, and Society misses never went out without a chaperone or a footman dogging their heels. And he'd not seen it even at the other end of the social spectrum, in brothels. If a man made unwanted advances there—or advances he wasn't prepared to pay for—the madam would toss him out if the girl herself didn't do it.

But in the middle—the shopgirls, the governesses, the maids—the women who had only themselves to rely on? Yes, he'd seen men flirt—and rather more than that—with them. He'd thought the girls had been flattered.

Perhaps he should have paid closer attention.

"My knife is only good as a surprise, to free myself. It's useless if I have no safe place to run to. I'm strong, but not strong enough to fight off an angry, determined man."

She took a deep breath and then let it out slowly. "I had to fight a man off once. I'm not sure I would have succeeded if someone hadn't happened by at the crucial moment."

Zeus!

Caro's eyes glinted with fire, but there was something about them that looked haunted, too. "The miscreant said that I'd asked for it. That I'd *wanted* it." Her voice grew stronger. "I did *not* ask for it, Nick. I did not want it. There was nothing amorous about the experience. It was an *attack*. And I'm convinced any pleasure the blackguard got from it was the pleasure of power, of domination. The pleasure of cruelty. The sort of feeling I imagine boys get from torturing a stray animal."

Dear *God*. "I'm sorry." The words seemed laughably inadequate.

She pressed her lips together, looked away—and then shrugged as if that physical movement could shed the painful memory.

"So, perhaps you can understand my concern. Your house is large, Nick. There are too many dark corners and deserted corridors where the Weasel could waylay me."

Yes, there were.

"I'll banish *him* to the stables."

Caro shook her head. "Even if you did, it wouldn't solve the problem. To be honest, the rest of the company doesn't give me much confidence—including your invited male guests." She raised a brow. "They *are* here for an orgy."

"Er, yes." Lord, that sounded bad. What had he been thinking?

To cock a snook at Leon.

No.

Well, yes.

Am I going to let Leon rule me from the grave my entire life?

Nick frowned and pushed the thought aside.

"I'm afraid the orgy *was* rather my idea," he said, "but I swear it was all in, er, good fun." How daft did that sound?

And why the hell was she suddenly smiling in a conspiratorial sort of way?

She leaned closer. "I know, Nick. And I can help you. My plan will work to both our advantages."

His brainless cock perked up. *Help with an orgy? Yes, please.*

He was quite, *quite* certain that was not the sort of help she meant.

Unfortunately.

"Excuse me?" he said. "I'm afraid I don't follow."

Her expression gentled, her eyes filling with . . .

Oh, bloody hell. That looks like pity.

"Your, er, *friend* Livy told me about your problem."

"My p-problem?" His heart—and a lower organ—cringed. So, Livy *had* been talking to Caro, or, if she hadn't been talking to her directly, Caro had been in the room where the horrible words had been said. Caro wasn't deaf—or stupid.

Though she *was* unmarried. She couldn't know what Livy had meant by *limp*, could she?

She did have all those brothers. Worse, she'd said she'd had to fight off a male attacker. . . .

"Yes." She glanced at his lap.

He crossed his legs.

Bloody, bloody *hell.*

"Since I know I have nothing to fear from you—"

Because, for all my sins, I don't attack women, not because there is anything wrong with me.

Though of course, he couldn't say that.

He took a steadying sip of brandy.

"I'm happy to play the role of your besotted lover."

He sprayed the brandy that didn't shoot up his nose over his breeches.

"L-lover?" He pulled out his handkerchief to mop up the mess.

"Yes." Caro smiled at him as if he were a bit slow-witted. "And you will pretend to be besotted with me. We will be inseparable."

"Ah." Inseparable.

Do not *think of her naked. In bed. On her back, legs—*

Too late.

But he would not act on that thought. Unless she invited him to. Which she was *not* going to do.

Also, unfortunately.

"I think it will work splendidly, don't you?" She grinned, clearly pleased with her plan and expecting him to fall in with it with equal glee. "No one will bother me if you're by my side. And once we've persuaded everyone we are involved in a torrid, passionate affair, I should be safe even when you aren't right next to me."

His mouth had gone too dry for speech, so he just nodded and reached for his brandy, took a sip—

"And you'll benefit, too, of course. I'll make it as clear as I can that you are satisfying my every need. No one will think for a minute you're impotent."

There went the brandy again, up the nose and over the breeches.

He put the glass back down. Obviously, drinking was hazardous while Caro was going on in this vein.

"This is not a topic I am prepared to discuss," he said firmly, "but I'm not . . . incapable of, er, *anything*."

She actually patted his arm as if he were a distressed child. "It's all right. I don't think any less of you."

He opened his mouth to argue, but nothing came out—if one didn't count the peculiar sort of gasping growl he emitted.

"I've observed enough lovesick fools to have a good idea how to go on," she said, "but you may have to give me pointers if we're stranded here very long."

"Gah." Pointers. He glanced down to be certain his cock wasn't pointing anywhere. No, thank God, though it felt as thick and tall—and *obvious*—as the Monument to the Great Fire of London.

"You can put me in the viscountess's room. That will save either of us having to traipse through the corridors at night to keep up the fiction." She grinned. "Everyone can just imagine for themselves what we are doing behind closed doors."

He was trying very, very hard—ha! He shifted his position to take some pressure off his hardest organ. He was trying very diligently not to imagine anything about the matter—and failing miserably.

He would call her bluff. "With the servants coming in and out to attend to the fire and such, you will probably have to spend some time in my bed to make the charade believable."

That would scare her off.

It didn't—though she did look a little uncomfortable. "Very well."

Now what? He cleared his throat. He should tell her he'd been joking—except it was true that the plan would work perfectly if her goal was to convince this Weasel beyond a shadow of a doubt that they were engaged in a heated affair.

"Er, won't it ruin your reputation and require a brisk trip to the altar?" Why wasn't *he* appalled by that thought? He should be breaking out in a cold sweat—and yet, he wasn't. If anything he felt rather . . . excited.

Perhaps snorting brandy up one's nose disabled rational thought.

Or perhaps his cock was the disabling agent.

Caro waved away his concerns. "Don't be ridiculous. No one in Little Puddledon cares about my reputation—except my reputation as a brewer and an honest businesswoman." She shrugged. "I'm thirty, long past the age when one thinks of marriage."

He was two years older and, while he didn't think of *marriage*, he thought quite a bit about the activities of the marriage *bed*. He was thinking about them now. With Caro. In rather too much detail.

And yet nowhere near *enough* detail. *If only I could get her out of that drab frock . . .*

He jerked the reins on his unruly imagination. He could not travel that road, no matter how much he wanted to.

It was a shame that a woman as passionate about life outside the bedroom as Caro seemed to be couldn't experience passion inside it, in bed, sprawled hot and needy and welcoming on—

He jerked his imagination's reins again.

He might need to jerk something else later.

Yes, he could use Livy to find his release, but that felt wrong when his mind and emotions were so focused on Caro. Livy might be a whore, but she was more to him than a convenient female body. She was a friend.

And his cock might humiliate him again and refuse to play with Livy.

But he couldn't engage in sexual congress with Caro, even if she was willing and naked in his bed. She wasn't a professional light-skirts. He'd be shocked if she knew how to prevent conception, and he was not about to risk bringing a child into the world outside of marriage. A child needed a father as well as a mother. Look at poor Mrs. Dixon. He didn't know her situation, but the fact that she was traveling in a snowstorm without the protection of a husband—or of the children's father—made him think she was on her own.

No, more to the point, look at me.

Yes, he was legitimate—he didn't have that burden to carry. He'd had a father and a mother for eleven years, but then they'd died. He'd been alone, stripped of his parents' warmth and support, forced to live with a stern, cold uncle. If *he* were ever to have a child, it would be in a family.

Which would mean he would have to marry.

Which he was not going to do.

Why? Are you really going to sentence yourself to a lonely life of pleasant but superficial encounters just to spite a dead man?

Put that way, it did seem beyond stupid.

"We just need to come up with a plausible story," Caro said, tapping her finger against her lips.

Her very lovely, very kissable lips.

Stop!

No. He could admire a woman—even entertain lascivious feelings about her—without trying to seduce her. He wasn't a randy youth.

"There's no need to fabricate any sort of story to explain my infatuation," he said, trying to sound amused instead of lustful.

She gave him a wary look. "What do you mean?"

He forced a grin. "Every man here needs only to look at you to know why I'm besotted."

She scowled at him. "That's ridiculous."

"No, it's not." He waggled his brows. "And I suppose the reason for your interest in me couldn't be as obvious?"

That made her laugh, as he'd hoped it would.

"I am not so swayed by a pretty—that is, a *handsome* face."

"And enticing figure?" He pulled back his shoulders, puffing out his chest theatrically.

She laughed again, but only briefly, her thoughts clearly moving on. "Yes, yes. You are the model of male beauty as I'm sure more than one female has told you."

He felt a flash of pique. He wanted to hear *her* tell him that. He wanted to see if he could—

No, he'd already admitted he couldn't try to lure her into sexual congress.

Zeus, it was going to be devilishly difficult to play the role she was assigning him.

"We knew each other as children—that part's true," she was saying. She bit her lip, obviously running a plan or two through her head. "It would be nice if we could pretend to a long, er, *passionate* correspondence, but I doubt anyone would believe that. Your friends know we didn't immediately recognize each other." She shook her head. "I thought you were the butler, for heaven's sake."

True. "So we hadn't exchanged miniatures."

She looked hopeful for a moment, but then shook her head. "I would think we would have if the correspondence was passionate, wouldn't you?"

"Y-yes." He grinned. "We'll just say we fell madly in love with each other's minds so neither of us cared what the other looked like."

She rolled her eyes just as he expected she would.

"We *did* know each other as children. It's not as if we had *no* idea of the other's appearance."

She snorted. "Right. Just not enough of an idea to recognize each other."

She had a point. He shrugged and then smiled a bit salaciously. "We'll just have to be so convincing as to our current passion that people will not question our story. It's not as if we have to maintain the charade for weeks. The snow should stop and the roads clear in a few days."

She sighed. "Yes. I think that is what we will have to hope." She frowned. "And I imagine I should know why you are called Lord Devil." She looked at him a bit sternly. "Why *are* you called that?"

He spread his hands as if to hold off her implied criticism. "Not because of my sins, I assure you." Well, he should be honest. "Or not *just* because of my sins. My uncle was dubbed Lord Pious. I swear he could make ale freeze in its tankard just by stepping into a room."

"Oh." She seemed very shocked at that, but then she *was* a brewer.

"*I* do not make ale freeze," Nick assured her.

"I should hope not. I—"

An insistent scratching on the door to the corridor interrupted her.

Nick frowned. Was something amiss—something beyond having a motley assortment of guests dumped on his doorstep? "Come."

Mrs. Brooks burst in, Edward behind her.

Nick surged to his feet in alarm. "What is it?" He glanced at Edward and then back to Mrs. Brooks. Edward looked much calmer than his housekeeper, but there was only one reason he could think of for the boy to be here. "Is Mrs. Dixon all right?"

"And the baby?" Caro asked, going over to Mrs. Brooks.

She looked as if she'd like to shake the answer out of the poor woman.

She managed to restrain herself, at least for the moment.

"Yes. Well, no. That is . . ." Mrs. Brooks actually wrung her hands and moaned. Nick had never seen her so distressed.

Of course, since he never came to Oakland if he could avoid it, he hadn't seen her more than a handful of times since she had assumed the duties of housekeeper.

"Mrs. Brooks, please. You are not making much sense," he said. "Take a deep breath and compose yourself."

"It's just that . . ." She bit her lip.

"It's just that Mr. Simpson is Grace's papa," Edward said.

Chapter Six

"Felix?" Nick asked. "Are you certain?"

Simpson had mentioned in passing that he knew the area, but he hadn't said anything about having a son and daughter nearby.

No, not a son *and* a daughter—a daughter only. Edward had called Simpson *Grace's* papa.

Edward nodded. "Yes, I'm certain."

Anger blinded Nick briefly. If Simpson were going to have an ongoing relationship with Mrs. Dixon, he'd bloody well better be prepared to be a father to Edward, too.

Edward was even younger than Nick had been when he'd been orphaned.

He knew many people would say Edward was none of Nick's concern. That Edward's mother would look out for him. That Nick shouldn't get involved. All that was true, but made no difference. Nick *would* involve himself because he knew what it felt like to be fatherless.

Though saying anything to Felix would likely be as productive as spitting into the wind. The man could be an amusing companion when one was up for a lark or, like this excursion, wanted to engage in a bit of scandalous behavior, but he lived very much in the present moment. Nick would be shocked if Felix had ever given the future a passing thought.

Unlike you who are so determined to deny the future you refuse to live fully now—all to settle a past score with a dead man.

Zeus! Is that what I'm doing?

No, of course not. His decision about marriage and procreation had nothing to say to the matter. This was Edward's present he was considering—and Felix's. Not his.

The sad truth was, Felix was not a man Nick would choose for anything like fatherhood that required responsible behavior. And yet Felix *was* a father. He'd chosen to take Mrs. Dixon to bed. He should have foreseen the consequences.

Hell, it wasn't a question of foreseeing but of *seeing*. Mrs. Dixon had been a mother when Simpson bedded her. Had the fellow ignored Edward completely?

"I thought his name was John Thomas," Edward said. "That's what he called himself when he visited Mama. We were going to Marbridge to meet him so he could see Grace and have Christmas with us." Edward's narrow shoulders slumped. "Except I don't think he was going to Marbridge at all."

Curse Simpson to Hades! The bloody—

Wait. . . .

Nick thought back to London. Felix had been at his party—that's how he'd ended up coming to Oakland with him. Nick would swear the man had never mentioned a newborn daughter, but had he said anything about leaving London for Christmas?

He might have, actually. Nick's memories of that night were hazy—he'd been drinking rather a lot. And then the dog had wreaked havoc—havoc that reeked so badly Nick had had no choice but to flee to Oakland at once.

It was possible Felix had been planning to come this way

all along and had just been swept up in Nick's uproar. Then, when the snow had started falling so heavily, Felix might have concluded Mrs. Dixon wouldn't make the journey to Marbridge—that was certainly a reasonable assumption—and so had decided to stay at Oakland to enjoy the orgy.

But he'd swear Felix hadn't mentioned a baby. *That* he would have remembered, drunk or not.

He was getting ahead of himself. Perhaps there was a perfectly simple explanation.

"Do you think you might have mistaken Mr. Simpson for this Mr. Thomas, Edward?" Though it would be just like Felix to use a nickname for cock if he wished to hide his identity. "People sometimes look very much alike. I've made that error many times myself."

Edward shook his head vigorously. "I *know* he's Mr. Thomas. He's got that hairy mole on his cheek." Edward wrinkled his nose. "Mama always laughs and calls it a beauty mark. It matches the one on his arse."

Ugh. Nick did not want to know how the boy knew about the lower mole, but it was true. Felix *did* have a distinctive mark on his face and—as Nick had discovered from too many raucous nights with the likes of Livy and Polly and Fanny—one on his rump as well.

"Is he with them now?" Caro asked, urgency in her voice. She glanced from Edward to the housekeeper and back as if she were choosing which of them to shake the information out of.

Mrs. Brooks nodded. "As far as I know. That is, he's with Mrs. Dixon. I know he's not with little Grace. Miss White's got her."

Some of the stiffness left Caro's body. "Well, thank God for that." She looked at Nick. "We should check on Mrs. Dixon."

She didn't spell it out in so many words, likely because

of the boy, but Nick got the distinct impression Caro was worried about the woman's safety.

"Where do you think we can find them, Mrs. Brooks?" he asked.

The housekeeper frowned. "I'm not certain, milord. When last I saw them, they were on the third floor of the east wing—near the room where I've put Mrs. Dixon and the children—heading toward the servants' stairs."

Caro grabbed Nick's forearm, her voice tight with anxiety again. "We have to hurry, Nick."

Mrs. Brooks's brows shot up at Caro's use of his Christian name.

Ah, well. If we're going to pretend to be lovers, I suppose we should begin at once.

"The blackguard—" Caro glanced at Edward and changed tone. "That is, I don't trust Mr. Simpson not to, er, injure Mrs. Dixon."

"Oh, you don't have to worry about Mama," Edward said. "Mr. Simpson won't hurt her."

Nick's and Caro's and Mrs. Brooks's attention snapped to the boy.

"Why do you say that?" Nick asked.

Edward shrugged. "Mama knows how to tell if a man's bad. She said, after my papa, that she was never going to let a man hit her again." He smiled. "And she hasn't."

Each calm, matter-of-fact word fell like another rock on the growing pile in Nick's stomach.

"How old are you, Edward?" Nick managed to ask, hoping the boy was merely small for his age and not as young as he looked.

"Seven—but I'm *almost* eight. My birthday is next month."

Seven! Good God.

And Nick had thought *he'd* had a horrible childhood. At least he'd had eleven good years. When he'd been Edward's age, he'd still had his mother and father and his happy life in warm, sunny Venice. He'd been blissfully carefree, spending his days playing ball, sailing toy boats, running races with his friends, or just exploring. He'd not given his parents much thought, mistakenly assuming they'd be with him forever—or at least until he was grown with children of his own.

He hoped he was managing to keep his dismay off his face.

"And Mama was chasing Mr. Simpson," Edward said, "not the other way round."

Nick looked back at his housekeeper and lifted a brow in inquiry. He didn't trust his voice.

"Mrs. Dixon wasn't precisely chasing Mr. Simpson, milord," Mrs. Brooks said. "She was . . . Well, I'd just stopped by her room to see if she needed anything more when Mr. Simpson walked by with Miss White. When Mrs. Dixon saw them"—Mrs. Brooks pressed her lips together—"she was not pleased."

"Mama yelled some bad words," Edward said, "and grabbed the first thing at hand."

"A pillow, fortunately," Mrs. Brooks said. "She went after Mr. Simpson, flailing at him and screaming to wake the dead. Mr. Simpson put his hands up and was trying to apologize as he backed down the corridor, but Mrs. Dixon wasn't having it. That's when Master Edward and I came to see you, milord, while Miss White stayed with little Grace."

"I see." That sounded . . . not terrible. But if tempers were high, anything could happen.

"Edward," Caro said, managing to keep her voice calm this time, "where do *you* think your mother might be?"

The boy frowned as he mulled the question over. "I think she must be back in our room. When she's argued with Mr.

Simpson in the past, she's gone to bed to cry, and he always gets in with her to make up."

The boy's shoulders slumped again. "But I don't think he can get her to forgive him this time. She was *very* angry."

Mrs. Brooks put a motherly arm around Edward.

"And she'd been so happy," Edward said. "She'd got a letter from Mr. Simpson last week and took it straight to Mrs. Wilks—Mrs. Wilks owns the dress shop in the village and Mama does piecework for her—so Mrs. Wilks could read it to her. When Mama came home, she said Mr. Simpson was going to marry her and we would live in a cottage in the country and not have to worry about anything anymore. We'd have a garden and maybe some chickens, and Mr. Simpson would teach me to ride and shoot and play cricket and do all the things boys with fathers do."

Zeus! Edward's words stabbed Nick in his heart so he felt physically breathless. He knew that longing feeling all too well.

The boy blew out a long breath. "Now I don't know what will happen, especially to Grace. I can look out for myself, but Grace is just a baby."

Bloody hell! Nick wanted to throttle Felix. Well, first he wanted to beat him within an inch of his life.

Or . . . Drawing and quartering suddenly seemed like a splendid practice.

"Your mother might forgive Mr. Simpson, mightn't she?" Caro said, her tone not quite hiding—at least from Nick—that she thought forgiving Felix would be a very big mistake.

"M-maybe. She's been mad at him before, though not *this* mad." Edward shrugged. "She always says men are single-minded snakes that want only One Thing—whatever that is." He smiled, but his expression was apologetic. "She was very happy Grace was a girl."

Zeus! The boy was clearly parroting his mother's words,

and while it might be understandable that Mrs. Dixon wouldn't value the male of the species, she *must* see that she was raising a boy who would become a man. Did she not stop to think how her words would affect her son?

Caro put her hand on Edward's shoulder. She looked sad and sympathetic. "Do *you* like him?"

Edward frowned. "I don't know. I thought I did. I wanted to, especially if he was going to marry Mama. But I'm afraid . . ." Edward bit his lip as if searching for the right words. "I'm afraid he's like all the other men, like an apple that looks juicy and sweet, but when you bite into it"—he wrinkled his nose in disgust—"it turns out to be nasty."

Mrs. Brooks made a small cluck of dismay—and not just about Felix Simpson. "You come down to the kitchen with me, Master Edward. We'll find you something good to eat."

Nick's Italian grandmother had also thought food would soothe many of life's tragedies.

Edward's grin lit his face—but vanished as quickly as it had appeared. "Thank you, Mrs. Brooks, but I had better go see how Mama is."

Blast it, the boy needed a chance to be a child, responsible for no one but himself.

No, not even for himself. At his age, his mother should be looking after him, not vice versa. Nick wished there were something he could do to resolve the problem. . . .

Well, he could have a word with Felix. And he could give Edward Christmas. They would gather armloads of greenery on Christmas Eve to make Oakland smell—and look—like the holiday.

And he could try offering a little gustatory comfort himself.

"Suppose once we've seen that all's well with your mother, Edward, we find our way down to the kitchen?" Nick smiled at the housekeeper. "Could you meet us there in a little while, Mrs. Brooks, and give me your report on how the new guests are settling in?"

Mrs. Brooks smiled widely. "Yes, indeed, milord. Cook will be delighted to see you. She's started her holiday baking and was just wondering this morning if you had any favorites you'd like her to prepare."

"Favorites?" He didn't have a favorite anything from his years at Oakland.

Mrs. Brooks frowned, but seemed to know exactly what he meant. "Oh. Ah, no. That's right. The old lord didn't much care for treats, did he?"

Or jokes or laughter or merriment of any sort.

"No. He didn't."

"But Mrs. Bishop—you'll remember she was Cook then—always made treats for the staff." Mrs. Brooks frowned and looked a little uncomfortable. "Your uncle didn't approve, but Mrs. Bishop threatened to leave if he forbad her baking. He gave in." She smiled. "He liked her roast pheasant and potted hare too much to risk losing her."

Nick wasn't surprised. Uncle Leon had been a bully and, as true of most bullies, had collapsed like a house of cards at the first sign of determined resistance. Nick had finally figured that out.

As much as his uncle might bluster and threaten to do it, he'd not really cut Nick off without a *sou*. He wanted his direct line to continue too much.

Ha! It had driven him mad that he couldn't force Nick to marry and have a son to ensure that.

Which is why my revenge will be so sweet.

Except today it tasted oddly bitter. And stale. As if it should have been thrown out long ago.

I'm just a bit off-balance because of all the unexpected guests and Oakland and the holiday.

"Very good. We'll be off then. Edward, will you lead the way?"

They started for the door.

"Oh, milord, before you go . . ." Mrs. Brooks glanced at Caro and back to him. "I've not yet shown Miss Anderson her room."

Would Mrs. Brooks balk at installing Caro in the viscountess's bedchamber?

It was time to find out.

"Right. I was thinking the connecting room would do very well."

"Oh." Mrs. Brooks looked at Caro.

Nick looked at Caro, too. She *was* an interesting sight, managing to look defiant, self-assured, and embarrassed all at once.

"Is that to your liking, Miss Anderson?" Mrs. Brooks's tone was carefully polite and deferential.

"Er, y-yes. That is . . . it seems . . . I mean . . ."

What *was* Caro doing? Her simple "yes" would have done the job nicely, but now she seemed intent on digging herself a deep, dark hole. Had she heard in Mrs. Brooks's voice some note of judgment that was inaudible to the male ear?

He was often mystified by the complexities of female communication. Even his friends who were married admitted they didn't always understand their wives. One newlywed fellow had amazed a group at White's by recounting how his wife had sent him off with a flea in his ear when, after an argument, she'd said she wished to be left alone—and he'd left her alone! Apparently in that instance *go* had really meant *stay*.

It was far better, in Nick's poor male opinion, to say clearly and precisely what you meant rather than expect someone to guess your point from your tone or expression or some other obscure clue.

"Lord Oakland was my brother Henry's childhood friend." Caro finally managed to say. "He used to spend holidays with us."

"Oh, yes." A smile blossomed on Mrs. Brooks's face. "I remember now. Of course. I'll have your things brought up and the room set to rights at once."

Caro followed Nick and Edward down the corridor to Mrs. Dixon's room.

I'll have to be a better actress if I'm going to persuade anyone Nick and I are lovers.

Lovers! Ack!

She felt a hot blush flood her face even as a heavy ball of ice formed in her belly. She swallowed a moan. *Oh, why, in all that is holy, did I suggest such a stupid, stupid plan?*

Because it would work splendidly, that was why. She'd have Nick by her side all day, and people—in particular, the Weasel—would think he was there all night as well. She'd not have to be constantly on guard.

Nick did say I'd have to spend some time in his bed to convince the servants. . . .

Unease and something else—not excitement, surely not that—twisted around the ice ball.

No. He *must* be wrong. Or . . . or perhaps they could just disarrange the bedclothes to make it look like she'd been there.

Her face burned so much she thought it might burst into flame.

She needed to get over her embarrassment. For the ruse to work, she would have to play her part convincingly.

And this was not just for herself, she must remember.

Her act was for Nick, too. They had an agreement. He was protecting her in exchange for her protecting him.

People believed their eyes over their ears. If they saw she was besotted with him, they'd discount any whispers they heard about his, er, limitations, especially since the words would come from Livy, his displaced lover.

Yet how could Caro convince anyone she was in love—or even in lust? She'd rooted out those emotions thirteen years ago, had shredded and burned them and left their ashes in London. Not one seed remained in her soul to coax into any sort of believable masquerade.

She would just have to take her lead from Nick. He must know how to go on. He'd lived among the *ton* where masks of all sorts were common. No one showed his or her true feelings in London.

He was attractive—handsome, really. Perhaps she could start there. He wasn't flashily good-looking the way Lord Der—

As always, she shied away from thinking about the bloody marquess.

No. She couldn't do that any longer. It was time to face her unpleasant past, especially if that past was going to keep her from helping herself and Nick.

Nick was not as remarkably good-looking as the despicable Marquess of Dervington, the man who had flattered her, had told her that they were meant for each other, and had persuaded her to be his mistress.

Briefly. Very briefly. And if she hadn't been seventeen and a country bumpkin dazzled by Dervington's rank, she wouldn't have fallen for his blandishments and made such a terrible mistake.

At least, she hoped that was true.

"This is it," Edward said, stopping about halfway down

the corridor. He didn't push open the door, but looked up at Nick instead.

Was he afraid of what he might find in the room?

"I don't hear any shouting," Nick said, smiling. "That's a good sign, don't you think, Edward?"

"Y-yes." Edward shifted from foot to foot. "Perhaps they have made up. I'm not supposed to bother them when they are in bed together." He frowned. "Though I heard Mrs. Wilks tell Mama—we stopped by her shop on the way to catch the coach to tell her Mama would be gone for a few days. I heard her tell Mama to remember it was too soon after Grace's birth to let Mr. Simpson back into her bed."

Dear heavens.

Caro thought Nick had flushed, too, though the light was too weak for her to tell for certain.

"I understand, Edward," Nick said, "but we need to be sure your mother and sister are all right." Then he turned and rapped on the door.

Nothing happened.

He looked at Caro and then down at Edward. "You're certain this is the room?"

Edward nodded.

Nick knocked again, harder this time.

Still no answer.

"Maybe Mama *did* forgive Mr. Simpson," Edward said in a small, uncertain voice. "Or maybe they went for a walk."

Nick's jaw tightened. "Not in a blizzard."

"I-I don't think he would hurt her." Edward looked up at Nick. "Do you think he would hurt her?"

Caro felt her heart twist as she stepped closer to touch Edward's shoulder. But what could she say? Edward might be a child, but he'd seen enough of life not to believe false reassurances.

Nick's eyes and mouth hardened into a starkly grim

expression. "He had better not." Then he pushed on the door.

It didn't open.

"There's something in the way." Nick's voice was clipped. This time he put his shoulder against the wood and threw his whole weight into it as Caro pulled Edward back, pushing his face into her body to shield him from seeing whatever was in the room.

The door gave way suddenly, and Nick fell forward—which saved him from having his head bashed in with a candlestick.

"Polly!" Caro said.

"Lawk-a-daisy!" Polly gaped at Caro and then down at Nick, who was picking himself up off the floor. "I thought you were Felix."

"Is my mama all right?" Edward asked, pushing forward to peer around Polly.

"Oh, yes, deary. No worry of that. She was just a bit low, so I gave her a drop of laudanum to take the edge off." Polly gestured toward the bed. "She's sleeping soundly."

A gentle snore confirmed the accuracy of that statement.

Nick and Edward went over to check on Edward's mother.

Caro hung back. "And Grace?" she asked. "How is she?"

"Slept through the whole fuss and bustle. Look, here she is."

Polly led Caro over to a small box, sitting on the floor in a corner of the room. "Mrs. Brooks found this, but she said she thought there was a proper cradle up in the attics. She's going to send someone up to look, once things aren't all at sixes and sevens."

"The attics?" Nick said, coming over with Edward. "I used to love to go up there and poke around when I was a boy." He smiled down at Edward. "Shall we search for this cradle after we have something to eat? It will be dark, but we'll take some candles with us."

Edward's eyes lit up, and he grinned—but then sighed, his mouth and shoulders drooping. "Thank you, sir, but I have to stay here to watch over Grace and Mama."

Caro opened her mouth to volunteer—but then remembered the Weasel. She didn't think he'd find her in Mrs. Dixon's room, but she wasn't entirely sure about that. And she'd have to leave at some point. Would Nick think to come fetch her? If he didn't—

Fortunately, Polly offered. "Tsk, go along, Edward. I'll keep an eye on your mama and sister."

"Really?" Edward sounded hopeful. "You don't mind?"

"Not at all. If I went downstairs now, I might murder Felix Simpson, and I'm thinking I should leave that pleasure to your mama."

Edward shifted from foot to foot. "I don't think Mama would try to kill Mr. Simpson, Miss Polly."

Polly smiled rather kindly. "Of course she wouldn't. And I wouldn't either—though I *would* enjoy scratching his eyes out. I may not be a model of proper behavior"—Polly snorted—"but I will not—" She stopped as if suddenly remembering exactly to whom she was speaking. "Well. Let's just say Felix should have been with your mama—and you and Grace—rather than with me."

Just as Dervington should have been with his wife.

Shame, anger, and disgust flooded Caro. She hadn't felt this surge of self-loathing in years, not since . . .

Not since she'd come to the Home and started the brewing program. Her friends and work had saved her—perhaps her work most of all. Creating and then perfecting and selling Widow's Brew took all her focus. She'd no time or energy to dwell on the past.

Until now when her friends and her work were out of reach.

"Caro?"

She felt Nick touch her shoulder—and was horrified to discover her eyes were wet.

But only wet. She hadn't shed any tears—and she wouldn't.

"Are you all right?"

Though if Nick kept talking to her in that gentle, caring tone, she might break down and throw herself sobbing on his chest. How mortifying would that be?

"I'm fine. Let's go find something for Edward to eat."

Chapter Seven

The moment Nick stepped back into the corridor, he realized he wasn't entirely certain how to get to the kitchen. He'd been there only once, one cold, dreary winter day several weeks after he'd first arrived at Oakland as a boy.

He'd not thought of that day in years. He'd been missing his parents and extended Italian family with an intense, unrelenting pain. Everyone he loved, everything warm and bright and joyful in his life, had been torn from him, and he'd been thrown into hell—a cold, dark hell. He'd been desperate to find even the faintest glimmer of happiness.

That particular day, he'd been remembering how his parents and grandparents and aunts and uncles and cousins had used to gather in his grandmother's bright, airy kitchen to talk and laugh as his grandmother and mother and aunts cooked. He'd thought he might find some of the same joy in the kitchen of this huge, joyless building, so he'd given his glum tutor the slip and gone looking.

Caro had been right about the dark corners and deserted corridors. His parents' house had been small—nothing like this labyrinth—so it had taken him quite a while to find the kitchen. He'd almost given up several times. And when he had found it . . .

It hadn't been as warm and bright as his grandmother's, but it had been busy, filled with noise and people and the familiar scent of food cooking. Mrs. Bishop, the cook, had been quite surprised to see him, but had smiled and given him a slice of seedcake and some lemonade and let him sit in the corner and watch all the activity—until his tutor had tracked him down and dragged him away. When Uncle Leon had got wind of the escapade, he'd been furious. Apparently, a member of the nobility was never to besmirch his exalted position by venturing into a lowly kitchen or scullery or servants' hall.

Nick grinned. He was going to violate another of Uncle Leon's rules—if he could just manage to figure out where the kitchen was.

"*Are* we going to the kitchen?" Caro said rather tartly.

At least she'd got back her prickliness.

Something Polly had said in the bedroom just now had called up an emotion in Caro other than defiance or determination. He thought he'd seen tears shimmer in her eyes before she'd blinked them away.

It was probably just his imagination or a trick of the candlelight. The woman frowning at him now would scoff at the notion that she'd succumb to anything as weak or sentimental as tears.

"I'm afraid I'm not sure how to get there," he admitted.

Her eyes widened.

Well, yes, he supposed it did seem odd that he didn't know where the kitchen was. She and her brothers had roamed every corner of their house, and she must know her way around the place she lived now. What had she called it? The Benevolent Home for the Maintenance and Support of Spinsters, Widows, and Abandoned Women and their Unfortunate Children.

Is she happy there?

Regret nudged him again. *Why didn't I seek her out when she first came to London to warn her about Dervington?*

The answer came back quick and unpleasant. *Because you were too busy being a drunken, whoring, irresponsible embarrassment to your uncle.*

He grimaced. Sadly, that rang true.

"You could ask him," Edward said, pointing farther down the corridor to where a young footman had suddenly appeared.

The footman wouldn't know if Caro was happy—

Oh, right. Ask him where the kitchen was.

"Good idea. You, there," Nick said, heading toward the fellow.

The footman looked startled and a bit alarmed. "Y-yes, milord?" He tugged nervously on his waistcoat. "Mrs. Potty sent me up to see if Mrs. Dixon needed anything, milord, but I'm not certain which room is hers."

"Ah. Mrs. Potty?" Who the hell was that?

"The cook, milord."

"Right." By the time the snow melted and the roads were passable, he might finally have learned all his servants' names.

You're the lord of the manor. You should already know them.

He pushed that thought—and the guilt—away.

He was doing an awful lot of that these days.

"We just came from looking in on Mrs. Dixon. She and the baby are resting. Polly, however—" How should he refer to a London whore when speaking to a country footman?

That etiquette question was beyond his ability to answer. Best to err on the side of formality.

"That is, Miss White, one of my, ah, friends from London—"

Of *course*, this man knew precisely what sort of *friend*

Polly was—and likely had a definite opinion on the matter of whores and orgies at a peer's country estate.

Is he shocked? Disgusted?

More guilt seasoned with a dash of shame nudged Nick, and he pushed it away yet again. It didn't matter what the fellow thought. It wasn't important. . . .

And Uncle Leon's very dead opinion is?

Bloody hell.

"Miss White is keeping an eye on them both," Nick said rather sharply and gestured at the door.

The footman's eyes widened at his tone, though the man quickly recovered and reverted to a bland, suitably respectful expression.

Oh, Lord. I'm just making matters worse.

Nick forced himself to smile and say more pleasantly, "You might see if she needs anything."

"Very good, milord." The footman moved to step around them, likely eager to be on his way.

"But before you go, ah . . ."

The man understood Nick's problem. "Thomas, milord."

"Thank you, Thomas." Nick filed the name away, determined to remember it. "Before you go, could you show us how to reach the kitchen? Edward here is hungry, and Mrs. Brooks is meeting me there shortly to report on how our new guests are settling in."

Thomas glanced toward Mrs. Dixon's door and then back to Nick. "I can take ye, milord."

"No, no, that won't be necessary. I was there once, years ago. If you'll just point me in the right direction, I believe I can manage."

Thomas looked rather relieved that he wouldn't be required to spend any more time with a man he must think an irresponsible and unpredictable master.

"Very good, milord. If ye just continue down the corridor,

ye'll come to the stairs." He frowned and eyed Caro's skirt. "They're a bit worn and uneven, madam, so ye'll want to take care. When ye reach the bottom, turn right, and follow the corridor round till it ends. That's the kitchen." He glanced toward Mrs. Dixon's door again and then back at Nick. "Are ye certain ye don't wish me to show ye the way, milord?"

"Perfectly certain. It sounds simple enough, now that I know where to begin. I think I can recognize a kitchen." He grinned. "And if we get lost, I'll just shout for help. I'm sure someone will hear me."

Thomas stared at him, clearly appalled at the vision of Viscount Oakland standing in the middle of some dingy service corridor, yelling.

"Don't worry," Caro said. "I know how to find a kitchen."

"And I do, too," Edward added.

Nick laughed. What else could he do? It was embarrassing, but there was no arguing with the truth. "So, you see, I am in excellent hands."

Thomas still looked a bit doubtful, but must have concluded that as long as Nick didn't wander out into the snow, he couldn't get into too much trouble. He bowed. "Very good, milord."

Thomas set off for Mrs. Dixon's room as Nick turned in the other direction.

"Lead the way," he said to Edward. "And don't bother to wait for us." Surely the boy could stand to burn off a little energy after his journey, the stress of the stagecoach accident, and his worry for his mother.

And I'm going to burn off a little energy, too, as soon as I see Felix, the blackguard.

Felix might well laugh at him, and Nick would admit he'd not been the model of responsibility himself in many respects. But on this point, he had no doubts.

Children needed parents. Plural. A mother and a father.

Nick would grant that Mrs. Dixon seemed to have done a good job so far with Edward, but they still had a very rough road ahead of them. And now she had Grace to care for as well. Felix needed to face his responsibilities.

Edward was looking at Caro as if asking her permission.

"Go on," she said. "You can be our scout."

Nick choked back a laugh as Edward took off at a run. "But we *will* follow him," he said when the boy was out of earshot.

Caro frowned at him. "W-what? Oh!" She laughed, too. "Henry did try to use that ploy to get rid of me, didn't he?"

"Yes, he did." It hadn't worked after the first time, though. Caro had caught on quickly. Even then, she'd been nobody's fool.

They started down the corridor after Edward.

Nick hadn't minded having Caro join him and Henry when they were children. She hadn't fussed about getting her clothes dirty or held them back—Henry would have left her behind if she had. On the contrary, Caro had often been the first to do everything—climb a tree, balance along the top of a stone wall, cross a stream on a fallen trunk. She'd been fearless.

He'd not really thought of her as a girl.

He glanced down at her. There was no overlooking the fact that she was a girl, now.

His memories—old and childish as they were—overlay the face and form of the woman at his side, making him feel . . .

What? He already felt desire. That had been a constant, familiar thrum from the moment she'd pushed back her hood in the entry. But now he felt something else as well, something unfamiliar.

In some odd way, it felt as if the memories of their shared

childhood adventures deepened and broadened his reaction to her.

Well, to be blunt, it was extremely odd to feel *anything* for a woman who wasn't a light-skirts. Since he'd decided long ago that he wasn't going to produce an heir, there'd been no point in wasting any thought on females whose price for bed play was a meeting at the altar and an exchange of until-death-do-we-parts. And, from his admittedly limited observation, Society girls, especially, struck him as silly and superficial and boring.

Caro's not silly or superficial, and she certainly isn't boring.

Nor was she available for bed play without a church blessing, unfortunately.

He felt surprisingly regretful about that. He almost wished he *were* the marrying sort.

Edward must have found the stairs. He'd disappeared from sight.

"I'm surprised you don't know where the kitchen is," Caro said. "Didn't you grow up here? I mean I know you were born in Italy, but weren't you ten or eleven when you came to your uncle?"

"Eleven."

And that was another reason he'd sworn off marriage. He'd seen the way well-bred women looked at him. He might have been a viscount's heir—and now a viscount—but he still had his mother's Italian, plebeian blood flowing in his veins. The few times he'd ventured into Almack's hallowed halls, the best families had kept their daughters away from him as though he were an unwashed beggar. The less exalted—or just more desperate—ones had choked back their revulsion, held their collective noses, and hoped his title and income would settle their collywobbles.

No, thank you.

Caro had never seemed to care about Mama's family.

True. But then why would she? She'd been just a girl—a country girl at that—and he'd been just her brother's schoolmate.

Though Henry hadn't seemed to care, either. He'd been one of the few boys at school who'd befriended Nick. And as for Mr. Anderson—even a mixed-blood viscount was still a viscount.

"Uncle Leon had very strict ideas about what was appropriate for a future Viscount Oakland. Visiting the kitchen was not on the list of approved activities."

"Oh." A line appeared between her brows. "That's . . ." She shook her head, and her frown deepened. "I was going to say it was odd, but it's more than that. It's rather dreadful."

It *would* seem dreadful to her. Her family's kitchen had been almost as warm and jolly as his grandmother's.

"Yes. Everything about my uncle was rather dreadful."

And there I go, sharing feelings again. Hell!

He tried to lighten his tone. "I assure you I was very happy to be able to escape him by coming home with Henry."

He hadn't thought about those visits in years. He tried hard not to dwell on the past at all, but Caro's appearance had apparently unlocked those memories.

It was true that holidays spent with her family had been the bright spots in a dark time. They'd got him through until he could defy his uncle and live on his own.

Though even then I was still living on Uncle Leon's shilling, wasn't I?

They'd arrived at the stairs. Nick could hear Edward's heels rapidly clacking down the stone steps a flight or two below them. He must be running, but then, he was seven—*almost* eight. Boys that age ran everywhere.

They would take their time. The footman—Thomas—

had been correct. The steps were worn and uneven, but at least they were wider than usual for servants' stairs. They could walk two abreast.

"Here, take my arm," he said. "And you might wish to hold up your skirt so you don't trip."

Caro grumbled, of course. Clearly, she was just as unwilling now as she'd been as a girl to admit her gender constrained her in any way.

She took his arm, and he got a whiff of her clean, light scent. She lifted her skirt, and he got a glimpse of her well-turned ankle.

Ahh.

"It's terribly unfair that women are forced into dresses, you know. We should be able to wear breeches as men do." She grinned up at him. "I'd wear breeches in the brewery, but I'm afraid it would give Albert, my elderly assistant, heart failure."

"Um." Nick felt as if *he* might be on the verge of heart failure. He'd swear all the blood in his body had just rushed in one great wave to his cock. Her scent and the sight of her ankle had combined to create an all-too-vivid image in his suddenly randy mind of her long legs encased in breeches—and then the delicious next step of sliding those breeches down over her rounded rump, revealing the sweet, secret place at the junction of her—

He stumbled, and her hold on his arm tightened.

"Perhaps you should take *my* arm." She laughed at him—but then must have discerned, even in the flickering candlelight and shadows, the heat in his eyes, because her face stilled and she looked away.

Don't be afraid of me, Caro. I won't hurt you.

Instead, he said, "Perhaps I *should* take your arm," and was relieved that his voice wasn't thick with lust.

If I annoy her enough, she'll forget to be uncomfortable.

He dropped his voice so his words wouldn't reach Edward's tender ears, though from the clattering coming from that direction, Edward's ears were safe from all but the loudest of shouts. "Don't you think men would be too distracted to accomplish anything if women wore breeches?"

Caro snorted and shot him a quick look of disgust before turning her attention back to the stairs. "Nonsense! Women manage to function very well, and we have to look at men in breeches all the time. Why can't men do the same with women? It's not as if you don't know what we have under these layers." She lifted her skirt higher to emphasize her point—and revealed a shapely calf. "Legs, just like you."

No. Not at all like mine . . .

This conversation might be making Caro more comfortable, but it was making him decidedly less. His cock and ballocks had hardened further and were now threatening to explode.

"If men can walk around with their legs clad in separate, er, *sleeves*, as it were, women should be allowed to do so, too."

"Erm." *Think of something to say, you idiot!*

It was hopeless. Like a dog that had found an exotic scent, his imagination would not leave the sweet, intoxicating vision of Caro's legs, no matter how hard and how often he jerked on its lead, trying to haul it away.

Hard. Jerked.

Oh, dear God, this was ridiculous. He was a man of thirty-two, not a boy of sixteen. He'd seen women's legs before and had been between quite a few of them.

And why the hell couldn't my blasted cock have been this enthusiastic last night with Livy?

It must be just that he'd known Livy—in all senses—for a long time, while Caro was new. . . .

No. Caro wasn't some new, alluring light-skirts, a challenge to seduce. She was *Caro*. Henry's sister. His childhood friend.

Though they *had* agreed to pretend to a grand passion. No one was going to believe they were lovers if he didn't show some desire for her. He wasn't a shy schoolboy or a bloody poet, worshiping his muse from afar. *And* he wasn't trying to fool a collection of nuns and monks. He didn't know about the stagecoach passengers, but his invited guests had come to Oakland for an *orgy*. It was *good* that he could feel—and thus show—some lust for Caro.

As long as he remembered he was acting . . .

Zeus, it would help if his emotions weren't in such a complete, befuddling jumble.

"You don't agree?" Disdain dripped from Caro's voice.

"Ah . . ."

"Mark my words, if men were forced to wear dresses for just one day—ha! for just one *hour*—dresses and related feminine whatnots would be consigned to the sartorial trash heap."

They'd reached the bottom of the stairs where Edward was waiting for them, so Nick was saved from having to respond.

"I can hear and smell the kitchen," Edward said excitedly.

Nick could hear and smell it, too—the clatter of dishes, the scent of . . . Could that be the same sort of seedcake he'd had the last time he'd visited the Oakland kitchen? He rather hoped so. It had been quite good—though, of course, he'd been only eleven, with a boy's unsophisticated tastes.

"Yes, indeed," Nick said. "It must be very close now."

Edward nodded and took off. Nick followed with Caro, though she'd dropped his arm the moment her foot had cleared the last step.

He missed her touch, the feel of her much-maligned skirt brushing against his leg, the occasional press of her hip against his. She was the perfect height for him—not too short nor too tall. She'd fit against him—

Remember—this is only a game. A charade to fool the other *men. Don't fool yourself.*

He looked around, trying to redirect his unruly thoughts. The corridor, plain with pale green, unadorned walls was quite narrow. The ceiling seemed low, too.

"It's smaller than I remember," he said with surprise.

Caro laughed. "It's just that you're bigger. As I recall, you were rather short and scrawny when last I saw you."

He nodded. "I grew late." Being small hadn't helped him at school either; it had just painted one more target on his back for the bullies to take aim at. It wasn't until he'd got his height—and had proven to be good at cricket and boxing—that the other boys had finally stopped tormenting him, at least to his face.

They turned a corner and bumped into Edward—literally.

"I waited for you," Edward said, and pointed at a door about ten feet ahead. The noise—and smell of seedcake—were definitely coming from there.

Nick nodded and stepped past him. The kitchen seemed smaller, too, though he'd still call it a good-sized room. He remembered the flagstone floor, the long pine worktable, the big fireplace, the shelves of dishes. A stout woman in a black dress and white apron, a white mobcap covering her graying hair, was inspecting the dishes. She must have heard him come in, because she turned. . . .

"Eek!" She clutched her hands to her breast—and then laughed and curtsied. "Oh, milord, ye gave me such a fright." Her eyes lit up when they landed on Edward. "And ye have a boy with ye"—she smiled at Caro—"and a lady as well."

Nick bowed, not being quite sure how to go on. While he knew he was technically the master here, he felt more like an interloper in this woman's domain. And she definitely seemed to be the person in charge. "You must be Mrs. Potty?"

She curtsied again. "Yes, milord."

Three kitchenmaids, standing at the worktable, had stopped their friendly chatter when he'd come in, freezing like startled deer, and were now staring at him.

"And this is Annie and Bess and Mary."

Each one dropped a nervous little curtsy when she heard Mrs. Potty say her name.

And then the cook frowned, raised her chin, and looked him in the eye. "They are good girls, milord." Her gaze sharpened. "If ye know what I mean."

Unfortunately, he knew precisely what she meant. *Why* had he thought bringing rakes and whores to his country home for an orgy was a good idea?

Because you still think of Oakland as Uncle Leon's. And you still want to thumb your nose at him.

Good God, surely not.

"Yes. Well, then." He turned to Caro and Edward. "This is Miss Anderson and Master Edward Dixon, two of the passengers from the stagecoach. You do know about the accident and our surprise guests?"

Mrs. Potty nodded. "Yes, indeed, milord. Thomas told us."

"Well, then, Edward here is a mite hungry, and we were wondering—"

Those were the magic words. Motherly concern flooded Mrs. Potty's face, and a stream of words poured out as she led them over to a table in the corner, likely the same table Nick had sat at years ago.

"And here I am standing around talking. Of course yer hungry, Master Edward. Boys are always hungry. Ye've probably missed yer dinner, what with all that traveling and the nasty weather as well. And such a shock it must have been to have landed in a ditch. And then to find out that nasty Mr. Simpson was—"

She stopped abruptly, gave Nick a quick nervous glance, and went on, changing course. "Yes, well, it must all have been very unpleasant. I'll get ye a nice bit of meat pasty, shall I? And some lemonade. And perhaps a slice of seedcake?"

Edward nodded enthusiastically. "Yes, please."

She looked cautiously back at Nick. "And would ye and Miss Anderson like anything, milord?"

"Yes, thank you." He smiled. Perhaps a bit of charm—no, friendliness—would smooth matters over and earn him, if not forgiveness, then at least a little less dislike and distrust. "I don't suppose the seedcake is the same that I had when I was a boy and Mrs. Bishop was Cook, is it?"

Mrs. Potty's face lit up with her wide grin—and he made a note that the way to a cook's heart was through *his* stomach. Flatter her food, and she might forgive him anything.

"It is, milord. I was one of the kitchenmaids when Mrs. Bishop was here. She lives in the village now, ye know. The old lord pensioned her off a few years ago."

He nodded. He hadn't known that.

But I should have. . . .

Guilt swept through him. Again. It was becoming an all too familiar sensation.

He beat it back. He didn't need to know such details. Pearson ran things here. He did a good job. Nick had heard no complaints. It wasn't as if he'd ever wanted to be the viscount and responsible for all these people.

He turned to Caro. "Then I can recommend the seedcake wholeheartedly, Miss Anderson. You should not pass up this opportunity to try it."

Caro smiled at Mrs. Potty, who was now practically

glowing with pride. "Then yes, thank you. I'll have a small slice."

"And I'll be getting ye some tea, too, to go with yer cake, shall I?"

"That would be lovely."

"And ye, milord? Would ye like a nice dish o' tea as well? Or perhaps a glass o' ale?"

He grinned when he saw Caro's eyes light up at the mention of ale.

"I'll have a glass—and would you bring a small glass for Miss Anderson as well? Though I doubt our brew will be up to her standards. She's quite the expert—oversees the brewery at the Benevolent Home for the Maintenance and Support of Spinsters, Widows, and Abandoned Women and their Unfortunate Children in Little Puddledon." He looked back at Caro. "Have I got that right?"

She nodded and addressed Mrs. Potty directly. "We make and sell our ale, Widow's Brew, to benefit the Home. I was just in London trying to interest a tavern keeper in offering it." Caro scowled. "I'm afraid my trip was a complete waste of time, however."

Mrs. Potty clucked sympathetically and went to get their food and drink.

"I'm glad you were on the coach, Miss Anderson," Edward said earnestly. "Grace might have been hurt if you hadn't held her. And Mama said if you hadn't gone up to the house, no one else would have." He looked at Nick. "Everyone was too scared of you, Lord Oakland."

Oh, hell. *More* guilt.

Caro look surprised and a bit disarmed by Edward's words. "Oh. I'm glad I was able to help."

And then Mrs. Potty and one of the kitchenmaids—Annie, he thought—came back with their food, Annie hovering behind Mrs. Potty as if she were afraid Nick might suddenly leap up and attack her.

This time guilt plopped its fat rump right on his heart and settled in. Clearly, he needed to do something about his reputation. He might not care about getting an heir and passing the title and property on, but that didn't mean he wished the people who worked here to see him as some sort of ravening, immoral scoundrel, seducing the innocent and barring his door against distressed travelers.

Edward took a large bite of his meat pie, and Mrs. Potty sighed with pleasure.

"It's so nice to have a hungry boy in the house again. Mrs. Bishop used to say it was a terrible shame that the old viscount wouldn't let ye spend time in the kitchen the way he and yer father did."

Nick's brows shot up. Had he heard correctly? "My uncle came down to the kitchen?" Then why had the old man told Nick such behavior was below what was expected of a viscount?

"Aye. Yer father more than the old lord, but he came too, on occasion. At least that's what Mrs. Bishop said. I was only a girl myself then."

"That, ah, surprises me." Flabbergasted might be a better description of his feelings.

Mrs. Potty nodded. "Ye didn't know him when he was young." She shook her head. "Oh, he was never up for a frisk and a frolic like yer da was. The old lord was a serious boy, always a bit worried—that's what Mrs. Bishop says. But he wasn't gloomy and sour then. It was the tragedy that made him so."

She started to turn away.

"Wait." Nick had to restrain himself from reaching out to grab the woman's arm. "What do you mean, Mrs. Potty? What tragedy?"

She turned back, her brows raised in surprise. "Surely ye've heard the whole, sad tale?"

"No. Or at least, I don't think so. I don't remember my father ever talking about his brother." But then his father had been an artist—a painter—not one to worry about anything that wasn't right in front of him, able to be captured with brushstrokes on canvas. Mama had been the practical one.

And for his part, Nick hadn't thought to ask about his English relatives. Why would he? England had been little more than a word to him, some odd, distant, unpleasant place that his father had said was always cold and damp and cloudy—nothing like Italy. And Nick had had his Italian family—his grandparents and aunts and uncles and cousins—around him. He hadn't felt a need for more people in his life.

If anyone had mentioned a tragedy once he'd come to Oakland, he didn't remember it.

Of course, he'd been living his own tragedy then.

Mrs. Potty nodded. "No, I suppose they wouldn't have discussed it around a young lad. Ye see . . ." Mrs. Potty sighed. "Yer father left on his Grand Tour shortly after his brother married. It didn't take long after the vows were said for the new Lady Oakland to be expecting. Everyone was so happy and excited—and rather proud that the viscount had done his duty so promptly. But then, when the poor woman was almost seven months gone, she took a terrible fall down the grand marble stairway. Mrs. Bishop said there was blood everywhere."

Caro made a sound of distress. "Oh! How horrible."

Mrs. Potty nodded. "Aye. Milady took to her bed at once, but it was no good. She lost the baby—a boy."

Good Lord! Uncle Leon would have had his own heir, but for one misstep. *And I wouldn't be saddled with the title.*

And he'd have an older cousin.

He felt disoriented, as if he'd just turned a kaleidoscope and seen the picture fall apart and reform.

"Everyone was very sad, o' course, but no one was worried. The lord and his lady were young and in love. There would be other babies." Mrs. Potty visibly drooped. "Except there weren't. No matter how careful poor Lady Oakland was, she always miscarried." Mrs. Potty shook her head sadly. "One baby after another after another. Seven more babies lost."

Nick's stomach clenched. Zeus! He'd no experience with nor interest in having children himself, and he'd never met his aunt; she'd died before he'd come to Oakland. But still, the story was beyond tragic—and might go far to explaining his uncle's dark and dour disposition.

"I do believe her spirit was broken after the last miscarriage. She started on a decline that she never recovered from." Mrs. Potty shook her head sadly. "And it didn't help that the London doctor told the old lord that he had to stay out of her—" Mrs. Potty looked at Edward and changed conversational direction. "Ah, that he had to stay in his own room. So, the man turned to religion as if his sins—or, more to the point, Lady Oakland's—were to blame for the babies' deaths. It was a terrible time."

She sighed and looked at Nick with what might be pity. "We'd hoped yer coming would cure him of his blue devils, but it wasn't to be. Mrs. Bishop used to say yer family was cursed, milord. So many deaths. First the babies', then Lady Oakland's, and then yer parents'. And the old lord who was dead inside long afore he stuck his spoon in the wall."

She shook her head—and managed to swallow what she must be thinking, that Nick was dead, too, dead to all sense of responsibility and propriety.

"But now Christmas is coming. It's time to be merry.

Have some more seedcake, milord. And ye, too, Miss Anderson." Mrs. Potty smiled at Edward. "And I've some special pudding I'm sure ye'll like, Master Edward."

And with that Mrs. Potty hurried off to find some sweets to counteract all the sour tales she'd just told.

Chapter Eight

Caro stood in the drawing room with Nick. They'd decided, once they'd met with Mrs. Brooks, not to search for the cradle tonight. Even with plenty of candles, the attic would be too dark and shadowy to find anything, especially as Mrs. Brooks had said the cradle, unused since Nick's father was a baby, was likely hidden away in a far corner. And Edward, who wanted to help, had been practically falling asleep in his pudding.

So, Mrs. Brooks had taken the boy upstairs, and Caro and Nick had come here, stopping only so Nick could have a word with his estate manager, Mr. Pearson, and his butler, Mr. Brooks. There'd been no point in going to their rooms to change. Caro had nothing suitable to change into, and no one else in the motley collection of uninvited guests would have packed with the thought of sitting at a viscount's table. . . .

Blast it! I should have stopped to get my knife out of my cloak pocket.

It was too late now. The Weasel would be here at any moment.

Anxiety tightened her chest. She—

She felt a warm hand on her elbow.

"Don't worry." Nick had leaned over to murmur the words by her ear. She felt his breath on her cheek.

"I'm not," she lied, and slipped out of his hold, moving a step away. She didn't like having men loom over her.

Except . . .

Much to her surprise, she realized Nick's touch had been comforting. She'd moved from habit, not from need.

And he let me go without my having to "ask" with the point of my knife.

She looked up at him. His eyes—puzzled, but not angry—studied her.

"What's the matter, Caro? I thought you wanted me to protect you from this, er, weasel."

"Yes." That's right. She'd made a promise, too. "And I'll protect you from gossip about your—"

"Right." He flushed slightly and waved away her words. "But if we are truly going to pretend to a grand passion—and a sudden one at that—and be at all convincing, you'll have to let me touch you. You'll have to look like you *want* me to touch you. That you are *desperate* for me to do so."

He smiled a bit ruefully and shrugged. "Not that I have personal experience with grand passions, you understand. Any, er, passion I've engaged in has been with women like Livy and Polly and Fanny, when the matter is a simple business transaction. Coins, not sighs or longing looks, are the currency in that sort of arrangement."

Caro understood good, hard coin far better than she did sighs and longing looks.

But Nick was right. No one would believe they were engaged in a heated liaison in private if she shied from his touch in public. She must remember she was playing a part here and act accordingly. Convincingly. Only . . .

She hadn't thought this plan out very well.

Of course she hadn't. It had been very much a spur of the moment thing. Still, she'd given her word, and she wasn't one to back out of an agreement. She'd have to rise to the occasion. And she *did* need Nick's protection. Oakland was a large house. *Remember the dark and deserted corridors.*

She hoped she was wrong about the Weasel, but her gut told her she was right.

And the other men, particularly the drunken bucks, might prove difficult as well.

"Yes. Of course you're right." She forced herself to put her hands flat on his chest. The wool of his coat was rough under her palms. "I don't have any experience with sighing and longing and grand passion either, but I'll try my best to be convincing."

His hands came up to cover hers, the warmth and strength of his grasp reassuring. If she looked, she could see, under the strong planes and angles of the man's face, the boy she'd known. He was much taller, of course, his voice deeper, his shoulders broader, but his eyes and his smile hadn't changed so very much.

Careful. He's a man now, not a boy. You don't know him—and you didn't know him well when he was young.

Perhaps not. She'd only seen him for a few days here and there on Henry's school holidays. But she'd felt like she'd known him. And she'd liked him. He was different from the other boys—different from her brothers, as well. He hadn't tried to keep her from coming along with him and Henry when they'd gone off exploring. He hadn't scoffed at her or belittled her as boys usually did. He hadn't treated her as an annoying girl whose place was in the house with her mother, tending children, but as a competent person with interesting opinions. As an equal.

Yes, but today he was hosting an orgy, and he clearly hasn't been a thoughtful or responsible landowner.

True.

It didn't matter. She needed his help. She couldn't leave Oakland until the roads were passable.

And she'd said she'd help him. They had a contract.

I'll trust Nick, but not blindly.

"We don't have to be giddy about it," he was saying. "We aren't youngsters. But we should seem . . ."

His thumbs slipped under her hands and stroked her palms. The slight pressure was both comforting and . . . distracting in an oddly fluttery sort of way.

"Enthusiastic. As you said earlier, we can't pretend our affair is longstanding, so I think we will have to give the impression that our feelings are so intense they overwhelm our good sense." He grinned. His mouth was only inches from hers. "Well, overwhelm *your* good sense. No one will doubt *my* motivations."

Dervington's smile had never been warm and open like Nick's. No, it had been . . . *wolfish* was the adjective that came to mind. She'd been both thrilled and fearful the first time he'd turned its full force on her.

In the end, she'd just been fearful. And disgusted—with him and with herself.

"Hey, now," Nick said softly, concern suddenly shadowing his eyes. "Are you all right?" His hands moved to rest on her shoulders.

"Y-yes." She couldn't think of Dervington. She—

"Nick," someone said from the doorway, "I—oh."

She startled. Nick's hold on her tightened briefly in a quick warning, and then he put her hand on his arm and turned to face the fellow, who was still gaping in the doorway. She recognized him as one of the men who'd come into the entry after she'd arrived with baby Grace.

"Hallo, Bertram."

The man grinned in a lascivious but good-natured way. "Fast work, Nick."

She felt Nick stiffen. And then the man leered at her—well, she thought that was what he was trying to do. His expression was more good-natured than licentious. He bowed. "I'm happy to entertain you, madam, should Nick fail you."

She swallowed a laugh. The fellow wasn't a boy by any means, but he had a boyish quality about him. She felt certain he wasn't a threat, even if she were to encounter him in a dark corner.

"Thank you for the offer, sir, but I mustn't let you hope. I've no interest in anyone but Ni—"

She paused. Should she call Nick by his title?

No. If this fellow used his Christian name, she would, too. She'd used it in front of Mrs. Brooks. That was how she thought of Nick—how she'd known him as a child.

And remember, we are trying to pretend to a grand passion. Surely, I'd not "my lord" Nick in the midst of . . .

Her imagination failed. The two times she'd had Dervington in her bed there'd been no passion, grand or otherwise, at least on her part. The business had been painful, unpleasant, and embarrassing.

"I've no interest in anyone but Nick," she said and made a show of gazing up at him in what she hoped was a suitably besotted fashion.

From the way Nick raised an eyebrow, she guessed she might be overacting her part.

Caro looked back at the other man. "Nick is an old friend I'm delighted to have rediscovered."

"Ah, but I'm sure you must want new friends, too." The man tried to leer at her again—and only reminded her of how Bumblebee, Jo's horse, looked when she thought you might be hiding an apple or carrot in your pocket.

Caro was no expert, but she'd say the fellow needed to work on his flirting skills.

Then again, the man had come to attend an orgy. Flirting was likely superfluous in such a situation—not that she knew anything more about orgies than she did about flirting, thank God.

"Leave off teasing Miss Anderson, Bert," Nick said, annoyance sharpening his voice and sending Bert's brows shooting up to meet the lock of brown hair on his forehead.

Caro was surprised by the testy tone as well. She glanced up at Nick. He was smiling now, but his eyes still looked hard.

Does he think me a bone to be fought over?

She did not like that notion at all. She would just—

No, she wouldn't. Much as she hated feeling like a tasty scrap Nick was defending from the other dogs, that was what she was at the moment. It was infuriating and annoying, but it was necessary. This boy-man was likely harmless, but the Weasel and the others might not be. She needed Nick.

And Nick needs me.

That thought salved her pride.

"Miss Anderson, may I introduce Mr. Bertram Collins? Bertram, Miss Anderson." Nick's voice was still tight. "Do come in, Bert, and stop blocking the door."

Mr. Collins threw Nick a cautious glance as he stepped into the room. "My pleasure, Miss Anderson. I apologize if I gave offense."

And now how should she react?

Oh, bother. She was never going to get through this if she questioned her every action.

"No offense taken, Mr. Collins." *Might as well be blunt.* "But it's true. I'm not in the market for dalliance." *Can I manage a coy look?*

Likely not, but she would try. "At least not with anyone but Nick."

If that wasn't jumping in with both feet, she didn't know what was.

Nick smiled at her, but managed at the same time to give her the impression he was rolling his eyes—though of course he wasn't actually doing that.

She looked back at Mr. Collins.

His eyes had widened. "Ah, well, then. I'll just say that Nick's a lucky fellow."

Nick finally took up his role in this farce. "Indeed, I am." His free hand came up to cover hers on his arm. "I used to spend school holidays with Miss Anderson's family, but the last time I saw her, she was only a girl—which is why I didn't recognize her at once." He grinned at her. "You've grown up quite nicely, my dear."

Now it was her turn to give the impression of rolling her eyes without actually doing so. "As have you. I remember you as short and scrawny and spotty."

His eyes narrowed, promising she'd pay for that comment later. Oddly, the notion didn't frighten her or even make her uneasy. Instead, she felt . . .

Excited? Is that what this peculiar, fluttery sensation is?

"Surely not spotty, but I will admit I grew late. I believe I was just fifteen when last you saw me."

"Yes, I believe you were. I—"

Someone cleared his throat—

Dear God! She'd been so focused on Nick, she'd completely forgotten about Mr. Collins standing not three feet from her. That would never do. She was only playing at being a lovestruck fool; she wasn't *really* such a poor creature.

Keep your wits about you!

That had been her mistake with Dervington—not staying alert. Well, she'd thought he'd gone out that day. And she'd never expected to encounter him on the servants' stairs.

Lesson learned. She'd vowed never to put herself at such risk again.

"Do you know where Felix is, Nick?" Mr. Collins was asking. "I thought he must be, er"—he sent her a cautious look and revised his words—"cavorting with Polly, but when I said as much to Fanny, she told me Polly was in Mrs. Dixon's room with the baby."

Nick scowled. "He must be in the house somewhere—it's snowing too hard for him to have been daft enough to go outside—but he'd do well to play least in sight."

Mr. Collins's brows shot up, likely as much in reaction to Nick's harsh tone as his words. "Oh? Has Felix offended somehow?"

"You're bloody right he has. He's the baby's father, Bert."

Mr. Collins's eyebrows almost flew off his forehead at that. "Are—are you certain? Felix didn't say anything about a baby."

"I'm certain. Edward recognized the moles on Felix's cheeks—*both* sorts of cheeks."

Caro flushed. She really wished she hadn't heard that. She did not want to contemplate Mr. Felix Simpson's naked hindquarters or speculate how Edward had seen them.

Bathing. It must have been bathing. Please, God, let Edward have seen the man in his bath or perhaps swimming in a pond.

The sound of voices in the corridor claimed their attention then. Caro must have tightened her hold on Nick's arm, because Nick bent his head close to hers again.

"Don't worry," he murmured so only she could hear him.

Or at least she hoped only she could hear.

The first two people through the door were the idiots who had driven the coach into the ditch. They looked to be in their early to mid-twenties—certainly old enough to have known better.

"Lord Devil!" the shorter one said, grinning. "What luck to have landed on your doorstep. I'd heard you were having a Christmas orgy." He leered at Caro—a real leer, nothing like Mr. Collins's awkward attempt—and whistled. "Are all the fillies like this one?"

If Nick had stiffened at Mr. Collins's words, he turned

to marble now. Caro swore she could feel waves of anger radiating from him.

Mr. Collins inspected an invisible spot on his coat.

The speaker's companion must have noticed their reactions, because he put a hand on the man's arm. "Er, Archie, we don't want to annoy Lord Oakland."

Archie laughed and shrugged off his friend's hold. "Lord Devil never turns snappish over a bit o' fun, Oliver. Do you, Devil?" He finally stopped ogling Caro to look at Nick.

His expression froze, mouth dropping open slightly.

If Nick carried a quizzing glass, he didn't employ it, but he did somehow manage to look down his nose at Archie—a feat that, until this moment, Caro had thought was merely a figure of speech.

The silence was quite, quite deafening.

"Er," Archie said. "D-didn't mean to offend, of course. A th-thousand apologies if I did. I mean, it was all over Town, you know, that the Devil was hosting a Christmas orgy at his family seat. Fellows thought it a capital joke, just what you'd do, don't you know?"

Nick kept staring at him in silence.

"I-I . . . th-that is . . . D-didn't mean to intrude. 'Twas an accident. The snow. The stagecoach. The d-ditch."

The fellow might have babbled on for the rest of the evening if Nick hadn't finally, blessedly, cleared his throat and stopped the flow of words.

"I don't believe I know you, do I?"

Caro shivered at Nick's tone. He could have been addressing a pair of loathsome bugs that had had the effrontery to invade his home—not that Nick talked to bugs, of course.

She felt some sympathy for the two men shrinking in on themselves in front of her eyes.

"N-no, my lord. You—you don't, my lord," the other

fellow stammered before executing a jerky little bow. "Mr. Oliver Meadows, my lord." He glanced at his friend.

Archie looked to be struggling with a combination of anger and mortification.

Anger won. The man's chin came up. He almost succeeded in looking haughty—would have succeeded if his Adam's apple hadn't started bobbing rather wildly and his voice had been steadier. "I-I'll h-have you know, I'm L-Lord Archibald T-Turner—"

Oh, God. Oh, God.

The roaring in Caro's ears prevented her from hearing anything else the man said, but it didn't matter. She knew who Lord Archibald was—the Marquess of Dervington's second son.

He won't recognize me.

She hoped. Archibald and his brother, the heir, had been away at school the whole of her very, *very* brief stint as their half-sister's nursemaid. She'd left London immediately after quitting their father's employ, so hadn't been in Town for anyone to point out.

But will he recognize my name?

I just need to keep my composure—not let on . . .

Nick's thumb stroked her hand in a firm, calming sort of way—and she realized her fingers had tightened so they might leave imprints on his skin even through his jacket and shirt.

She tried to relax her grip.

"Ah. Yes," Nick was saying. "I can see the family resemblance." His tone made it very clear that was *not* a compliment.

Before Archie could puzzle out a proper reply, the rest of the company arrived—minus Felix, Polly, Mrs. Dixon, the children, and the coachman. It said something about Caro's emotional state that the Weasel's unwelcome presence did little to increase the violent storm raging in her.

Nick turned his attention to the room at large, but kept his broad, strong hand on Caro's. Normally, she'd have stepped away from him, or at least reclaimed her hand, but she needed something—someone—to hold onto.

Am I really so weak?

Sadly, yes. But she would get over it. It was just the surprise that had thrown her. She would collect herself and come up with a plan.

Another plan. At the moment she had to focus on convincing the onlookers that she and Nick were undertaking a passionate affair.

Perhaps I'm holding up my end of the bargain by letting Nick hold me up now.

"I am Lord Oakland," Nick said. "Welcome to my home. I'm sorry your stagecoach ended in a ditch, but—"

"But it wouldn't have happened if not for those two ruffians!" The clergyman jabbed his finger at Archie and Oliver. "Call the authorities, my lord, and have these men locked up! Remember, the Good Lord's commandment: *Thou shalt not steal!*"

"We were only borrowing the coach," Archie said, unwisely.

Fortunately, that reply enraged the clergyman so much that he was rendered mute—which, unfortunately, gave the Weasel an opening.

"I see ye didn't waste any time scooping up this tasty piece, milord," he said, baring his teeth at Caro. "Didn't ye land on yer feet, girl—or should I say yer back?"

Caro saw Nick's jaw clench as he worked to control his temper. The Weasel must have seen it, too, because his twisted grin wavered, and he took a step backward.

Which reminded Caro it was time for her to step forward, onto the stage to recite her lines.

She attempted a giggle—and thought she was rather

successful. She'd got Nick's attention, at least, though he still looked angry—and rather taken aback. In the heat of the moment, he must have forgotten their plan.

"If you mean am I happy to have encountered Lord Oakland again, then yes, I am. We were friends as children, but lost track of each other over the years." And now it was time for another besotted, adoring gaze into Nick's face.

Nick's mouth twitched as if he were suppressing a grin, and his eyes once again gave her the impression they were rolling on the inside.

"And here he is"—she ran her free hand down his coat—"all grown up."

She half expected to hear applause for her dramatic performance. Instead her audience greeted her acting skill with grunts, snorts . . . and a sigh from one of the women. She glanced over at the group—and happened to catch Livy's eye.

Livy gave her a knowing and strangely satisfied look—and a *wink*. Good Lord!

Caro looked back up at Nick. Was that a flicker of heat behind the humor in his eyes? Oh! It made her feel very . . . odd.

It was definitely heat. Nick's mouth slid into a slow, intimate smile. His voice when he spoke was low and, er, *sultry*.

"Yes, I'm all grown up now, aren't I? As are you." His look got even hotter. "I can't wait to play, though our games will be rather different than they were when we were children, won't they?"

Dear Lord, she was going to die of embarrassment or melt into a hot, steaming puddle on the floor.

He looked back at his guests—thank God, because if he'd kept looking at her, she wasn't certain what she would have done, but she was afraid it would have been something extremely embarrassing.

"As the snow shows no signs of letting up," he said, "I'm afraid we shall very likely be stuck here together for Christmas. We would all do well to try to get along, make the best of things, and help out in any way we can."

There was some grumbling over that, but Caro thought everyone saw the truth in what Nick said.

"So, let's begin by introducing ourselves. As you know, I'm Lord Oakland, and this is Miss Caroline Anderson."

Caro held her breath, looking at Archie out of the corner of her eye to see if he would recognize her name and leap to reveal her sordid past. He didn't, though he did frown as if a chord in the farthest recesses of his memory was vibrating.

She hoped the sound was faint and faded quickly, but she would be on her guard nonetheless.

They went around the room. First Livy, then Fanny, and then the clergyman—Tobias Hughes, who was between positions.

That did not sound good. The Little Puddledon vicar was between positions, too, because he'd attacked her friend Pen, now Lady Darrow, last summer. Caro made a note to watch out for the clergyman as well as the Weasel.

The Weasel was Uriah Woods, a wainwright by trade.

"Splendid!" Nick said. "Perhaps you can figure out how to repair the stagecoach so it will be ready when the snow stops and the roads clear. Mr. Pearson, my estate manager, tells me my men and the stage's coachman were able to tow it up to the stables, but, after inspecting it, they fear it's beyond their abilities to fix."

Mr. Woods grinned, which made him look much less threatening. "I'll be happy to see what I can do."

"And I can help with the baking, milord. Ye can't have Christmas without Christmas pies," Humphrey said. "I'm Humphrey Parker, milord, and this is me wife, Muriel. Muriel's a dab hand in the kitchen, too, I'll have ye know.

She helps me with me baking, but she can also make a tasty meal out of all sorts of odds and ends."

Muriel nodded. "Aye, that I can. I'll be happy to help out, if yer cook would like. I'm always in the kitchen when I visit me sisters in Marbridge. It's not Christmas without the smell of meat roasting and Humphrey's pies baking. And he always makes a special treat for the children." She looked around. "Where are the boy and his mother and the baby?"

"Mrs. Dixon and her family are resting in their room," Nick said. "I suspect it's well past Edward's bedtime. One of my guests, Miss Polly White, is acting as a temporary nursemaid until Mrs. Dixon recovers her strength." He frowned. "The only other guest who's not in the room at the moment is Felix Simpson."

Nick did not mention Mr. Simpson's connection to Mrs. Dixon and her family.

"I say, Mr. Parker," Mr. Collins said enthusiastically, "I don't suppose you can make a Yorkshire Christmas pie, can you?"

"O' course, I can, sir. Me wife says I make a bang-up Yorkshire pie, don't ye, Muriel?"

Muriel nodded. "The best I've tasted."

"That sounds splendid," Nick said. "Anything we can do to make the holiday merry. I have to confess that I'm not usually here at Christmas, so I've no traditions of my own to follow. I welcome your suggestions."

"Holly and ivy," Oliver Meadows said. "You have to have holly and ivy hanging about."

Fanny nodded. "And mistletoe. I used to love making kissing boughs when I lived at home."

"Right." Archie, Dervington's son, grinned rather salaciously.

Ugh.

"I could direct a Christmas play, if you'd like," Mr. Hughes offered. "Not a mummer's play, but a short Nativity reenactment—for the boy more than anyone. Children should learn the Christmas story."

"And we have a baby to play the part of Baby Jesus," Livy said.

"We could have games." That was Mr. Collins. "I used to enjoy playing snapdragon and blindman's bluff."

"And don't forget the Yule log," Fanny added. "Christmas isn't Christmas without the Yule log."

Caro wished she could offer to brew some Christmas ale, but she hadn't any of the ingredients. She could, however, offer to mix up some wassail. She did that for the Home's inhabitants every year—though this year someone else would have to fill that role.

She opened her mouth to suggest it, but Mr. Brooks came in then to announce dinner. Oh, well. She would mention it to Nick later.

She walked on his arm past Archie. Oh, blast. Archie's brow was furrowed, and she felt his eyes follow her. Clearly, he was still trying to puzzle out who she was.

Her stomach twisted as she took her place at the table on Nick's right, and what little appetite she had fled.

There was no getting around it—she would have to tell Nick about her time at Dervington's London house. Not the whole story—there was no need to do that. But enough of the tale so that if Archie *did* remember who she was and said something, Nick wouldn't be taken unawares.

She stared glumly down at her plate. She was not looking forward to that conversation.

Chapter Nine

Nick shrugged out of his coat and hung it over the back of the chair to his writing desk. If anyone had told him this morning that he'd sit down to a meal with company that included a baker, a wainwright, a clergyman, and two whores, he'd have thought they were drunk as an emperor. And yet he had. And the experience had been surprisingly pleasant—a regular Christmas miracle!

He grinned as he unwound his cravat. Christmas stories had dominated the conversation, tales of the various ways his guests celebrated the season now and in the past. He hadn't had much to add since Uncle Leon had frowned upon Christmas cheer, deeming all nonreligious festivities pagan, if not outright demonic. There had been no wassail bowl, no caroling, and certainly no games at Oakland when Nick was a lad. He'd spent every English Christmas head bowed, mind wandering as his uncle read from the Bible.

In Venice, however . . .

He smiled at his father's painting of the Grand Canal as he tugged his shirttail out of his breeches. Christmas in Venice had meant Carnival—masks and music, jugglers and acrobats. A feast of sound and color as unlike an Oakland Christmas as chalk to cheese.

And yet . . .

What would Christmas at Oakland have been like if his aunt hadn't fallen and lost her baby, his uncle's heir? Or if she'd been able to carry another infant to term?

Mrs. Potty had said Uncle Leon had never been as light-hearted as Nick's father—well, Nick would admit, looking back, that Papa might have bordered on the irresponsible—but it seemed very likely his uncle wouldn't have been so grim if he hadn't had so much tragedy in his life.

Nick pulled his shirt over his head and dropped it on the floor as he looked at the connecting door. Something had been bothering Caro at dinner, though she had perked up a bit as the meal went on and the conversation got merrier.

What was the problem?

She'd said earlier that she was concerned about the Weasel, but he'd wager it was Dervington's whelp that had upset her the most. She'd almost driven her fingers through his forearm when the fellow had told them his name.

She was strong. He looked at his forearm and was surprised not to see bruises.

I bet the rest of her is strong, too. All that work in the brewhouse. She must have strong arms. Strong legs. A strong, lovely body . . . mmm. Does she wear a virginal nightdress with a high neck and long sleeves? Or nothing at all—

Stop it!

Of course she wore a nightdress. And if she didn't, it was none of his concern. They were only playing at being lovers.

His cock would certainly like to play. It was long and hard, pushing against his fall now, eager to be set free.

This bloody masquerade was going to be hell.

He stomped over to the bootjack and jerked his boots off with more force than necessary. Then he sat down on the bed to tug off his socks.

His large, soft, comfortable bed—or rather, Uncle Leon's large, soft, comfortable bed. The man likely had worn a hair shirt to counteract the worldly pleasure of such luxury at night.

Though maybe not. There *were* those obscene statues. Perhaps the old goat had held a nightly party of one here on his mattress.

Poor lonely, old man.

For the first time he could remember, Nick felt pity for his uncle.

He frowned at a bedpost. Had his parents ever discussed Leon, Lady Oakland, and the babies?

Not that he remembered, though the first baby's death and likely some of the miscarriages must have happened before he was born. And it was possible his parents *had* discussed the matter, and he'd just not paid attention. He'd been a young boy, after all, far more interested in playing than in listening to boring tales about people he didn't know in a faraway, unpleasant-sounding place. Papa had always talked of England as if it were perpetually gray and cold and rainy—which it mostly was.

Though eventually, his father might reasonably have concluded that odds were good Nick would be the next viscount and brought some of this up.

No, not Papa. His father had lived very much in the moment, never planning for the future. He had been like an overgrown boy in that regard. When he was painting, you could have set off a small bomb in his studio and he'd not have noticed. When he was between paintings, he'd been up for any sort of lark. He'd go punting on the canals or fishing in the lagoon or exploring Venice's maze of *campi* and *calli*—small squares and narrow streets.

And surely Papa never thought he'd die so young. He'd—

Zeus! Papa had been only a few years older than I am now.

Nick did the calculations several times in his head—and then resorted to counting on his fingers. The result was always the same.

He'd thought Papa old, but he hadn't been.

And he'd only one son—me.

Why? Papa and Mama had seemed very much in love, not that Nick had paid a great deal of attention as a boy. But they'd always been touching and smiling and whispering together, and his grandparents and aunts and uncles had often teased them about it. He'd learned to avoid their bedroom in the night or the early morning—and even, occasionally, in the afternoon. Whenever the door was closed.

Much as he hated to contemplate it, his parents had obviously been doing what needed to be done to get more children—and yet they hadn't.

Had Mama miscarried?

No. He would have known if she had. That wasn't something she could have hidden in their small house, especially surrounded as they were by Mama's mother and sisters.

Perhaps the St. John seed was weak or damaged. . . .

He stood up and dropped his stockings on top of his shirt. It didn't matter, at least to him. He wasn't in the market for an heir. Let his distant cousin worry about continuing the line.

He felt a nagging whisper of guilt again, blast it. A worry about Mrs. Potty and the Brookses and old Pearson. Would the distant cousin look after them?

Surely, he would, though Nick supposed he should investigate the matter and find out precisely what sort of man was in line to be the next Viscount Oakland. He wasn't even entirely certain of the fellow's name. Was it Jonas or Jonah St. John? Or perhaps it was Joshua. And had Pearson said the fellow was an Oxford don? That would never do. Dons took vows of celibacy, didn't they?

Oh, blast. Well, Nick would give Pearson the Christmas gift he'd always wanted. As soon as Nick got rid of his guests—invited and not—he'd stop putting the man off and would sit down with him to discuss estate business for as long as he wished.

He pulled off his breeches and drawers and dropped them on the pile of discarded clothing.

All he knew for certain was that *he* was not going to be the one to father the next viscount.

Unless . . .

He glanced at the connecting door—

No. Don't be an idiot.

Ha! He was safe. Even if he *were* interested in marrying Caro—which he was not. Of *course* he was not. They hadn't seen each other since they were children, for God's sake. But *if* he were interested, Caro would set him straight at once and save him from himself. She obviously had no thought ever to marry.

A pity.

He heard a faint noise. Was it a knock at the door?

No. Now he was so randy, he was hallucinating. Worse, his cock had sprung to eager attention at the imagined sound.

He groaned, closing his eyes. Hell. Clearly—*painfully* so—even though he had no interest in fathering a child, the organ that had to do the work had a keen desire to undertake the task. If only Livy were here now—

"Oh!"

Oh? Who'd said oh*?*

His eyes flew open to see Caro, standing in the open doorway, staring at—

He lunged for the counterpane, pulled it off the bed, and wrapped it around his middle. Fortunately, there was plenty of extra fabric so his large and getting larger erection didn't make an obvious tent in the cloth.

"Uh. Er. What's the matter, Caro? Why are you—"

Idiot! There could be only one reason Caro would invade his room; the Weasel must have invaded hers.

"Don't worry. I'll deal with him." He started forward.

"But, Nick. I'm mean, I'm sorry. I—oh!"

Caro had been right when she'd said if men were ever forced to wear skirts, the bloody things would have been shredded, burned, and banned eons ago. His first step caught the frigging counterpane. He took another, trying to catch his balance, and only made things worse.

There was no hope for it. He had to abandon the bedclothes and all sense of modesty and propriety before he measured his length on the floor.

He dropped the blasted coverlet, but that didn't help. The damnable cloth still tangled about his feet like a mass of vines—or a seething ball of serpents. He pitched forward—

Caro, the daft woman, came running to help him.

"Oh, Nick. Watch out! Let me—"

He grabbed her shoulders—he hadn't much choice, she was in his path. He had some confused notion that he might be able to push her away and save her from disaster, but it was a vain hope. His momentum carried them onward.

By some miracle, he managed to keep upright as he hopped and skipped and stumbled, until they crashed into the wall, Caro's back flattened against it, his front flattened against Caro.

Mmm. He'd answered his question as to what she wore to sleep in. She was clad only in a thin nightdress. It was not as wonderful as having her naked, of course, but it was still very wonderful not to have a dress and stays and chemise between them—well, or his coat, waistcoat, shirt, breeches, and drawers, either.

She was soft—and yet, firm, too—and curved and warm. Her glorious hair, tumbling loose over her shoulders, smelled of lemon and soap.

Fortunately, his heart was pounding so hard from the

wild, bizarre dance they'd taken that it had stolen all the blood from his cock. He might be flattening her, but he wasn't also spearing her.

Yet.

"Are you all right?" He whispered the words into her hair. He should push away, but his hands had somehow got trapped between her and the wall.

And I'm naked, remember.

And she was in a nightdress. A thin garment that did nothing to hide her lovely, soft curves, that could be easily removed on the way to the wide, comfortable bed just steps . . .

No! Think with your brain, not your cock. This is Caro. *Henry's sister. Your childhood friend. She's clearly had bad experiences with men. Don't add yourself to her list of blackguards.*

He leaned back a little so he could see her face. Her eyes were wide, blue pools, fringed with absurdly long, dark lashes, but he thought he saw only surprise there, not alarm. "*Are* you all right?"

And was there also a little flicker of . . . need? Was she panting just a little? Her mouth was *so* close. It would take bending only a fraction of an inch to capture her lips.

No, no, no.

"Y-yes."

Yes?! So, he *could*—

Bloody *hell*, it was hard to clear the fog of lust from his brain. Caro meant yes, she was all right, not yes, take me to bed and have your wicked way with me.

Unfortunately.

Though she did seem to be darting glances at his neck and shoulders. And she wasn't struggling to get free, nor did she seem alarmed by her position in his arms, pressed against his naked body.

Because she trusts me.

He was shocked to realize that the thought of losing her trust was more painful than that of the agony he'd feel upon receiving a knee to his most sensitive organ.

He'd hate it if Caro looked on him as an enemy rather than a friend.

"I apologize. I'm not, er, dressed for company," he managed to say in spite of his dry mouth and thick tongue.

Humor sparked in her eyes. "I noticed."

Perhaps that was the answer—keep it light. "Was there a particular purpose for your call?" He waggled his brows theatrically. Might as well admit what must be becoming embarrassingly obvious. "If you were looking for a bit of diversion, I will be most delighted to provide it."

She laughed, as he'd hoped she would. "No, thank you."

And then she frowned and pressed against him.

His foolish male organ jumped with hope and excitement.

"You don't feel like you're impotent." Her tone was accusatory. "And you certainly didn't look like you were when I came into the room."

"Er." Should he say she'd misunderstood Livy? But she hadn't misunderstood. He'd been as limp as boiled asparagus when he'd had Livy in this room last night.

She pushed on his shoulders. He hesitated a moment and then decided to let her take the lead wherever the hell she wanted to go. If she brought a fit of the vapors on herself, then so be it.

He stepped back. His thick, swollen cock stood boldly at a right angle to his body, pointing directly at Caro. If that didn't send her screaming back to her room—

It didn't. She was staring at his male member as he imagined she might study a brew that hadn't turned out as expected. He felt an odd mix of embarrassment, titillation, and curiosity.

Curiosity won. He would wait and see what she did next.

She glanced up at his face. He thought—or perhaps it was just that he hoped—her eyes held more than scientific interest. And yet, she wasn't being flirtatious. He felt *quite* certain of that. She didn't want him to seduce her.

Sadly.

"May I touch?"

His cock nodded—and then his head did, too, even though he couldn't believe he'd heard correctly.

She reached—slowly, tentatively—toward his brainless member, which, if it had been a dog, would have been whining and jumping and begging, in a frenzy to be petted.

He bit his lip as her fingers grazed his skin, tracing his length from his root to his tip.

His knees were going to give out if he didn't lie down at once. "Uh, the bed?"

Caro snatched her hand back, alarm flashing through her eyes. "No. I-I didn't mean . . . That is, I don't want . . . I really am not interested in . . ."

He would put her out of her misery before she strangled on her own tongue.

Don't think about tongues.

"Caro, I won't touch you unless and until you ask me to do so. But if you want to continue to touch *me*, I need to lie down. Or sit. I suppose that might work. Or, well, I could *try* holding on to a chair while standing. I might be able to keep to my feet with support."

She eyed him cautiously. "The bed, then."

He hobbled—partly to make her laugh and partly because walking *was* uncomfortable—over to the bed, got carefully onto it, stretched out on his back, looked up at the ceiling, and threw his arms wide. "Now, have your wicked way with me."

She laughed again, but this time the sound had a nervous edge to it. A nervous and *distant* edge.

He turned his head to look at her.

She hadn't followed him across the room.

Clearly, she was having second thoughts.

Since he had no idea what her first thoughts had been—beyond being certain she hadn't come into his room to ogle him or invite him to engage in some spirited bed play—he regretfully decided he needed to stop whatever it was they were doing until he knew what she wanted. He carefully propped himself up on an elbow.

"Does it hurt?" She was staring at his cock again, which only made the blasted organ swell more.

"Well . . ." He would not resort to polite lies.

Polite?! The present situation was far, far outside the boundaries of polite.

"It *is* uncomfortable, but it will, er, subside with time."

How familiar was she with the male anatomy? She wasn't reacting like he imagined a virgin would. Well, if the rumor he'd heard years ago in London was true, she *wasn't* a virgin. But she wasn't acting like an experienced woman either.

Clearly, whatever Dervington had done to or with her hadn't sold her on the notion of sexual congress. Hell, she carried a knife around to defend herself from men—though she obviously didn't have it with her now.

And you don't want to do anything to make her wish she did *have it with her.*

True. He sat up, grabbed a pillow, and put it across his lap, giving his cock some privacy to shrink back to its normal, polite-company proportions.

"Pardon me for asking, and not that you aren't welcome, but why are you here"—*keep your tone light*—"if not to have your wicked way with me?"

She laughed—but flushed, too. "I knocked. I thought you . . ." She looked away, shrugged, looked back at him. "Well, I suppose you just grunted, but I thought you'd indicated I could come in. I'm sorry I intruded. I'll just go—"

"No." If she went back to her room now, leaving him ignorant—and aroused—he'd not be able to sleep.

More to the point, if what she had to say was important enough for her to brave his bedchamber, it was too important to leave unsaid.

"What did you want to tell me?"

This was so embarrassing. And odd. And . . .

Exciting?

Surely not. And yet a host of emotions she'd thought long dead had woken in her.

She'd not seen a man naked before. Oh, she'd caught glimpses of her brothers in the buff. She'd even seen their dangly bits a few times—but the bits had definitely been dangly, not long and thick and stiff like Nick's. The two times Dervington had come to her bed, he'd kept his shirt on. There had been a few kisses, a quick fumble as he'd pulled her nightdress up, and then—

That memory quickly killed her reanimated desires.

To think that huge thing had been shoved up inside me . . .

She shuddered. *Now* she understood why what Dervington had done had hurt so much, especially that first time. The second time hadn't been quite so painful, and there'd not been blood all over her sheets. But the first time . . .

No wonder she'd bled like a stuck pig.

If I'd seen Dervington's bit beforehand, I would never have let him near me.

"Caro, what is it?"

She blinked and came back to the present and Nick, sitting naked—except for the carefully placed pillow—on the bed. He was looking at her, really looking at her, as if he saw her and not just an attractive female body that he wanted to use for his own amusement.

I can't let myself be fooled again. . . .

"Tell me." He sounded as if he truly cared.

She trusted herself to size up customers interested in her ale. She'd become a much better judge of character in thirteen years. It was far harder to hoodwink her now.

Hoodwink? Ha! Dervington hadn't had to do much on that score. She'd fooled herself. She'd written the play, and Dervington had happily donned the costume she'd handed him. He just hadn't acted the role in the way she'd imagined.

And this was *Nick*. When they'd been together in his room earlier, he'd not attacked her. On the contrary, he'd given her that statue to use as a weapon if she felt she needed one. And he'd clearly been aroused when she'd come in here—she eyed the pillow again—and had even been pressed up against her, and yet he'd not hurt her. She'd not even felt threatened.

She flushed. Lud, he'd let her *touch* him. And he'd still not taken that as an invitation to attack her.

Enough. She'd come in here with the single goal of telling Nick enough about her time in London to forewarn him if Archie remembered and started talking—and she was going to do that.

I just wish I knew how much of the sordid tale Archie knows. . . .

Likely not so very much. Remember, he was a boy at the time.

She would tell Nick as little as possible. Just enough for him to understand the problem. There was no need to share any unsavory details. It wouldn't be sporting not to tell him something. Having the story sprung on him with no warning would be uncomfortable for them both.

She needed an ally. And they had an agreement. He would look out for her, and she would look out for him.

And if she *couldn't* count on him, the sooner she knew that, the better.

Sadly, odds were good he *would* turn on her. Women

were supposed to save themselves for marriage. Or at least for love. They weren't supposed to be curious or . . .

She still didn't understand why she'd done what she'd done. Yes, she'd overheard her brothers talking and joking—they often forgot to watch what they said around her—about all the exciting, dangerous things they did in London, including their various bedroom adventures. So perhaps that had motivated her. She'd wanted to do something more exciting than tend a baby; she'd done so much of that at home. And she wanted to be more in control of her life. She wanted the power to make choices. Decisions.

Even foolish ones, apparently.

It was very unfair that men weren't held accountable for their actions in the same way women were. No one expected men to be virgins when they married.

Hmph! If men *were* made to follow Society's rules for women, it would be just like forcing skirts on them—things would change.

Though, to be honest, men didn't run the same risks women did. If a bedroom adventure resulted in pregnancy, a man could deny he was the father or just fade out of the picture. The woman was left literally holding the baby. Just look at poor Mrs. Dixon.

"It's not just the Weasel I need to worry about."

"Ah." He frowned. "Is it Archie, too, then?"

She felt her eyes widen. "How did you know?"

He shrugged—and she was annoyed with herself that she watched with far too much appreciation the movement of his shoulders and chest.

"You dug your fingers into my arm so hard when he introduced himself, it's a miracle you didn't leave a mark." He examined his naked forearm and then showed it to her.

Ah. It was broader than hers, covered with light brown hair and curved slightly by muscle. His upper arm bulged with muscle, too.

He'd have no trouble rowing the mash or moving casks of ale.

"And then you went so pale, I was afraid you might faint." His voice was calm. Kind. "What I don't know is why. What is Lord Archibald to you, Caro?"

This was the perfect opening. "He . . . That is, it's not him, precisely. It's his . . ." *Oh, dear God, how am I ever going to get the words out?*

"Just say it, Caro."

Nick was right. She should just say it. She wasn't usually one to beat about the bush. It was just that this particular topic was so difficult. It was embarrassing both due to what had actually occurred—well, that was shocking as well as mortifying—but also because she'd been so stupid to do it. Inconceivably stupid . . .

Inconceivably. Oh, God.

And she'd done it *twice*. She didn't count the time Dervington had tried to take her against her will.

"It's . . ." She swallowed. Tried—and failed—again.

"It's his father, isn't it?"

She froze. Her face must have revealed the truth because Nick sighed and seemed to droop.

"So, Dervington attacked you, did he, Caro?"

All words—all air—whooshed out of her.

And then she started to cry. Hell! She never cried. She *hated* crying. It made her feel ill, with a stuffy nose and cloudy head.

Arms came round her—naked arms—and gathered her gently against a naked chest.

She'd locked her feelings about that horrible time away deep, deep inside her, but now they broke free, splintering the box she'd kept them in. There would be no forcing them back into that dark place.

No. It's not that bad. I can handle this. I just need a minute. I'll be fine in a—

"It's all right, Caro. It's all right." Nick rubbed her back in a soothing way.

She had no idea how long they stood there—her crying, Nick murmuring—but finally either his calm presence settled her or the storm blew itself out on its own. Her sobs turned to snuffles and painful, stuttering gulps. She pulled back—and Nick loosened his hold on her. She felt certain he would drop his hands completely if she gave him the smallest sign that she wanted him to do so.

She wasn't yet ready to give up the warmth and comfort of his touch.

Nonsense! I don't need him or anyone. I can handle this myself.

The only move she made was to wipe her nose on her sleeve. And then she told Nick the truth.

"Yes, it was Dervington." It was easier to look at his chest than his face.

His *naked* chest with its hard muscle, warm skin, and dusting of soft, springy hair.

"And yes, he attacked me, but it's more complicated than that." She paused, pressed her lips together—and then the story started to spill out. "I seduced him—"

Nick snorted!

That was not the reaction she'd expected. She looked up at his face.

His expression wasn't what she'd expected either. Instead of revulsion, she saw . . . compassion?

Perhaps he'd misunderstood.

"Didn't you hear me? I said I seduced Dervington"—she'd be painfully clear—"*twice* the week before he attacked me."

Nick still looked . . . well, perhaps sad now, but sad *for* her, not sad about her.

She didn't know what to make of that. Best just get to the point of this embarrassing confession so they could move on to discussing how to handle matters if Dervington's son became a problem.

"Archie was away at school when it happened, but I'm sure he must have heard the story. If he connects me to the disreputable nursemaid, he might conclude I'm no better than I should be."

She finally stepped back out of Nick's hold and looked him in the eye. She wanted absolutely *no* confusion about her position on her past, er, indiscretions.

"Which might have been true then, but it's not true now." She wrinkled her nose. "I am not interested in any sort of dalliance. The two times with Dervington were more than enough to convince me I do not like such activities *at all*."

Chapter Ten

Oh, Lord.

Nick had been in some dangerous situations before, though up until this moment they'd all involved drunken men and flying fists.

This was a different sort of danger. He was afraid that saying or doing the wrong thing would hurt Caro and damage the tenuous connection between them.

He'd rather take a fist to the jaw than do anything to push Caro away.

Why?

He wasn't certain. He only knew what his gut told him, and he trusted his gut. It was often a better guide than his brain—and a *much* better guide than his cock.

But where to begin? There were so many ways to put a foot wrong.

"I very much doubt you seduced Dervington."

All right, *that* had been the wrong place. Caro's brows had shot up—and then slammed down into a fierce scowl. At least she seemed too annoyed to be embarrassed. On balance, he supposed that was a good thing.

"Excuse me? I think I know whether I seduced the Marquess of Dervington or not."

She poked him in the chest—and then snatched back her hand as if she'd just realized he was still naked.

Of course, that didn't stop her.

"Do I need to spell it out for you, Lord Oakland?"

Zeus! Of all the times to be referred to by his uncle's title, this had to be the worst. Not that there was anything amorous going on here—despite his lack of attire—but that didn't mean he wanted his uncle's ghost to join them.

Caro seemed to understand, or that's how he interpreted the expression that flashed across her features—as one of regret. But then she was right back to her argument.

"Do you think I don't know what seduction is? Then let me disabuse you of that notion." Caro's voice was hard. Tense. "I allowed Lord Dervington into my bed." Her jaw tensed, too, and she said, through clenched teeth, "Into my *body*. I gave him my virginity. It was bloody horrible. Painful and, well, just bloody."

Don't flinch.

"And then, when he swore the next day and the day after and the day after that, on and on, that it had only hurt so much because it was my first time, that I shouldn't be afraid, that I would like it if I would only let him do it again . . ." She stopped. Swallowed. "He flattered me. He begged and pleaded. So, I let him do it again."

Her scowl grew fiercer. "He was right that it didn't hurt as much the second time, but it hurt badly enough. I did *not* like it. Not. At. All."

Nick was not surprised. Dervington was a selfish, coarse braggart outside the bedroom, and Livy had told him he was just as unpleasant inside it. She'd had the misfortune of encountering him early in her career. He'd been rough and boorish and, once she had her own, er, business, she'd struck him permanently from her list of potential clients.

Which might be one reason Dervington seduced his servants—he couldn't get any but the most desperate professionals to take his coin.

"You misunderstand me. I believe you when you say you went to bed with Dervington. I just wouldn't call what happened seduction, and I certainly wouldn't say you were the one doing the seducing."

"I assure you, I was."

"Oh? And what exactly did you do to lure Lord Dervington into your bed?"

She blinked and then stared at him blankly. "Do? I didn't *do* anything. I, er, didn't need to."

He nodded. Sadly, he could guess how it had gone. "So, he flattered you, did he? Told you how beautiful you were?"

"Y-yes." She flushed. "He said he couldn't think of anything else when he saw me. That I drove him mad with desire."

Right. That sounded revoltingly like what Dervington—and other unscrupulous men of Nick's acquaintance—would say, the selfish blackguards.

"I see. And then you dragged him up the stairs and into your bedroom."

She snorted. "No, of course not." She flushed. "And do put some clothes on, will you?"

He grinned. "Your wish is my command." He scooped his shirt off the floor and slipped it over his head, its long tail falling down to safely cover his cock.

Well, perhaps not so safely. His shirt wasn't as cloaking as the counterpane—which was still lying in a heap where it had fallen in his mad dance across the room.

He picked it up and put it on the bed as he gestured with his head toward the chairs by the fire. "Have a seat while I pour you a glass of brandy. You look like you could use a little liquid warmth."

He'd like to give her some physical warmth, as well—of a brotherly nature only!—but didn't want to risk sending her running back to her room.

He pulled on his breeches as she looked at the chairs, hesitated . . .

"I can get one of those obscene statues out of the cabinet if you feel the need of a weapon."

That made her laugh. "Don't be ridiculous," she said, and finally sat down.

"My point is," he continued as he walked over to pour them both some brandy, "Dervington was the one at fault. You were just going about your business, doing your job." He handed her her glass. "Isn't that right?"

She opened her mouth—to argue, he suspected—but then stopped and frowned.

Good. Perhaps she was reconsidering the way she'd thought about this over the years.

He sat and took a swallow of brandy. "I assume you wore the Dervington livery?"

"Yes. Of course."

"So . . ." He shrugged. "There's nothing very revealing about that uniform, is there? I believe it's the standard long-sleeved, high-necked gown and mobcap?"

"Y-yes."

"So what else were you supposed to do to keep from inflaming Dervington's passions? Wear a mask and cape? I imagine that would have made tending the baby a bit difficult."

She laughed. "I think poor little Alexandra would have been terrified to see such a figure in the nursery." Then she frowned and took a sip of brandy.

"Precisely." He would give her more to think about. "And consider this. You were—what? Seventeen? Dervington already had Archie and his brother from his first wife. He must have been old enough to be your father."

The look of revulsion on her face then was almost comical. Clearly, she'd not thought in those terms before. She took a rather larger sip of brandy.

"And he was your employer *and* a marquess—a powerful man in a position of power over you. You were completely dependent on him, even for the roof over your head. You were away from home for the first time—and taking care of his child. If he'd had a scintilla of honor, he'd not have touched you even if you'd danced naked across his sheets."

She looked torn, as if she saw his point but was, perhaps, reluctant to give up the guilt she'd harbored for so many years.

"Erm. Y-yes." Her voice grew stronger. "But I should have remembered my *own* honor and refused him."

Ah, that had been another thing he'd so liked about Caro as a girl—she'd had a fierce integrity. Her word was her bond, as good as any boy's and better than that of many, and she was passionate about doing what she believed was right, no matter what anyone else thought or said.

"Well, yes, you can argue that, but . . ." He held a mouthful of brandy on his tongue as he tried to find a way to say this as gently as possible. "Dervington was—is—a practiced rake, Caro. He knows precisely how to manipulate women, especially young women. In fact, he takes a fiendish delight in it. You were far from the first or the last to fall victim to him. For years, the betting book at White's has been full of wagers as to how long it would take Lord D to seduce Miss A or C or V."

Blech. And why didn't I find that repellant?

Because it had just seemed like a game. Nick had never thought of Miss A or C or V as a person, a woman like Caro who might be hurt.

And when I heard the rumor about Caro?

He'd told himself the damage was already done, she'd left Town, she wasn't his responsibility.

Shame twisted in his gut, but he tried to ignore it. Caro was here now. He needed to focus on her.

"It would have been a minor miracle if you'd been able to resist him."

Caro shrugged one shoulder and scowled into her brandy glass. "I *should* have resisted. I should have considered Lady Dervington's feelings. She could not have liked her husband to, ah"—Caro waved her hand vaguely—"do what he did with me."

Caro did not know the *ton*. "I suspect she liked it quite well. I've heard that while Lady Dervington enjoys being a marchioness in the ballroom, she's delighted when she can skip her duties in the bedroom."

Caro snorted. "I can believe that. I don't see how any woman puts up with that sort of mauling."

Dervington should be damned to hell for giving Caro such a poor introduction to the bedroom arts, serving her old, tough mutton when a more skilled man would tempt her with roast pheasant and pineapple and champagne.

She had no idea what pleasure could be had between a man and a woman. She might still reject carnal relations, but she should at least know what it was she was rejecting.

I could show her—

No! Don't even think of that.

"I suppose it's the price they must pay for a comfortable, secure existence," Caro was saying. "I was very lucky to find the Home." She shrugged. "And I suppose some do it for the babies." She looked at him. "Which is another reason I shouldn't have done what I did. I was very lucky I didn't get pregnant."

He experienced a sudden jolt of . . . desire? Was that

what he felt at the thought of Caro big with child? Whatever it was, it was a very odd, very intense sensation.

He shoved the peculiar emotion back into the roiling cauldron from which it had bubbled up.

Only to have it replaced by the memory of little Grace lying in her makeshift cradle in Mrs. Dixon's room. She'd been so tiny, with such a perfect little nose and mouth. . . .

Zeus! He wasn't usually so . . . maudlin.

His normal state—bosky and in the company of dissolutes—was far less challenging to his peace.

The dead are *quite peaceful. . . .*

I'm not dead!

No?

Was his soul showing some signs of rigor mortis?

Of course not. It was merely that, up until now, he'd not given babies any thought—besides deciding he would not contribute to making one. He wanted no heir of his body.

But he'd always thought of an heir as an adult male, waiting in the wings for him to die. He'd never thought of—never *pictured*—a baby.

In his normal life, he'd been able to avoid small children. No one brought an infant to White's, thank God, or to his more disreputable haunts. And yet now, here, for Christmas, he was host to a baby and a boy and a desperate mother.

And an irresponsible, self-centered father.

He would have a word—several words—with Felix in the morning. The man had money enough to gamble and carouse and go whoring. He could share some of that with Mrs. Dixon and her family.

Caro finished the rest of her brandy and handed him the glass.

"More?"

She nodded.

He got up to pour her another and then decided just to set the brandy bottle on the table between them.

"To return to your concern about Archie," he said. "I'm afraid if he realizes you were a nursemaid in his father's house, he'll assume you were his father's mistress. All the nursemaids were."

"Oh." Caro let out a long breath—and took another, rather large swallow of brandy.

She was managing the strong spirits rather well. Perhaps it came of being a brewer and, he assumed, frequently taste testing her brew.

"Y-yesh."

Well, perhaps not *that* well.

"Now I see why Mrs. M-Morris wasn't surprised when I ran into her office."

"Who's Mrs. Morris, and why did you run into her office?" This did not sound good.

Caro blinked at him. The brandy was definitely having an effect.

"She's Der-ving-ton's"—she pronounced each syllable carefully—"housekeeper." She took another sip. "I ran to her after he tried to r-rape me."

"Rape?!" The word came out in a croak. Rape had never been part of the rumors.

Of course, it had been men telling the tales. . . .

His heart stilled as he remembered drunken boasts about reluctant girls "persuaded" by a kiss or two.

Caro nodded. "It was a very near thing." She looked at the fire, her words chillingly clear now. "It was my day off." She glanced at him and then back at the fire. "The day after he mauled me for the second time. I thought he'd gone out to one of his clubs. I never thought he'd be on the servants' stairs, so I wasn't paying attention."

She looked at him again, her eyes cold and bleak. "You can be sure I've never made *that* mistake again."

He nodded, not trusting his voice. He didn't want to hear this—and yet he *had* to hear it. He gripped the arms of his chair.

"I was thinking about what I should do," she continued, looking back at the fire. "I'd told him that I never wanted to do . . . what we'd done again, but I knew he wasn't going to give up and leave me alone. He was going to keep asking—or maybe start taking what he wanted. There was no lock on my bedroom door."

She paused. Pressed her lips together. He wanted to reach out and touch her hand, but was afraid to distract or, worse, upset her.

"So, I was going down the stairs, wondering whether I should try to find a new position in Town or just give up and go home—whether I *could* go home—when I heard someone coming down the stairs behind me. I-I thought it was just one of the footmen."

She stopped again. Stared at the fire, a muscle flexing in her jaw as if her teeth were clamped together.

He waited. The seconds felt like minutes—no, like hours. A hard ball of ice formed in his belly.

Finally, she let out a long breath. "It wasn't a footman, of course."

He saw what he thought was pain flush over her features—to be replaced by steely determination.

Good for her.

He was impressed—awed—by her strength of will.

"He grabbed me when I reached the landing. He pushed me up against the wall. He put his mouth over mine so quickly, I didn't have time to scream. And then he . . ." She bit her lip.

She looked at Nick, eyes haunted. "When Dervington's hands closed round me, I was literally so weak with fear I could barely stand. I knew how rough he was when he wasn't angry. How much more would he hurt me if I fought him? I'd already given him my virginity, so what did one more time matter? And I'd need a reference to get another position. I was afraid to risk being let go without one."

She looked back at the fire, pain twisting her mouth. "I decided it would be better not to fight—to just give in, let him do what he wanted. It would be over soon enough. It always was. I could endure five minutes of—" She grimaced. "I could endure five minutes."

What could Nick say to her? He wanted—needed—to *do* something to fix her pain, but there was nothing he could do. He could only listen.

"He'd pulled my skirts up, got his fall unbuttoned, and then I heard someone—two sets of footsteps—coming down the stairs. Footmen, talking. Dervington heard them, too. He turned his head to shout at them to go away, and I saw my chance." Her jaw hardened. "I took it. I screamed and drove my knee up between his legs as hard as I could."

As much as he despised Dervington—and felt a savage satisfaction that Caro had done him an injury—Nick still flinched in fellow feeling at that.

"Dervington let go of me to shield his precious jewels. The footmen came running down the stairs, shouting." Caro smiled rather grimly. "Looking back, I think they helped me escape by getting in Dervington's way."

She reached for the brandy and poured herself some more.

Nick did the same. After listening to that story, he might need several more glasses to be able to sleep tonight.

"I ran like all the demons of hell were after me, down the stairs to Mrs. Morris's room. She sent Arthur—he was the biggest, strongest footman—up to my room with me so I could get my things. Gave me money for the stagecoach." She glanced at him. "Within the hour, I was standing in the yard of the Golden Cross, my satchel on the ground beside me, just enough money to purchase an inside seat on the stagecoach clutched in my hand."

He nodded. "And then you went home—"

She snorted. "Oh, no, I didn't. I was going to. I had no other option at that point. But fortunately, I struck up a conversation with a young, well-dressed woman who was also waiting for the stagecoach. Jo, Lady Havenridge, was newly widowed and had come up to London to meet with her benefactor, the Duke of Grainger—the former duke, not the current one—to talk about turning her house into a Benevolent Home for women and children in need."

Caro took another sip of brandy and smiled. "She was very impressive. And persuasive. When I told her I was rather in need myself, she invited me to come back with her to Little Puddledon and help her get her charity going. I took a chance and threw my lot in with hers."

Caro's smile widened, and the confidence he'd got used to seeing in her reasserted itself, albeit with perhaps a touch of brandy-induced swagger. "That was the *best* decision I've *ever* made. We struggled in the beginning, but once Pen—Penelope Barnes, now Lady Darrow—arrived and we hit upon the notion of getting the brewhouse going, everything began to fall into place. We can always do better, of course, but things are definitely looking up. Even if the new Duke of Grainger pulls his support, I'm certain Pen will see that her husband, the earl, continues his commitment."

Caro grinned at Nick. Oh, Lord, was she going to try to pick his pocket again? He didn't want to discuss that now.

"I'm sure your family would be proud of your accomplishments, if they knew about them, Caro."

Hell, that had been the wrong thing to say. Caro's face fell, and she took a long swallow of brandy.

"No."

"You must be mistaken. I mean, I suppose it's not the

usual way of things for women to run their own businesses, but surely your parents would see it as quite an accomplishment."

"I'm *not* mistaken." She emphasized her point by poking a finger at him. "I wrote my father to tell him where I was. He—" She pressed her lips together for a moment before she completed the sentence. "He refused my letter. Sent it back unopened." She pressed her lips together again, nostrils flaring as she took a sustaining breath. "With his own letter, unfranked."

"Oh." *Bloody, bloody hell.*

"I had to pay to receive the unpleasant news that he'd already heard from the marquess, so he knew I was no better than a—"

She sniffed. Swallowed. Took a deep breath.

No. She can't be going to say—

"That I was no better than a wh-whore."

"Caro!"

She pushed on. "He told me I'd sullied our name, embarrassed my brothers, and should no longer consider myself his d-daughter or, indeed, any part of his family."

She sniffed again, several times. "I did as I was t-told. I n-never wrote any of my family again." She raised her chin, her voice stronger. "I've done very well without them."

"The bloody, fuc—" Nick clenched his jaw, paused for a moment, and then said, with barely suppressed violence, "Your father is a black-hearted scoundrel."

Caro's eyes widened. "I-I wasn't exactly surprised. I know what I did was unforgiveable."

Anger surged in him again. "It was *not* unforgiveable. You were young and completely at a practiced rake's mercy."

She frowned. "I should have been stronger."

"All right, maybe you should have been. So, you made a mistake, one you regret. We've all done that." He certainly had—and he could feel more regrets coming on, starting with his harebrained notion of hosting a Christmas orgy. "You were young," he said again. "Inexperienced. I'm sure you'd stand up to Dervington if he tried his game with you today."

Caro laughed. "Oh, yes. I'd castrate him and nail his bits to the front door to use as a knocker."

Nick squirmed a bit at the thought, and then leaned toward her, trying to will her to believe him.

"It is what Dervington did to you that's unforgiveable, Caro. Your father should have gone up to London and horse-whipped the man."

She looked at him cautiously, as she might eye a madman. "But I'm ruined."

"You don't look ruined to me." She looked very, very attractive—not that he could act on that attraction.

"I'm not a virgin."

"Neither am I."

She laughed. "Not that I'm in the market for a husband, but no one on the Marriage Mart—in London or in the country—cares about a man's virginity or lack thereof."

"No, but they care about other things. A man's purse, his social standing, his bloodline. No one except the desperate wants to give his or her daughter over to a half-Italian mongrel."

Oh, God. Why did I say that?

He hadn't meant to. It had just spilled out. And he didn't care about such things anyway. He wasn't going to marry. It had nothing to do with whether any woman wanted him or not. It was all about denying Uncle Leon an heir.

Bloody hell, is that sympathy in Caro's eyes?

"I'd marry you, Nick," she said, patting his arm as if he were a sad, little boy in need of consolation—and for one, bizarre moment, he *felt* like a little boy, an eleven-year-old orphan. . . .

Stop. Don't be ridiculous.

"*If* I liked that sort of thing." She pulled a face. "But I don't."

Zeus! If Dervington were here now, Nick would beat the blackguard to a bloody pulp.

"And now I should go to bed." She stood up. "Oh!" Her eyes widened, her hands reaching out to find only air. "The room is spinning."

He jumped to his feet in time to catch her as she listed to the side.

She braced herself on his chest and blinked up at him. "I-I think I might have had a little too much brandy." And then the color drained from her face. "I'm afraid I'm going to be—" She put her hand to her mouth.

He grabbed the chamber pot just in the nick of time.

Chapter Eleven

Nick's eyes snapped open. He'd heard something. . . .

Zeus! Had that been the creak of a door opening?

And now he heard footsteps in the viscountess's room.

He tensed. If the Weasel or Archie had sneaked into Caro's room—

Thankfully, they'd not find her there.

Unless she had gone back to her own bed in the middle of the night.

Nick turned over and propped himself up on an elbow—and was relieved to see Caro was still there beside him, mouth slightly open, snoring softly.

After she'd got sick, he'd helped her into his bed. It was a testament to how ill she'd been that she'd not argued with him about that. Then he'd dumped the unfortunate contents of the chamber pot out the window—checking first to see that no poor servant was standing in the snow below him—so the lowly receptacle would be ready in case it was needed again.

Fortunately, she'd made it through the night without any other unpleasant eruptions.

He studied her. Asleep, she looked young, fragile—

He almost snorted at that, but managed to stop himself in time. He didn't want to wake her. Still, he could just imagine how she'd rip up at him if he were daft enough to say something like that aloud.

There was nothing fragile about Miss Caroline Anderson.

Well, except for her stomach and head. They might be a trifle fragile this morning.

He supposed he should have tried to stop her from drinking so much last night—not that she would have taken well to that, he was *quite* certain. But he'd been too caught up in—and appalled by—her story.

The embers of last night's anger blazed up again. Bloody Dervington! He deserved to roast in hell for wounding Caro as he'd done.

And then the wound, left untreated, had festered.

You know something of festering wounds, don't you?

He frowned. Perhaps he did.

His attention snapped back to his surroundings—the footsteps were coming toward the connecting door.

He sat up. He couldn't believe any man would have the audacity to look for Caro in his room, but apparently—

No. It was just the maid come to check on the fire. Her eyes widened when she saw him—and she saw quite a bit of him, as he'd dispensed with his shirt and breeches once Caro had fallen asleep. They were far too restrictive to sleep in and he'd not packed a nightshirt. He'd thought he was going to be hosting an orgy, not a hodgepodge of stranded travelers.

Then the maid saw Caro, and her eyes widened further.

Oh, blast. Well, at least the fiction that he and Caro were involved in an affair would be flying through the household without any effort on their part.

Too bad it's a fiction—

Zounds, where the hell had that thought come from? Of *course,* it was a good thing it was a fiction. If it weren't, he'd be forced to meet Caro at the altar and recite his vows.

And would that be so bad?

He blinked. Yes. Yes, it would be disastrous.

The rock-solid conviction he always felt when repudiating the wedded state was conspicuously absent this morning.

He gave the maid a brief smile and lay down again, pulling the covers up to his chin so as not to further offend her sensibilities.

She went about her duties and left.

Caro slept soundly through it all. She must have been completely exhausted last night—in addition to having had a few too many glasses of brandy.

She hadn't told him all the details of her encounter with the disreputable London tavern keeper, but if she'd had to use her knife to protect herself, he could guess the general outlines of the matter. And then she'd had the stagecoach journey, the Weasel, the crash, taking charge of baby Grace, tramping through the snow, and finally and perhaps most unsettling of all, discovering Dervington's son among Nick's unplanned guests.

He propped himself back up on his elbow to look at her again. Normally when he woke with a woman in his bed . . .

Well, actually, he'd never woken with a woman in his bed. After a bout of enthusiastic, energetic coupling, he always went home to sleep by himself.

Hmm. What *would* it be like to be married and wake every morning next to the same woman? Or would he follow the pattern of so many titled men and go back to his own bed after each conjugal encounter? That must have been the arrangement here. . . .

No. Having two bedrooms in the master suite didn't mean they were both used. If Mrs. Potty was to be believed, once upon a time his aunt and uncle had been very much in love.

And then they'd lost baby after baby after baby. God, that must have been horrible.

So, Uncle Leon had been wounded, too. Mortally wounded. As Mrs. Potty had said, he might well have been dead long before his body stopped breathing.

Long before I came to Oakland.

And hard on the heels of that thought came another.

Am I letting an old wound kill me?

He frowned. Of course not.

Caro gave a little sigh—followed by a soft snore.

If I did *marry, I'd be very unfashionable—very* common—*and share a bed with my wife every night, like Mama and Papa did.*

He frowned. Since he wasn't ever going to wed, it was a complete and utter waste of time to entertain such thoughts, and yet . . .

Last night Caro said she'd marry me.

She hadn't meant it. Hell, she'd said it in *pity*.

Ugh. He felt as if a leaden ball had just dropped into his gut.

Well, if Caro *were* his wife, she'd be naked now, not clothed in a high-necked, long-sleeved nightdress.

He smiled, imagining the scene. He'd lean over to wish her a good morning by brushing his lips over hers. Then he'd wake the rest of her with a long, slow stroke from her lovely breasts to the tangle of curls above her entrance. And if, when he gently dipped the tip of his finger inside, he found her damp and ready, he'd ease her leg over his hip and slowly, leisurely slide deep, deep. . . .

And now his cock was fully awake and ready to play.

I wish . . .

He wished he could show her that her experience with Dervington—the supposed seductions, not the attack on the stairs—wasn't representative of carnal relations. That love between a man and a woman could be deeply satisfying—

Love?

Physical love. That was all the love he knew.

It was a bloody shame she'd had such a bad time of it. The Caro Nick had known as a boy had been deeply, fiercely passionate. And, clearly, she was still passionate—about the ale she brewed, the Home where she lived and worked, even people she hardly knew. Look how she had defended baby Grace, Edward, even Mrs. Dixon.

She should be passionate about passion, too.

And, yes, perhaps that argument was more than a little self-serving, but he sincerely wanted Caro to be happy. She was someone—a *friend*—

A friend? He stared at her while the truth hit him.

Zeus, I have no friends, do I? No real friends.

The leaden ball was back in his stomach and heavier.

It was true. He had plenty of acquaintances, but no one with whom he could share more than a drunken evening—or a spirited romp in bed. No one he'd miss if he or she vanished from his life—or who would miss him. Livy probably came the closest, but he was always aware of the business aspect of their relationship. If he didn't pay her, she'd—regretfully, perhaps—bid him adieu.

But Caro was different . . . *might* be different. He could—

Zeus, am I really considering marriage?

No. Or, well, maybe. First, he needed to know if Caro could put aside her distaste for physical, er, *affection*. He might care for her—he thought he *did* care for her—but he couldn't marry a woman he couldn't bed.

And get an heir?

Ahh . . .

It was too early to think of that. First, he would see if

he could give Caro pleasure. It would be his Christmas gift to her. . . .

Ha! The Almighty should strike him dead—or truly impotent—for entertaining such a profane thought. Still, desire hummed through him. His cock was all too eager to leap gleefully to business.

Fortunately, his brain—and his heart—held the reins, which they now pulled back on sharply.

It didn't matter what he or the Almighty thought. This was *Caro's* decision. If she said no, then that was the end of the matter.

She stirred then, mumbled a little, opened her eyes. . . .

"Oh!" Alarm flashed across her face.

He sat up to give her more space, and she scrambled to sit as well, sliding away. . . .

"Careful. You'll fall off the bed."

She stopped—and glared at him, of course, as if it were his fault the mattress wasn't wider.

He grinned back at her. He'd take anger over fear any day.

Caro had had the oddest feeling that someone was watching her—and someone *had* been. Nick. A *naked* Nick. Had he . . .

No. She would have known if he'd touched her. There was none of the discomfort and unpleasant mess between her legs that had been there both times Dervington had been in bed with her.

And Nick was grinning at her in an amused, not a lascivious, way.

But what's he doing in my bed?

She looked around.

This was not her bed.

"You had a bit too much brandy last night," Nick said.

"You, er, weren't feeling well, so it seemed wiser to have you here with me in case you needed any, ah, help."

Lud! She closed her eyes. Now she remembered. Nick had held her hair back for her as she'd puked into his chamber pot. Could anything be more embarrassing?

"How do you feel now? Stomach all right? Any headache?"

"I'm fine."

And she hadn't just puked up the contents of her stomach. Oh, no. She'd vomited up far too many details of her encounters with Dervington.

She hadn't meant to do that. She'd meant only to tell Nick the bare minimum so he'd be prepared if Archie remembered anything. She'd meant to say only that she'd, ah, *sinned* with Lord Dervington. She was mortified. . . .

She blinked.

No, she wasn't. Well, yes, she was embarrassed, but her predominant feeling was one of . . . relief? Like a burden she'd been carrying so long she'd forgotten it was there had suddenly been lifted off her shoulders.

Or her heart.

The box where she'd kept those dark feelings locked away hadn't just splintered, it had turned to dust, pulverized, and the feelings had flown free like a flock of birds. . . .

Or, perhaps more accurately, a cloud of bats.

Not that the winged creatures hadn't left a mess behind to be cleaned up, but that could be attended to later. At this particular moment she felt wonderful. Strong and brave and capable and . . .

She looked at Nick—at his naked shoulders and chest.

And lusty? Was that what this feeling was? Surely she felt curiosity. . . .

Curiosity is what got you into trouble thirteen years ago.

But this is Nick.

Nick felt safe. It might be foolish of her, but she trusted him.

"What happened to your shirt?"

She definitely felt something that wasn't fear or distaste. It might be a tug of attraction. A warm little ember of desire flickering to life.

"I took it off after you fell asleep." He smiled, though his eyes watched her as if he were afraid she might take fright. "And I took off my breeches, too. They weren't comfortable to sleep in." His smile widened, but his eyes stayed watchful. "I didn't bring a nightshirt—I hadn't planned on having you visit my bed."

And she hadn't planned on being here, but now that she was . . .

No. She pulled her thoughts back from the primrose path they seemed determined to travel.

She was definitely in an odd mood this morning. She should get out of this bed immediately and go to her own room—but something in her didn't want to do that very sensible, prudent thing.

She looked away from Nick and noticed the painting on the wall across from the bed, a picture of a broad canal and gondolas and buildings and blue sky and white clouds. "Oh! That's lovely."

"Do you like it?"

Nick's voice was warm with happiness and . . . pride? He must feel a special connection to the picture. Odd, because he hated everything else about Oakland.

"Yes. I'm not educated about art—you must know that. The few paintings we had at home were dour portraits of Papa's ancestors. But . . ." How to put what she was feeling into words? "This painting is so bright. Or, well, the light seems so clear. I can almost feel the heat of the sun and smell the water."

He laughed. "You probably wouldn't want to smell the water."

She looked at him. He was grinning as he used to as a boy.

And then her eyes dropped to his shoulders and chest again before scurrying back to the painting.

Nick most definitely wasn't a boy any longer. *And I'm not a naïve seventeen-year-old girl.*

A shiver of . . . something went down her back. Excitement? Anticipation?

It definitely wasn't fear or revulsion. And it found an unlikely home in the place where Dervington had entered her all those years ago.

Even more shocking, that thought didn't dispel whatever this new sensation was. Dervington's long shadow must have flapped away with the bats.

Good. It was past time for that to happen. Out with the old, stale ale, she always said. Time to brew some new memories.

With Nick?

She glanced at him again. Perhaps. It was Christmas, after all.

She let herself remember, for the first time in a long, long time, how magical the holiday had been when she was a child and the house had been transformed by the sights and scents of greenery and cooking. The games. The laughter. Even her parents had joined in their play. Rules and regular order had been put aside from Christmas Eve to Twelfth Night.

At the Home she was too busy working to spend any time playing.

She wasn't at the Home now. She had no work to do.

Perhaps this Christmas, she would play, and the holiday could be magical again. The stagecoach crash had given her this brief opportunity. She should take it.

And how are you going to play with Nick?

She couldn't risk pregnancy, but, over the years, she'd heard the women at the Home talking about other ways a man could give a woman pleasure. She hadn't believed them. She'd been certain *pleasure* and *men* did not belong in the same sentence.

This might be the perfect time—her *only* time—to find out for herself the truth of the matter.

"Is it Venice?" she asked, trying to ignore the warmth that was beginning to spread from her core to her breasts.

Nick nodded.

"Did your father paint it?"

He nodded again. "Yes. I don't remember him doing it, but it bears my father's mark, down in the lower left corner."

He pointed.

She admired his muscled arm—and then forced her eyes back to the painting.

"Papa must have sent it to Uncle Leon at some point. I found it hanging in the back of Leon's dressing room after he died." He grimaced. "If he'd liked it enough to keep it where he could see it, you'd think he would have hung it in a more prominent location. I'm certain everyone would have been happy if he'd taken down one of the many depressing paintings cursing Oakland's walls to make room for this one."

"Did I hear you tell Edward *you* took them down? What did you do with them?"

"I'm surprised you heard me over the screaming baby." He grinned. "Did you think I'd sold them for funds?"

"N-no." She hadn't had time to think anything about it, though it was true the estate had a bit of a shabby, neglected air to it that all the blank, painting-sized squares of darker wallpaper contributed to.

He snorted. "Right. No one would have bought them. I was tempted to throw them on a bonfire, but decided that was more trouble than it was worth. Instead I had them packed away in the attics. The next Viscount Oakland can deal with them."

He said that as if he didn't intend the next viscount to be his son. That seemed . . . sad.

"I hung this one here so I would see something warm and happy the first and last thing each day."

He looked at her, and there was an odd pause, as if they were both thinking of some other warm and happy way to start and end the day.

Not that there'd been anything warm and happy about what Dervington had done to her, but with Nick . . .

Now was her chance to find out. Soon the snow would melt and she'd go back to the Home and her real life.

"The maid came in while you were asleep," Nick said, bringing her thoughts back to more practical matters.

"Oh." Caro frowned. "Did she see me?"

He nodded and then added, a cautious note in his voice, "I'm afraid by the time we leave this room, the story of our night together will have run through the servants and probably many of the guests. No one will think we were just sleeping."

Well, that would certainly make their charade more believable.

And I'm staring at Nick's naked neck and shoulders, again.

Perhaps she shouldn't fight it. Feeling this, er, spark could only help her performance. And. . . .

Curiosity reared its head again. *Might as well be hung for a sheep as a lamb.*

She looked up at Nick's face. He was watching her cautiously.

"That was the plan, wasn't it?" he asked. "*Your* plan. To pretend to an affair?"

"Y-es." *Wait a minute.* "But when I suggested it, I

thought you were impotent." She frowned at him. "You aren't impotent"—she glanced down at the bedcovers, half expecting to see them tented by Nick's . . . enthusiasm—"are you?"

She'd seen his *enthusiasm* with her own eyes. She flushed. She'd *touched* it.

He flushed, looked away—and then met her gaze squarely, if with obvious discomfort. "No, I'm not. Or at least, I'm not usually. I did fail to"—he cleared his throat—"rise to the occasion with Livy the night before last."

"Oh." So, Livy hadn't lied to her. "Why?"

"Why what?" He sounded a bit techy.

She did suppose it wasn't a proper question, but she was curious. "Why didn't it"—she gestured to where she guessed the relevant organ was hiding under the bedclothes—"work with Livy?"

Nick ran a hand through his hair, and his chest and arm muscles shifted quite entrancingly. He'd definitely be an asset in the brewhouse.

"I'm not a machine, Caro. I suppose I was . . . I don't know. Tired perhaps. Or maybe I had one too many glasses of brandy."

"Oh." He wasn't tired or bosky at the moment. "Is it working now?" It would be better for her plans if it weren't, but best to find out beforehand.

His brows shot up, and then he grinned. "Would you like me to show you?"

"No!" Her courage deserted her in a rush.

He must have noticed, because his expression gentled from teasing to concerned. He brushed her hair back from her face, tangling his fingers in it, cupping her cheek—and then said something completely unexpected. "You told me last night you'd marry me. Did you mean it?"

"Urgh. Ah. Er . . ." She hadn't expected the conversation

to take *this* turn. *Had* she meant it? Surely, she'd said it only because she'd felt badly for him.

Buy time.

"You haven't asked."

No, she shouldn't dodge the question. His lips were smiling, but his eyes . . . They looked like they wanted—*needed*—an answer.

"I never thought to wed." *Point out the obvious, which he must have forgotten.* "I'm ruined, remember."

He snorted.

All right, so that argument didn't persuade him. "And I have a job that I like very well."

"Perhaps I can offer you a better position."

"As viscountess? *Are* you offering, Nick?"

Did she *want* him to offer?

Lud! I don't know.

He looked just as taken aback as she was. "I think maybe I am."

Shock or confusion or panic—whatever this churning feeling was—sent her to her usual defense mechanism: sarcasm. "Now *there's* a proposal for the record books."

He laughed, apparently not put off by her tone or words. "I'm sorry. I never thought to wed, either."

She believed he was sincere, so she should be, too. "I'm not at all certain I'm the marrying sort, Nick. I didn't like what Dervington did to me, and I don't think I'm one to grit my teeth and endure just to give you an heir."

His eyes widened at *heir*. Ha! That would get him to change his mind.

It didn't.

"I don't care about an heir, Caro. I've actually never wanted one. I've always been content to let some other relative assume the title once I'm gone." He shook his head. "This is all new to me, too. But I will tell you this. I'm not like Dervington. I won't hurt you."

It might already be too late. . . .

Nonsense. I haven't seen Nick in years and have spent only a few hours with him now. I can't *care about him.*

That's what her head said. Her heart—and the rest of her body—begged to differ.

Her head must rule. It could very well be that the problem was deeper than one—or two—bad experiences. Yes, she felt some odd sensations now, but they could well vanish the moment Nick touched her.

"I'm just not certain I want to submit to any man." She flushed. "I don't think . . . That is, I don't . . . I don't feel things the same way other women do."

Or at least the way other women *said* they felt. She'd always wondered if they were, if not out-and-out lying, then at least greatly exaggerating.

His thumb was stroking her cheek now, setting an odd warmth fluttering in her stomach.

"Sexual congress isn't a matter of submission, Caro. Or at least, it shouldn't be."

She grunted. "Easy for you to say. You aren't the one having what feels like a log shoved up inside you."

Nick flinched. "All right. I see your point. What if we try a little experiment? I'll touch you, and you can tell me what, if anything, you like."

And if I like nothing?

Best to find that out now, rather than wonder forever after.

She'd never been one to fear experimentation before. It was experimentation—trial and error—that had perfected Widow's Brew.

And there were a lot of brews I threw away as failures.

"Very well. You may try—as long as you stay above my waist and don't be too long about it." She looked at the clock on the mantel. "Remember you promised Edward you'd take him up to the attics this morning to look for that cradle for baby Grace. He's probably waiting for you."

Nick grinned. "Very true. Thank you for reminding me. Shall we say no more than fifteen minutes? That won't inconvenience Edward too much, I hope. And I'll even stay above your shoulders. How's that?"

She could endure anything for fifteen minutes, especially if he didn't stray below her shoulders. It was hard to imagine how he could fill even five minutes with that restriction.

She nodded. "Fifteen minutes, beginning now." And then she closed her eyes and braced herself for the attack.

She didn't expect to hear Nick chuckle.

She opened one eye. He hadn't moved. "Shouldn't you get on with it?"

He grinned. "That eager, are you?"

She snorted. "Suit yourself. You have fifteen minutes"—she glanced at the clock—"no, fourteen minutes now. If you wish to spend it staring at me, go right ahead."

"Ah, there's another challenge—one I will have to take some other time. Today I wager I'll have you sighing my name before fifteen—pardon me, *fourteen* minutes have passed."

Aha! Even better. "A wager you'll lose."

He just smiled and leaned closer.

She looked at the clock again. "Thirteen minutes now. You—eek!"

He'd brushed his lips over a spot just below her ear that she'd exposed by turning her head. It had felt very . . . unsettling.

She inched away from him.

He inched closer. "I hope you don't intend to make me chase you around the room, Caro. I hesitate to remind you, but I am as naked as the day I was born under this coverlet."

Which made her look down over his broad shoulders, muscled chest and arms, and narrow waist to—

The coverlet.

"Shall I push it aside?"

"No!" Even she heard the nerves in her voice. She forced her eyes up to look him in the face. "No, thank you. I prefer to have that part of you covered."

His expression was . . . kind? As if he really saw *her*—her thoughts and fears—and accepted her in spite of—or, rather, along with—them.

What a peculiar thought.

"Your decision." He leaned forward and kissed her cheek. "Which you can change at any time." His lips brushed her temple.

"I—oh." His mouth touched the angle of her jaw. "I won't. . . ." He was back to a spot under her ear. "That is . . ." And now the base of her throat. "Ohh."

What is he doing to me?

She felt so odd. And, oddest of all, the place between her legs where Dervington had been felt swollen and . . . tingly.

"Trust me," Nick murmured.

Trust him?

She wasn't one to trust, especially men. Trusting men had never got her anything good. She'd trusted Dervington. Ha! She'd trusted her father, and he'd turned his back on her. She'd trusted the Westling Mr. Harris and had hied off to London only to have to use her knife to fend off his brother.

The only person she trusted was herself.

Except at the moment her body felt most untrustworthy. Her neck arched without her conscious will to give Nick's clever mouth more room to explore.

Stop. I need to stop this.

But her treacherous body argued back. *It's only for a few more minutes. You can last that long. You don't want Nick to win the wager, do you?*

Somehow her hands had moved to steady herself by grasping Nick's arms—his warm, naked, muscled arms.

"Don't worry." His tongue traced her collarbone. "You are safe with me, Caro."

"I . . . I . . . Ohh." The words came out thin and high. Her breasts felt odd now, too. Heavy and full. Her nipples had tightened into hard nubs. The place between her legs was *throbbing*.

She should be mortified. Or terrified. But the feeling pounding through her, keeping time with her heart and her . . . lower organ was desperation. She *needed* Nick.

"I won't do anything you don't like."

She heard the words through a haze. He had lit this fire. He needed to put it out before it consumed her. "Nick."

He kissed one corner of her mouth, nibbled her lower lip.

"Nick." She was panting, lips parted, waiting for him to—

"Oh, look," he said. "Our fifteen minutes are up."

Chapter Twelve

Nick unlocked the heavy wooden door that closed off the storage section of the attics from the female servants' rooms. Judging from all the giggles and surreptitious looks they'd got as he and Caro—and Edward—made their way here, the tale of Caro's being in his bed this morning had already spread far and wide.

Good. That should put not only the Weasel and Dervington's spawn but also Felix and Bertram and all the other men on notice that insulting Caro would earn them his wrath.

Unless . . .

What if the other men thought Caro was no more to him than Livy or any of the many other women he'd bedded over the years? He *was* known as Lord Devil.

A wave of shame and regret washed over him, followed by a familiar sense of ill-usage. *If Uncle Leon hadn't—*

No. He couldn't blame Leon any longer. Look how Caro had recovered from her experience with Dervington. She'd more than recovered—she'd flourished.

Oh, God. I've spent years wallowing in the mud made of old pain and dreams of revenge, haven't I?

Yes, he'd had sorrow and challenges, but, unlike Edward,

Nick had had eleven years of happiness and then, even at Oakland, food on the table and a roof over his head.

He was grown now. He should take control of his life just as Caro had taken control of hers. It was long past time to stop living in Uncle Leon's shadow.

Especially now that he knew what a dark, painful shadow Leon had lived in. Soul-crushing loss and dashed dreams had twisted his uncle, robbing him of love—

Is that what I'm letting happen to me?

He frowned. No. Of course not.

Living to spite Leon certainly sounds like it.

Well, perhaps.

Marrying Caro—

No! He should *not* jump into marriage. Even thinking about taking such a plunge so abruptly seemed beyond foolhardy.

That was his brain talking. His heart felt differently.

Eh. Or maybe it's my cock.

He watched Edward wade into the hodgepodge of odds and ends, some likely consigned to the attics generations ago, and then Caro follow him, seeming not to give a second thought to the dust and dirt collecting on her skirt.

Of course she didn't think of it. She wasn't some Society miss, caring for her appearance. She was an independent businesswoman, used to getting dirty, focused on her work, not her wardrobe.

She didn't need him. She didn't need any man. She was doing quite well on her own.

But he was beginning to think he needed her.

And I can *offer her something she doesn't have—pleasure.*

Edward had picked up some object he found interesting and was showing it to her—and she was listening and smiling.

She'd be good with children. Unlike him, she'd grown up

in a family with siblings—well, brothers. If they were to have—

And now I've jumped to considering an heir?

Good God!

Edward and Caro moved farther into the jumble. He started to follow, but bumped against—

Lord, here was one of the pictures that had given him such nightmares as a boy—a nasty, dark depiction of the fallen angels, tumbling into hell. How had Papa created such joyful paintings after growing up with this sort of gloom hanging on every wall?

Perhaps it was the darkness that had motivated him to try to capture brightness and light in his own art.

I need to focus more on brightness and light.

He looked over at Caro again and remembered, far too vividly, the warmth of her skin this morning, the sound of her little pants and moans, the way she'd moved to give him easier access to her neck—and the confused and then annoyed look she'd speared him with when he'd called time.

And yet, it wasn't just those fifteen minutes that had seduced him. It was the conversation that had happened before as well—then and last night. Something more than physical pleasure had sprung up between them.

At least, it had sprung up in him. He hoped Caro had felt some of the same emotions.

She *had* felt pleasure. He grinned. He'd won their wager.

But would she want to do what they'd done again—and more?

He liked to pride himself on his bedroom skills, but he suddenly realized they'd never been tested. Livy would act satisfied even if he failed miserably.

He *had* failed miserably, so miserably no amount of acting could hide his, er, *flaccid* performance.

But this morning hadn't been about performance at all.

It had been about something else—something deeper. And it had been about *Caro*. He'd wanted to bring *her* joy. He'd barely thought about himself.

Well, it was almost Christmas. He would hope for a Christmas miracle. And, yes, he supposed that might be profane, but it didn't feel profane to him at the moment.

"Look!" Edward said. "A sled."

Happy to leave the painting of newly minted demons, Nick snaked his way over to where Edward and Caro stood. There was indeed a sled leaning against the wall.

"I'd forgotten about that. My uncle gave it to me when I was a boy."

Well, Uncle Leon had *tried* to give it to him.

There'd been a snowstorm just a few weeks after Nick had arrived at Oakland, and his uncle, with a bit of a flourish, had presented him with this sled. Leon had said it had once been Papa's. His uncle had had the estate carpenter refurbish it for Nick.

Nick picked up the sled, examined it. He hadn't thought about it in years. It was much smaller and lighter than he remembered, but then he'd been much smaller and lighter then, too.

Had his uncle thought it a way to bridge the chasm between them? He vaguely remembered Leon's saying he and Papa had used to slide together down the long slope in the north field.

If forging a connection had been Leon's intention, it hadn't worked. Nick had not been able then to see anything beyond his own misery and loss. He'd wanted his *papa* back—not some wooden sled. His papa and his mama. He'd wanted to go home to Italy where it was sunny and warm and he had aunts and uncles and cousins.

He'd wanted nothing to do with the strange, cold, wet snow.

He'd burst into extremely unmanly tears and had refused even to touch the sled.

That had not sat well with his uncle. Nick might not remember the man's expression when he'd given him the sled, but he remembered all too clearly how Uncle Leon had looked at Nick then. His mouth had twisted with distaste.

And hurt?

Nick frowned. Perhaps. Looking back from an adult's vantage point, he thought that possible.

Uncle Leon had said that only girls cried and only weaklings quailed at a little snow, that Nick was an Englishman now, not some bloody Italian, and should behave like an Englishman—an Englishman who would one day be Viscount Oakland.

At that, Nick had turned and run. He'd wanted to get as far from his cold, English uncle as he could. He'd run down one cold corridor after another, past countless dark and ugly paintings, until he'd been completely lost.

After what had seemed like several hours, but likely hadn't been even one, a footman had found him huddled in a corner in the east wing and had guided him back to the schoolroom where his dinner of mutton stew was sitting on a tray, stone-cold.

He'd choked down every gelatinous spoonful and had vowed never to cry in front of his uncle—or anyone else—again.

He'd tried the sled several days later, mostly to show his uncle he could. And then he'd never touched it again.

Until now.

He could appreciate good workmanship when he saw it. The sled was well made and, he'd wager, sturdy even after all these years.

"Does it still work, do you think?" Edward asked. "I've never ridden on a real sled—only on old boards and such."

Nick looked down at the boy, impressed that he could sound so excited and happy after the shocks of yesterday's events.

"I imagine so. Shall we take it downstairs? You can try it out when the snow stops."

Edward grinned. "And will you come, too, milord?"

"Er . . ." Nick didn't want to disappoint the boy, but he still hated the cold. And this was Felix's duty. Felix might not be a blood connection to Edward, but he was Edward's . . . stepfather, of a sort. He was responsible for Edward and his mother and sister's being at Oakland. If Felix hadn't misled Mrs. Dixon about his intentions, she would not have set out in an impending blizzard with her small family.

Where *was* Felix? The bounder had been playing least in sight since yesterday and the arrival of their surprise guests.

I need to have a word with him.

It's not really my concern . . .

But it was. The drama was playing out in his house on his land. He was the lord of the manor, much as he might wish he weren't.

Do *I still wish that?*

Of course I do. I must. I . . .

Lord, this was so confusing. Something he'd known as a certainty for years suddenly seemed not so certain at all.

Caro came to his rescue on the sledding part, at least.

"Lord Oakland lived in Italy when he was your age, Edward. I believe he's never completely adjusted to England's winters." She looked at him and raised a brow, inviting him to confirm her words.

"Right. I'm sorry, Edward. No matter how many layers I put on, I'm still chilled to the bone if I spend any time in the cold."

"Oh."

Hell, Edward looked so disappointed. Nick hated to fail

him. But what could he do? He couldn't offer Felix as an option. There was no guarantee he could find the bounder, especially if he didn't wish to be found—Oakland was large and Nick didn't know it much better than he had as a boy. And even if he did corner Felix, he couldn't compel him to do the right thing.

But he *was* lord of the manor. "Perhaps we can find a footman to go out with you."

Edward brightened, though his expression was still a bit wistful.

"And I promise to brave the snow tomorrow to collect holly and ivy and the Yule log."

That earned him a smile.

Nick turned to see that Caro was smiling at him, too. He grinned back at her.

And mistletoe. I'll find some mistletoe, as well.

It would be expected, if they were decorating for the season, to include a kissing bough. He'd just keep a sharp eye out to be certain none of the other men ambushed Caro under it. He, however, planned to take the opportunity for a kiss. People would expect it, given their sham affair.

Which might not be a *complete* sham . . .

"Oh! Look what was under the sled." Caro stooped to pull a cloth off a long, narrow object.

"What is it?" He looked down. "Ah, the cradle. Splendid. I'll send a footman up—"

"Nonsense. It's not that heavy. I can carry it." Caro picked the cradle up and tucked it under one arm. "And I have a hand free to manage my skirt on the stairs." She laughed at what must have been his befuddled expression. "Brewing is hard work, Nick. I'm not some London hothouse flower."

"So, I see." And he'd like to feel—feel her strong arms around his neck, her strong legs around his waist. . . .

And he'd better think of something else. At least the sled provided an excellent shield to hide his body's enthusiastic reaction.

On their way down the stairs, they encountered the footman who'd directed them to the kitchen the day before. He looked young enough to be able to take Edward sledding. Nick stopped him, relieved he managed to recall the man's name.

"Ah, Thomas."

The footman's eyes widened. He clearly was as surprised as Nick that Nick remembered his name—and possibly also surprised to see Nick carrying a sled.

"Y-yes, milord?"

"Have you ever gone sledding around here?"

The footman's eyes opened wider. "Er, yes, milord. I grew up at Oakland."

"Splendid. So, you must know all the good hills?"

"Yes, milord. I think so, milord."

"Then could you take Master Edward out?" Nick glanced out a nearby window. "It looks as if the snow has finally stopped."

"Yes, milord. It stopped about half an hour ago. Mr. Brooks is of the opinion that the worst is over."

"Excellent." Nick looked at Edward. "Your mother won't object, will she?"

Edward shook his head. "Oh, no. Mama is used to my going my own way."

Right. Edward wasn't the heir to a viscountcy. His mother worked, so the boy must spend much of his time unsupervised. Quite possibly he helped out as he could, earning a few pennies here and there.

Nick turned back to the footman. "So, Thomas, if you would be so kind?" He handed Thomas the sled.

"Very good, milord." Thomas looked down at Edward. "Come along, Master Edward."

"Ah, before you leave, Thomas," Nick said, "could you tell me where I might find Mr. Simpson?"

Thomas's eyes flicked down to Edward and then back to Nick. "I'm sure I can't say, milord."

Blast, that must mean Felix is with Mrs. Dixon.

Well, Nick would find out soon enough when he delivered the cradle.

"Ah, very good. Thank you."

Thomas went off with Edward and the sled. Nick turned to take the cradle from Caro.

Of course, she didn't give it up. She stepped back, out of his reach. "I can carry it."

She certainly was a prickly, independent female.

Which is surprisingly seductive.

"Yes, I'm sure you can, but please think of my reputation. People will talk if I am seen walking along empty-handed while you tote that bulky cradle."

Caro scowled at him. "Who is going to talk? We're in your house—not on some London street."

"True, but remember, we are supposed to be besotted with each other. Every lovesick swain I've ever observed treats his beloved as if she were a delicate flower to be protected from the slightest breeze."

Caro's face was the picture of disgust. "That sounds revolting."

Nick laughed. "Yes, I think it rather silly, too, but I still wish you to give me that cradle."

She scowled at him a moment longer. He began to weigh the wisdom of taking the blasted thing out of her hands. He could do it easily enough—but was it worth brangling over?

Fortunately, he didn't have to put it to the test.

"Oh, very well." She shoved the cradle into his hands and continued down the stairs ahead of him.

Caro reached the floor Mrs. Dixon's room was on and hurried down the corridor. She wished to put as much distance between herself and Nick as she could. Now that Edward was gone and she didn't have the cradle as a shield, she felt . . .

What? Nick isn't going to attack me.

Yes, she knew that, but . . .

What did he do to me this morning?

Nick had barely touched her, and yet those fifteen—*thirteen*—minutes had changed something deep inside her. He'd woken parts of her she hadn't known were there and made her feel a host of new, intense sensations.

For a few moments, her body had ruled her mind. She hadn't been afraid or nervous. She hadn't analyzed Nick's actions. She'd just *felt*. Just ached and throbbed and *yearned*.

She hadn't even minded that he'd won their wager.

The experience had been nothing at all like the two times Dervington had visited her bed. Those had been painful. Deeply distasteful.

This had been. . . .

What Nick had done with her had been wonderful, as satisfying as sipping her best batch of Widow's Brew.

Except Nick *hadn't* satisfied her. He'd . . . tantalized her. She'd wanted more. There must be more. But what was it?

Her steps had slowed while she considered the matter, so Nick had caught up to her. She glanced at him. *What other delights can he offer me?*

Pen and many of the other women at the Home seemed to enjoy sexual congress.

Could I enjoy it, too?

Nerves danced in her belly, but whether they were from anxiety or excitement, she couldn't say.

Everyone thought Nick and she were lovers. That had been their plan, and it had worked flawlessly. On their way to the attics, she'd noticed the female servants' giggles—*and* their looks of envy.

Nick *was* very handsome with his broad shoulders, which were even more attractive in the, er, *flesh*. She flushed, remembering all the handsome flesh she'd seen last night and this morning. Even his naked cock had been strangely appealing.

And his face was very easy to look at, as well. His warm, brown eyes and faintly olive skin gave him a slightly exotic, exciting appearance. And when he smiled—mmm. She loved his dimples and the way the corners of his eyes crinkled.

She even loved his voice. It was deep, but not too deep, and warm.

But, more important than his appearance was his . . . kindness. He'd been kind to her last night as she'd emptied her stomach into his chamber pot and kind this morning even when he'd been touching her. He'd been kind to Edward in the attics. She smiled. She suspected he would ultimately have gone sledding, no matter how much he hated the cold, if they hadn't encountered the footman.

And he'd mentioned marriage—

"Penny for your thoughts?"

She startled and felt a hot blush rush over her face—and likely every other inch of her body.

His brows shot up. "It looks as if they are worth far more than a penny."

"Oh, stop it."

He grinned, but took pity on her and didn't press her.

She *had* to get out of here. The snow had stopped. Once the sun was out, it would begin to melt. Soon she'd be able to flee Oakland and get back to the Home and her sensible, steadying routine. Then all these odd feelings would subside, and she'd be cured of whatever this madness was that Nick had infected her with.

And the pang she felt at *that* thought would fade as well.

They reached Mrs. Dixon's room. Nick raised his free hand to knock—and then lowered it again and looked at her.

"I don't know if you caught Thomas's drift, Caro, but I suspect we're going to find Felix Simpson in the room with Mrs. Dixon."

She nodded. "Yes, I gathered that."

Nick frowned. "I'm afraid I have no clear idea what to say to her—or him. I have no power to force Felix to take responsibility for Grace and her mother—and Edward—if he doesn't wish to. I can't even throw him out until the roads clear." He shook his head. "I suppose I can confine him to his room if that will ease Mrs. Dixon's mind, but"—he inclined his head toward the door and shrugged—"my guess is, if he's in there, she doesn't want that."

Likely true.

"So, what do you suggest I do?"

Caro blinked, surprised Nick would ask her advice. In her experience, men assumed her gender robbed her of any valuable opinions, unless the subject was something within feminine purview like cooking or cleaning.

Or, in her case, brewing.

Though Nick likely saw Mrs. Dixon's problem as a feminine one, so she shouldn't give him too much credit.

In any event, she had no good suggestion to offer.

She shook her head and shrugged. "I don't know what to say."

"Could she go to your Benevolent Home?"

Unfortunately, that wasn't an option. "I'm afraid we don't take boys."

Nick's brows shot up.

It did sound odd, but there was a good reason for the rule.

"The Home isn't large, Nick. There's no room for two separate dormitories, one for boys and one for girls. As it is, the girls all sleep in what was originally the Long Gallery."

He was frowning. Surely he understood?

"And boys are very active—just think of my brothers. They were always fighting or wrestling, climbing or throwing things. Boys require more space than we have."

"I-I suppose I see your point."

"And we don't get many mothers with boys. Those women seem to be able to find husbands easily." She snorted. "Men prefer women who are proven breeders of sons. Daughters are only useful if they can be sold off as wives to other men and thus increase their father's wealth and connections. If a girl makes the great mistake of squandering her virginity before—"

Oh, God, where was her mouth taking her? She pressed her lips together, took a long, deep breath through her nose, and focused on the door rather than Nick. "That is, I'm afraid the Home isn't an option for Mrs. Dixon, unless she gives up Edward, which I can't imagine she'd do. She seemed very devoted to him on the coach yesterday."

There was a beat or two of silence, long enough for Caro to brace herself for Nick's response, but, blessedly, he let her comment on lost virginity pass.

"I suppose I can offer her a position of some sort here, if need be," he said, "but I do hope Felix comes through and does the right thing." Then he raised his hand and knocked.

They waited. No one came to the door.

He knocked again.

Still no answer.

"Perhaps they're not there," Caro said.

"Right. We'll just go in and leave the cradle." He reached for the door latch.

Another thought occurred to her, and she put her hand on his arm to stop him. "Or perhaps *are* there, and they're, er, *busy*."

Nick looked down at her. "Then they will have to interrupt themselves. We went to the trouble of getting this cradle, and I'm not lugging it back upstairs. The baby still needs a comfortable, safe place to sleep, doesn't she?"

"Y-yes." And, now that Caro considered the matter further, a more sinister possibility occurred to her. What if Mrs. Dixon was in need of rescuing?

"You're right." *She* reached for the latch.

But the door opened before she could touch it. Mr. Simpson stood there, hair askew, shirttail hanging over his breeches. Clearly, he'd scrambled into his clothes.

"Oh. Nick," he said, "and, er . . ."

"Miss Anderson," Nick said. "Miss Caro Anderson."

"Sorry." Mr. Simpson grinned, looking quite happy and rather boyish. "I'm bad with names." He looked over his shoulder. "It's Lord Oakland and Miss Anderson, Emma."

Mrs. Dixon was sitting in the middle of the bed, her nightdress askew and her hair tumbled over her shoulders, but her smile was so wide and bright, it distracted completely from her dishevelment.

"We found the cradle for Grace in the attic," Caro said. How could Mrs. Dixon be so happy? It was obvious she and Mr. Simpson had been in bed together, and, given the fact that they'd produced Grace, it was unlikely that they'd just been sleeping.

She must have enjoyed what they'd done.

"Excellent. Thank you." Mr. Simpson reached for the cradle, but Nick stepped past him into the room.

Caro followed. She didn't know what Nick meant to

do, but she wasn't about to be left in the corridor—and in the dark.

"I wanted to let you know, Mrs. Dixon, that Edward has gone out sledding with one of the footmen," Nick said. "I hope that's all right?"

Mrs. Dixon nodded, blushing. "Oh, yes. And it's not *Mrs*."

"Not yet," Mr. Simpson said. "I've asked Emma to marry me, Nick."

Nick smiled, but his eyes were still guarded. "I'm glad to hear it. But what of Edward, Felix? Will you take care of him, too? He might not be your son, but he seems to be in need of a father." Nick looked back at Mrs.—no, *Miss* Dixon. "Pardon me, madam, but I got the impression from Edward that his father wasn't part of his life."

Miss Dixon scowled. "You are right about that. The skunk took a swing at Edward when Edward was still in leading strings." She shook her head. "It was bad enough the blackguard hit me, but when he tried to hurt my boy—"

Caro sucked in her breath at the thought of a grown man hitting a child. Fortunately, no one paid her any attention.

Miss Dixon pressed her lips together, brows meeting over her nose so she looked very fierce. "I wouldn't put up with that. I packed up and left that night, as soon as the scoundrel had fallen asleep in his usual drunken stupor."

Nick nodded. "You did exactly right." Then he turned to look at Mr. Simpson.

"*Do* you plan to be a father to Edward, Felix?" Nick's voice was suddenly taut with emotion. "It may not be my place to say anything—well, I *know* it's not—but I feel I must speak up for Edward's sake. I lost my father at a young age, though not as young as Edward, thank God. I know what it feels like to be fatherless." He frowned and then said, his words clipped, "My uncle was not an adequate substitute."

Oh! Caro felt the pain in Nick's words like a stab to her heart. She'd known he'd not got on well with his uncle—well, he'd told her yesterday how bad that had been—and she'd known he was always very happy to come home with Henry on school holidays, but she'd never *really* considered how it must have felt to suddenly lose both parents and have to leave everything and everyone you've ever known to come to a strange country, even though that country was your father's native land.

She'd lost her parents, in a manner of speaking, but she'd been an adult and in control of her life when her father had disowned her. And, she'd been partly to blame. Even so, it had hurt terribly.

It still hurt.

Felix ran his hand through his hair and looked at Miss Dixon. "I know I've made mistakes—serious mistakes—and I haven't been very responsible, but Emma has accepted my apology, and I've promised to do better. I'm going to try to be a good father to both Edward and Grace"—he grinned—"and any other children we might have."

Nick grinned back at him, shook his hand, and slapped him on the back. "That's all anyone can do, Felix. Resolve to try one's best."

And then Grace let out a wail, and Felix jumped.

"She's probably hungry," Miss Dixon said. "She's always hungry."

Felix nodded, Caro and Nick's presence forgotten as he reached in and carefully lifted baby Grace out of her box. His hands looked so big, the baby so small.

How would Nick handle an infant?

No. She shouldn't be thinking that. It was ridiculous.

"We'll see you downstairs later," Nick said, heading for the door.

Mr. Simpson grunted, but Caro would wager he hadn't

heard a word Nick had said. His attention was all on his baby and his baby's mother.

She felt as if she were intruding on a private moment.

And she felt something else, something that felt painfully like envy.

Chapter Thirteen

"Do you think Mr. Simpson is sincere about trying to be a good husband and father, Nick?"

They'd just left Mrs.—*Miss*—Dixon's room and were walking back down the corridor.

"Yes." Nick glanced at Caro briefly and then focused again on a point in the distance. He should say more—he didn't mean to be abrupt—but the domestic scene he'd just witnessed had unsettled him.

Why?

Because it's yet one more thing that makes the life I'm leading, a life of mindless drinking and whoring, of living in the present and not thinking about the future seem . . . foolish at best.

Since he'd passed his thirtieth birthday—especially since he'd succeeded to the title—the small, annoying voice of . . . maturity, adulthood—whatever you wanted to call it—had started to whisper more and more insistently in the back of his thoughts. He'd always been able to drown it out with another glass of brandy.

Until now.

It had got louder when he'd arrived at Oakland, far removed from the frenetic energy and distractions of Town—and far too close to his largely ignored responsibilities as a landowner. It had got louder still with the arrival of the coach passengers—and had turned surprisingly persuasive this morning in his room. In his bed. With Caro.

And after seeing Felix with his baby and future wife?

It was bloody shouting.

Nick rubbed the back of his neck. If anyone had bet him *Felix* would turn into a devoted husband and father, Nick would have taken the wager in a heartbeat—and expected to collect handsomely. He'd thought Felix irresponsibility personified.

He'd been wrong.

Do *I want what Felix has? A wife-to-be. A family. The beginnings of an orderly, settled existence.*

Perhaps he did.

He'd been alone for so long—really since his parents had died and he'd left Italy. And while he had plenty of acquaintances now, people with whom he enjoyed drinking or swiving—depending upon their gender—he'd not miss any of them if they all vanished from his life today.

Except Caro.

How can that be? She's been here less than twenty-four hours. We haven't seen each other—or likely even thought of each other—for years.

He didn't know the why of it. He only knew how he felt. And speaking of feelings . . .

He glanced down at Caro again. Had she felt the same odd pull he had back in the room with Felix and Miss Dixon and Grace? Was she beginning to change *her* feelings about marriage?

Or am I just letting the oddness of the situation—the snow, the children, Christmas—bewitch me?

He certainly was acting as if he were bewitched. His proposal this morning had been made without conscious thought. He'd been surprised—shocked—to hear the words as they'd tumbled out. He hadn't been certain then that he'd meant them—and he wasn't completely certain now.

But he was *almost* certain.

Yet I vowed never to marry. I don't want to carry on Uncle Leon's line, remember?

The swell of glee—he'd admit, *evil* glee—and satisfaction that always came with that thought didn't come this time. Instead he felt . . . empty. Wistful. Now that he knew how Leon had suffered . . .

When he'd made his pledge to remain single, he'd been young, driven by his own pain to defy his uncle and pay him back for . . .

What? Taking me in? Doing the best he could, perhaps? Zeus!

He didn't yet forgive the man, but perhaps finally, he understood a little why Leon had acted as he had.

Seeing baby Grace had impressed on Nick what small, helpless creatures babies were. And Leon had lost *eight* babies. He'd seen his wife, whom Mrs. Potty had said he'd loved, suffer, and he'd been powerless to help her or do anything to stop the horror—besides avoiding her bed.

Nick closed his eyes briefly as he imagined the torment his uncle—his uncle and his aunt—must have felt for years.

But when Nick was young, he'd been unable to see past his own pain. Instead, he'd fanned it to an anger that had burned so fiercely he'd thought it would light up the night. It *had* lit his nights at first as he'd careened from one wild escapade to another. And while his anger had dimmed over the years, it had never burned out completely.

Perhaps it was time to snuff it for good—it and the pain that had fed it—and try to feel some sympathy. Just as Caro needed to stop letting her long-ago encounters with Dervington keep her from experiencing passion.

Though she'd done much better than he had at rising

above her past. At least she'd built a satisfying, productive life for herself.

They'd reached the end of the corridor where a window looked out on the grounds.

"That must be Edward and Thomas." Caro pointed to two small figures in the distance, trudging through the snow, dragging what appeared to be sleds behind them. Thomas must have found another sled somewhere.

"Yes, I think it must be." Nick didn't quite manage to hide the shudder that went through him at the thought of being out in the cold and the wet, nasty snow.

Caro laughed up at him. "You need to get used to the English winters, Nick. Are you going to enlist a footman to take your own son sledding someday?"

"Ah." *His son.* A jolt of some strong emotion shot to his cock—and his heart. It was lust, yes, but it was also a new, more profound desire. He wanted sexual congress, but, even more, he wanted a connection to a woman—*this* woman—that lasted more than a few minutes.

He *did* want a family. Even a son—an heir.

Or a daughter. I might have only daughters.

He laughed inwardly. He could marry and have children and yet *still* have the title go to a distant branch of the family.

Or I might not have any children. Look at Uncle Leon. Even Papa and Mama had only me—and that hadn't been for lack of trying.

Zounds! Now he found the thought of *not* having children lowering.

It was all so confusing. He'd mull it over later. Caro was looking at him now, likely wondering why he hadn't answered her question.

"I'll wager most English viscounts do indeed enlist a footman to take their children sledding," he said.

Caro snorted derisively.

He agreed. *If* he had a family, it would be like the family he'd had in Italy. He would be very much a part of his children's lives.

Though he probably still wouldn't go out to play in the snow.

He smiled down at her. "Perhaps my wife will teach me to enjoy—or at least tolerate—the cold."

"Mmm." Caro flushed and stared out the window as if she were examining something far more interesting than a vast expanse of snow with two specks.

Ah! This is promising. She didn't snap at me and tell me to go to hell.

"Do *you* want a family, Caro?"

That got her to look back up at him—with suspicion, eyes narrowed. "Are you proposing again?"

He was not going to be lured into brangling with her, much as he might enjoy it. There was something very . . . stimulating about matching wits with Caro.

"If I were, would you say yes?"

"No."

He grinned, suddenly even more hopeful—though why, he couldn't say. "Then, no, I'm not proposing."

She looked frustrated, as if she'd wanted a nice verbal brawl.

He watched Edward and Thomas slide down the hill. It looked like fun—until you remembered about the cold and wet.

"I always envied you Christmas," he said. "Henry would come back to school and tell me about all the fun he'd had—tell me about all the decorations, the games, the food."

Caro's eyes widened. "Didn't you celebrate Christmas?"

He shook his head. "We *observed* Christmas—it's not at all the same. My uncle believed the holiday should be a *holy* day—a time of prayer, spent in church. He had no patience for what he saw as the pagan practices of decking the halls with greenery and engaging in any sort of merrymaking."

"Oh." Caro frowned. "So, there was no Yule log?"

"None. Nor boar's head nor Yorkshire pie nor plum pudding. And nary a twig of holly or ivy in any corner of the house." Nor any kissing boughs, but he wouldn't mention those.

"Oh. That's . . ." Caro seemed for once to be at a loss for words. "Ah, that's too bad."

It *had* been too bad. He'd noticed how the servants were making merry as Christmas approached, and he'd wished he could go down to their hall to join them or could visit one of the tenants' houses, but he'd never even asked permission. He'd known his uncle would forbid it.

He grinned. "But this year is going to be different." Yes. This year, for the first time, Christmas—*real* Christmas—was coming to Oakland.

Caro walked downstairs with Nick, thinking about how he'd described his Christmases as a boy. She hadn't thought about her own family's Christmas celebrations in years.

She hadn't thought about her *family* in years—at least not before yesterday. Whenever one of her brothers or her parents popped into her thoughts, she shoved them right back out. They were dead to her.

Or, more accurately, she was dead to them.

A thread of doubt twisted through her. *I am, aren't I? Nick* couldn't *be right. Papa and the others would never forgive me or be proud of what I've done.*

Her father had made his feelings abundantly clear when he'd returned her letter.

But that had been thirteen years ago.

Is *Papa still angry with me? Does he ever think about me? Does he—*

She froze, putting a hand out to steady herself.

Oh, Lord. Is he even still alive?

She hadn't considered that her father—or her mother—could have died, and she'd not know it. She'd just assumed . . .

She'd assumed they were all frozen in time—that they were exactly as they had been when she'd last seen them.

"Are you all right, Caro?" Nick's voice held concern.

It was then she realized that when she'd put out her hand, it had landed on Nick's arm. Now he covered her fingers with his.

The warmth of his touch was comforting. Steadying.

"Yes. I'm fine."

Except she wasn't. Her world had suddenly turned topsy-turvy.

I'm an adult. I don't need my parents or my brothers.

And there was no reason to think the members of her family weren't happily going about their business, not sparing her a single thought. She was letting her imagination run away with her.

She wasn't usually so daft. Perhaps there was some madness afoot here at Oakland—some evil Christmas spirit haunting the halls. One might expect such a guest at what was supposed to have been a Christmas orgy. She'd be fine once she got back to the Home.

And away from Nick.

She looked at her hand on his arm. *He asked me to marry him.*

He hadn't meant it.

Except, for some reason, she thought he *had* meant it.

I could have a family of my own with Nick.

Nonsense. The evil spirit had addled Nick's wits as well. Viscounts didn't marry women who weren't virgins.

And why the hell not?

She bit back a giggle.

Nick's brow winged up. "Now what?"

She shook her head. "Nothing."

He gave her a skeptical look, but didn't press her.

Why the hell not? she thought as she continued down the stairs with him, leaving her hand on his arm. As Nick said, *he* wasn't a virgin. Why should she be?

She'd never accepted Society's dictates on anything else, and yet she'd believed all these years, deep in her heart, that she was . . . dirty. Damaged goods. All because Society had taught her to think that—well, and her father had written it.

But now that she finally considered the matter from a mature point of view, she realized she didn't need to believe such twaddle. Yes, some people might judge her if they discovered her history, but such people would probably also be put off by the fact that she worked as a brewer and lived at an establishment called the Benevolent Home for the Maintenance and Support of Spinsters, Widows, and Abandoned Women and their Unfortunate Children.

She could be the most virginal virgin in Christendom, and the arbiters of propriety would still pull their collective skirts back and give her the cut direct.

So be it. I don't need them.

She felt immeasurably lighter.

She smiled as a daring thought popped into her head. She had at least one more night with Nick. She was going to enjoy it—to continue the experiments of this morning and see what she discovered.

Excitement shivered down her spine.

They reached the bottom of the stairs just as the Weasel—well, she should call him by his name now that she knew it—just as Mr. Woods and the clergyman, Mr. Hughes, along with Polly and Fanny, came into the hall from the sitting room, talking in an animated fashion among themselves.

Nick pulled his arm closer to his body, thus pulling her closer. She felt protected and . . .

Claimed?

The notion was oddly exciting—and annoying. She *wasn't* Nick's. She didn't belong to him as a wife belonged to a husband. . . .

Ugh! She'd never liked that about marriage—that a woman lost so much of her identity and power to a man.

Perhaps she was fortunate to have avoided parson's mousetrap.

And she should not *have* to be protected. She should be able to feel confident that no one would accost her—or that if some man did, she could deal with him herself.

Though it was a good thing not to have to carry her knife with her everywhere.

Mr. Woods gave her only a cursory glance before focusing his attention on Nick. "Milord, Mr. Hughes asked me to build a stage and some other things for his Nativity play. Would that be all right?"

"Not a large stage," Mr. Hughes hastened to add. "Just a small one. I find having a stage helps the actors and the audience. It makes the play feel more like a real production."

"Stage?" Nick sounded more than a little bemused. "Actors? Christmas Eve is tomorrow."

"Yes, yes," Mr. Hughes said. "There won't be any practice needed—or only a very little bit. Everyone knows the Nativity story. And there won't be any speaking parts—I'll read the tale from my Bible." He smiled hopefully at Nick. "It would be good for the boy, don't you think?"

"Er, I suppose so."

"We always had a Nativity play at home." Fanny sounded rather wistful. "All the children liked it. The adults, too."

"Fanny and I'll make the costumes," Polly offered. "I did

the sewing for our village Christmas plays afore I went up to London."

Fanny nodded. "Polly's quite good with her needle."

The thought of two whores making Nativity costumes—

Well, why not? The Bible had all sorts of disreputable people in it. Wasn't Mary Magdalene a prostitute?

"Can ye ask Mrs. Brooks if she has any scraps of fabric we can have?" Polly asked. "Or maybe there's some old costumes stored away somewhere? We always saved ours from year to year, back home. Sometimes the moths got to them, o' course, but even so, we could usually find some bits to use."

"Ah." Nick sounded overwhelmed.

Mr. Hughes reclaimed Nick's attention. "And we thought to have the play in the Long Gallery, milord. Is that where it usually is?"

"I don't know. My uncle wasn't interested in any sort of theater, even religious plays, so there weren't any such entertainments when I was young."

Mr. Hughes looked horrified, but quickly schooled his features to pious melancholy and shook his head sadly. "That's a terrible shame." He heaved a heavy sigh, and then smiled. "But nothing to be done about it now, eh? Better to begin again."

"Er, right."

"So, you've no objection to our using the Long Gallery?"

"N-no." Nick turned to the Weasel. "Mr. Woods, before you get too involved in this project, can you tell me how repairs on the coach go? I would think those should take priority. Now that the snow has stopped, the roads will clear, and you'll all want to be on your way."

A hollowness opened in Caro's stomach.

Ridiculous! This was *good* news. She needed to get back to the Home as soon as possible.

And leave Nick . . .

Yes, and leave Nick, especially if she were developing some bizarre attachment to him. Even if he were serious about his marriage proposal—which was very hard to believe—she had the Home to think of. Jo needed her, particularly now that Pen had married and gone off. Someone else was going to have to look after the hop plants to be certain they stayed pest and blight free—and Caro intended to look after that person to ensure she did a good job. No hops meant no Widow's Brew.

"The coach is fixed, right and tight, milord. Or at least me and the coachman and yer man Walters jury-rigged something that should get us to Marbridge, where they can do a proper repair."

"Ah. Very good. Then I see no problem in your building the stage."

Caro—and she suspected Nick as well—expected the little group to be on their way then, but they didn't move.

"Is there something else?" Nick asked.

The men exchanged a glance, but Polly was the one who spoke up.

"Could ye ask Mrs. Brooks now? Christmas Eve *is* tomorrow, so there's no time to lose."

Mr. Hughes nodded. "And perhaps she knows how things were done before your uncle was viscount. It wouldn't hurt to inquire."

"Aye," Mr. Woods said. "And if they had a stage in the past, I'd like to see where they put it."

"We could come with you," Polly said.

"To save time," Fanny added.

The small group smiled expectantly at Nick.

Just then a very bedraggled but excited Edward came bounding into the entrance hall.

"Milord, you must come out sledding. It's great fun. Thomas has a—oh!" Edward finally noticed the other people.

"Apologies, milord," Thomas said, catching up to Edward, "but the lad was that excited, he had to tell ye at once. I'll take him off now and get him washed up."

Nick nodded. "Very good, Thomas." Then he smiled at the boy. "You'll want to get into dry clothes, Edward, and tell your mother how you fared."

He didn't mention Mr. Simpson. Well, of course, he didn't. That was Edward's mother's place to explain.

"And then you can come tell me the full tale."

Edward had been looking rather abashed, but at those words he grinned. "Oh, yes. I will."

"Oh, and Thomas," Nick said as the footman started to usher Edward away, "could you ask Mrs. Brooks—and Mr. Brooks and Mr. Pearson, too—to meet me in the Long Gallery?" He gestured to the small gathering. "We are trying to make some Christmas plans."

Thomas grinned. "Very good, milord. I'll let them know as soon as I've delivered Master Edward to his mother."

Thomas and Edward left, and then the small group set off for the Long Gallery, Nick leading the way with Caro at his side and the rest following. They passed the billiards room just as a game was breaking up. Mr. Collins, Mr. Meadows, Lord Archibald, and Livy came out, Livy hanging on Lord Archibald's arm.

If Archie had been looking for female companionship, it appeared he had found some.

Livy smiled and gave Caro a knowing look.

"Are we missing a party?" Mr. Collins asked.

"We're going to plan Christmas Eve, Bertie," Fanny said. "We're going to have a Nativity play!"

The billiards group grinned.

"That sounds like fun," Livy said.

"And will there be singing?" Dervington's son asked. "There should be singing."

"Archie and I love to sing," Mr. Meadows said.

And with that, Lord Archibald started in on "While Shepherds Watched" in a beautiful tenor. Mr. Meadows joined in, singing baritone, and then Livy added her soprano. They sounded like an angel chorus.

"Gor! That's prettier than the church choir back home," Polly said.

"Lovely, indeed!" Mr. Hughes looked at Mr. Collins. "Not a bass?"

Mr. Collins shook his head. "No. When I sing, the dogs howl."

"Ah. Then perhaps you can take a part in the play," Mr. Hughes said diplomatically.

Mr. Collins nodded and then grinned. "Are we going to have games as well? I hope we do. I can thrash old Felix at snapdragon."

"Ha!" Lord Archibald said. "I'm the king of snapdragon. I'll take you both on."

Mr. Meadows snorted. "King? More like court jester. I'll beat every one of you to flinders."

"You're on." Mr. Collins slapped Mr. Meadows and Lord Archibald on the back. "Prepare to taste ignominious defeat."

Caro bit back a grin. Suddenly, these men reminded her of her brothers, verbally jousting with one another. Inevitably, one of her brothers—usually the youngest—would lose sight of the fact that the teasing was all in good fun and tackle someone. Then they'd all be at it, rolling around on the floor, whaling away at one another until someone got hurt and ran crying to Mama.

Christmas at home had been a noisy, boisterous affair.

The pain of that memory took her breath away.

I could have my own family. . . .

There was that evil Christmas spirit haunting her again. There was no point in thinking about marriage and a family. The Home was family enough. She was needed there. She had a job to do.

She dropped Nick's arm, ignored his questioning glance, and went with the rest of the party into the Long Gallery to await the Brookses.

Chapter Fourteen

Nick untied his cravat. He had so many thoughts buzzing around in his head, he might not be able to sleep for hours. Normally he'd have stayed downstairs drinking in the library with Bertram and Felix. . . .

No, Felix wasn't in the library. He'd come down briefly before dinner to announce to the company at large that Miss Dixon had agreed to be his wife and that they planned to marry as soon as he could get a license and have the banns read. Everyone had drunk to their health, and then Felix had gone back upstairs to eat in his wife-to-be's room with his small family. He'd looked happier and more content than Nick had ever seen him.

I'm envious.

He snorted. If anyone had told him just two days ago that he'd envy a man whose days of freedom were so numbered, who would soon be chained to a wife and baby and young boy, living somewhere in the country far from Town, Nick would have thought the fellow mad.

Good God, what is *the matter with me?!*

He heard Caro moving around in the room next door. *She* was what was the matter with him, the reason he wasn't downstairs. If he hadn't promised to keep her safe and pretend to an affair, he'd be drinking with Bertram and Archie and Meadows—and Livy and Polly and Fanny. Perhaps even Hughes would join them. And Woods. Hell, they might as well call in Brooks, Pearson, Thomas, and anyone else within shouting distance.

Perhaps it was to be expected that a gathering that had begun as an orgy would end in breaking down the usual walls between the classes.

He pulled his shirt over his head and dropped it on one of the chairs.

No, that wasn't it. It was Christmas, not the orgy, that was to blame—or to thank—for bringing them together.

The mood in the Long Gallery earlier had quickly turned to one of boisterous good fellowship. The Brookses and Pearson had been full of stories of past Christmas cheer. Apparently, Nick's grandparents had loved Christmastide and had celebrated the season with great enthusiasm. And much to Nick's shock, his uncle had kept up those traditions the first Christmas he was Viscount Oakland.

But then had come the viscountess's fall and their firstborn's tragic death. Mrs. Brooks said that the lord and his lady had been devastated—of course they had been—and had wanted no merriment that year. So, the servants had celebrated Christmas quietly in their own quarters, hoping the next year would be better.

It wasn't.

Year after year, miscarriage after miscarriage, Leon and his wife had been battered by horrible loss, falling into such deep dismals, they'd never wanted anything even the least bit merry around them.

When the viscountess died, too, Leon's dark mood got even darker.

And then Nick had been deposited on Oakland's doorstep. The servants had all hoped that *finally* things would change, that their lord would try to find joy for Nick's sake—but that hadn't happened, either. It was then that they'd realized that as long as Leon was lord of the manor, Christmas's joy would never be welcome abovestairs.

When Nick had succeeded to the title, they hadn't known what to expect. Would he stay in London as had been his habit for years or, now that Leon was gone, come to the country? And if he did, would he let Christmas take over the house again?

Mr. Pearson, the Brookses—all the servants—had been dismayed when they'd seen his coach pull up and he and his unruly guests tumble out, but not because he was going to host an orgy. Or, not only because of that. No, they'd been dismayed because it had looked as if Christmas would still have to stay hidden away in the servants' quarters.

They were overjoyed to discover otherwise. Mrs. Brooks, in particular, could hardly contain her enthusiasm as she rattled off all the ways they'd celebrated in the past. Nick had been swept along by her words, struggling to keep from being drowned by all the details. He'd agreed to every suggestion. What did he know of cold, English Christmases?

Nothing.

He pulled off his boots and then sat down to take off his stockings. He'd like a glass of brandy. Just one. If he were downstairs with the other men, he'd have several.

Ha. He'd drink himself into a stupor, stumble upstairs, and fall into bed to wake foggy-headed in the morning. He'd been doing that far too often of late. He should—

"Oh. Er. Ah. Argh."

The grunts and squeaks were coming from Caro's room! He leaped to his feet, bounded for the connecting door—

And paused with his hand on the latch.

He'd have sworn Caro wasn't in any danger from Woods or Archie or the other men, given the Christmas merriment and fellow feeling that had overtaken everyone in the Long Gallery earlier—and the fact that the rumor of his affair with her had spread throughout the house.

A rumor that, oddly enough, Mrs. Brooks seemed quite happy about.

He *must* have imagined the sounds. He didn't hear anything now. He put his ear to the door to check . . .

Zounds! That was a yelp followed by a thud!

His heart jumped into his throat, and he threw open the door—

To see Caro sitting on the floor, scowling up at him, the neck of her dress twisted around as if she were trying to strangle herself.

There was no one else in the room.

"Caro! Are you all right? What are you doing?"

She *was* alone, wasn't she? Should he look under the bed? Or in the wardrobe?

"What does it *look* like I'm doing?" She sounded very annoyed.

"Er, sitting on the floor?"

She appeared to grind her teeth at this inanity before saying, with barely restrained temper, "Of *course* I'm sitting on the floor. Any *idiot* can see that." She tried to get up, but accidently put her hand on her skirt, pinning herself to the spot.

He approached her cautiously. "Would you like some help?"

"No." She tried to get up again, but with just as little success. "Oh, fiddle. I told you skirts were the work of the devil."

He bit his lip so as not to laugh and extended a hand wordlessly.

For a moment he thought she might bite his fingers, but then she sighed and let him pull her to her feet.

She stumbled—well, he might have pulled a *little* harder than necessary—and braced herself by putting her free hand on his chest.

His bare chest. Zeus! He felt the imprint of her palm and each of her fingers as if they'd burned themselves into his heart—and a far less noble organ.

She snatched her hand back. "*Must* you go around naked?"

He laughed, though the sound was a little shaky even to his ears. "Are you asking me to shed my breeches, Caro? I will be delighted to do so, if you insist."

"What?" She glanced down as if to confirm that his lower regions were still properly clad.

Perhaps she wouldn't notice, but he feared his fall was bulging conspicuously. It felt as if his cock had swollen to several times its normal size.

Her cheeks flared bright red.

She'd noticed.

She looked back up into his face with . . . alarm? He hoped not.

Compassion tempered desire. "Don't worry," he said gently. "I won't hurt you."

She snorted, though her eyes shied from his. "I'm not w-worried. Of course I'm not. How ridiculous."

She *was* worried. She was afraid of him—or perhaps not *afraid*, but not at ease, either.

He suddenly remembered how she'd stared at him—and at a particular part of him—last night when she'd come into his room, and an audacious thought presented itself. Perhaps she needed to feel her power. She did seem to like to be in charge of things.

He'd be happy to give her that opportunity. It might be difficult, but he would rise to the occasion.

The most relevant part of him already had.

"Since you're here," she said rather waspishly, "you may

as well make yourself useful." She tilted her head forward to reveal the top of her dress. "I was trying to untie my tapes when I lost my balance. I'm sure they are knotted."

"Ah." His eyes focused on her skin instead, on the nape of her neck, on the sensitive spot just under her ear that his lips had brushed that morning . . .

"Well, are they?"

They? What—oh! The tapes.

"Yes." He cleared his throat of the desire clogging it. "They *are* knotted."

She tried to crane around to see, but only succeeded in lurching up against his chest again—with more than just her hand this time. He steadied her, held her . . .

He thought he felt her relax, but he might have been mistaken, the sensation was so fleeting.

"Oh!" She pulled back, and he let her go.

He smiled. "I see how you ended up on the floor."

He got a scowl in reply.

"Turn around and let me look at the knot again, will you?"

She growled low in her throat, but did as he asked.

Mmm. Her twisting about had sent one lock of hair tumbling down her back. He ran his fingers through it. It was so heavy and silky . . .

"What are you doing?" She sounded more annoyed than nervous.

"Moving your hair so I can see the knot better."

"Well don't take all night about it."

He'd love to take all night. . . .

Hell, it might take that long to undo the knot. "I need better light. Come into my room. I've got an Argand lamp on my desk."

He put his hand on the small of her back to guide her—and she didn't object, though she didn't seem to be especially pleased by his touch, either.

"Right over here," he said. He pulled out the chair at his writing desk and had her sit sideways on it so he could reach her back easily. Then he knelt down and moved the lamp closer. He had to push or pull on her shoulders a few times to position her precisely where he could get the light most focused on the knot.

"Don't set me aflame."

"I won't as long as you sit still. You're not making this any easier, you know, with all your squirming."

"I'm not squirming."

He could make her *really* squirm, but, sadly, that would also make her angry. It certainly wouldn't help him get her tapes untied and free her from her dress.

His cock perked up in interest again.

So she can go to bed.

His cock endorsed that thought enthusiastically.

To sleep! Nothing else.

Unless . . .

He put the thought aside to attack the knot. He tried with his fingers, but they were too fat. He needed something sharp, but he'd trimmed his nails just before he'd left London. . . .

There was only one solution.

Caro jumped as he leaned closer.

"What are you doing?!"

"I'm not a vampire, if that's what's worrying you. I'm just trying to loosen the knot."

"With your *teeth*?"

"Yes. Haven't you ever done that?"

"N-no."

"No? Perhaps you keep your nails longer than I do."

He inhaled, filling his lungs with the scent of her soap and hair and *her*. Then he bit one strand and worried it, brushing his cheek against her skin.

He might have prolonged that effort a bit. Her skin and hair were so soft. He could feel her tension, hear her sharp intake of breath, smell her desire. . . .

No, I can't. I'm not a dog, either.

But he still thought she was . . . Well, *aroused* might be too strong a word. Interested?

Finally, he had to admit he'd loosened the knot enough that his fingers could finish the job. Regretfully, he leaned back and pulled the tapes apart.

"There you go."

"Thank you." Caro bolted out of her chair.

Sadly, her bodice was not loose enough to droop in any significant way.

But she also had tapes at her waist.

"Let me get the other ties for you."

She flushed. "I can manage by myself."

He raised an eyebrow, and she laughed.

"Oh, very well. I suppose you can play lady's maid if you insist." She presented her back to him, a stiff, slightly trembling back.

She wasn't afraid of him, was she?

Perhaps she's afraid of herself.

Right. That was his cock talking.

"These are in better shape. At least I won't need to use my teeth to loosen them." He tugged a few times, and—voila!—Caro was free. The back of her dress opened—to reveal stays and shift.

She grabbed her dress as she spun around to face him. "Th-thank you."

He smiled, staying where he was and trying to appear as unthreatening as he could. "You're welcome. How do you manage normally?"

She looked toward her room as if she'd like to flee.

"Oh. I-I don't usually have any problems. I'm just a little n-nervous now."

"Why?"

She frowned at him. "I . . . I'm not used to sharing, ah, *space* with a m-man." She took a deep breath and then said so quickly the words almost tripped over one another, "I think the danger is past, N-Nick. Mr. Woods hardly looked my way in the Long Gallery, he was so intent on the Christmas preparations. And if Archie said anything, it made no difference. Everyone is talking about you and me. Our charade is a complete success. We don't need to act it out in private any long*er*."

Her voice squeaked up at the end of her little speech. She swallowed rather convulsively and took another deep breath.

He spoke before she could try to drown him in another verbal deluge.

"What's really bothering you, Caro?"

"I told you."

One of the man's evil eyebrows arched up.

Oh, blast. Yes, Nick was right. She hadn't been thinking of the Weasel or Archie or the success of their charade when she'd managed to knot her tapes so thoroughly. She'd been thinking of *him* and how he'd made her feel this morning.

And her decision to experiment.

What had seemed so splendid and brave on the main staircase didn't feel quite so brilliant in Nick's bedchamber.

She wasn't usually so totty-headed. It must be the bloody holiday. The hideous merriment. The hail-fellow-well-met jollity. It had been so thick in the Long Gallery earlier she could barely breathe. And it would only get worse. Tomorrow they were going to gather holly and ivy—and mistletoe!—

and sing carols and have that stupid Nativity play and light the Yule log just like they used to do at home.

At her *family's* home where she hadn't been in thirteen years.

She much preferred Christmas at the Benevolent Home. Things there were so much tidier. They had committees to handle everything: decorating, baking, making presents for the children. There weren't all these loud men.

Maybe that's what was reminding her of her family—the men. The Home had only single women. Friends.

Well, perhaps not friends, precisely, but they were all in the same boat—or at least the same flotilla, charting their course across life's stormy seas.

"Caro . . ."

Nick took a step toward her. She took a step back, holding up her hand to stop him.

And then she had to grab at her dress again to keep it from—

What? It had long sleeves and a high neck. It wasn't going to fall off.

"Caro," he said again, his voice gentle and . . . kind?

It was rather disarming, that note of kindness.

There'd been no kindness with Dervington.

Kindness? Ha! Kindness required seeing someone as a *person*. She finally understood that Dervington hadn't seen *her*. He'd seen a female body. He'd been feeling goatish and had decided to make use of her, just as he would eat a joint of beef if he were feeling peckish. Their two encounters had been only physical—no more than what animals might do.

She had no interest in ever again submitting to that sort of mauling.

And yet . . .

For years, she'd listened to women at the Home talk about carnal relations with enthusiasm—and had shaken her head in disbelief. She was certain they must be engaging in puffery if not out-and-out lying, like her brothers had used to do to make themselves sound braver or faster or stronger than they were and so earn their friends' admiration and envy.

What the women said couldn't be true. But if it was? Then she must be fundamentally different from them.

She hadn't thought herself a rara avis. Neither Pen nor Jo had shown any interest in male companionship in the years Caro had known them. Pen had a daughter, so she'd obviously experienced a carnal encounter or two. Jo was a widow who, Caro surmised from things she'd said, didn't miss her marital duties in the slightest.

But then the Earl of Darrow had come to Little Puddledon, and everything had changed. Pen—the Home's skilled, smart, responsible, hop grower—had succumbed to love, throwing away everything she had, everything she'd worked for, to be with the father of her daughter and live happily ever after.

Blech. It didn't even make a believable fairy tale; it was too hackneyed and mawkish.

Still, Caro had been deeply, deeply shaken. And skeptical. She'd felt sure Pen would have a rude awakening, face reality, and come back to Little Puddledon and the Benevolent Home, tail between her legs, soon enough. And Caro would happily—graciously—welcome her back without a single I-told-you-so.

Except Pen *hadn't* come back. She married the earl and, according to her last letter, was enceinte and deliriously happy.

Anyone could feign happiness in a letter.

But I saw *Pen that night when she'd got back from, ah, visiting the earl at the guest cottage.*

There had been nothing feigned about Pen's joy then.

She'd been . . . Well, the only word for it was *glowing*. And now she was pregnant. There was only one way *that* could have happened.

Caro had to admit, much as it pained her to do so, that she was more than a little envious of Pen. And she felt . . . off-balance. Forced to question things she'd thought long-ago decided.

Here's my chance to see if I can feel what Pen and the other women at the Home said they've felt.

It might be her only—or at least her best—chance to see what all the fuss was about carnal relations. Should she take it?

Her body said yes. Her mind said . . . maybe?

"Caro?"

She looked at Nick, at his handsome, kind, familiar face.

Perhaps she'd been wrong to shut and lock that door thirteen years ago. Perhaps it had been Dervington's loutishness that was to blame for her distaste and disappointment and not the deed itself.

The same malt, hops, and water could produce a superlative pint or undrinkable swill depending on the brewer's skill—or lack thereof. Perhaps it was the same with bedroom matters.

"Let me show you pleasure, Caro."

Nick's voice was kind, too. He looked calmly back at her. He didn't move; he wasn't trying to force her. He was just waiting—with those warm, sympathetic brown eyes.

Well, more than warm. Hot, but not in an alarming way. And intense, as if he was entirely focused on her.

A thread of excitement or anticipation shivered through her. She'd wager Nick was very skilled in bedroom matters.

She'd liked what he'd done with her that morning. He'd made her feel warm and a bit . . . tingly and had reminded her that years ago, before her brief time in London, she'd dreamed of a husband and children.

Not that she had those dreams now. Oh, no. Her life was full enough without adding a man to it. She had her friendship with Pen—well, only with Jo now—and her work and . . .

And her work.

Perhaps she was a *little* lonely, but only occasionally. She was too busy to be lonely. The Home needed her. Jo needed her. If Caro left, who would do the brewing?

Bathsheba and Esther and old Albert.

No. Well, yes. All three had helped Caro almost from the beginning. They could probably take over if they had to.

Stop it. You just want to experiment. To explore. To let Nick show you pleasure. You aren't committing to anything.

Looking at Nick certainly gave her pleasure. She let her eyes travel from his handsome face and warm eyes over his broad shoulders and muscled chest, flat belly . . .

Bulging fall.

She winced.

How could copulation *not* hurt?

"You aren't afraid, are you, Caro?"

"Of course not." She said it automatically—she never admitted to fear—but then realized she meant it. She *wasn't* afraid of Nick. She might be uncomfortable at the thought of his male bit and not particularly enthusiastic about ever encountering it, ah, *intimately*, but she wasn't afraid of him.

And remember, she *wouldn't* encounter it intimately. She couldn't. She had to be very clear about that.

And *that* would likely put paid to the entire experiment.

"Did you like what we did this morning?"

Her chin came up. She *had* liked it. "Yes."

Nick smiled. "Then let's pick up where we left off."

Anticipation fluttered low in her belly.

She pushed it aside and called on her practical business sense.

"I can't, Nick. I can't risk getting pregnant. I've seen the troubles single mothers face, both for themselves and their children. I've had a front-row seat on too many performances of *that* tragedy."

She was incredibly fortunate she hadn't conceived either of the two times she'd been mauled by Dervington. She would be mad to roll that die again.

"I would marry you, Caro, if that happened. I've already said—"

She put up her hand to stop his words. "Yes, I know you've mentioned marriage, but you're not really certain you want that, are you?"

She saw the truth of the matter—the hesitation and unease—in his eyes.

"And I'm not certain I want it, either. I'd hate to *have* to marry you, Nick."

Nick nodded. "I understand. But there's much we can do that won't put you in danger of pregnancy."

"Oh? What?"

Nick grinned. "Let me show you."

Hmm. To have the sensations Nick had already evoked in her without risking a child?

That would be an experiment she was willing to undertake. . . .

Ah, but once an experiment was begun, it was sometimes difficult to control. Just look at what happened when fermentation went awry. She'd spat out far too many mouthfuls of sour brew, especially when she was still learning her craft, not to have learned that lesson thoroughly.

And yet, she didn't want to miss this opportunity. . . .

"All right, as long as you swear to stop if I ask you to. The *moment* I ask you."

Nick's smile didn't waver. If anything, his expression seemed gentler, as if he understood what she was feeling.

Which he couldn't, of course. He was a man.

"I give you my word, Caro, that I'll stop *before* you ask if I have the faintest suspicion you aren't an enthusiastic participant in what we're doing."

A *participant*? What did he mean by that? She hadn't been a participant with Dervington. She'd been a receptacle into which he could stick his—

Yes. Well. She'd just tried to lie still and endure. Fortunately, Dervington had been quick about the business.

"I'll keep my breeches on and buttoned." He smiled and held out his hand to her. "How's that?"

She looked at him suspiciously. What could he do without his cock?

He'd done lovely things this morning with his lips. . . .

She studied him as he stood quietly waiting for her to make up her mind. He was sinfully handsome—*and* a peer. Just like Dervington.

No, not at all like Dervington. Nick wasn't married. He wouldn't be breaking any vows no matter what he did with her. And she knew him in a way she'd never known Dervington. He was the orphaned boy Henry used to bring home at school holidays, who'd been smart and funny and kind to her and had always seemed a little sad—alone and lonely.

She thought she saw traces of the same sadness, the same loneliness in his eyes now.

He's offering me a rare opportunity, a chance to explore something I've long wondered about.

She trusted Nick. And she felt . . . something else for him as well. It might be love. She certainly cared about him. This wasn't the silly daring or cockiness—ha!—she'd felt when she'd let Dervington into her bed.

She would be brave, as fearless as she'd been as a child, as fearless as she was in her brewing and business dealings.

She would say yes.

She gave Nick her hand.

"Y-yes."

Chapter Fifteen

Caro's fingers were ice-cold, and her mouth, her eyes, even the way her nostrils flared radiated tension. She made him think of a wild creature, a doe or a hare, poised to bolt at the first sign of danger, even if the "danger" was no more threatening than a stray leaf blown across the ground.

An odd warmth filled his chest.

He wanted her. Well, that was nothing new. . . .

No, this wanting *was* new. It was far more intense than anything he'd felt before. It was . . . starvation compared to being just a bit peckish.

He'd always considered himself a lusty fellow. He might have grown late and so started his amorous explorations after some of his friends, but he'd quickly made up for lost time. He'd enjoyed earning his nickname—and not just because it scandalized his uncle so thoroughly.

But after a while, even a Lord Devil found tupping a different woman every night tedious. When, after one pleasant swiving, he went to bid his delightfully naked companion adieu and realized he couldn't remember her name—Was it Jane or Joan?—he had decided it was time for a change.

Now he had, well, not a mistress—nothing so settled as that—but Livy and one or two other women he visited regularly to satisfy his needs. He considered them friends, but he'd admit it was a shallow sort of friendship. His motivations were largely physical and theirs, monetary. But it had worked well . . . until this trip.

No, now that he considered the matter, he saw that he'd been losing interest in his carnal encounters for a while—even before his embarrassing failure with Livy in this very room. Lord Devil had become an act, one that was getting harder to perform.

Harder? Ha!

But did he *really* wish to entertain the thought of marriage?

He smiled at Caro and stroked the back of her hand with his thumb. Perhaps he did. All he knew for certain now was that he was here, alone in a bedroom with a woman he wanted intensely—*painfully*—and yet was not going to have. His cock and ballocks were going to ache like the devil, and he'd probably have to pleasure himself for the first time since he'd lost his virginity if he wanted to get any sleep tonight.

And it didn't matter.

That was the oddest part—the fact that he knew he'd get no physical satisfaction and it truly did not matter to him in any significant way. If he could bring Caro pleasure, that would be enough. *That* would be his satisfaction.

It was a peculiar—a foreign—notion, and yet it was true. Why?

He had no idea. He'd think about that later. Right now he had a woman—no, he had *Caro*—to . . . seduce? Serve?

Make love to?

Yes. He might not know anything about the love poets wrote of, but he knew something of loving the female body.

"Let's finish getting you out of that gown, shall we?"

That earned him an alarmed look. She pulled her hand out of his, but at least she didn't run to her room and slam the door behind her or even step back out of his reach. Her eyes just got wider—he could see her wrestling with her nerves.

"You don't want to sleep in your dress and stays," he said calmly. Matter-of-factly.

She frowned at him. "What about my shift?"

Might as well be honest. He grinned. "I hope that will come off, too, but I'm not going to ask you to do anything you don't want—*enthusiastically* want—to do."

Her frown deepened to a scowl. He waited while she considered the matter.

"Oh, all right. Or, at least all right to everything but the shift." She tugged on one sleeve.

He put his hand over hers. "No. Let me. I'm your maid tonight."

She scowled at him a moment longer and then rolled her eyes and shrugged rather gracelessly. "Suit yourself."

Her dress was already untied, so it was quick work to send it sliding down to puddle at her feet.

She stepped free before he could help her and started to bend over—

"No," he said again, putting a hand on her upper arm. "I— oh. You've muscles." The words slipped out without his meaning to say them, he was that surprised. He'd not encountered muscles in a woman's arms before. It was rather . . . exciting.

"Of course I have mus*cles*."

Caro's voice had started out annoyed, but it rose at the end as he traced her biceps, stroking her inner arm with his thumb.

"It takes s-strength to b-brew. There's a lot of lifting and carrying and stirring and pouring."

"Mmm." Was she breathing a little faster? Could he kiss the pulse he saw beating in her throat?

No. Not yet.

"I can't leave my dress in a heap," she said, frowning

down at the discarded fabric. "I didn't pack with the thought that I'd be gone several days." She tried to bend over again, and again he stopped her.

"Oh, no, milady. Remember, I am your maid tonight. I will attend to your clothing."

She snorted—and then laughed as he made a show of picking her dress off the floor, shaking it out, and draping it carefully over his desk chair.

He turned back to her and bowed theatrically. "And now, milady, your stays."

Her laughter stopped. She flushed and took a step backward. "I-I . . ."

"Courage."

Her chin came up defiantly. "I'm not afraid."

He smiled, saying soothingly, "Of course you aren't."

But am I?

He froze, shocked at the unexpected thought—and shocked even more that it might be true. Why the hell would *he* be nervous?

"You must do this with many women." Her voice was tight and rather sharp, as if she wanted to provoke an argument, perhaps hoping to distract him.

He was not going to be distracted.

He looked at her, looked into her eyes, and thought he saw some of his own confusing uncertainty reflected there.

"I told you I'm not a virgin." Though he might as well be one from the way his nerves were vibrating.

"I'm not a v-virgin, either." She said the words defiantly, but he thought he heard notes of regret and pain, as well.

How to respond? "That is technically—or perhaps I should say *physically*—correct. Your maidenhead is gone." He frowned. "From what you've told me, I'd say you were robbed."

Her brows shot up.

"Or at least you made a very bad bargain."

Her brows slammed down, and he had to swallow a chuckle. Clearly, she did not care to have her negotiating skills disparaged.

"What do you mean I made a bad bargain?"

He shrugged, keeping his voice light. "Dervington took your virginity, but gave you nothing in return."

"Thank God!"

What the . . . ? Oh. Right.

"I don't mean a child." To his surprise, mixed in with the relief he felt on her account was a throb of sadness.

Which made no sense at all. He *must* be losing his mind.

"I mean pleasure. Dervington gave you no pleasure in exchange for your virginity. So, in that regard—in the area of true carnal knowledge—you *are* a virgin." He grinned. "That's the situation I hope to remedy."

She was still frowning. "And what about you?"

"Me? What do you mean?"

"What are *you* getting in return? Surely you don't intend to make as bad a bargain as I did."

Hoist with my own petard.

"I'll get pleasure from giving you pleasure."

Her right brow winged up skeptically.

Yes, he'd admit that was difficult to believe—he'd likely not believe it himself if someone said the same to him. But he knew in his gut that it was true. How to explain it so she would believe him?

"Consider me a teacher—your teacher, Caro. Teachers get enjoyment from teaching their pupils new, ah, material, don't they?"

She didn't look completely convinced.

"Don't you get pleasure from teaching people about brewing and your ale?"

That struck a chord. Her face lit up. "Yes. Yes, I do. I enjoy sharing what I know, my skill . . ." She looked at him, an odd expression—a mix of disapproval, perhaps, and curiosity and . . . desire?—on her face. "And I suppose you have a lot of skill in c-carnal matters."

Did he? He would have said yes even as recently as an hour ago, but now he wasn't so certain.

"Let's see, shall we?" He grinned. "I have it. Don't think of me as a teacher. Instead, think of me as a . . . salesman, but instead of selling ale, I'll be trying to sell you the benefits of physical pleasure. In the end, you'll be the judge of whether I succeeded or not." His grin widened. "I'll look for you to evaluate my performance. And feel free to give me instructions or suggestions for improvements as we go along."

That made her giggle. "All right." She lifted her chin and waved her hand rather regally. "You may begin."

"Splendid." He tugged open the bow on her stays and made quick work of unlacing her; he did have experience with such things, though he'd say Caro's stays were plainer and stiffer than the ones he was used to. Practical, not decorative.

Of course they were. Caro didn't expect anyone to see her underthings, while the light-skirts he consorted with dressed to be undressed.

"Ohh." She gave a small groan of pleasure as her laces loosened.

The sound went straight to his cock. Had he heard such a noise before?

Not that he could remember, but then again, every other time he'd been in a bedroom with a woman, his focus hadn't been on undressing his companion—or even on his companion, he suddenly realized. No, he'd been thinking entirely of himself and his anticipated satisfaction.

Selfish blackguard.

Or just paying customer?

Zeus!

This would be nothing like any of those times. This time his focus would be entirely on Caro.

This time he might be as virginal as she.

"It feels so nice to be free of my stays at the end of the day."

"Ah." He'd not considered what it would be like to go about encased in stiff fabric and bone or wood.

She laughed and stretched. "You have no idea what—oh. You are looking at me."

"Guilty as charged." When she'd moved, her lovely breasts had moved, too, pushing against the shift's thin fabric. He reached out—slowly so she could stop him if she wanted—and lightly traced the outline of one breast.

"Ohh."

That was Caro moaning, though it could have been him.

He saw her nipple peak, and he touched it, again lightly and with just the tip of his finger.

Caro inhaled sharply. Her eyes drifted closed; her teeth caught her bottom lip.

His cock felt as if it were going to explode. He'd be lucky to be able to waddle over to the bed when the time came.

He stroked the side of her breast, and she moaned again. Her head tilted back slightly, and he thought she arched into his touch. Her breath came in short, little gasping pants.

He might be having a little trouble breathing himself.

She was so beautiful. So responsive. He felt powerful and awestruck and overwhelmed all at the same time. He wanted this woman with a fierce need, but he wanted her for more than just one night. He wanted her forever.

Are you mad?!

Perhaps, he was. Or perhaps he was just caught up in the madness of desire. He'd never before felt it this intensely.

Anything so intense must pass.

No . . .

It didn't matter. Nothing that happened here was permanent. No need to think of the future. He would just enjoy the present.

He brushed Caro's temple with his lips—and earned a

small sigh as his reward. He inhaled her scent as he kissed her cheek, her jaw, the spot on her neck just below her ear with light, teasing touches.

Her eyes drifted shut. Her hands came up to brace against his chest, and he felt again as if she were branding him, both palms, each finger, burning their mark into his skin.

Into his heart?

Bah. He'd never been one for such poetic folderol.

Except it feels true. . . .

He brushed the thought away as he brushed his mouth over Caro's—and was rewarded with another sigh.

"Do you like this?" He breathed the words as he dusted small kisses over her forehead. He certainly did. Who could have guessed how erotic restraint could be?

"Mmm."

He took that as a yes. He stroked her breast again.

"Mmm mmm." That was almost a purr.

He kissed the base of her throat. "Think how much better my lips and hands would feel against your bare skin."

"Mm—" Her eyes flew open, and she frowned at him—though her cheeks were flushed and her breath still came in little pants.

"Remember, I'm keeping my breeches buttoned. You're in no danger—unless melting from intense pleasure qualifies as danger." He nuzzled her neck as he slid his hands down her back to cup her lovely, firm rump. "And there's this, too: I can't present my most persuasive arguments in favor of physical pleasure while you're wearing any clothing. It wouldn't be sporting of you to make me try."

Caro snorted.

He straightened to look her in the eye. "It's true. It would be like you trying to sell your ale to someone who refused to taste it. You might be able to do it, but you certainly wouldn't be able to make your best case—or your best deal. Isn't that right?"

She frowned, and then nodded slowly, almost as if against her will.

He saw uneasiness and indecision and, yes, passion swirling in her eyes, shading the blue to gray. He wanted to seduce her, to use her body to overwhelm her reservations, but he knew *that* wouldn't be sporting.

So, he waited.

Finally, she smiled in a lopsided, tentative way. "I wouldn't want to be unsporting." The smile wavered, and she looked away. "So, yes. All right. I'll take off my shift as long as you promise to keep your breeches buttoned."

Elation performed a spirited reel in his chest, but he tried to keep it from leaping into his expression. "Very good. Let's repair to the bed then, and I shall assist you out of your shoes and stockings and shift."

Her frown was back. "I can do that myself."

"Yes, of course you can." He put his hand on the small of her back and urged her toward the bed. "But I am playing lady's maid tonight, if you will recall. And undressing you is also part of my sales pitch for physical pleasure."

She snorted. "How can taking off a shift have anything to do with that?"

"You'll see." He would, too. He'd never done anything like this before, but he was oddly eager to experiment. "Now, if you will please sit on the edge of the bed?"

Caro looked at him as if he were dicked in the nob, but she did as he'd directed. Then she held out her foot.

"Here you go."

Her voice hardly wavered at all.

Her shoes were sturdy, sensible, exactly what he'd expect a working woman to wear. He slipped the first one off, and then massaged her foot—heel, arch, ball, toes.

"Mmm. That's lovely." Her eyes were half-closed. She looked almost blissful.

"You must be on your feet a lot."

She nodded. "Especially when I'm in the middle of a brew. But I live in the country. I walk everywhere."

So, were her legs as strong and curved with muscle as her arms? He slid his hands up her calf, over her practical cotton stockings, taking the shift with him.

Yes, they were.

Caro's eyes widened as his hands moved higher and higher. "Oh. Oh!"

He slid his fingers above her knee to her garter, untied it, and then started the journey back down, peeling the stocking off, moving over skin instead of cotton.

Was the room getting warmer? He certainly felt as flushed as Caro looked.

He pulled the stocking off, dropped it on the floor, and moved on to the second, pushing Caro's shift a little higher so he could kiss her inner thigh just above her knee.

"Ohh."

Her small moans went straight to his cock. He thought he could smell her desire, an intoxicating, musky scent far more entrancing than any perfume.

This restraint was going to be torture, but it would be worth every minute.

He slid the second stocking off. "And now your hair. You can't go to bed in your pins."

She looked at him blankly, eyes slightly unfocused, lovely bosom heaving.

Excellent. She was already befuddled by passion.

He sat beside her on the bed, took her shoulders, and turned her slightly so he could reach the back of her head. He pulled the first pin loose.

"Don't lose it," she said, rather breathlessly.

"I know—you don't have extras. Here, we'll collect them in your lap, shall we?"

She'd crooked one leg on the bed, forming a triangle in her shift, and had braced herself with her hands on the mattress.

"Oh. Y-yes. All right."

He reached around to drop the pin in her lap, and then slid his fingers back into the silky mass. "How many are there?"

"Um. Ah. S-six. I-I can do it myself, you know." But her hands stayed where they were.

"Yes, but tonight I am your maid, remember." He whispered the words by her ear, brushing her skin with his lips as he reached around to drop another pin onto her lap.

Had she pressed back against him? Perhaps. He'd swear he'd heard her breath hitch.

"My job is to minister to your needs." He kissed the spot behind her ear before he pulled out another pin. "*All* your needs."

He half expected her to protest, but she didn't. Instead she gave a soft, little moan and tilted her head, wordlessly—and perhaps unconsciously—inviting him to kiss the sensitive spot again.

He did. Zeus! This slow, deliberate, careful bed play was going to kill him. It was nothing like his usual lusty romp. This time his mind was involved—and he rather thought his heart, as well.

He took his time, running his fingers through her soft, thick hair, finding the sensitive points on her scalp. Her eyes drifted closed again as if she were concentrating on his every touch.

He found the last pin, dropped it in her lap, and combed through her hair with his fingers one last time.

"Mmm. That feels good."

That was Caro talking, but it could have just as easily been him.

"I-I should braid it." She smiled, her eyes still closed. "I'm guessing that's beyond your skills?"

He chuckled. "Yes, I'm afraid it is." He brushed her hair aside to kiss the spot under her ear again. "Leave your hair down tonight, Caro. It's lovely."

"It will be a tangled mess tomorrow if I do." She said the words as if she'd already resigned herself to that fate.

He nuzzled the top of her neck. "If it is, I will be happy to help you comb it."

"Mmm. I hope you are as good at untangling snarled hair as you are at unknotting dress tapes. I—ohh!"

His fingers had moved from her hair to her lap. One hand cupped the outside of her leg, holding it still, stroking it, while the other chased the hairpins down her shift, closer and closer to her core. The pins were small, and his fingers felt large. Thick and clumsy.

Something else felt thick—and was rapidly growing thicker as Caro moaned and fidgeted against him.

He'd not paid attention to other women's scents or the texture of their hair or the changing colors of their eyes or the subtle shift in their voices as their passion grew. He'd been too focused on getting his cock inside them to notice such details.

With Caro, he wanted to memorize every nuance.

"Pesky pins," he murmured as he drew one slowly up her thigh.

"Um." She pressed back against him.

Did she know she'd tilted her hips up slightly? Perhaps her body had taken over from her mind. . . .

It's Caro's mind I most have to woo.

He pursued the last pin down the valley of her shift,

dipping deep to trap it gently against her body—and then he waited to see if she would startle.

She didn't. If she moved at all, it was to press against his touch.

He smiled and drew his finger slowly up, brushing over the seam of her opening, until he could pinch the pin between his thumb and fingertip.

She was panting again. Her head had fallen back against his shoulder, her lovely breasts thrust out, her nipples forming little peaks in the thin fabric of her shift. He couldn't resist—he cupped one breast with the hand not encumbered with pins and stroked the nipple with his thumb.

Caro caught her breath, eyes flying open.

"Shh," he said, stroking the side of her breast this time. "You're safe. I have you."

She must have decided to trust him, because he felt her body relax—until he tried to touch her with his other hand, the one with the pins.

"Careful! You'll spill them."

He chuckled. "Of course. Pardon me. I will put them away safely."

He disentangled himself, and then made a great show of carefully laying each pin on the bedside table.

She pulled a face, and he laughed. Warm affection flooded him, diluting and softening his pounding need.

Odd. He'd never before felt this way in bed.

Or out of bed, for that matter.

"And now, milady, it's time for your shift to come off. I'm sure you have only the one with you. You'll want to remove it so it will be aired out by morning."

Uneasiness and indecision clouded her eyes again. He would give her a gentle push in the right direction.

"Remember, you agreed it would be unsporting to keep

it on and hobble my efforts to sell you on the wonders of physical pleasure."

She nodded slowly. Reluctantly?

He would reassure her.

"And remember as well that I've promised to keep my breeches on. You will be completely safe from anything of that, er, nature."

She looked at him guardedly, and he waited while she made whatever calculations she needed to. This had to be something she chose freely—not something he seduced her into that she'd regret later.

But he could still present arguments, couldn't he? She was undecided, which meant part of her wanted to go down this path. And it was quite possible that *not* going forward would be what she'd regret later. She could always turn back if she changed her mind. His breeches were buttoned and would stay buttoned.

Perhaps appealing to her business sense once more would work.

"This is an exceptional offer, you know. You may never have this opportunity again—to have a man at your beck and call, willing and eager to be your lady's maid in *all* things."

Doubt still flickered in her eyes, but he thought he saw curiosity—and passion—there, too.

"I promise to stop the moment you say the word, just as a good servant would." And he'd learned this morning that she liked to be challenged. "But I wager instead you'll beg me to keep going until you scream my name in ecstasy."

She snorted, skepticism suddenly writ large on her features. "You'd lose that wager."

"I think not."

Her eyes narrowed. "All right. I'll bite. What are your terms?"

Aha! He had her. He just had to offer her something so enticing she couldn't refuse. But what . . .

Of course!

"I'll order a dozen casks of your Widow's Brew if I lose."

She snorted again and rolled her eyes. "And what do I owe you in the unlikely event I'm the loser?"

What did he want? Nothing besides the reward of bringing this difficult woman pleasure. "You'll have to thank me politely."

Her mouth fell open, she gawked at him—and then she grinned. "You're on."

And with that, she scrambled off the bed and grabbed the hem of her shift, almost as if she were afraid that if she waited, she'd lose heart.

Or perhaps she just wanted to be in control.

Or . . .

Coherent thought evaporated as Caro pulled the shift up and over her head.

"Here you go," a beautiful, wonderfully naked Caro said as she handed him the garment. "Hang it up so it doesn't wrinkle, if you please."

Chapter Sixteen

Lud! Her heart was pounding so hard, Nick would have been able to see it if he were still staring at her. Instead, he was across the room by the hearth, making a show of draping her shift over one of the chairs—the chair she'd been sitting in when she'd told him about Dervington's attack and her father's letter and then had drunk far too much brandy, got sick, and spent the night next to him. In bed. In *this* bed.

He'd been naked then—

Dear God, I'm *mother-naked now!*

She was never completely naked, except in her bath, and she always hurried through that.

She scrambled back onto the bed, dove under the coverlet, and pulled it up to her nose.

And then peered over the edge to watch Nick walk back toward her.

His body was very nice—tall and lean and muscled. She eyed his fall, and for a moment wished he would unbutton it and let her see his hips and thighs. And his cock, poor ugly—*enormous*—thing.

She shifted on the bed, remembering the feel of Dervington's—

No. Nick has promised to keep his breeches on.

"Don't be afraid, Caro," Nick said, sitting next to her, his weight depressing the mattress so it sloped slightly toward him.

She inched away and moved the coverlet down to her chin to say, "I'm not afraid."

The lie was automatic. It didn't fool either of them.

"Ah. So then why are you hiding under the bedclothes?"

Did he expect her to flounce around the room? "I might be a little nervous. I'm not used to this sort of thing."

He smiled in an understanding, comforting sort of way. "I meant it when I said I'll stop at once, the moment you say the word." His smile widened. "*If* you say it."

And then he just looked at her and waited.

Oh, hell. She *was* afraid—and she hated being afraid.

I trust Nick as much as I trust anyone. . . .

The truth hit her so hard it took her breath away.

I don't really trust anyone, do I?

Why should she? Her family had turned its back on her. Her friends . . . well, her only friends were Jo and Pen, and Pen had married and left her and the Home.

Caro knew she shouldn't feel betrayed by that, but she did. Stupid! Pen had her own life to live. Everyone did. It was the way of the world.

Ever since she'd fled Dervington's London house—if not before—she'd known she couldn't rely on anyone but herself.

The thought made her oddly melancholy. And . . . lonely.

She shook the feelings off. She would rely on herself now—on her own judgment—and she judged she could trust Nick. After all, he could have taken whatever he'd wanted last night when she was asleep.

He was offering her an exceptional, once-in-a-lifetime opportunity. For years she'd suspected other women were lying when they said they enjoyed bedroom activities, but it was galling, at the advanced age of thirty, not to know the truth of the matter.

She couldn't let a little case of nerves keep her from finding out once and for all.

Nothing Nick had done so far had been anything like what had happened with Dervington. *And* if Nick failed to show her passion, he'd promised to buy her ale. That would be a win right there.

Enough! She was tired of being afraid or nervous or whatever this fluttering feeling was. And she was very tired of being ignorant.

"All right," she said, a bit roughly, trying to mask her unease. "We have a wager. You might as well see if you can win it." She lifted a brow, but kept the coverlet firmly under her chin. "Is there a time limit? I assume you'll need more than fifteen minutes since you spent that long this morning with your"—what to call it?—"foolishness. However, I *would* like to go to sleep tonight."

He grinned at her. "You are endlessly entertaining, Caro."

She frowned. She had not said anything entertaining—she'd been rather caustic—and she knew Nick was smart enough to have heard the edge in her voice. Yet he was still grinning at her and seemed genuinely diverted.

"I definitely don't want to inconvenience you," he said. "How does this sound? If you are bored and still wishing to go to sleep in thirty minutes, I will concede defeat, and you may charge me for those casks of ale."

This was going to be too easy. Only thirty minutes and she'd earn a tidy sum for the Home. And if Nick liked their ale, she might have got a new customer. Perhaps several new customers, if he shared it with his London friends and *they* liked it.

This ill-fated journey might turn out to be profitable after all.

The thoughts passed through her mind—but like lessons learned by rote, recited by habit. The feelings of pride and satisfaction that always accompanied them were strangely muted today.

This time the notion of winning felt more like losing.

Balderdash. She was just out of her element. . . .

Ha! She was *naked* and in *bed* with a man. She couldn't be more out of her element if she sprouted wings and flew into a tree.

"Very well. I can expend half an hour on this project. Proceed."

And that made Nick laugh!

"No, don't frown," he said, still grinning. "You have set me quite a challenge, but I accept it."

Nick looked over at the clock on the mantel, the one that had been flanked by the oddly blissful shepherdess and the statue he hadn't let her see. "We've just hit the hour." He looked back at her. He was still smiling, but now his eyes had an intent, sharply focused look. "Let's begin."

"All right. It's—oh!"

Nick didn't waste any time. He stretched out on the bed, which caused her a moment of anxiety, but when he didn't shift his weight on top of her, pushing her into the mattress so she couldn't breathe—

"Shh." He stroked her cheek. "Don't worry. Nothing unpleasant will happen." He pressed his lips to her forehead. "Trust me."

There it was again—trust. She *wanted* to trust Nick.

I trust tavern keepers to pay their bills. . . .

That wasn't the same thing at all.

"Remember how you felt this morning?"

This morning *had* been very nice.

"And just a few moments ago when I was taking out your pins?"

That had been nice, too.

"Loosen the tight rein you've got on your feelings, Caro. Let your body guide you." He brushed his lips against her jaw. "Be brave."

I want to be brave.

"Be fearless."

I want to be fearless.

"Be passionate."

Passionate? "I . . . I don't know how." The "how" came out on a bit of a wail.

"I'll show you." He stroked her hair, kissed the corner of her mouth. "Will you let me?"

She wanted him to show her. She wanted to know what it was like. "Yes."

He smiled, and then his mouth brushed hers. The touch, light as it was, shot through her like lightning, incinerating all her hesitation and fear. And when his fingers pushed aside the coverlet, she didn't protest. No. Suddenly, she wanted his clever hands to move lower.

They did. His fingers brushed the side of her breast, and the slight friction of his skin against hers caused both her nipples to tighten into hard, aching nubs. The channel between her thighs where Dervington had been ached, too, not in pain but in . . . need. As if it were empty and crying for Nick—and Nick's long, thick cock—to fill it.

Good God! She shuddered—but in anticipation, not horror.

She'd felt none of these sensations with Dervington. He'd fumbled under her nightdress, slobbered a kiss or two on her lips, and then climbed onto her and shoved his way in. She'd felt nervous and anxious, and then she'd felt pain the first time, discomfort the second. There'd been none of this . . . excitement.

"Stop thinking of Dervington, Caro."

"I'm not."

Nick chuckled, seeing right through her lie. "Perhaps it will help if you think of the, er, brew that Dervington served you as vastly inferior, tasteless small beer. What I'm offering now is a sample of high-quality, robust ale."

She snorted. "Aren't you cocky."

He grinned. "Oh, yes. *Very* cocky."

The way he said it made her think of his swollen organ, of course. A hot tide of embarrassment swept up from her. . . .

Er, perhaps the hot flush wasn't embarrassment.

Nick glanced at the clock and then down at her again. "I'd best begin in earnest if I'm going to win our wager."

"Ha!" Caro couldn't take that lying down—well, yes, she *was* lying down. But she couldn't lose a wager—

Perhaps this is one you want to lose . . .

Nonsense! "You haven't a chance of winning tha—eek!"

His lips brushed the side of her breast, and her nipples tightened again. She needed him to touch *them*. To lick them—

What an odd idea—but an exciting one. Should she mention it to Nick? He did say she could give him suggestions.

Perhaps he'd come up with the notion himself. His lips were moving in that direction, but he was taking *so* long. So *maddeningly* long.

She was going to lose her mind if he didn't hurry.

He didn't. His lips kept up their glacial progress, inching closer and closer to one nub, while his fingers stroked nearer the other—which, oddly enough, only made her ache more.

She moaned again and arched up, encouraging him to touch her *now.*

He *chuckled*.

"*Nick.*" She grabbed his hair and tugged, trying to pull him over to where she needed him.

"Patience, love."

Love.

It was just a casual endearment. She knew it meant nothing. But she wished . . .

Her thoughts spun away as Nick's mouth and fingers finally reached their destinations. His tongue glided over one aching nipple as his fingers tweaked the other.

"Oh! Ohh. Oh, Nick."

She gripped his shoulders as a drowning man—or woman—might grab a tree limb to keep from being swept away by a flood. Her hips twisted on the bed. Each stroke of his tongue, each brush of his fingers made her breasts—*and* channel—ache. How had Nick forged that link?

She opened her legs to cool the heat and, yes, invite him to visit—

Lud, am I damp *there?*

She should be *dying* of embarrassment, but she had no room for anything but need—mindless, compelling, demanding, and, yes, *drenching* need.

This was *nothing* like her experience with Dervington.

Another stroke of Nick's tongue, and she couldn't even remember the marquess's name.

And then Nick's hand started to move. It slid slowly over her ribs, over her belly, nearer and nearer to where she most ached for him. . . .

And stopped. His fingers tangled in the curls right above her entrance—right above another throbbing nub.

She needed him to touch her *there*.

Now.

She opened her legs wider to give him a hint.

She moaned. Whimpered. Tried to tilt her hips up, to close the small space between her ache and his finger, but Nick's hand held her still.

"Patience," he murmured again, his mouth moving back to hers.

Patience?! Was he mad?

She dodged his mouth.

"No. No patience. Now. I need you *now!*"

"Oh? Where do you need me?"

This was no time for a bloody conversation. They weren't taking tea, for God's sake.

"You *know* where. Move your finger."

He'd propped his head up on one hand, the other being engaged—well, *not* engaged—elsewhere, and smiled at her, a lazy sort of smile, just a pulling up at the corners of his mouth. His eyes watched her intently. He looked so . . .

Familiar.

No, that wasn't it—or not only it. Rather, he looked as if he cared about her. As if he wanted something for her that she'd want for herself if she only knew it existed.

Well, she knew *one* thing she wanted.

"Move. Your. Blasted. Finger."

He grinned. "I love how demanding you are, Caro. How strong." His grin softened into . . . tenderness? Was that what this expression was? She was quite, quite certain no one had ever smiled at her this way before.

And then all coherent thought dissolved as his finger finally moved, the tip sliding below her curls, brushing ever so lightly over her aching flesh.

"Oh!" The sensation shot to her breasts as well—and Nick kindly leaned forward to flick his tongue over one nipple. "Oh!"

"Do you like that?"

Like it? It was agony. And heaven. She looked at him through a haze of desire. "Ahh."

That was all she could manage.

Except . . .

His finger had gone still once more! It rested against her desperate flesh, taunting her. She tried again to arch her hips up, but again his hand kept her from moving.

His strength was both oddly comforting and infuriating.

"Still impatient, are you?"

Was there humor in Nick's voice? Perhaps, but she thought she heard a note of need there, too, so she forgave him—a little.

"Yes! Move your finger again. *Now.*"

He brushed her lips with his. "I have a better idea. I'm going to kiss you there, all right?"

She gaped at him. There? He couldn't mean *there*. The notion was shocking. Embarrassing. Wildly improper.

Oh, who the hell cared?

"Yes. Yes. Just *do* it, Nick."

"Your wish is my command."

His mouth started down her body, kissing, licking, stroking, following the path his hand had taken earlier, moving closer.

Closer.

She panted, arched her back, willed him to hurry—and yet take his time. . . .

He nuzzled her curls. He was *so* close. She felt his warm breath on her. . . .

"Nick . . ."

He looked up at her, grinning again. "Yes? Did you wish to discuss something?"

"Nick!" She'd pull his hair if she could reach it.

"Or were you asking me to use my tongue for other matters?"

His tongue? What did he mean by—oh!

The warm, wet tip dipped down to touch her. Ohh. *This* was what she needed. This was exactly what she needed. She'd had no idea. . . .

"Nick! Oh. Oh, Nick."

Her world shrunk to Nick's tongue sliding over and around her, drawing her tighter and tighter.

"Nick. Dear Lord, Nick, please. Please."

"Shh." Nick lifted his head, taking his lovely tongue away from the magic it had been making in her.

She wanted to cry.

"Shh." He stretched out next to her again, wrapped an arm around her, and held her close as his finger took up where his tongue had left off.

"Oh." She pressed her face into his chest, breathing in his scent, warmed and comforted by the touch of his skin. "Oh. Oh, Nick."

His finger dipped and stroked and pressed. She wanted it to move faster and yet slower. She wanted whatever was coming to come and not come. She wanted—

"Nick!" It was coming. There was no stopping it. She was going to shatter into a million pieces and never be the same again.

"It's all right, Caro. Let go. I have you."

"No. I can't. I—Nick. Oh, God, Nick. *Nick!*"

She shouted his name and let go. She had no choice. The force growing inside her was too strong to resist. She let go, and something inside her convulsed. Pleasure exploded through her, wave after wave after wave of overwhelming, deeply carnal pleasure.

And then she collapsed against Nick, limp, completely spent—and totally changed.

No. It's an illusion. I haven't changed at all.

Liar.

She felt changed. Whether the change would last . . . That she didn't know.

If I can stay with Nick . . .

No. That was foolishness. Nick was a viscount. She had a business to run. Jo needed her. Nick didn't.

Nick's hand stroked down her back. She felt his lips brush her hair.

"Good?"

"Yes." Tomorrow was Christmas Eve. The day after was Christmas. She would allow herself to live this fantasy for that long. And then the snow would melt, and she'd go back to her real life at the Home in Little Puddledon.

"I believe I won our wager," Nick said.

Wager? Oh, yes. She *had* screamed his name, hadn't she?

"And now you must pay up. I await your polite thanks."

She heard amusement in his voice, but also a note of strain.

Right. *He* hadn't had any glorious release—or any release at all.

She tilted her head to look up into his face. He was smiling, but there was definitely a tightness to his expression. And need in his eyes and . . . loneliness?

An unfamiliar feeling welled up in her breast. She cared how Nick felt. She wanted to make him feel better. But how?

Sexual congress would surely do the trick. She'd even be willing to put up with the discomfort. It couldn't hurt as much as she remembered.

Maybe there wouldn't be any discomfort this time. Perhaps—

No. Even if the experience proved to be as wonderful as what she'd just felt—almost impossible to imagine—she couldn't risk pregnancy. Yes, Nick had said he would marry her if she conceived, but she wasn't totty-headed enough to chance changing her life for a few minutes of, well, sympathy.

Perhaps a hug, as small as that was, would help. She leaned into him—

And he flinched. Oh! She'd put pressure on the place where his poor cock was hiding under his fall.

Well, not hiding very well. His fall was definitely bulging.

"Careful," he said. "I'm a little, er, sensitive there."

Sensitive. She'd heard women at the Home talk of how sensitive a man's organ was. How much it liked being stroked and kissed and . . . licked.

She'd assumed they'd been making some lewd joke, but perhaps not.

Nick kissed me that way. I should kiss him back.

Fear flickered to life, but she snuffed it quickly. She was not going to be ruled by fear any longer. She was done with giving Dervington any power over her. She was older and wiser now, and she trusted Nick. She was going to be fearless. Bold.

If other women could kiss a man's cock, she could, too—that is, if Nick would like it.

She put her hand gently on his fall and felt his organ twitch—eagerly, she thought. She stroked it—and smiled when she heard Nick suck in his breath just like she'd done when he'd touched her.

"May I thank you impolitely?"

"Ahh."

Was he shocked? Disgusted? Perhaps she should—

Be bold. Surely what was sauce for the goose was sauce for the gander.

"I'm not certain that is a good idea."

She heard yearning in his voice. She searched his face again—a face that was becoming all too dear to her—and saw yearning there, too.

"Why isn't it a good idea?"

He frowned. "You aren't a light-skirts, Caro. You're a—"

"Brewer. Don't worry. I'm not planning to change careers."

His eyes widened. "I didn't mean to suggest such a

thing! It's just that, no matter what you say, you're gently bred. Such behavior can't be appropriate for a gently bred female."

"Why not?"

That stumped him. He blinked, his mouth dropping open slightly.

"If you insist on talking about propriety, Nick, a gently bred female would not be naked in bed with a man who's not her husband nor would she have allowed any of the liberties I just allowed you."

Does he look abashed or regretful?

That would never do.

"Liberties I *thoroughly* enjoyed," she added quickly. *She* would not regret what they'd just done. She'd felt a lifetime's worth of regret and shame over the Dervington business, and where had that got her? Bah! She was as done with those feelings as she was with fear. This had been her choice. She'd made her decision freely. She would stand by it.

She suddenly felt rather powerful.

Nick did not yet look convinced, but she thought he was wavering.

"You made me an offer, Nick—a truly exceptional offer. As you said, I may never have this opportunity again." She grinned. "Never again have a man at my beck and call."

And there would be something . . . healing, perhaps, in taking control of matters. She'd had so little control thirteen years ago.

"I would like to experiment—if that's all right with you, of course." She wanted to stroke him again, but she restrained herself.

She'd asked. Now she had to wait for his answer.

"Are you quite, quite certain, Caro?"

"Yes." Ah. Best to clarify precisely what she was certain about. "That is, I am certain I want to do to you what you did to me." She grinned. "Just lie back. I shall do all the, ah, *work* this time."

His answering grin made her surprisingly happy. "Very well. Shall I remove my breeches first?"

"Yes. I'm naked. You should be, too."

He stood and unbuttoned his fall—and his cock leaped out, apparently delighted to be freed from confinement.

To think I once—well, twice—had something this long and thick inside me . . .

Instead of shrinking at that memory, the relevant part of her body gave a little shiver of excitement. Because this was Nick, and the man attached to the organ made all the difference.

Nick would have filled my emptiness just now . . .

Right. And possibly given me a child. Get your head out of the clouds!

She watched Nick's cock waggle about as he climbed back into bed. What an ungainly organ it was. Rather homely and quite ridiculous really. Even when Nick stretched out on his back, it didn't lie down quietly, but bobbed about.

She touched it cautiously—and it jumped with apparent eagerness.

She circled it with her finger and thumb, measuring its girth—which seemed to increase as she held it—and then traced its length from tip to base.

She heard Nick suck in his breath—and she smiled. He liked what she was doing.

She stroked him again, exploring. Experimenting.

How different his body was from hers.

Of course it was. Male and female were made to fit together to make children.

It would be nice . . .

No, it would *not* be nice to have a child, especially without a husband. Children were a lot of work; she knew that from tending her siblings and from living at the Home. Children needed care and attention. They needed to be fed and clothed and educated. They were a distraction from one's work. A worry. Look at poor Mrs.—no, Miss—Dixon.

Yes. Look at her love for Grace and Edward. Look at Pen's love for Harriet.

And Mama's love for me?

Oh! She'd thought, growing up, that her mother—and her father—had loved her. She'd assumed it, counted on it—and then she'd got that horrible letter disowning her.

I'm just as alone as Nick. . . .

She pushed the thought away. She had a once-in-a-lifetime opportunity here. She needed to get on with it.

She stroked Nick again—and he moaned.

Must it be just a once-in-a-lifetime experience?

She *shoved* that thought away, even though it seemed her heart wanted to grab onto it and never let go.

Her heart was a fool. Yes, Nick had mentioned marriage. Once by accident—he'd admitted to being shocked himself by the offer. And once as a way to fix a mistake should she conceive. Neither had been accompanied with professions of undying love.

It only made sense that he would wish for their connection to be nothing more than an amusing way to pass the time. Her arrival had interrupted his orgy, after all. He'd been at loose ends, deprived of his sport, and she'd walked right into his arms with her daft charade suggestion.

But—

No! She must use her brain, not her heart. It didn't matter what Nick wanted. *She* didn't want to leave the Home. She had important work to do there.

And she had "work" to do here, too.

She focused on the organ awaiting her further ministrations.

An organ attached to Nick . . .

She told her heart to be quiet as she continued her experiments—stroking, gently squeezing, growing bolder with each of Nick's indrawn breaths, each gasp, each moan. She was in control now, just as Nick had been in control before.

Could she make him feel all the wonderful things she'd felt? He was a man. . . .

She grinned down at his cock, swallowing a giggle. Yes, indeed, he was most definitely a man.

She would follow his lead. She'd kiss him as he'd kissed her. She'd use her tongue as he'd used his.

She licked his entire length as if he were a tasty, melting ice and she needed to capture every drop.

"Uhh!" Nick's hips lifted off the bed.

Her grin widened. She was succeeding—and it made her feel very, very powerful. *Oh, look. Here's a real drop at his tip.* She lapped it up.

Nick moaned again, his hips lifting, twisting. "Caro. Oh. God. Caro."

Yes, he appeared to be driven just as mindless as she'd been earlier.

She licked him again, letting his sounds of desire guide her.

"Caro. I—oh. Ah. *Ahh.*"

He stiffened. She pulled back in time to see his cock tighten and then pulse, a thick fluid spurting onto his belly.

This must be what causes a child to begin.

She felt oddly sad that it had spilled out here where it had no hope of bringing life. . . .

Have you lost your mind?

Yes, perhaps she had. Her heart had pushed to the fore again. This wasn't just some man; this was Nick. Whom she cared about. Whom she felt even closer to now.

Nick will make wonderful babies, handsome strong sons and beautiful strong daughters. He'll love them and care for them and raise them to be good men and women.

His wife, whomever she would be, would be very lucky.

I wish . . .

No, I do not *wish. Remember the Home. Remember Widow's Brew.*

And remember that even if she were willing to give up her current life, she'd never be accepted by Society. Yes, she'd been born to the gentry—unlike Pen who was a farmer's daughter—but Caro had been disowned by her father and had broken one of Society's most fundamental rules by giving Dervington her virginity outside of marriage. Pen, at least, had eventually married the man she'd "sinned" with.

Nick was a viscount, albeit a somewhat disreputable one. He could not like to have his wife given the cut direct at every turn.

He was smiling at her now, warmth and something else in his eyes. . . .

Oh, God, he's not going to ask me to marry him again, is he?

She couldn't let him do that. She didn't trust herself at the moment to do the honorable, sensible thing and say no.

And she would *have* to say no. She couldn't desert the Home. And she couldn't bear to be the anchor keeping Nick from moving forward in Society, especially now, when it looked as if he was ready to take charge of his estate and other responsibilities.

Apparently, this was another danger of intimate activities. Besides risking pregnancy, they made people think foolish thoughts. Imagine connections that weren't there.

The snow, the forced togetherness, and, perhaps most of all, the bloody Christmas merriment weren't helping either. The Christmas season could make even the most practical person dream of families and babies and miracles.

She had to break this spell before Nick did something he'd forever regret. How better than to state the obvious, no matter how impolite?

"You're rather a mess."

Nick's eyes widened, and then he laughed. "Yes. Could I trouble you to hand me my handkerchief? It's in my breeches pocket."

Chapter Seventeen

Do I really want to marry Caro?

Nick wrapped a muffler several times around his neck. It was Christmas Eve morning, and he was standing with his guests as they donned coats, hats, and boots, readying to go out into the nasty, bitter cold to gather holly and ivy and other greenery with which to festoon the house.

And mistletoe. We'll need mistletoe for a kissing bough.

It was a very good thing he'd already put on his greatcoat, because the thought of kissing Caro had an all-too predictable effect on his cock.

I almost asked her to marry me last night, but I lost my nerve.

And then she'd gone back to her room to sleep.

Just as well. That had given his better sense a chance to reassert itself. He'd never had any occasion to doubt his decision not to marry and get an heir until Caro had appeared on his doorstep less than forty-eight hours ago.

He should be highly skeptical of such an abrupt change of mind. It was likely some sort of holiday mania. He was being swept up in the Christmas jollity he'd not experienced since he was a boy in Venice. That was the problem. Once the holiday was over and the roads cleared, Caro would leave, and things would go back to normal.

The thought was not comforting.

He closed his eyes briefly, remembering last night.

It had been heaven—with apologies to the Almighty for thinking of something so carnal in spiritual terms. But there *had* been a spiritual aspect to it. It certainly had been nothing like any other encounter he'd ever had with a woman. It had been far more . . . *personal* than those.

Zeus! It was hard to explain, but he'd felt close to Caro in some way that went beyond physical.

He snorted—earning a startled look from Bert, who was pulling on his gloves next to him.

Nick smiled and made a show of studying his own gloves.

Beyond physical? Hell, their bodies hadn't even joined.

But our . . . souls did. . . .

Good God, what poetic claptrap! A holiday mania, indeed! He should see about a spot in Bedlam. He'd clearly lost his mind.

And yet . . .

Some sort of connection had been made—or strengthened—last night. He'd felt a part of Caro, even though his cock hadn't had the pleasure of coming calling, of sliding through her entrance, deep inside her warmth. . . .

His cock *wasn't* showing, was it? It felt large enough to make a tent even in his greatcoat.

He glanced down to be certain there were no suspicious bulges.

Even though he'd not entered Caro, he'd felt as if they were . . .

The only word he could come up with was *wedded*.

The experience had been very, very good. It was probably

fortunate he'd not risked souring it with a marriage proposal. Caro might have said yes, and that would have been wonderful—or at least it would have seemed wonderful at the time. But she could just as easily have said no. After all, she was an independent woman with her own life—and she hadn't jumped at his first offer yesterday morning.

Well, yes, he'd admit he'd bungled that quite thoroughly.

And his second offer—saying he'd marry her if she conceived—didn't really count.

If he'd asked again . . .

Third time lucky?

What was lucky? A "no" last night would have murdered the warm, deeply contented happiness he'd felt and have left him a bloody emotional mess. But a "yes" would have condemned him for life.

He waited for a sense of relief at his near escape to flood him, but instead he felt . . . empty.

Forlorn?

He glanced at Caro. She was smiling, chatting with Polly. She certainly wasn't sending *him* any longing looks.

She's probably regretting the whole thing.

Of course she was. She *had* left him last night, right after handing him his handkerchief so he could clean himself up.

Gah, *that* had been embarrassing.

If she'd stayed, he might have asked her then, soiled handkerchief still crumpled in his hand. Or this morning, in bed, warm under the coverlet.

Why did *she leave me to sleep alone?*

Maybe it wasn't that she'd regretted what they'd done. Maybe she'd been confused and uncertain, too. Maybe she'd been worried that if she stayed with him the whole night, he'd try to engage in some more serious lovemaking.

To be honest, he'd have been tempted to do so.

On the other hand . . .

Zounds! He needed fifteen hands to manage all these silly arguments. He wasn't used to dithering like this.

Well, he had a bit more time to mull the matter over. The roads wouldn't clear right away. At the very least, he'd have today and tonight with Caro. Perhaps by then he'd know his own mind.

He looked around to see if everyone was ready to venture out into the cold. Caro and Polly and Livy and Fanny all had their coats on, as did Bertram. And Thomas, the footman—he was going along to show them the best places to find what they needed.

Felix was busy helping Edward put on his outerwear. Nick shook his head. If anyone had told him *Felix* could be domesticated so quickly, he'd have laughed and thought them mad. And yet, there Felix was, helping a young boy sort out his mittens.

Nick felt a twinge of . . . what? Jealousy? Envy? Edward had been *his* shadow yesterday. He'd rather liked it.

But this was far better for the boy. Felix was going to be Edward's stepfather. It would be splendid if Felix could bring himself to treat Edward as his own son and spare him the sort of lonely, loveless boyhood Nick had had after his parents had died and he'd come to England.

It looked as if everyone who had chosen to "enjoy" this freezing entertainment had assembled. The Weasel—Woods, that is—wouldn't be joining them. He was still working on the stage. And Hughes was polishing his plans for this afternoon's Nativity play. Parker and his wife were probably in the kitchens—that's where they'd been since yesterday afternoon—helping prepare the Christmas Eve feast. And Dervington's spawn and his friend . . .

They were likely still abed.

"Shall we—" Nick heard a clatter as if someone—or two

someones—were running down the corridor, and then Oliver Meadows and Lord Archibald burst into the room.

"Sorry we're late," Oliver said.

"Stayed up drinking," Archie said.

Oliver frowned at Archie. "*And* practicing our singing."

"Right." Archie nodded. "We're ready to perform. Now we want to help gather the greenery."

"It was one of my favorite things to do at Christmas when I was a lad," Oliver said.

I've no favorite memories of the holiday in England. Nick couldn't keep from looking at Caro. *At least not yet.*

This Christmas's memories might be wonderful—or horrible.

"Very well," Nick said. "However, as you can see, we are on the point of departure."

"We'll be quick." Archie grabbed his greatcoat.

The two men *were* quick, and in very short order they all set off into the cold and snow.

Ugh. Will I ever get used to English winters?

Doubtful. Nick had lived here almost twice as long as he'd lived in Italy, and the cold still sliced through him.

If I had Caro to keep me warm . . .

He looked ahead to where she walked with Polly. He'd meant to offer her his arm, but of course she'd not waited for that. She must have concluded she no longer needed his protection. After all, she *had* gone back to her own bed last night.

Well, there was no question she was safe out here in the snow and ice. They weren't polar bears. If nothing else, the multiple layers of clothing—the coats and hats and scarves and gloves—would limit the amount of insult any man could offer her.

She laughed at something Polly said and his heart—and even his poor frozen cock—lifted.

He *would* try his luck and ask her to marry him. He'd wait until tonight, when they were in their rooms—

"You seem happy."

He startled. He'd been so lost in thought, he'd not noticed Livy approach.

Livy grinned knowingly, blast it. She was far too sharp-eyed to have missed his reaction. In her line of work, she needed to pay close attention to people, especially men.

"Of course I'm happy. It's Christmas Eve."

She rolled her eyes.

Well, yes, he deserved that. She knew he didn't put any stock in the holiday—he'd invited her here for an orgy, after all.

She nodded toward Caro. "You can thank me for telling her your cock wouldn't crow."

Oh, Lord. Normally he'd raise a quelling eyebrow, but he'd never been successful at quelling Livy.

Plus his eyebrow was as frozen as the rest of his face. He doubted he could move it.

It was safer not to look at Livy at all. He watched Caro instead.

Caro really was remarkable—a woman from the gentry who could converse so easily with everyone. She would make him an excellent wife, even outside the bedroom. She'd be a partner in running his home and estate.

She'd have much to teach him about those duties, to be brutally honest.

"I thought at the time she was afraid of the mattress jig," Livy said, "so I figured telling her you couldn't dance it would put her at ease." Livy sent him a sidelong, knowing look. "I'm guessing both her problem and yours are solved, eh?"

He shrugged. He was not going to share any details

with Livy. What had occurred between him and Caro was private.

That was new, too. In the past, he'd not cared who knew about—or even who observed—his couplings.

And he *hadn't* coupled with Caro. Not exactly.

Not yet.

"You should marry her."

Had he been so transparent, then? But he was still surprised Livy would say such a thing. She knew he'd sworn off marriage. "Why?"

Livy smiled. "I like her—even though she may be stealing two of my best workers."

"Oh?" He looked back at Caro. Fanny had now joined her discussion with Polly, Bertram following a few steps behind.

Livy sighed. "Yes. Fanny's heart hasn't been in the business for a while, not since she lost her baby."

Good God! Fanny had miscarried? He'd not known that. He'd not known she'd been increasing. He never. . . .

Well, he'd assumed light-skirts knew how to prevent conception.

No, it was worse than that. Shame flooded him as he realized he'd never given a thought to what happened after he finished a bedroom romp and pulled his breeches back on.

How could he not have?

Here I am judging Felix when I might have committed much the same sin.

He'd always thought he'd been careful, but, well, especially when he'd been younger and establishing himself as Lord Devil. . . .

He couldn't swear with one hundred percent certainty that none of the many seeds he'd sown had taken root, could he?

"Fanny has been wanting to leave, but she's had no place to go. Caro's Benevolent Home sounds like the perfect solution."

"Ah. Yes. I suppose it might be."

I might have a child somewhere—a child without a father.

His stomach twisted.

What can I do?

Nothing. Even if he tracked down every woman he'd ever had relations with—an impossible task—there was no way of knowing, if she had a child the correct age, whether that child was his.

He stared blankly ahead, appalled.

And then his resolve stiffened. He couldn't change the past, but he would change the future. The present. Today. He hoped Caro would marry him and he'd put his raking days behind him, but if she wouldn't, well, at the very least, he would be far more careful in his liaisons.

And perhaps he would also contribute to this Benevolent Home as a small way of making amends to women and children in general. If Caro was involved with the enterprise, it must be a deserving, well-run charity.

"Caro says the Home's hop grower just got married," Livy was saying, "to the Earl of Darrow, if you can believe it. So they need someone to help tend the plants. Fanny's father was a farmer, and her mother had a big flower garden that Fanny helped with, so Fanny knows something about growing things."

Livy smiled, perhaps a bit sadly. "She's quite excited. Says she wants to go there straightaway. Now that Emma Dixon will stay with Felix, Fanny can take Emma's seat on the stagecoach when the roads clear."

Or Caro's seat, if I can persuade Caro to marry me.

Livy sighed. "But now Polly wants to go, too. She's always loved to cook and has even done some brewing."

Ah! Caro might be more willing to marry if she knows there's someone who can take over her brewing duties. . . .

This was an excellent development—for him.

He looked down at Livy and frowned. "Will you be all right? I would think it hard to lose two of your girls at once."

Livy didn't keep a brothel, but she did depend on her portion of the income her girls generated. Losing two popular, er, employees at the same time couldn't be comfortable.

She shrugged. "Aye. I'll miss them—I liked them, and they did well for me—but I can find new girls. There are always women coming to Town, eager to live their lives independently, free of overbearing husbands or fathers." She raised a somewhat cynical brow. "And as long as there are rich, titled men looking for amusement, I can find them work."

Right. Rich titled men like me.

Ice formed in his stomach to match the cold outside.

She gave him a sly look. "I asked Caro if she'd like to work for me."

"You did *what*?!" Fortunately, that came out as a hiss rather than a shout. What had Livy been thinking of?

Her profits, of course. She was as much a businesswoman as Caro.

Livy grinned. "Oh, she turned me down. Unfortunately. She really is remarkably lovely." She laughed. "As I suspect you've noticed. She would have been very much in demand had she accepted my offer."

Words clogged his throat. He was angry, and yet he realized he had no standing here. Caro was neither his sister nor his wife—nor, he suspected, would she thank him for interfering even if he *were* related to her. Still, he—

Livy shrugged. "I'll admit I'd hoped at first that after you introduced her to sexual pleasure, she'd reconsider."

Horror overcame anger. How *could* Livy think he'd have anything to do with persuading Caro to join the ranks of the fashionable impures?

That's a mite sanctimonious, isn't it? Don't turn into Uncle Leon.

He couldn't very well disparage a group of women he'd spent so much time with, enjoying precisely the skills his inner Leon was now turning his dead nose up at.

Though there were those obscene statues on Leon's mantel . . .

"I'll miss you, Nick," Livy was saying now. "You were always one of my favorite bedmates."

Anger and horror changed abruptly to a warm, less-strident emotion. He and Livy *had* been friends of a sort for years. She might be a whore, but she was also a good person. She'd been kind to him, and she had always looked out for her girls, sometimes in an almost motherly way. Look at how she was willing to let Fanny and Polly go free, thinking of their needs before her finances.

"I'll miss you, too, Livy." *Best not be at all ambiguous.* "But if Caro will have me, I mean to be faithful."

Livy nodded. "I never imagined otherwise." She patted him on the arm—not that he felt her touch through his many layers of clothing. "I've always thought you a monogamous sort. Not all men are, you know."

Why would Livy think that? He'd railed against his uncle, marriage, and the succession for as long as she'd known him. He—

"Now I remember who you are."

Blast, that was Archie's voice. Nick's attention snapped back to Caro. Dervington's spawn had come up to her.

"You're one of my father's whores."

If Nick had thought he was angry before, he was mistaken. Blind fury exploded through him.

Here I do *have the standing to intervene. This is my estate. Caro is my guest.*

He would brook no insult. He started forward.

"No, I'm one of your father's *victims*," Caro said—and then shoved the slimy little blackguard into a nice, deep snowdrift.

"I *do* like her," he heard Livy say from behind him, "but the real reason you should marry her is because *you* like her. In fact, I think you love her."

Caro sat in the flickering candlelight of the Long Gallery, clapping along with everyone else. The Nativity play had just concluded, and Mr. Hughes and the cast were taking a few well-deserved bows.

The Weasel—no, she really should call him Mr. Woods from now on—had built a sturdy stage along with a rough stable and other bits of scenery to evoke the proper atmosphere. Mrs. Brooks had found a trunk in the attic full of Nativity costumes from when Nick's father and uncle had been boys, and Polly and Fanny had mended any that needed attention.

Mr. Hughes had read the story from his Bible so no one had been required to memorize any lines. Still, Mr. Woods, playing the angel Gabriel, had been overcome by what appeared to be fright the moment he'd seen the audience. Perhaps he hadn't expected so many people; all the servants were there to watch. In any event, he'd swayed, turned an un-angelic shade of green, and bolted—to the jakes, most likely—leaving his robe and halo behind.

Livy had leaped into the breach—or, rather, onto the stage. She'd plucked the halo and robe from where Mr.

Woods had dropped them and, wings a bit askew, had swaggered into his abandoned role.

That casting had been exquisitely ironic for this particular gathering, though Caro doubted Mr. Hughes approved of it or of the absurdly dramatic way Livy played her part. The audience loved her, though, cheering and whistling whenever Gabriel was in a scene—and he (or, in this case, she) managed to flit, uninvited, into every scene.

Emma and Felix had played Mary and Joseph, of course, with Grace as Baby Jesus, and Edward had been a very serious, conscientious shepherd supported by his co-shepherd, Thomas. Bertram, Mr. Brooks, and, much to the servants' delight, Nick had acted the parts of the Magi. Archie and Oliver—plus Gabriel/Livy—rounded out the cast as the choir of angels.

To everyone's great good fortune and relief, Baby Jesus had slept through the entire performance only waking now—and squalling—in response to the audience's applause.

"Thank you to all our actors," Nick said as Emma hurried the baby offstage and out of earshot, "for a fine performance. Thanks also to Mr. Hughes for directing the production, and to . . ." He looked around.

"Well, it appears Mr. Woods has not yet returned, but he deserves thanks for this fine stage and scenery as do Mrs. Brooks"—Nick removed his elaborate headdress and bowed theatrically to the housekeeper—"and Miss Taylor and Miss White"—he bowed to Polly and Fanny as well—"for the costumes. Now if you'll give us a moment to change, I believe Lord Archibald and Mr. Meadows plan to sing a few duets for us."

Caro had put her shawl on the chair next to her to save it for Nick. She hadn't discussed the matter with him beforehand—well, she'd been rather dodging him all day. But they were still carrying on their public charade, weren't they? Surely Nick would want to sit next to her now.

Her shoulders slumped. Or perhaps not. She *had* fled his room last night. She'd felt overwhelmed and had needed to be alone. And it had been the right thing to do if he'd really been on the verge of mentioning marriage again.

She still felt overwhelmed—and confused—but her desire to spend time with Nick, especially as she might have only a day or two left, was stronger than either of those feelings.

"Is this seat taken?"

She looked up to see Nick and grinned. She couldn't stop herself. Her entire face must be glowing.

I'm losing my grip on reality—and perhaps on my sanity.

At the moment, she didn't care.

"I was saving it for a handsome Magus."

He grinned back at her. "Well, I hope you mean me. I suspect Mrs. Brooks will take offense if you have designs on her husband."

She snorted. "Mr. Brooks is quite safe."

Nick had managed to arrange his expression to look serious, but his eyes laughed. "And while Bert may be unattached, I think you *must* have better taste than to favor him over me."

"Oh, yes. Much, much better." Mr. Collins was handsome enough, she supposed, but her heart didn't leap nor little shivers waltz up and down her spine when she saw him.

And it wasn't Nick's appearance, splendid though it was, that drew her—or at least not *only* his appearance. It was far more than that. It was his kindness—to Edward and his mother. To her. His gentleness. The odd feeling she had that he understood her in a way no one else did.

And his loneliness. That drew her as well. Perhaps it resonated with her because she was lonely, too.

She loved Nick for *who* he was, not—

She blinked. Do *I love Nick?*

She knew nothing about love, and yet . . .

Good God! That must *be what this intense, mad, confusing feeling is.*

Nick sat down next to her—she was happy that their seats were close enough that his arm brushed against hers—and turned his attention to the stage. Archie and Oliver were beginning.

She allowed herself another moment to admire Nick's profile, and then she, too, turned to face the performers.

The men had lovely voices that complemented each other extremely well. If she closed her eyes, they almost sounded as if they were indeed part of a choir of angels.

She felt her heart lift with the beauty of the music.

And then she opened her eyes to see Archie, and her heart jolted back to earth.

She studied him. His expression was one of focus and, yes, joy. Unlike Mr. Woods, he clearly relished performing. And he was quite gifted. That would be evident to anyone with ears. She thought he must truly feel the emotions in the music to convey them so well.

But it was also evident that he'd studied and worked to perfect his gift—just as she had studied and worked to perfect her brewing. He had the air of confidence that came with competence.

He seemed so much more mature now, singing, than he had when he'd used his beautiful voice to call her a whore.

It had been extremely satisfying to send him into that snowdrift. And she'd been very lucky. She'd caught him by surprise. He'd been off-balance—literally and figuratively.

To his credit, he hadn't tried to strike back, even verbally. Yes, seeing Nick standing next to her, glowering at him, must have encouraged him to rein in his temper, but she also thought—hoped—he'd realized himself that holding his tongue was . . . kinder.

A man who could sing like an angel should have at least a glimmer of a soul.

She frowned. She'd been so focused on herself, on her worry that her past would get out, that she hadn't thought about Archie. It must have been hell for a boy as musical and sensitive as he appeared to be to have grown up with Dervington for a father. Had the man recognized his son's gift at all?

Perhaps, but she doubted it. The marquess struck her as someone who valued boxing, not ballads.

Well, it would be hell for any child to have Dervington for a father, given the man's proclivity for swiving the nursemaids. And Nick had said the marchioness was just as happy to have her husband busy with the servants.

Clearly, there'd not been much love in that house. She hadn't realized it at the time, but looking back, she could see how that lack of love—or even of respect—between the master and mistress had fostered the tension and anxiety that had permeated everything.

What sort of a home was that for a child to grow up in?

In any event, she'd told Archie, calmly and firmly after he'd picked himself out of the snow, that she was not now and had never been a whore. That she'd been only seventeen when his father had—

When the events had occurred.

She'd been tempted to tell him exactly what she thought of the marquess, but she'd stopped herself. Dervington might be the worst sort of snake, but disparaging him to his son helped no one.

Archie had listened and apologized. She thought he was sincerely regretful for what he'd said.

Sometimes just a little change in the ingredients—in

the hops or the malt—or a change in temperature or a new cask could make a brew taste different, better or worse. She supposed it was the same with people. Everyone was a unique brew of their past experiences and future hopes. Each day was a chance for new ingredients to be added.

Look at how a few unexpected events had changed her. If there'd been no snowstorm, if Archie and Oliver hadn't taken the stagecoach reins and sent them into a ditch, she'd not be here. She'd not have met Nick again, not have kissed him or done what they'd done last night.

And would do tonight?

She felt a thrum of excitement.

She should thank Archie for that.

Archie and Oliver had started their performance with beautiful but complicated songs of soaring notes and intertwined harmony, but now they'd moved on to simpler, more familiar tunes so the audience could join in.

Caro couldn't carry a tune to save her life, so she just smiled and enjoyed everyone else's singing. Nick, as it turned out, had a very nice baritone. Not trained like Archie's and Oliver's, but still very pleasant.

She relaxed, breathing in the familiar scents of evergreens and candles, the scents of home, of when she'd been young and life had seemed so safe and uncomplicated. She'd been lucky to have had a happy childhood. Nick hadn't been so blessed, at least not after he came to England. And poor Edward certainly hadn't, though things would improve for him if Felix turned out to be a good husband and father.

Nick will make an excellent father . . . and husband.

Her heart gave a little leap—and she frowned. He'd make an excellent husband for *someone else.*

Nick was a viscount—a handsome, wealthy viscount. Once he decided for certain that it was time to give up orgies and start his nursery, he'd have his pick of the well-bred, well-connected girls on the London Marriage Mart. He'd not, in normal circumstances, consider marrying an old, slightly soiled spinster, no matter how much he enjoyed frolicking with her.

If he did offer her marriage, she must hold firm, do him a kindness, and say no.

Not that what they'd done could have been impressive "frolicking" to him. A man who engaged in orgies must find what had happened between them last night quite tame. Enjoyable, perhaps, but only in the way that even small beer could be enjoyable when one was *very* thirsty. It wasn't something anyone would choose when there was better brew available.

Not that it mattered to her, of course. She had no intention of marrying anyone. She was needed at the Home. Her role was important—crucial, really—to their economic well-being. And now she might have convinced Polly and Fanny to join her. They would be assets to her brewing program, but they would need training. She definitely had her work cut out for her once she left Oakland.

The thought wasn't as exciting—or motivating—as it should have been. Instead, it was slightly depressing.

Dear God, I don't want to leave.

No. She couldn't think like that. That way lay madness. She had to take herself in hand and—

She felt a hand on her arm and looked over to see Nick smiling at her, a question in his eyes—and on his lips, though for some reason she thought it wasn't the same question.

"Ready to go down to the servants' hall to light the Yule log and candle?"

Tonight might be her last chance for any . . . frolicking. She did not want to miss it.

She would indulge in a day—or night—or two of madness before the snow melted and she went back to being the Home's responsible, level-headed brewer.

"Yes," she said, answering both questions—the one he'd asked and the one she thought she saw in his eyes. "I'm ready."

Chapter Eighteen

Nick, Caro at his side, paused on the threshold of the servants' hall, taken aback by the crowd in the room. Yes, he'd followed everyone—guests and servants—from the Long Gallery, so he shouldn't be surprised, but he was. And slightly overwhelmed.

Perhaps it just seemed so crowded because the room was smaller, the ceiling lower. They were actually missing a few people. Felix and Emma Dixon and the baby had gone back to their room, though Edward was here. Thomas had taken charge of him so the boy could see the festivities.

And Mr. Woods had yet to reappear.

Oh, Lord. Now everyone had stopped talking and was staring at him.

At them.

He glanced down at Caro. She seemed a bit taken aback, too, but she smiled up at him in an encouraging way.

He forced himself to smile as well. Act confident. These were his guests, his servants.

It was his servants he focused on, the people who worked for him, who depended on him, many of whose names he had yet to learn.

Well, that would change. He'd begun, finally, to take up his responsibilities.

He crossed the black-and-white stone-flagged floor, his steps echoing in the quiet, toward the hearth where Pearson was waiting for him with Mr. and Mrs. Brooks nearby. Nick was very glad he had Caro with him. Her presence was steadying. She was from the happier times of his life, when he'd been away from Oakland, spending school holidays—save Christmas, of course—at her parents' house. . . .

No, he needn't look that far back, either in time or distance. Less than twelve hours earlier, in a room just two floors above them—in his uncle's room . . .

No, in my *room. I'm the viscount now.*

In *his* room upstairs, he'd been far, far happier than he could ever remember being before. Because of Caro.

I'll ask her to marry me tonight, and this time I won't hesitate or leave her in any doubt that I want her as my wife.

Happiness filled him, spilling over in what he guessed must be a foolish grin. Once they were married . . .

If *we are married.*

He looked down at Caro. She was smiling at Pearson and the Brookses now.

She might say no. She would be sacrificing a lot if she said yes. She would have to give up her place at the Home, her work, her friends.

Yes, but there would be new work for her here, as viscountess. He would even see if they could get the old brewhouse operational, if she wanted. And she would have him . . .

He frowned. That was another issue. They had not settled the question of marital relations last night. He thought she'd enjoyed what they'd done—*he* certainly had—but it had not been complete sexual congress. If he were going to take up the duties of viscount, he would have to consider the succession and—

Succession be damned. The real problem was he *wanted* Caro. What they'd done last night was not enough for him.

He wanted—*needed*—to dive deep into her and feel her come apart around him as he spilled his seed, hoping it would take root and give them a child. A family.

He wanted all of her—and to give her all of him. He wanted her to welcome him in enthusiastically. Lustily. He wanted her passion. He needed it. He couldn't live as a monk, especially not if Caro were in the viscountess's room.

If she couldn't open her body to him, he might. . . .

No, he'd not turn back to whores. He'd be breaking his marriage vows, sinning before God and Caro. And he couldn't risk bringing a fatherless child into the world.

Not to mention Caro would likely murder him in his bed if he even considered that course of action. He was quite, quite certain she'd not approve of his taking lovers. *She* was not a jaded Society woman like the Marchioness of Dervington.

And he was not going to venture down whatever odd path Uncle Leon had with those peculiar statues.

There was no point in thinking about it now. He would propose to her tonight, lay out his arguments. She was a businesswoman. She must be used to looking at all the pros and cons before accepting—or rejecting—an offer.

They reached the group by the hearth.

"My lord," Pearson said, grinning widely, "I am so glad you'll be the one lighting the Yule log and Yule candle this year. We were afraid you might share your uncle's distaste for the traditional ways."

Nick looked around. His guests must have moved to the back of the room. All he saw were his servants, smiling as if they, too, were happy to have him officiate at this ceremony.

How many other duties have I neglected?

Probably several score. He'd been rather single-minded about ignoring the estate.

No more, no matter what Caro decided. As long as he

was alive, he was the viscount. These people depended on him. He was honor bound to look out for their welfare.

Though he *did* hope Caro agreed to marry him. Beyond the fact that he wanted her in his bed so desperately that he literally ached with it, he could use her help. She had far more experience at managing people and financial affairs than he did.

"I'm afraid I don't know what I'm supposed to do, Mr. Pearson," Nick said. "Things were different in Italy and, as you say, Uncle Leon didn't observe any Christmas traditions. I'll have to throw myself on your mercy and ask you to guide me."

Pearson nodded. "Of course, milord. I am happy—*delighted*—to do so."

If it were possible to smile any wider, Pearson managed it. All the servants were grinning.

Except Mrs. Brooks. She emitted a rather forceful grunt.

Her husband stiffened. "Now, remember, Mrs. Brooks," the man said hurriedly. "We discussed this. You said you weren't going to—"

Mrs. Brooks waved a hand, brushing aside her husband's words. "I know what I said, Billy—"

Nick saw the eyes of the two footmen standing behind the housekeeper widen. They likely hadn't known Mr. Brooks had a first name, let alone what it was.

Nick hadn't known it, either, but that was neither here nor there.

"But I can't keep quiet a moment longer." Mrs. Brooks turned her gaze on Nick. "Milord, I'm sorry to speak ill of the dead, but your uncle was a cold-hearted villain."

"Cecilia, love—"

The footmen's eyes opened even wider at hearing Mrs. Brooks's Christian name.

"Think. . . ."

"I *am* thinking, Billy. I've thought about this for years."

Mrs. Brooks turned back to Nick. "I *know* the master suffered when his lady lost all their babies, but how he could have treated you as he did and you just a little boy—" She pressed her lips together.

"Ah. Yes. Well, it was a difficult time, to be sure," Nick said. It seemed a weak response to such passion, but he didn't know what else to say. He looked at Caro to see if she had any suggestions.

Oh, hell. She was looking approvingly at Mrs. Brooks and nodding.

He'd thought he wanted sympathy, but now that it was being served up in such a heaping, public helping, he discovered he had no taste for it.

"Oh, yes. I *know* it was a difficult time." Mrs. Brooks's tone indicated she found that a poor excuse. "We could all see how the old lord suffered, but he was your *uncle* and you were an *orphan*. You were all he had of your father, his only brother. And he was all you had." Mrs. Brooks shook her head as if words failed her.

Unfortunately, they hadn't. Before Nick could say something to turn the tide, she continued.

"I just want to say, milord, that I'm so very, very sorry *I* didn't do something to make you happier—though I *was* only a chambermaid back then. But still, I wish I'd done *something*."

"You did do something, Mrs. Brooks," Nick managed to squeeze in. "You brought me sweets when you came back from visiting your family. I much appreciated it."

"Oh, yes. A few sweets." She made a scoffing sound. "That was not enough. Milord, I tell you, it has bothered me for *years* that you had such a hard, sad time of it. We knew that was why you went so wild once you got to Town."

Dread grabbed him by the throat. *She's not going to list all my sins, is she?*

No, thank God. She stopped there.

And smiled at Caro.

Oh, hell. He was afraid he knew what was coming. His mouth went dry—too dry to manage a single syllable, not that anything was going to stop Mrs. Brooks.

"I am so very glad you have finally found some happiness. And I do hope—no, it's my Christmas wish—that you have a long, happy marriage blessed with many healthy children."

"Cecilia!"

That was Mr. Brooks, but it could just as easily have been Nick. Things were going to be *very* awkward if Caro turned him down.

He looked at her out of the corner of his eye. She didn't look angry or embarrassed. She looked, if anything, stunned.

"Er, thank you," Nick began—and was fortunately interrupted by a shout from one of the maids who'd been looking out the window.

"Mr. Pearson, the sun is close to setting!"

"Ah, then there's no time to lose. Here, my lord." Pearson handed Nick a long, thin splinter of wood. "From last year's Yule log, as is the kindling." He gestured at the fireplace.

"Ah." Nick took the sliver of wood from the man and looked for the first time at the enormous log Thomas had helped them find when they'd been out in the frigid cold earlier. Nick probably should have stayed and watched the men of the estate cut it down and haul it in here, but he'd already been out in the beastly cold far longer than he'd wanted.

Well, five minutes was longer than he wanted.

"That's a very large log," he said, stating the obvious.

Mr. Pearson nodded, kindly not rolling his eyes. "Yes, it is. Now, if you don't mind, my lord, as time is of the essence—tradition has it that both the Yule log and candle must be lit by sunset—I will say the blessings. I've said them for years, so I have them by heart."

"Yes. Of course. That's fine." Nick, recognizing his complete ignorance and not wishing to disappoint his servants or otherwise take a wrong step, was more than willing to go along with whatever Pearson said.

Pearson turned to the long wooden table nearest the hearth. On it were three shallow dishes; a short, lighted candle; and a large, unlit white candle—the Yule candle, Nick surmised.

Pearson reached into each of the dishes in turn as he recited the blessings. "May the new year bring all who live here wisdom." He sprinkled salt on the log. "Life and strength." Wine came next. "And"—he grinned at Nick before sprinkling the last, oil—"fertility."

Oh, God. Things were going to be *very* awkward if Caro decided she couldn't marry him.

"And now, my lord," Pearson said, "if you will light the splinter of last year's Yule log and then light the new log." A slight frown creased his brow. "And do keep hold of the splinter as you'll need it to light the Yule candle."

That Nick could manage. He *had* lit a fire before, just not one so impressive. The kindling caught, burned hotter. . . .

Everyone cheered as the flame licked up around the Yule log.

"How are we doing, Margaret?" Mr. Pearson asked the maid at the window as Nick straightened.

"It's time," she called back. "The sun is just going down."

"Splendid."

Nick thought it splendid, too, as the burning splinter was getting shorter and shorter.

Pearson gestured to the large candle on the table. "Now, if

you'll light the Yule candle, my lord, we will have completed tonight's ceremonies."

Nick set the splinter to the wick, which caught quickly, to more cheers. Then he threw the burning bit of wood onto the Yule log before his fingers got singed.

"And now," Mrs. Brooks said, "it's time to eat."

Nick had taken the seat at the head of the table, of course, and had put Caro in the place of honor on his right. He'd kept her close to his side for the lighting of the Yule log and the Yule candle, too. She'd thought he'd needed—or at least wanted—her support, and she'd been happy to give it.

And it wasn't as if there was a woman of higher—or of any—rank present to take offense.

Mrs. Brooks sat on Nick's left, her husband next to her. Mr. Pearson took the seat on Caro's right.

At the Home, they made no distinction between nobility, gentry, and lower class, but that was not the usual way of things in England. Not that Caro had any extensive experience with the behavior of the nobility. She'd eaten in the nursery during her brief stay in Dervington's house.

She glanced down the table to see how Bertram and Archie and Oliver were taking the arrangement.

They were taking it very well—and she was reminded again how much more freedom Society men had than their female counterparts. Bertram was in close conversation with Fanny, Oliver was flirting with Polly, and Archie was saying something to one of the maids that caused the girl to blush.

Hmm. That would never do.

She glanced at Mrs. Brooks to see if she had noticed. Nick was talking to her, so she might not have.

Mrs. Brooks had noticed all right. She was an excellent

housekeeper, awake on all suits. She was sending someone a very significant look. Who?

Caro followed her gaze. Ah. Mrs. Potty. Mrs. Potty nodded and gestured to another servant—an older woman with graying hair and a bit of a squint—who went over and changed places with the younger girl.

Archie looked rather annoyed, but there was nothing he could do besides appeal to Nick—and fortunately he had more sense than to do that.

Also fortunately Livy decided to help out. As Caro watched, she turned her attention from the handsome, but clearly overawed footman on her one side to Archie on her other.

Livy might be the proprietress of her business, more a manager than a worker these days, but she hadn't lost her touch. In a matter of seconds, she had Archie eating out of her hand, the young maid forgotten.

Caro turned her attention back to her immediate companions—and caught Mrs. Brooks beaming at her.

Oh, blast, this was bad. Unless she'd completely misunderstood or imagined the exchange earlier, the housekeeper thought Nick planned to marry Caro—and, inexplicably, *approved* of that plan.

How could that be? As a respectable, God-fearing woman, Mrs. Brooks should be thoroughly repulsed by the notion that Caro might one day be her mistress. Mrs. Brooks didn't even need to know about Caro's past indiscretions to form that opinion; she had the evidence of her own eyes—or, rather, ears. She must have heard the chambermaid's story—everyone else had—and must know Caro had been in Nick's bed.

Mrs. Brooks *should* think Caro little better than a whore.

Lud! Her "brilliant" scheme to save Nick's pride and herself from Mr. Woods's attentions had misfired spectacularly.

What were those lines of poetry Jo had read aloud one night a few weeks ago? Ah, yes.

Oh! what a tangled web we weave
When first we practice to deceive!

Sir Walter Scott definitely knew what he was writing about.

And Nick's problem was all a hum anyway. There was nothing wrong with his—

A cheer went up, and she looked over to see Mr. and Mrs. Parker walking in beside a huge Yorkshire Christmas pie, carried on a tray by two footmen. The pie was at least a foot high and as big around as the tun she used for brewing test batches of new ale recipes.

Now she knew what the couple had been so busy doing since the stagecoach had landed in the ditch.

The men carefully put their burden down on the table in front of Nick.

"Mr. Parker, Mrs. Parker," Nick said, looking sincerely impressed, "this is magnificent. I've never seen such a splendid Christmas pie."

Neither had Caro. Mr. and Mrs. Parker might be annoying travelers, but they appeared to be extremely skilled bakers.

"It is even more beautiful inside, milord," Mrs. Parker said, "and tastes like heaven. Humphrey here is a wizard in the kitchen."

Humphrey blushed at his wife's praise. "I couldn't have done it without Muriel, milord." He glanced around the room, smiling. "And Mrs. Potty and her staff helped, too, of course."

"Here, milord," Mrs. Parker said, handing him a large knife. "Do cut the first slice."

Nick took the knife and then looked at the pie again. "Oh, I don't know, Mrs. Parker. I hate to disturb such perfection."

"It's meant to be eaten, milord," Mr. Parker said.

"And if ye don't cut it, everyone will go hungry." Mrs. Parker gave Nick an encouraging smile. "Go on."

"Very well, since, as you point out, everyone's stomach is depending on me."

That provoked general merriment.

Nick stood, rested the knife on the pie, took a deep, theatrical breath—and bore down once, twice. Then Mrs. Parker plated the resulting slice, holding it up so everyone could see the neat layers of pigeon and goose, partridge and turkey, and likely several other types of fowl.

"Huzzah!" Archie shouted—Livy might have encouraged him to drink a bit more wine than was sensible on an empty stomach—and then everyone else joined in.

"Huzzah! Huzzah!"

Mrs. Parker put the slice in front of Nick. "There ye go, milord—the first one's for you. Now we'll cut the rest." She gestured to the footmen to transfer the pie over to the sideboard.

"Do I understand you're a brewer, Miss Anderson?" Mr. Pearson asked as they watched the pie being cut and distributed.

Ah, a safe topic. "Yes, indeed. I run a small brewhouse at the Benevolent Home for the Maintenance and Support of Spinsters, Widows, and Abandoned Women and their Unfortunate Children in Little Puddledon."

Mr. Pearson blinked at the Home's name as a footman put their slices of Christmas pie in front of them.

"I make and market Widow's Brew to earn money to defray the Home's expenses. We do have two noble patrons—the Duke of Grainger and the Earl of Darrow—but we want to be as self-sufficient as possible." She smiled. "The ale's quite good—though I will admit I'm more than a little prejudiced. I was on my way home from London after trying to interest a tavern keeper there in carrying it, when the coaching accident occurred."

Mr. Pearson nodded. He could probably understand her concerns better than most people. An estate manager had to be aware of costs and economies.

"Caro was asking about our brewhouse, Pearson," Nick said, leaning toward them. "I told her I thought it was used for storage now, since my uncle Leon disapproved of alcohol so strongly, but that she should ask you if she wanted to be certain."

Mrs. Brooks had leaned forward, too, her eyes darting between Caro and Nick, no doubt hoping to spot the slightest sign of romance.

Caro looked back at the estate manager. He was a far safer focus for her attention than Nick or Mrs. Brooks. "*Has* it been turned to storage, Mr. Pearson?"

The man nodded. "I'm afraid it has, Miss Anderson."

"Oh." That was what she'd expected, but it was still painful to hear. "And was all the equipment sold off, then?"

What a terrible waste, but she supposed she could understand. If you didn't have a brewer or anyone interested in learning the trade and you had the means to purchase your ale elsewhere, why bother with a brewhouse?

But Mr. Pearson was shaking his head!

"I don't think so." He smiled. "Would you like to have a look? Not tomorrow, of course, since it's Christmas Day, but sometime later in the week?"

When I'll be gone . . .

She glanced at Nick, but luckily, he was having a word with Mr. Parker and so wouldn't hear her answer.

She turned back to Mr. Pearson and opened her mouth,

expecting to decline regretfully, but for some reason her lips formed entirely different words. "Yes, thank you."

She froze, appalled. *Why did I say that?*

Perhaps she *wouldn't* be gone. The snow might not have melted enough for the coach to get through. Or perhaps it would have melted *too* much, turning the roads to ribbons of wheel-sucking mud.

Her spirits rose—and then she took herself to task.

No, the sooner the roads were passable, the better. She should *not* want this visit prolonged another moment, let alone another day.

Certainly not another night.

But she did.

Anticipation hummed through her, centering on a very embarrassing part of her body.

She prayed she wasn't blushing.

Mr. Pearson leaned closer. "I hope I'm not getting ahead of matters, Miss Anderson, but I must tell you I'm very happy Lord Oakland is finally settling down. We all are."

Aiee! Her inner self screamed and spun around in frantic circles, looking for some way to escape this conversation.

"Oh?" Her outward self remained calm.

She'd experienced this dichotomy between her thoughts and her words in the past, but usually only when negotiating a deal, when she didn't want to tip her hand. This was different. This felt as if she had somehow trapped a wild animal inside her—or as if *she* were the wild animal.

Well, she *was* trapped—in this seat next to Nick's estate manager.

She looked at her wineglass and contemplated spilling it on herself.

But it's red wine, and I have so very few clothes with me. . . .

Which was why she'd consented to remove her shift last night.

No, it wasn't. She'd taken her shift off so Nick could show her pleasure, wonderful, soul-shaking, name-screaming pleasure.

Don't think about last night!

Or what might happen tonight. In just a few hours.

The hum of anticipation grew to a full-throated chorus with orchestra.

Stop it!

She was afraid to look at Nick—and afraid of what Mrs. Brooks's eagle eyes might see.

She should just tell Mr. Pearson that there had been some misunderstanding. She'd never had any difficulty being blunt before.

She was having enormous difficulty today. She sat tongue-tied as Mr. Pearson swept on down this dangerous conversational path.

"Lord Oakland had a very unfortunate childhood, Miss Anderson, as I'm sure you know. Mrs. Brooks was quite right in that. His uncle had turned into a hard, bitter man by the time Master Nick came to live with us." Mr. Pearson took a sip of wine and shook his head slowly.

She couldn't help herself; her curiosity was piqued.

No, it was more than curiosity—at least of the idle variety. Mrs. Potty had told her some of the story, but she wanted—*needed*—to know more about Nick's history.

"Did you know Lord Oakland's uncle as a boy, Mr. Pearson?"

He nodded. "Aye. My father was estate manager before me. I used to play with Leon and his younger brother, David—Nick's father." He sighed and gazed into his wineglass.

"Leon was never as happy-go-lucky as David. Well, of course he wasn't. He knew from the time he was in leading strings that he would inherit the viscountcy, and he took that responsibility very seriously indeed. David was free to go off painting and traveling, to fall in love with an Italian girl and never come home, but Leon had to stay at Oakland and learn about crops and drainage and roofs and rents. He had to marry and get an heir."

Mr. Pearson looked at her as if asking whether she understood.

She thought she did. She certainly knew what it was like to feel fierce loyalty to a place—or an enterprise, like the Home. She and Jo and Pen had worked so hard to get it started, to manage it, to keep it afloat financially. That was why she'd felt so betrayed when Pen had chosen the Earl of Darrow over them.

No, that wasn't fair. Pen had had her daughter to think of—Caro had always known Harriet came first in Pen's hierarchy of values.

But I have no children. I would never choose a man over the Benevolent Home.

Her eyes strayed to Nick—and she pulled them back, unsettled by a flutter of uncertainty. And need.

Remember, Nick should marry a young woman from a good family.

Who likely wouldn't know the first practical thing about running Oakland.

I'm needed at the Home.

The Home was only a place.

Yes, but Oakland is only a place, too. Nick can't leave it—leave his responsibilities. He should understand why I can't leave mine.

That argument seemed reasonable on its face, but it wasn't persuasive—or, at least, she had to admit she wasn't feeling persuaded.

I owe Jo my loyalty. She gave me a refuge when I most needed one.

Just as Jo had given Pen a refuge when *she'd* needed one, and yet Jo had seemed to understand—and be happy for—Pen when she married.

I have to go back to Little Puddledon. I just have to.

It would be easier—and far less risky—to go back to the Home. Caro worked hard there, but she understood her duties. She was comfortable. She was in control of things. She certainly didn't suffer from all this . . . emotional upheaval.

"Yes. Of course he had to marry," she said. "He was the viscount. He did just as he ought."

Just as Nick ought . . .

She jerked her thoughts away from Nick again and his viscount-ish responsibilities.

Mr. Pearson nodded. "Not that Leon viewed his marriage to Lady Oakland as just another duty, you understand. Not at all. She was beautiful, well-bred, charming. I think they truly loved each other when they married."

Mr. Pearson paused, as if remembering pleasanter times. Caro tried to—discreetly—glance Nick's way.

Oh, dear. Mrs. Brooks had seen her.

Her eyes scurried back to focus on Mr. Pearson.

"They were very happy," he said, "until that dreadful fall." His breath whooshed out in a long, heavy sigh.

No point in making the man repeat the sad story. "Yes, I know. Mrs. Potty told us—that is, Lord Oakland and me—about the accident."

Mr. Pearson nodded and took another swallow of wine. "The fall was the beginning of the end. Oh, at first it seemed that everything would be all right. Lady Oakland recovered, at least physically. Lord Oakland was very solicitous of her."

He shook his head. "But then she lost the next baby and

the next. With each failed pregnancy, Leon grew more bitter. He would shout at poor Lady Oakland, saying terrible things, blaming her for the miscarriages, for his lack of an heir."

"Oh!" Mr. Pearson's words hit Caro like a punch to her heart. How cruel. To attack a woman who'd lost a baby—*several* babies—that way . . .

In her mind's eye, Caro saw Fanny's face when she'd looked at Grace. Fanny's expression had been so full of yearning and loss and misery. "*Poor* Lady Oakland."

Mr. Pearson nodded. "It was ghastly. By the end they were barely speaking." He shrugged. "Well, by the end they barely saw each other. Lady Oakland had moved her things to the east wing when the London physician who Leon brought down to see her told him to stop all marital relations, that another pregnancy would kill her."

Mr. Pearson shook his head. "I think Leon went a bit mad with grief and enforced celibacy then." He grimaced. "Though I *will* give him credit for not taking advantage of the maids."

Unlike Dervington, the scoundrel.

"He fell into the deep dismals and—as you know—adopted a very bleak sort of religion."

Caro nodded. "And Lady Oakland? What became of her?"

"She just faded away. The poets would likely say she died of a broken heart. The physician said it was consumption."

"Oh! How sad." Tragic, really. The stuff of poems and plays, but acted out in real life.

"Aye."

They both took a long swallow of wine.

Poor, poor Lady Oakland. *This* was why Caro should go back to Little Puddledon. If she stayed here, if Nick actually asked her to marry him and she said yes . . .

She'd be at his mercy, physically, financially, and emotionally.

Her throat closed up in panic. *I can't do it. I can't. Even if I love him, I can't give anyone that much power over me again.*

"Lady Oakland had been gone about two years," Mr. Pearson continued, "when we got word the fever had taken David and his wife." He frowned. "Leon's first reaction wasn't sorrow so much as a sort of dark joy that he would finally have control of his heir."

"Oh." Poor Nick.

Mr. Pearson looked at her. "Even so, I think Leon tried to do the right thing. He'd just forgotten how to love. And that's what Master Nick needed most: love. He was all of eleven years old, suddenly orphaned, torn away from everything he'd known and dropped on Oakland's doorstep."

"The poor boy." The words just spilled out, wrung from her heart.

Mr. Pearson nodded approvingly. "As you might imagine, things did not go well. So, it was not a surprise at all that as soon as Master Nick was old enough to get free of Leon, he ran wild. For years all of us at Oakland have lived in fear that he would do something really dreadful. Gamble away all his money. Marry a notorious light-skirts. Even get himself killed."

She nodded. Of course everyone had worried. Their security depended on Nick.

No, that wasn't fair. From what she could see—and had heard in Mrs. Brooks's impassioned speech—the people here sincerely cared about Nick's welfare. Of course, they did. Most of them had watched him grow up.

"So, perhaps you can imagine our delight now that we see him showing a marked interest in such a sensible, practical sort of woman."

Ah, but they were fooling themselves, seeing what they wanted to see, what they'd long hoped and prayed to see.

"You don't know me, Mr. Pearson. None of you do. I've only been here—" She paused. How long? It had seemed like a lifetime. "Not even two full days."

His brow arched up. "You're Henry Anderson's sister, aren't you?"

"Well, yes."

And, after her brief stint in Dervington's house, many would say a light-skirts. *No need to mention that.* However, no one would dispute that she associated with that class of women.

"I'm also a brewer and work and live at the Benevolent Home. I sincerely doubt the *ton* would find me any more acceptable as Lady Oakland than they'd find Livy or Polly or Fanny."

Mr. Pearson waved such concerns away. "Perhaps the highest sticklers would cavil about your history, but they would likely also take issue with Nick's Italian blood."

"That's not the same thing at all." Though now that Pearson mentioned it, Caro remembered Nick saying something about parents of Society misses looking down their long noses at him.

Mr. Pearson favored her with a speaking look. "It is to some people. It was, unfortunately, to Leon. I'm afraid he made no secret of the fact that he wished Nick was one hundred percent English."

Nick had told her that, too.

"But it really makes no difference what your past holds, Miss Anderson. It's the present and the future that's important. You've already had a positive effect on Nick—we've all seen it." He grinned. "He's even agreed to go over the estate books with me—that's a Christmas miracle indeed."

She had to laugh at that.

"Oh, Mr. Pearson, surely Nick would have come around eventually." She hoped. She'd admit she had her doubts. "He hasn't held the title for even a year yet."

Mr. Pearson looked extremely skeptical. "Maybe. All I know is that he'd shown no signs of changing his ways until you arrived. I read the London papers, Miss Anderson. I know the wags call him Lord Devil. His name is never linked to any respectable female's." He snorted. "Well, look whom he brought home for Christmas—for a Christmas *orgy*."

Well, yes, there *was* that.

"Believe me when I say we will all dance for joy at your wedding and drink to your good health"—he grinned—"and fruitful union."

A confusing wave of emotions washed over her. Yes, she was needed at the Home, but she thought she was needed here, too. Nick needed her. . . .

Nick isn't the one talking to you, idiot!

Her good sense finally reasserted itself. Heavens, had she really been on the verge of believing the farce she was acting in? That would never do.

Mr. Pearson was looking at her as if he expected her to say something in reply, but what could she say?

She found she was completely incapable of maintaining the charade, either by denying that there was anything more than physical attraction between her and Nick or by encouraging Mr. Pearson to dream of a wedding.

She took refuge in the Christmas pie, forking a large bite into her mouth and smiling through the crumbs.

Chapter Nineteen

That had been quite a supper, Nick thought as he watched Caro pace back and forth across his room.

He'd watched her downstairs, too—watched her expression grow paler, tighter, more hunted-looking as, after all the food was eaten, the wassail bowl came out and toast after toast was made to their good health—and anticipated fecundity. His servants were clearly ecstatic at the thought of them marrying and, of course, his disreputable guests had joined in the merriment.

He'd not known what to do.

Well, what he *should* have done was nip the matter in the bud the moment he had first become aware of it. When Mrs. Brooks had wished him a happy marriage and many children just before the Yule log lighting, he should have corrected her—as gently as possible. But how would that have reflected on Caro? They had purposely led everyone to believe they were lovers. To publicly proclaim that they'd been swiving just for amusement would make Caro out to be a whore.

And there wasn't any way he could publicly announce that they *hadn't* done anything of a carnal nature. Who would believe them? They'd been seen together in bed.

And, in any event, it would be a lie. They *had* engaged in deeply carnal behavior. Not what people were imagining—and would gossip about—but behavior that went far beyond what an unmarried woman would engage in and likely even beyond what many *married* women would.

And it had been wonderful. What he'd done with Caro had felt far more intimate than any of his actual couplings.

No, to be completely honest, he'd stayed silent when Mrs. Brooks had wished them well and during the many toasts after supper, because he'd wanted what everyone had said to be true. He wanted to marry Caro and have sons—and daughters—with her. And something in the way she'd looked at him when they'd left the Long Gallery after the play and concert to go down to the servants' hall had made him think she wanted that, too.

He'd been very hopeful then that she'd say yes when he asked her to marry him.

He wasn't so hopeful now.

"Did you hear what they were *saying?*"

Caro's voice was shrill. Brittle. Was she going to cry?

Oh, Lord. He ached to wrap his arms around her, comfort her, take her to bed, and . . .

He clasped his hands behind his back.

And then focused on another ache.

He glanced down. His brainless cock was still obviously hoping to make Caro's close acquaintance very soon.

He clasped his hands in front of him and said, "Yes. I heard."

The comments had got extremely ribald by the end. That was when he'd decided it was time to retreat, even if that resulted in another round of good-natured, suggestive ribbing and sniggering.

Well, *he'd* thought the ribbing good-natured. He was fairly certain Caro had not.

"At least one good thing has come of this," she said, her voice still brittle. "There's no question that I no longer have to share your bed. Certainly Mr. Woods—and any of the other men—will not risk forcing themselves on Viscount Oakland's bride-to-be."

"Right."

She looked at him.

Best be clear. "Right that no one will dare to accost you now. Wrong about it being a good thing you don't have to share my bed."

Her look turned to a glare.

"That is, it's good you don't *have* to share it. But sharing would still be splendid." *You're going about this all wrong, you know.*

He smiled. Tried again. "I thought you liked what we did last night."

Now she was not only glaring, she looked as if she might spit at him or claw his eyes out.

Or cry.

"*I* certainly liked what we did last night," he said, probably putting the last nail in his coffin.

She chose anger over tears. Of course she did. She was Caro. And she didn't retreat. She attacked. She stepped closer and poked him in the chest. "I *told* you. I'm a brewer, not a whore."

He flinched at hearing that ugly word. "I know that, Caro." And no one had been saying that downstairs, but he had enough sense to see it would be counterproductive to quibble over that. "But what I was hoping—really, *really* hoping—was that I could persuade you to become a wife."

She stared at him. She couldn't be surprised by the proposal, could she? Surely, she must know he would have squelched all the suggestive talk in the servants' hall if he hadn't had honorable intentions.

It *did* look as though she was struggling with herself, which might mean she hadn't yet cast her decision in stone. He might still be able to persuade her.

Third time lucky?

Time to find out. He'd lay everything out while she was still speechless. She would probably scoff at him. A smart businessman—even a good card player—wouldn't reveal his entire hand at the beginning of the game.

This wasn't a deal or a game. He was telling her the truth—*his* truth. Much as he cringed to say it in such sentimental terms, he was opening his heart to her.

It was the most terrifying thing he'd ever done. She could very well reject him.

Zeus, if she does that—

No. If she rejected him, he'd find a way to get through it. Taking the coward's way out and not saying anything would be a thousand times worse. He'd torture himself forever with a litany of if-onlys and might-have-beens. Better to find the courage to ask now and know for certain rather than wonder forever.

"I love you, Caro." *Be* completely *truthful.* "Or, I think that's what I feel. I'm afraid I don't have much experience with love of any sort. All I know is that I've never felt this way before."

She stared at him. He couldn't read her expression, but at least she was no longer poking him in the chest.

"Mr. Pearson told me a little about your uncle," she finally said. "How he behaved when you came here as a boy."

Nick nodded. He'd thought that might have been what Pearson had been saying to her when they'd had their heads together during supper. "It was . . . unpleasant."

It had been far more than unpleasant. It had been a nightmare, a nightmare that had started months before in Italy.

He sometimes thought fondly of his childhood in Venice

or his school holidays with Caro's family, but he shied away from remembering the dark time when his parents had died and he'd had to leave Italy. He'd never talked about it with anyone.

If I want to share my life with Caro, I should share this, too.

"To be honest, it would have been hard for even a happy man with a wife and children to have dealt with me when I first came to Oakland. I was . . ." He shook his head. There were no words bleak enough to convey how he'd felt.

"Oh, Nick." Caro put her hand on his arm, but he hardly noticed.

"I got the fever first—I and two of my cousins. Mama nursed me, and then, once I was better, she fell ill."

Caro made a small noise, low in her throat. A sound of sorrow, sympathy, compassion.

"And then, Papa got sick, too." It had been so frightening. His entire world had tilted on its axis. His parents had always been healthy—strong and active, smiling and laughing. Full of . . . life. Now they just stayed in bed, pale and weak.

He kept thinking they'd get better like he had. That he'd wake up in the morning and everything would be back to normal. Papa would be in his studio painting. Mama would be baking and gossiping with her mother and sisters.

Nothing had ever been normal again.

"And then they died."

"Oh, Nick, I'm so sorry." Caro wrapped her arms around him. Hugged him.

His arms came round her, but he didn't feel her presence. Not really. He was still lost in the past.

"I blamed myself at first. Well, for a long time. If only I'd not got sick, my parents wouldn't have either. They'd still be alive." And he'd still be in warm, beautiful Italy.

"Nick! It wasn't your fault. How could it have been your fault? You were just a boy. And you didn't ask to take ill."

He nodded. "Yes. I know. I finally—years later—came to believe that. The fever ran through the entire village. Almost everyone got it—even my grandparents. Only my parents died."

Reason had helped him muffle the pain. These things happened. Sometimes—often—you couldn't control what life handed you. You could only adjust and endure.

But when he'd been a boy, when he'd touched his parents' cold, lifeless bodies, he'd been inconsolable—sad and angry and lost and afraid. Hopeless. He'd wanted to turn back time. He'd wanted to die himself. He'd cursed God and anyone who tried to help or comfort him.

He'd been wild, like an animal.

And then, when his fury had started to subside and every day hadn't begun with a howl of despair, when his loss had turned to a deep, constant ache instead of a sharp, stabbing, breath-stealing pain, Josiah Pennyworth had appeared, come to take him to England.

And his wound had burst open again.

"My uncle engaged a man—a traveling tutor—to bring me to him at Oakland. It was—I don't remember how long after my parents died. My grandparents argued that it was too soon, that I was too young, that I should stay with them for a while longer, but Mr. Pennyworth was adamant."

Nick still said that name with bitterness, though none of it had been Mr. Pennyworth's fault.

"He had a very official-looking letter with him from my uncle. I was the heir to the viscountcy. I belonged in England. He said we had to leave right then, before the weather changed and travel became too difficult. That my uncle wanted me at Oakland for Christmas."

Nick looked down at Caro. "Though I'm not sure why

Uncle Leon cared about that. It's not as if my presence would have made Christmas any less bleak a holiday for him."

Perhaps that was why he didn't like Christmas—it reminded him of all he'd lost.

He thought he saw sympathy and understanding in Caro's eyes. She hugged him tighter.

This Christmas could be different. It could change everything—will *change everything if Caro agrees to marry me. But if she says no . . .*

He closed his eyes as pain twisted his gut.

No. He couldn't think that way—the pain and despair were too like what he'd felt as a boy. He would just have to hope he could persuade her.

And if he couldn't?

He would face that if and when he had to.

"So, my grandmother helped me pack a satchel and sent me off." She'd given him a hug and a kiss as well, had cried over him, had told him to write.

But she'd still sent him away with a stranger to go to a stranger.

Dear God, I've never really forgiven her, have I?

That was something else he must do.

"By the time I arrived at Oakland, I was . . . Well, I was rather dead inside, I suppose. And it didn't help that England was so cold and damp and bleak."

And I've stayed cold all these years.

He hadn't realized it before. Why would he? The men and women he lived among, caroused with, were cold, too. They all lived solitary lives, even in the crowded halls of London. The connections they made were only physical—only body touching body—and over in a matter of minutes.

What he felt for Caro was different. It was deeper. It felt as if it would endure for years, until they both were old and gray. His heart and his mind were involved as much as—or more than—his cock.

Though his cock would dearly love to be involved as well.

He tightened his hold on Caro, buried his face in her hair.

She's alone, too, isn't she? Does she feel the same cold? The same loneliness? Or is the Benevolent Home—her friends and her work—enough?

It was time to find out.

Caro inhaled Nick's scent, her face pressed against his chest. He was holding her so tightly, it was difficult to breathe. And he was so tense with loss and pain and need. Not physical need. Not yet. His cock wasn't pushing against her. No, this was something deeper. And it called to her.

She wanted to hold the little boy who'd lost his mother and father and everyone and everything that had meant home to him. The boy who'd had to live here in a dark, gloomy house with his dark, gloomy uncle. The young man who'd fled to London and the harsh, soulless *ton*.

And now this man, who had been kind and gentle to her and was, she thought, deeply lonely. In need of a partner.

In need of her.

She closed her eyes, letting the warmth of his body comfort her, and surrendered to the truth.

She recognized Nick's pain because she felt the same ache. There was a hole in her life where her family had been. She'd plastered over it with work—getting the brewhouse running, perfecting Widow's Brew, training her assistants, selling the ale to more and more taverns, tracking expenses and income, even dreaming—against Jo's and Pen's advice—of getting into the London market. It wasn't until she'd been stranded here, far from the Home and her work, that the plaster had cracked and she'd seen the emptiness beneath it.

And it wasn't just her family that she'd lost. When she'd left Dervington's house, she'd left the hopes and, yes, the dreams she'd had as a girl behind. She'd gone to London with a hazy idea that she would find love, marry, have children, run her own household. Instead she'd made a terrible choice and had, she thought, ruined her life.

She hadn't. She'd survived—flourished even—and had built a new life. But now. . . .

She'd let all the talk downstairs—and the jokes—overwhelm her. She'd felt cornered. Pushed into a role she hadn't asked for. Pushed to give up the satisfying, independent life she'd made for herself.

But Nick wasn't pushing her. He was asking her. Offering her the opportunity to have something she'd forgotten she'd wanted.

Yes, it might make more sense for Viscount Oakland to marry a young, well-bred, pure-as-the-driven-snow girl, but *this* Viscount Oakland needed an older, not-so-pure, sensible brewer to help him manage his estate. A woman who knew what loss felt like, who could understand his pain.

Someone who loved him like *she* loved him, not for his title, but for himself. Who loved *Nick*, not Lord Oakland.

He loosened his hold on her enough that he could look into her eyes. "Marry me, Caro. Please? I love you. I'll admit I don't have much experience with love, at least recently. But I did have eleven years of love with my parents and grandparents and aunts and uncles and cousins. I've seen love—I just took it for granted before."

His words tumbled out—he wasn't giving her time to answer.

"You might like being a viscountess. There is plenty for you to do here. I need help with the estate—I admit that. I've been a terrible landowner. I turned my back on my responsibilities. I refused to deal with my unclc, to learn anything from him or from Pearson. But I mean to do better now. *Will* do better." His lips smiled, but his eyes were anxious. "We could see about reopening the brewhouse, if you like."

That made her laugh. "Well, then, of course I'll marry you."

Nick looked hopeful, but not entirely convinced. "You will? You mean it?"

The last shadows, the last lingering wisps of doubt from her time in London, dissipated like mist before the morning sun. She grinned. She hadn't felt this light—this young—in thirteen years.

"Yes, I mean it. I love you, too, Nick. I . . ." Emotion welled up, clogging her throat. She swallowed, struggling to regain her composure. She would say this—*had* to say it.

"I wasn't looking for love—I'm not sure I believed in it anymore. I certainly wasn't looking for marriage. Two days ago, I would have laughed had you said I'd be standing here with you now, telling you that I love you and, yes, I'll marry you."

Nick grinned, his face bright with happiness, but he didn't interrupt her.

"I thought I was happy with my life at the Home." She shrugged. "And maybe I was, then. But now . . ." She smiled. "Now I want more. I want you, Nick, and, God willing, children someday."

He let out a long, relieved breath and hugged her tightly. "Thank God. I don't know what I would have done had you said no, Caro."

She suddenly felt a bit daring—or maybe it was, ah, *cocksure*. . . .

She pushed on his chest so he loosened his hold on her. She looked up at him. "So, what are you going to do now?"

His expression froze for a second, and then his eyes lit up and he grinned. "Well, there is a bed, a very comfortable bed, quite close by. We could plight our troth in a carnal manner, if you would like."

Nerves twisted in her stomach. . . .

No, this would be good. It would put to rest finally and completely the bad memory of her encounters with Dervington.

"I would like—very much."

"Splendid!" He pulled the first pin from her hair.

His fingers felt wonderful.

"Think of last night," he said as he moved on to untie her tapes. "Remember how you felt." He brushed a kiss on her temple, and she felt his lips pull into a grin. "How you screamed my name."

She laughed at the reminder of how she'd lost that wager—and her body hummed with expectation.

The hum grew louder as her dress and stays and shift dropped to the floor. She didn't even care that her clothes would likely be wrinkled—her focus was on other matters entirely.

Nick has too many clothes on . . . And I have two hands and ten fingers.

Nick wasn't doing something *to* her—they were doing this together.

She started to untie his cravat.

His clothing was more difficult than hers to remove—or maybe it was just that she'd had no practice. She managed to get his cravat off without strangling him, but his well-tailored coat defeated her.

He started to laugh.

She growled with frustration. "If I'm to be naked, you must be, too."

He grinned. "Of course. I wouldn't want it any other way."

Then he stepped back, struggled out of his coat, and

quickly shed his shoes and stockings and breeches before pulling his shirt up over his head.

He was splendidly, gloriously naked from his broad shoulders and muscled chest to his flat stomach and . . .

Oh, my!

His cock was pointing at her, thick and long and eager.

Her stomach shivered, but with anticipation, not dread. She wanted to feel him against her, feel the friction of his skin on hers again, like yesterday.

And feel him in *me?*

Her stomach shivered with nerves this time, but she still knew her answer.

Yes.

She loved Nick. Even if that part was uncomfortable, it would be worth the discomfort to be close to him. And she knew he would make the rest of it good.

It had been very, very good yesterday.

She wanted to feel his touch again, to feel the tension grow until she couldn't bear it any longer—and then to have it explode through her in waves of pleasure.

"Let's go to bed," he said. He took her hand. "We'll go slowly. You'll see. It will be even better than yesterday."

In the end, they did not go slowly. Once Nick's clever mouth and fingers touched her skin, her need became an inferno, turning to ash any lingering threads of worry.

"You're beautiful," Nick said. "Beautiful and strong." His lips skimmed her cheek, touched her collarbone. Her nipples tightened into hard peaks, waiting for—

Ah! His mouth. His fingers.

Now the place between her legs throbbed. "*Nick.*"

His mouth moved down over her ribs, her stomach.

"Nick. Nick." She was mewling, begging, desperate. "Nick."

His tongue traced her opening. Stroked. Teased.

"N-Nick. Ohh. Nick!" Her hips wanted to dance and twist, but he held them still.

She felt his finger slide a little way inside her as he kissed her inner thigh.

"You're so wet. So ready. Shall I come in now?"

"Yes." She wanted Nick close, as close as it was possible for two people to be. "Yes." She tugged on his shoulders. "Yes."

He rose up over her. He didn't press her down into the mattress with his weight the way Dervington had; no, he kept his body away from hers, balanced on his arms, except for his tip at her entrance. And then he pushed in slowly. Carefully.

Oh! There was no pain. Just pleasure.

He slid deeper and deeper, stretching her, filling her, connecting her to him. Deeper and deeper until he couldn't go any farther.

She loved it. She loved *him*. Raw emotion welled up in her, so intense it spilled over in tears.

Nick stopped. "Caro." His voice was tight with concern. "Are you all right?"

She was too overwhelmed to do more than whisper, "Yes." And then she reached up and wrapped her arms around him. "Yes. I love you, Nick."

"And I love you, Caro," he said. "With my whole heart. My soul. My body. My life."

Then he moved again. In. Out. In. Each stroke wound her tighter and tighter and tighter.

She felt her release coming. She tightened her grip on him. She needed to hold on to Nick or she would shatter—

"Ohh!"

She *did* shatter just as she had the night before, but this time was better, because Nick was there with her. In her. Anchoring her.

And then she felt, deep, deep inside her, by her womb, the warm pulse of his seed.

Ohh! Unlike the time with Dervington, she *hoped* Nick's seed took root and gave her—gave *them*—a child.

He collapsed onto her then, and she hugged him close. His weight made it hard to breathe, but she just took shallower breaths, savoring his heat, his closeness, the feeling of being surrounded by him.

She wished he would never leave her.

He did leave, of course.

"I'm too heavy," he said.

"No."

But he'd already moved, sliding out of her, taking away his warmth, leaving her empty and sweaty and chilled. Alone . . .

But not for long. He stretched out next to her, wrapping his arm around her and pulling her close as he pulled the coverlet up over them.

She rested her head on his chest and listened to the steady, strong beat of his heart. She felt so close to him and so happy she thought she might cry again, and she was not—had never been—a watering pot.

She turned her face slightly to press a kiss on Nick's chest.

He hugged her even closer, his hand stroking her back. "I'll get a special license as soon as the snow clears."

"Mmm."

"Though I hope you won't make me wait until our vows are said to do this again."

"Mmm." She slid her hand down his body to cup his now-soft, relaxed cock. It stirred. "No waiting."

He laughed. "Zeus, Caro, there has to be *some* waiting." He kissed the top of her head and plucked her fingers away from his sleepy cock. "Have mercy."

She looked up at him. "How long do I have to wait?"

He grinned. "Insatiable, are you? I think I like that in a wife." A small frown creased his brow. "Are you certain you won't mind giving up your position as brewer?"

Would she? Two days ago—perhaps even as recently as yesterday morning—she'd have been unable to even imagine leaving the business she'd worked so hard to build, for which she had such high hopes.

But now? The choice was easy. Jo needed her, yes, but she wasn't irreplaceable. She was sending Jo Fanny and Polly. And Albert and Bathsheba and Esther had helped her with the brewing for years. They were very capable.

Well, to be brutally honest, they might be just as happy not to have her keeping such a tight hold on the reins.

"Yes." She grinned. "And you did say we might open the brewhouse here, didn't you? So, I'd not be giving up brewing—just changing, er, establishments."

He laughed. "Ah, I see how it is. All you want is my body and my brewhouse."

She knew he was teasing, but she didn't want there to be any doubt about her feelings. "And you, Nick. I want you. I *need* you. I hadn't realized how lonely I was until you showed me." She smiled. "I guess I should thank Archie and Oliver. If they hadn't sent the coach into that ditch, I'd be back at the Home now. But I wouldn't be *home*."

"Home." Nick's voice wavered on the word and he closed his eyes briefly. When he opened them again, they were full of . . . yearning and a little damp. "I want a home with you, Caro. A home like I had in Italy. A happy, warm, laughter-filled place with children, if we are so blessed."

His lips twisted. "And I suppose I should thank Archie and Oliver, too, though I'm fairly certain I can't bring myself to do so, at least in so many words." He grinned. "But I would say this is definitely a Christmas miracle."

His eyes darkened. "And if you'll forgive me for skating

very close to blasphemy, I believe another miracle has occurred."

"What? Oh." She laughed and looked down to see his cock had risen and looked eager to do again what it had just done. "Yes, indeed."

And then Caro pressed a kiss to Nick's chest, offering a silent prayer for yet another Christmas miracle more in keeping with the season—that a new life might grow from the seed planted tonight—before all her attention was taken up with far more earthly matters.